SYSTEM ERROR

SYSTEM ERROR

AARON SHIH

Podium

Podium

SYSTEM
ERROR

CHAPTER 1

Origin System Status

Ark'tis has fallen to the R System's Eternal King.

Estimated W Inertia lost: **92,204,373**

Notable B losses: Arthur Samson [**Wandering Hero lv. 198**], Kylie Ralston [**Stalwart Paladin lv. 177**], Sine [**Divine Core lv. 127**], Karl [**Rare Core lv. 377**], Alexander Kelsin [**Heretical Thief lv. 94**] . . . [expand]

Notable R losses: **<DATA LOST>**

Notable events: Personal Systems of 3,700+ Integrated returned the status **<ERROR>** upon attempting to analyze a [????] attack from the Eternal King. Attack power was later determined to have been equivalent in scale and power to that of a high-leveled [**Legendary**]- or [**Unique**]-class skill. All Personal Systems were disabled. Fatality rate 99.83%.

Response formulating . . .

Note: All Personal Systems available at the time possessed intelligence levels roughly equivalent to a [**Common**]-class human with 3 INT.

Conclusion: Personal Systems for B Integrated were insufficiently intelligent to handle edge cases where R skill complexity outclassed processing capability.

Proposal: Increase Personal System intelligence.

Examining feasibility . . .

Issue: Personal System intelligence cannot be raised through increased mana nor through increased W Inertia.

Proposal: Include reincarnated intelligence in Personal System.
Examining feasibility . . .

No immediate issues found.

Proposal: Initiate experiment with new reincarnation. Reincarnate one individual possessing high W Inertia with a [**Legendary**] class. Reincarnate a second possessing high natural INT and high W Inertia. Expend all mana resources necessary.

Proposal deemed feasible.

Initiating reincarnation process . . .

Target found!

Target Name	Jerome Smith
Target Age at Death	22
Target W Inertia	239,827
Target Natural INT	7

Abnormally high W Inertia detected. Natural INT insufficient. Prioritizing reincarnation as classholder advised.

Reincarnating target . . .

<ERROR: Reincarnation process failed. Reinitiate?>

Mana expended: 20

Increasing reincarnation parameters . . .

Reinitiating target's reincarnation . . .

<ERROR: Reincarnation process failed. Reinitiate?>

Mana expended: 200

[process collapsed for brevity]

Reincarnation succeeded!

Mana expended: 20,000

<WARNING: Reincarnation process consumed significantly over the standard mana limit for reincarnation.>

Initiating reincarnation process . . .

Target found!

Target Name	Parker Wu
Target Age at Death	19
Target W Inertia	38,317
Target Natural INT	17

High W Inertia detected. Natural INT sufficient. Stronger targets currently unavailable.

Reincarnating target . . .

P-System Log

What the fuck? I was walking down the street just now, I swear. Heard a truck of some kind coming my way, and now I'm . . . here?

What the hell is here, anyway? I can't see or hear anything, and I can't even feel my own body, but somehow I feel like I can perceive things. It's weird—I don't know how to explain it, but I can see without having actual visual sight? I have no idea what's happening.

Hold on. What's with this text? Are my thoughts being recorded?

Origin System Message

Reincarnation process complete.

Welcome to the Continent.

Your body in your homeworld has died. Your soul was selected to enter the Continent, a world of swords and sorcery in which the Eternal King reigns supreme.

There has been a deviation.

You will not be fighting the Eternal King yourself.

Your role will be to enable another.

You are now able to check your status.

Integration with target Jerome Smith will occur in thirty minutes.

<table>
<tr><td>P-System Log</td></tr>
</table>

Reincarnated into another world, huh? I've read and watched enough to see where this is going . . .

Matter of fact, even the enemy seems generic. Demon Lord, Eternal King, tomato, tomahto. It's just some big baddie that I'm gonna get tossed at.

But that didn't seem normal. Deviation? Enabling?

Integration?

I can . . . I still can't feel what's happening, but there's this innate sense I have, one that's gotten me to figure out how to open this log here. Can I use that to check my stats?

Parker [ALIAS: P-System]

Class	Race	Level
PERSONAL_SYSTEM	SYSTEM	-

Stat	Current	Maximum
W Inertia	38,317	38,317
Mana	-	-
Health	<ERROR>	<ERROR>

Skills	[W%M; G, P]
Titles	[System], [Reincarnator]

Other statistics have been deemed irrelevant.

<table>
<tr><td>P-System Log</td></tr>
</table>

. . . what the hell?

Whatever that was, I am pretty sure that wasn't what I'm supposed to be seeing. I just got reincarnated into a fantasy world, dammit! I should have special powers of some kind, some mission—

Well, I guess there is a mission. But what's up with that? The class and race classifiers looked like they were placeholders from some indie game that released their pre-alpha two months too early! That skill looks like a cat rolled over someone's keyboard! And who's this "System" to tell me that I shouldn't be allowed access to my stats?

Alright, Parker, think. You're not dumb.

. . . I'm talking to myself inside a blue box.

Never mind that. The "Origin System" there told me that I was going to need to assist someone else on their way to defeating the Demon—no, the Eternal King. Agh, the name is just so goddamn generic.

Anyway, that fact combined with my class being "PERSONAL_SYS-TEM" (oh, neat, I can capitalize my thoughts [and put parentheses here, apparently]), indicates a pretty obvious answer.

I haven't been reincarnated into a body.

I'm going to be another body's System.

Origin System Message

Mana allotted to [**Godkiller**] Jerome Smith.

Tutorial allotted to [**Godkiller**] Jerome Smith.

Ready for Integration process.

P-System Log

Hold on. Tutorial? Why don't I get a tutorial? Am I supposed to just figure things out as I go along? What even is my purpose here? Am I going to be stuck in someone else's body? Am I going to have to work? Will I even have any control over myself?

And why couldn't I have gotten a better class?

Origin System Message

Beginning Integration process . . .

<WARNING: Both targets possess high W Inertia. Integration may require significant mana.>

Mana consumed.

Mana consumed.

Mana consumed.

<ERROR>

Reconfiguring . . .

System Integration complete!

Jerome Smith

Class	Race	Level
Godkiller	Human	1

Stat	Current	Maximum
Mana	1,000	1,000
Health	500	500

Skills	[Magic Missile lv. 1]
Titles	[Reincarnator]

Stat	Modifier	Total
Strength	+10	25
Magic	+12	27
Insight	-5	10
Constitution	+8	23

P-System Log

I can see. Kind of. I've got a dome of perception right now, and some line of sight within it? The dome is strongest around a center point, and then it starts losing effectiveness maybe ten, twenty meters out. I'm going to have to test it out later. I've got the same sightless perception inside it, like I can feel everything, but my skin is really, really numb.

I think . . . I think I might have gotten attached to a guy. I just saw the stats of this Jerome fella pop into my mind, and it looks like he's looking at them right now.

If everything I was told was true . . .

I suppose there's worse people I could've gotten attached to. This guy's stats look pretty solid, at least. Then again, having not seen anything else in this world, I can't really judge for sure.

We—or he, I guess, I still don't have a physical body—are in the middle of a grassy field, one with blades that go past Jerome's hip. Looks like he got reincarnated with Earth-style clothes. Jeans and a long-sleeved shirt, which has got to be making him hot. Not that I can tell, since I can't feel the temperature without focusing on it.

There's a town off in the distance, I think, but it's kind of fuzzy. Some deep part of me tells me that the name of that town is Maplecrest, and I'm not sure if I like that. Having knowledge that I didn't even know about . . . that indicates something weird with the Origin System.

Speaking of which, I totally forgot to be mad at it for sticking me somewhere without my consent! Like, what the hell, man? I didn't even get a tutorial!

Oh hey. There's an animal approaching Jerome. I have that same numb-touch blind-sight sensation with it, but there's something more. Like I can connect to it. Hang on, I'll try.

Nameless Wolf		

Class	Race	Level
-	Wolf	1

Stat	Current	Maximum
Mana	0	0
Health	20	20

Skills	[Bite lv. 3], <HIDDEN>
Titles	-

Stat	Modifier	Total
Strength	-	<HIDDEN>
Magic	-	<HIDDEN>
Insight	-	<HIDDEN>
Constitution	-	<HIDDEN>

[**Magic Missile**] activating!

System Prompt

Activate a [**Magic Missile**]. Mana invested: 10

P-System Log

. . . how the hell do I do this?

CHAPTER 2

[**Bite**] dealt 9 damage to you!

P-System Log

Shit, shit, shit, shit fuck!
Thanks, *Origin System*. More like Origin Idiot, am I right?
. . . humor was never my strong suit.
Okay, Parker, focus.

[**Bite**] dealt 11 damage to you!

Hero's Personal Log 001

What the fuck! Okay, I finally figured out how to open this thing.
System, what the fuck?
It says [**Magic Missile**] in my stats. I have a decently high magic stat.
Where is my magic?

P-System Log

Oh, no no no no.
That wasn't me thinking there.
Was that . . . was that Jerome? The Origin System said that I was going to be his System, so I guess that's to be expected, but I dunno. I didn't really see that one coming.

[**Bite**] dealt 8 damage to you!

P-System Log

Agh! Okay, this is important!

It looks like the health pool is doing something. This obviously isn't my world—*duh, Parker, you're literally a disembodied voice floating around in blue boxes*—so I guess that makes sense, too. Jerome isn't taking the physical effects of the hits that he should be feeling, and all that's happening is his health is going down.

He . . . honestly doesn't seem that scared about the wolf that should be straight up mauling him. More annoyed than anything else, really.

Is he annoyed at *me*?

System Prompt

Activate a [**Magic Missile**]. Mana invested: 10

P-System Log

I understand, okay? Maybe if you'd given me a tutorial on how to do this shit, we wouldn't have a problem!

. . . okay.

How am I supposed to use magic? I assume the prompt is some pre-programmed stuff from the Origin System, making sure I'm not 100 percent on my own, but it would have been real nice if it could've come with an instruction manual.

I can figure this out. The numb-touch perception sense I've got going is probably the key here. I can tell what's happening and where things are. Sight in a different way from having eyes, I think. And I can identify more information from my surroundings than I could before I died. I can sense the air pressure, little changes in the rustling of the grass, the hairs on the legs of the flies that are flying through the fields . . .

And that's not to mention the stat sheets that I can just feel, waiting for me to open them.

Wait, I can detect something that wasn't here a moment before.

Uhhh . . .

[**Blazing Spear**] cast!

P-System Log

Hold on, that wasn't me. I detected the message in the same way that I saw the messages about [**Bite**] hitting Jerome.

This is someone else, then?

I'm gonna focus my perception just a little more . . .

Axel Anselton

Class	Race	Level
Apprentice Mage	Human	9

Stat	Current	Maximum
Mana	113	137
Health	77	77

Skills	[Magic Missile lv. 6], [Assess lv. 4], [Fire Resistance lv. 1], [Magic Resistance lv. 1], [Simple Shield lv. 2], [Blazing Spear lv. 2], [Acid Spray lv. 1]
Titles	[Student]

Stat	Modifier	Total
Strength	-	<HIDDEN>
Magic	-	<HIDDEN>
Insight	-	<HIDDEN>
Constitution	-	<HIDDEN>

[**Blazing Spear**] cast!

P-System Log

Okay! Finally, something is happening! I detected a few abnormalities in the air.

There was a distortion where the new figure came in from. Axel, I think. Not a reincarnator, from the stats, so I guess this is our first natural inhabitant of this world. Apart from the wolf, at least.

Yeah, this is definitely someone from this world. Either that or he's the most dedicated cosplayer I've ever seen. He has a whole setup with trousers, long-ass leather boots, and a cloak that wouldn't have been out of place at AnimeCon.

More importantly, he cast magic. I have that weird perception thing going, and I caught the spell (or skill, whatever they want to call it) forming. The air . . . warped, kind of, in a way that ripped apart cause and effect and made my numb touch go haywire for a moment. I don't know how I'm supposed to influence the world, but this Axel guy has to have a System, too, because I assume otherwise he wouldn't have a stat sheet.

That means I have a reference point on what I'm supposed to be doing.

Also, the wolf died. Didn't get a message for that. I *sensed* it happen, yeah, and I can perceive its dead body there, but I didn't get a direct notification. I got direct notifications for magic in the area as well as effects being applied to Jerome . . . I suppose I am supposed to be linked to him.

More pressingly, there's a conversation going on right now. I can hear it, but it's like I'm hearing it from every angle all at once at every volume and, well, it's a little discomforting. Still, this sounds important, and I feel like I should record it if I can . . .

P-System Log [Conversation Jerome–Axel 001]

Unfortunately, after a whole ten seconds of searching, I haven't found a way to create recordings of my perception. I did, however, realize that I can add a tagline to these message logs and look back at them, so that's good.

Nothing to be done about it. I guess I'll just try transcribing it here.

Jerome (oh, hell yeah, I can bold shit): Who the hell are you?

Axel: You must be a reincarnator. Master K'lon saw the magic signature flare.

Jerome: Magic signature?

Axel: Oh, you must be new. Haven't you used your, uh, tutorial? I think that's what they're called. Don't you have a guide to our world in your head somewhere?

Jerome: I kind of glazed over a lot of it, to be honest.

Axel: So you're one of *those*.

Jerome: What do you mean by that?

I'm not going to bother transcribing what they're saying right now. Just imagine that there's a bunch of back-and-forth with mild insults that I think Jerome is completely missing.

Future Parker is going to hate me, huh.

God(s. I guess. The being that put me here seemed awfully like one, at least), could I have at least gotten a smarter reincarnator?

Oh. Something's happening now. The weird ripping-in-reality sensation is there again. Another spell?

[**Assess**] cast!

P-System Log [nope nope nope nope]

I don't like that, not at all.

The warping effect is coming toward me. Feels weird. It's probably the clearest thing I've been able to perceive so far, along with the [**Blazing Spear**] earlier.

I don't want that shit to touch me. Lemme try and . . .

[**Assess**] spell blocked!

P-System Log [fuck you, Origin]

Oh, for fuck's sake. You can tell me that I blocked the spell but not how to block it? What kind of useless god are you?

I'm going to have *words* with the Origin System, whenever I connect to it again. If I do.

But that's not relevant right now. I think I just *did* something. Something important.

Not quite magic, but I did shape what I feel. Using my not-body to manipulate the not-air and slap that rip in reality.

I'm learning.

And it looks like that other guy realized it, too.

P-System Log [Conversation Jerome–Axel 001, cont.]

Axel: Hail, reincarnator! You must already be proficient in the use of the B System!

Jerome: What do you mean by that? Damn thing can't even listen to activate my most basic skills.

Axel: But you blocked my [**Assess**] just now! You must be skilled indeed.

Jerome (picture him confused and speaking all weird): I didn't do anything.

Axel: Hmph. If you say so. You said your System was working weird?

Jerome: It's not working. I tried a [**Magic Missile**] and it just . . . fizzled.

Axel: Odd. Perhaps Master K'lon can help you? I can escort you to him.

Jerome: Can he fix it?

Axel: Hopefully.

Jerome: Then yes. Take me to him.

Come on! I actually have reference for how magic works now! Gimme a chance, man . . .

Alright, to be fair, I did sit there and let him get mauled by a wolf. But still!

Wait, I'm still doing this in the conversation log—

Hero's Personal Log 002

Going to meet the village. Hopefully this exposition fairy can be more useful than the last one. [**Godkiller**] seems to be a really good class for leveling, but I gotta get my System in working order first. Useless piece of shit.

P-System Log

. . .
I resent that.
Guess we're going to the village, though. Yay?
Maybe I'll even figure out how to cast along the way!

CHAPTER 3

Jerome's been walking for a bit. My perception "dome" is following him. Another point for the Origin System being right. Looks like I really am attached to him.

Fuck me, man. Am I going to be stuck like this forever? It's neat, having this kinda semi-omniscient magic System thing going on, but do I really want to spend eternity stuck like this?

Questions for later, Parker.

For now, I have to figure out how the hell I can cast the magic that I'm supposed to be able to.

Parker [ALIAS: P-System]

Class	Race	Level
PERSONAL_SYSTEM	SYSTEM	-

Stat	Current	Maximum
W Inertia	38,316	38,317
Mana	-	-
Health	<ERROR>	<ERROR>

Skills	[W%M; G, P]
Titles	[System], [Reincarnator]

Other statistics have been deemed irrelevant.

P-System Log

Aside from the obvious—I don't have any stats like a human should—there's one key difference between me and Jerome.

The W Inertia stat.

I don't know what it does. I haven't been able to see what others have. But I can see my own. Is that what makes me a System? Or does it do something else?

I don't think I can truly understand what it means until I link up with the Origin System again and pick its brains. Still, I can maybe glean certain things from it.

It dropped by a single point. The only thing I can think of that might have triggered it was the bitchslap I gave to that [**Apprentice Mage**]'s spell. What does that indicate?

Inertia is the tendency of an object to stay in motion or stay at rest. Basically, how resistant it is to an outside force, or the angular momentum divided by the angular speed in circular motion. How does that relate to magic? It shouldn't be a consumable property, but I lost a point somehow. Is it going to come back? What did I even gain? Am I just substituting it for mana?

There's just too many damn unknowns. What W stands for, its specific purpose, what the term *inertia* even means in this context—come to think of it, I got transported to a fantasy world as a disembodied System, it's entirely possible that the word means something different here—and so much more.

Whatever the case, it doesn't look like I'm going to run out of it anytime soon. That might change when I learn how to make Jerome's spells actually become spells, but that's a problem for then.

P-System Log [important thoughts 1]

Do I even want to cast Jerome's spells? From all appearances, this guy's not the brightest, and he's kind of entitled, too. I wouldn't be surprised to see him go full murderhobo once I start casting spells for him, to be honest, and I don't know if I like the thought of that.

On the other hand, what happens if I don't? I know next to nothing about this world (thanks a lot, Origin). Maybe Axel's master is strong enough to forcefully recalibrate me. Maybe my ol' buddy Origin will step in if I'm not doing the right job.

I . . . I don't want that. Keeping myself alive and *me* is my number one priority, and from what the Origin System told me, one that I already managed to fail at last life. I'm not going to let that happen again.

Besides, I'm pretty sure I remember being told that Jerome's job was to defeat the Eternal King. Not sure what that entails, but the name sounds like an endboss that's guaranteed to have some level of cruel rule to its name. I'm not going to stand by and let people suffer, and if Jerome is going to be a force of enduring good, it should damn well be my place to enable it.

Also, I do have to admit that I like the idea of being able to cast magic. Even if it's not my own. So . . .

Guess that settles that for now.

P-System Log [poetry]

roses are red
violets are blue
Origin, are you listening?
if so, then fuck you

P-System Log

We're on our way to the village right now. It's not inside my dome, but I can kind of make it out off in the distance. Looks like a really bog-standard starting village, if I'm being honest. I can't make everything out, but it's got all the markings of one. We'll see more about it when we get there.

Axel and Jerome are having a conversation. Wonder if I can get any information out of it.

P-System Log [Conversation Jerome–Axel 002]

Jerome: Tell me more about this world.

Axel: The tutorial didn't cover that?

Jerome: It was . . . incomplete. I don't know how to describe it, but there were parts of it that I *know* were missing. Broken pieces flung off into the void.

Axel: Alright, I suppose I must provide.

Axel: The village of Maplecrest will welcome you with open arms. We receive many of your kind—

Jerome: Reincarnators? There's a lot of us, then?

Axel: Reincarnators, yes. We used to get more, but the rate has dropped off recently. Only about one a month, these days.

Jerome: So you're a starting village.

Axel: The hometown in which I was born and raised being referred to as a "starting village" rubs me the wrong way, but in essence, yes. We are one of the Edge Cities.

Jerome: Edge Cities?

Axel: We exist on the outskirts of the Continent. Here, we lie unmolested by the reaches of the Eternal King.

Jerome: Oh, I think I remember that from the tutorial. He controls a lot of the Continent, right?

Axel: Eighty-one percent. Legend says that the Eternal King himself exists at the very center of it all, in his Forgotten City, where the world itself crumbles away into nothingness.

Jerome: I was told my job here was to defeat him. Why should I? I wasn't told much beyond him being a fearsome force of darkness or whatever. Why should I care?

[Parker's note: Hey, the other reincarnator actually has some sense to him! Maybe his really shit Insight doesn't mean everything?]

Axel: The Eternal King and his forces are anathema to us Integrated.

Jerome: Integrated refers those of us with the System, right?

Axel: Correct. It is not exclusive to you reincarnators. The Eternal King brings with him an indescribable, inexorable, Integration-destroying force. Living in his domain is lethal to those of us native to these lands, and so we've largely been forced to the Edge Cities. Every day, another of our outposts falls, another Edge City falls to the Eternal King's march.

Jerome: So the System wants me to end the domain.

Axel: As a reincarnator, it is your purpose. The System sends us brave souls like yourself to liberate us from the Eternal King's wrath.

And how has that been going for you so far, huh? Forty-four percent left uninhabitable? Also, if these guys have Systems, too, are those Systems also people like me? I feel like the answer is no. I don't know where the feeling is coming from—information from the Origin System, maybe? Ugh, get out of my head.

Jerome: . . .

Jerome: Can I level up by doing this?

Axel: A question better left for Master K'lon. Between you and me, though, I think you can. I've heard tales about the great [**Wandering Hero**] Arthur Samson. He was a reincarnator that passed through this very Edge City, and I've heard that he's over level 150 now.

Jerome: I'm in, then. As long as I can get this stupid System of mine fixed.

Axel: For your sake and ours, I hope so, too.

P-System Log

Fantastic. More of what I already knew. I'm damaged goods right now. Hopefully meeting this new guy will help clear things up for me. At the very least, I'll be able to try a spell. The manipulation I did with the perception dome earlier seemed to do the trick for blocking the [**Assess**]—if I'm lucky, the same principle will apply to casting spells.

Just as important, though, is the information Axel just gave. The Origin System was awfully stingy when it was giving me details about what I was actually supposed to be doing here, but Axel has contextualized it some.

Final boss is the Eternal King, I already knew that, but the nature of its—or his, I guess—threat is nice to know. Self-preservation is a decent motivation for Jerome to go for it, but somehow I don't think that's going to be his focus. I could practically feel him light up inside when Axel was talking about leveling up.

Speaking of which, am *I* supposed to be handling levels? Apparently, I'm supposed to be casting his magic, so I wouldn't be surprised if there was even more that I'm supposed to do.

This isn't going to be the last time I complain about Origin, I don't think. Could I have at least gotten *some* direction? If I'm able to manage his level of power, can I just jack it up to infinity and then steamroll the Eternal King and be done with the mission?

The issue is I don't know how to do any of these things. I think I can approximate a spell now that I've witnessed a couple, but I have no idea what a level up looks like.

Looks like we're approaching the village. There are buildings in my perception dome now, quaint little wooden structures that really scream "generic fantasy village." I think I can perceive what's inside of them, and it's all common stuff like you might find in a procedurally generated home in one of the newer-gen open-world RPGs.

The warping sensation that I felt with the magic is back now. Are the items inside these buildings magic, too? No, it can't be that. I'm fairly sure that a loaf of bread doesn't have any magical properties to it.

Am I causing the warps? I'm gonna try focusing on them a little more. Focusing . . .

There's something there. In the warps. Almost solid, like I can reach out and touch it.

New skill unlocked: [**Assess**]

You may identify objects and enemies around you.

P-System Log

Well, that's something.

CHAPTER 4

P-System Log [Skill Discovered]

That message was as much a shock to me as it was to Jerome, it seems. Looks like both of us saw the pop-up at the same time, because he recoiled ever so slightly, and I'm pretty sure he was staring off into the space right in front of him.

Oh, conversation. This might be important.

Axel: Is something the matter?

Jerome: Uh, no, nothing at all.

Axel: Okay, he's not saying anything, but picture him squinting all suspicious-like.

Jerome: I think my System might be working.

Axel: May I examine your status sheet?

Jerome: Sure, I guess.

P-System Log

Uh-oh. He's going to use that same spell again, right?
I guess I can just let it pass this time. [**Assess**] isn't harmful, right?

[**Assess**] cast!

Jerome Smith		
Class	**Race**	**Level**
Godkiller	Human	1

Stat	**Current**	**Maximum**
Mana	990	1,000
Health	472	500

Skills	[Magic Missile lv. 1], [Assess lv. 1]
Titles	[Reincarnator]

Stat	**Modifier**	**Total**
Strength	+10	25
Magic	+12	27
Insight	-5	10
Constitution	+8	23

P-System Log [Jerome talks to Axel about me]

    I'm not going to bother tagging these with numbers anymore. I'm totally going to forget what each one refers to.

    Anyway.

Axel: Your status sheet seems to be in good shape, at least. And your class! It's **[Legendary]** level! Your mana is criminally high! Reincarnators, I swear . . .

Jerome: Yep. I just gained a skill. **[Assess]**, the System said.

Axel: Interesting. Were you, perhaps, perceiving something particularly hard? Many reincarnators begin without the most basic skills like that and the resistances, but they tend to gain them quite quickly.

Jerome: I suppose I was looking at the town a lot . . .

Axel: That might've done it.

Hey, that was all me!

Then again, I'm not sure how much of that really *was* me. I've been kind of playing it by ear, but from what I've heard, the Systems that handle each person's stats and magic and stuff should probably be displaying the message.

That message . . . It wasn't my choice to display it. Was that a gift from the Origin System, making sure I wasn't completely alone? Something to help guide the way as I figure out what I'm supposed to be doing?

Then again, it could just be an odd quirk of how this world works. I really don't know enough.

Damn it all, couldn't I have gotten a tutorial?

Oh, something just came to mind. Jerome spent ten mana. Was that me spending his mana on the [**Assess**] just now? Or was it the expended mana from the [**Magic Missile**] that I failed to cast earlier?

Questions, questions, questions, and none of them ones that I can actually answer.

Speaking of which, is what I'm doing mana manipulation? It's like, not *not* mana manipulation, as far as I can tell, but I don't know what mana is in this world. Have I been perceiving it this whole time? I think the surest bet for it is the rip-in-reality sensation I've got. Maybe messing with that counts as screwing with mana.

And what the hell is W Inertia?

[**Assess**] activating!

System Prompt

Activate [**Assess**]. Mana invested: 10
Object identified: **Wooden Door**

P-System Log

That's interesting. I could actually feel him initiate the spell, now that I know what he's trying to do, and I could feel where he was aiming it. There's a lot more data about that wooden door stored in my head (well, not quite a head, but you get the point) that didn't get to that screen, though. I can feel them, hiding just beneath the surface, like they're just waiting for me to dig a little deeper. Weird, useless stats, but they're still there. I'm going to reach just a little deeper . . .

Wooden Door

Attribute	Current
Type	Oak
Height	213 cm
Width	112 cm
<HIDDEN>	<HIDDEN>

Stat	Current	Maximum
Mana	-	-
Health	53	60
W Inertia	2	2
<HIDDEN>	<HIDDEN>	<HIDDEN>

Stat	Total
ATK	+2
DEF	-1
<HIDDEN>	<HIDDEN>

P-System Log

Hoooooly shit. Okay, okay, that was totally unnecessary. It's literally just a door, I don't need to know its entire historical bloodline!

Okay, I'm definitely being aided by the Origin System, right? Unless you're telling me that seeing these huge blue windows in my mind's eye—ones that have the audacity to tell me that *even more* facts about this goddamn door are being <HIDDEN> from me—is part and parcel of a normal life in this place?

I mean, I guess it is, but that's because of us Systems. As far as I know, I shouldn't have a System of my own, so the only proper conclusion is that Origin did something to me to help me comprehend all this raw data. I would be mad, normally, but I have to shift my goalposts a little. I'm not the person I was on Earth. Matter of fact, I'm not a person anymore. I'm going to have to get comfortable with a world with godlike entities like whatever's behind the Origin System.

Jerome doesn't seem to have reacted to the notification, and I feel like he would've if he'd seen whatever that mess was, so that probably means that was for me only.

That [**Assess**] did manage to bring up a few new questions, though. First off, the W Inertia stat. I thought that it was unique to me, since the two human stat sheets I'd seen hadn't mentioned W Inertia, but just glancing at this door particularly hard had revealed that it, too, had this stat. Something tells me that if I try to dig deeper into the stat sheets that Axel and Jerome have, I might find something similar. Why is that? Is it dangerous for people to know what it is? Is it a back-end kind of deal where only Systems can know and use it?

Too many questions and not enough answers. Basically the only thing I can conclude from this is a) the world is confusing and b) when Jerome casts a spell, it says [**Spell**] activating, while the window says [**Spell**] was cast if someone else does.

Oh, new person!

Hopefully this lady who just entered my perception dome can help us. She's outside a building. Focusing on that building gives me the sense that it's an Adventurer's Guild, by which I mean that it probably is, since I get that same impression of potential deeper [**Assess**] being available there.

The woman seems more important than the building, though. She's nearly as tall as Jerome is, and she's wearing long, dark-blue robes with a ponytail dyed the same color. If Axel was a suggestion that this world's fashion customs were different from ours, she seals the deal. This new woman looks like she could be commissioned art for somebody's D&D OC.

[**Assess**] activating!

Integrated identified: **Human [Mage lv. 26] Aster K'lon**

P-System Log

Oh, that's interesting. When Jerome activated the spell, I felt something from him, like he had half of a whole. I completed that half with around the same power, manipulating the not-air I can perceive to do so, and it looks like it came out to be a lower power than what I can do on my own.

I did it fast enough that the System Prompt didn't show up, but we didn't get a full status sheet from that. I guess it need [Assess] to be a higher level before it can do that. Which, y'know, I don't actually know how to increase, but we'll burn that bridge when we get to it.

Well, it's less cluttered, at least. Fun!

Looks like Aster is the "Master K'lon" that Axel was referring to. Let's see if Jerome can weasel any information out of her.

P-System Log [Introduction to Aster]

Axel: Master K'lon! I thought you were resting!

Aster: I felt the reincarnation occur. I could not remain resting while that happened.

Jerome: This guy here—

Aster: Axel.

Jerome: Yeah, Axel says you can help me. My System's broken or malfunctioning or something.

Aster: May I chance a look at it?

Jerome: Sure. I'm watching you, though. Don't try anything tricky.

Aster: Wouldn't dream of it.

[Greater Assess] cast!

P-System Log

. . . I'm just going to let this one hit me. No point in making this any harder than it should be.

Oh, she's saying something.

Aster: . . . incredible. Your System is deviant.

Jerome: Deviant?

Aster: I haven't seen it much, but it has occurred. In two other reincarnators, I saw them with a System that was *more*. Like it was a living, breathing being.

Shit. I'm not the first? Are there more of me?

Jerome: Is it a bad thing?

Aster: Far from it. One of them became one of the greatest heroes known to the Edge Cities, and his System only had a little bit of that feeling to it. Your System contains it in spades.

Wait, so are the other living Systems not human? Or, well, not originally human? Less than human? I dunno.

Jerome: Sure doesn't feel like it.

Aster: Patience. I am yet unexperienced with deviants, but both of those who passed through Maplecrest saw difficulty engaging with their Systems. Your time will come.

Jerome: How do you know it's a good thing? Can you prove that my System is different in a way that isn't just breaking it apart?

Aster: Come around to the back. I have something to show you.

P-System Log

Starting a new log, I'll tag the last one with something relevant later.

Something is happening. Aster is taking us—well, Jerome, I'm just here for the ride—to the back of the Adventurer's Guild. Still doing my best to not focus too hard on the building. Don't want to overwhelm myself with useless info again.

The building is *big*. Like, large enough to be a town hall big. For a village of this size, it's almost comical in how large it is, and even then it seems pretty populated.

I suppose adventuring is a popular profession around these parts. That . . . It says a lot about the world, at least. The Continent, if Origin is to be believed. Does this mean that adventuring can produce food and materials? If the incredible number of people entering my perception dome are anything to go by, the supermajority of the villagers are adventurers. There's no way that's sustainable if adventuring can't provide something other than money.

Oh, we're at the back now. Aster's unlocking a thick steel door that really looks like it's supposed to stay closed . . .

Aster: Try and use [**Assess**] on what's chained inside our laboratory.

That's a *lab*? From what I can perceive of it, it's no better than a dungeon, complete with steel bars, a rough dirt floor, and chains attached to each corner of it that are holding down . . .

Holding down . . .

There's a hole in my perception where the prisoner (lab experiment? unfortunate adventurer?) should be. It's the size of a human, I *think*, but it's painful to perceive and it feels *wrong* and **I hate it it should be killed and burned in the flames of**

Owwwwww, fuck. Didn't realize that I can still somehow feel pain despite not having nerve endings to feel it with. I'm gonna try to not perceive that, I think. I don't know what effect is causing that, but I can assume it's magical, and . . .

[**Assess**] activating!

P-System Log

Ah, shit.

I wonder if I just use the spell instead of trying to perceive it myself . . . ? If I do the magic, will it come out to be any less bad?

Integrated identified: **<ERROR> [<ERROR>] <ERROR>**

P-System Log

. . . that's not good. As much as I hate to do it, I kind of want to see what's inside there. It feels wrong to even perceive, and every part of me is screaming that I need to **destroy destroy kill burn end** it as soon as possible, but what could possibly cause an error?

The instinct to kill it isn't alone. I need to understand it need to know it need to evaluate need to eviscerate need need need—

I'm going to focus more attention on it.

P-System Log

Ow! Piece of shit!

<table>
<tr><td colspan="3"><ERROR></td></tr>
</table>

Class	Race	Level
<ERROR>	<ERROR>	<ERROR>

Stat	Current	Maximum
Mana	<ERROR>	<ERROR>
Health	<ERROR>	<ERROR>

Skills	<ERROR>
Titles	<ERROR>

<ERROR: REMAINING STATS NOT AVAILABLE>

THIS IS NOT ONE OF OURS

P-System Log

Not one of ours? Then what the hell is it? Also, what kind of error message is that?

I hurt. I hurt everywhere and nowhere. This is not something I should be doing, I *know* that, but at the same time, I can feel the urges of myself and something that definitely isn't myself pushing me along and I *need to see what this is*.

I'm going to look again, and I'm going to look harder.

System Prompt

<ERROR> encountered.

Recalibrating . . .

Recalibrating . . .

Recalibrated!

▼

Name: Bill Stonebreaker

Class: Thief | **Race:** Goblin

Level: 2 | **XP:** 12/110

Health: 32/60 | **Mana:** 20/20

Fortitude	10	Perception	5
Magic Power	12	Agility	5
Magic Regeneration	7	Strength	15

Skills

▼

CHAPTER 5

P-System Log

I feel like I've said "what the fuck" too many times already, so I offer an alternative:

What the balls?

It's *red*. Why the fuck is it red?

I've got this burning feeling in me. Like nothing else I've felt so far. Reminds me of how I felt when my professors back home were being utter dicks, but damn if it doesn't feel a hundred times worse.

I think it might be the lasting effects of good ol' Origin. Maybe the same effect as the wrongness I felt when I was initially perceiving this . . . thing.

But that's not important. Even if my anger at this thing is caused by a mental compulsion, I can't deny the fact that I absolutely *know* that it isn't supposed to be here.

I can make its figure out now that I've done a deeper perception of it. Still painful to think at, but I can mostly see its shape by examining the edges of the wrongness I can sense.

I want to kill it. I don't know how and I don't know if I can, but I want to rip it apart. Whatever that thing is, it should be *gone*.

P-System Log [exposition lady gives us exposition]

Lovely. Looks like our new friend Aster is telling Jerome what this is.

Aster: Did you feel that?

Jerome: Yes. Kind of. Was that my mana getting more intense?

Aster: Indeed. Your System reacted to it.

Jerome: What is that? It looks like a pretty average goblin to me.

Aster: You're one of the more adaptable reincarnators, then, if this doesn't surprise you. The last one we had ran away from this capture the moment he encountered it.

Jerome: I'm familiar with fantasy—er, these types of monsters.

Aster: This is a monster, yes, but not because it is a goblin.

Jerome: Goblins aren't evil?

Aster: They are good and evil just like humans are. This one, however, is truly destructive. It is what we call an R Beast.

Jerome: R . . . Beast?

Aster: Short for Red.

Hey, aren't those the same number of syllables? Why would they shorten it?

Ugh, it's not like I can ask.

Jerome: This is what the Eternal King wields?

Aster: The Eternal King wields power over many beings of this type. We know not of why they are anathema to our Systems, but most Systems will encounter difficulties when processing them, and many who come into contact with them perish shortly after.

Jerome: Ah, so I'm supposed to be killing a bunch of R Beasts?

Aster: More heavily phrased than I would have put it, but yes. As a reincarnator, it is ultimately your duty to save the Edge Cities from the Eternal King's R Beasts.

Ooh, exposition! That's nice to have.

Jerome (quietly, he's whispering): Thank fuck for exposition fairies.

Man, something about thinking the same way as that guy does not make me feel right.

Well, that's that, then. They're discussing more about how to determine what's wrong with me. Honestly, I'm just hoping that one of them casts a spell. I'll probably learn more from that than their conversation.

P-System Log

I need to kill the R Beast. It's a blight upon my perception, and if the wave of hostility I'm sensing from it is anything to go by, it's a blight upon this world.

It needs to die.

Can I replicate the [**Blazing Spear**] that Axel used?

I can recall what it felt like. Scarily well, actually. I kind of figured out how to do my own manipulation of my dome when I figured out [**Assess**]. For an offensively oriented spell, I should just need to direct that manipulation differently, right?

It's like I'm pulling on threads that aren't actually there.

If I do it just so, in the same manner that Axel did with his spell . . .

System Prompt

<ERROR: Authorization not obtained.>

Offensive spells require Integrated authorization!

Decasting spell . . .

Spell decasted.

P-System Log [oh screw off]

That's not even a prompt! That's just straight up an error message!

This is the second time I'm seeing a System Prompt that looked like that. I think it's safe to assume that this is an Origin System thing, because from what I've heard so far, most other Systems don't need this kind of guidance. Unless this is just a built-in thing.

Oh, talking.

Aster: Did you feel that?

Jerome: Kind of. What was that?

Aster: Half a spell. The execution half, missing your direction. Your System reacted instinctively to the R Beast, moving to attack it. The standard System that I, Axel, and the supermajority of the Edge Cities' residents possess would never do that.

Jerome: So it has a mind of its own?

Aster: Not necessarily. It may simply be more complex than other Systems.

Jerome: I see. So like an AI of some sort.

Aster: AI?

Jerome: Don't worry about it.

Okay! So he doesn't think I'm a person. Yay? Or not yay? I . . . guess I'll figure that out later. For the time being, I think I'm alright with not being identified. I want to at least figure things out and be an intact System before we get to that stage.

Some things never change, huh. I was a nervous wreck back on Earth and am still kind of one now.

P-System Log [Jerome, Axel, Aster speaking]

I should really go back to standardizing the tags on these, but it's so much more fun just thinking whatever and then putting that down.

Anyway, they're speaking, so here we are.

Jerome: So can you teach me about magic?

Aster: I may be able to, but I can only teach the basics.

Axel: Master K'lon enjoys a more practical method of teaching.

Aster: You can say that I just toss you into the dungeons, you know.

Jerome: Dungeons? You have dungeons here?

Aster: Indeed. They are autonomous, regenerating structures run by Dungeon Cores.

Jerome: Those are a thing here, too? I'm familiar with the concept.

Aster: Of course a reincarnator gifted with a [**Legendary**] rarity class would know. I'll detail them anyway, as you may be missing some critical details.

Jerome: Sure.

Aster: Just like with our classes, Dungeon Cores have rarities, which you can generally identify by the intensity and wavelength of magic they radiate. When you use an [**Assess**]-type spell on them, they'll usually return a color. White is [**Common**], green is [**Uncommon**], blue is [**Rare**], purple is [**Epic**], gold is [**Legendary**], and red is [**Unique**]. Maplecrest is one of the safest Edge Cities, furthest away from the dangerous borders near the Eternal King's domain, so we mostly have whites and greens around here. As you get closer toward the Eternal King's realm, the dungeons and monsters tend to increase in class, even if they aren't R Beasts.

Oof. That's a lot of information. It helps with some questions, at least, but as seems to be the trend right now, it opens up even more. The way she described it, it seems like a red class is more powerful—or at least rarer—than basically anything else. I don't *think* that applies to errors, because I don't think anyone else has been reacting to them. It might just be me that can see them.

More importantly, my class is [**PERSONAL_SYSTEM**]. That's red. Am I really that powerful? Sure doesn't feel like it.

Am I alone? I think I might be. Aster said there were others that had boosted Systems that weren't quite normal, but I'm getting the sense that they might not have been people like me, especially if this class is [**Unique**].

Ugh. The R goblin is making it hard to think. It's just . . . *there*, like someone is constantly breathing down my neck.

Well, not—okay, you get the point, future Parker. Hopefully when you look back on this one day, you'll be better at dealing with it.

P-System Log [learning magic]

The exposition is done, I think. The lady *finally* took us out of the Adventurer's Guild, so the feeling stopped. I still want to kill that piece-of-shit R Beast dead, but it looks like I literally can't take action unless Jerome wants to.

That's . . . really irritating, and kind of frightening. My actions being controlled by something beyond my power is really not something I'm a fan of, but man . . . I don't think there's anything I can do about it.

I can still be angry, though! >:((oh god what the fuck I can do emoticons this is terrible I'm never doing this again look away future Parker)

P-System Log [Learning Magic (for real this time)]

Okay. As I was saying. Perception dome is picking up a pretty flat meadow now. Lots of grass, rocks, and a few esoteric plants that are all clamoring for me to inspect further. I'm not going to make that mistake again, ya pieces of shit! I do *not* need to know the mana storage of a blade of grass right now.

Apart from those, I can sense a few other presences. Uhhh . . . I count three. They're kind of just milling about right now. Not human, if their movement pattern and size are anything to go by. They're remarkably blob-shaped.

Oops. I can sense Jerome starting a spell. Now that I know what it's like,

I can really identify it, and it *is* pretty obvious. Not quite sure how I missed this earlier.

[**Assess**] activating!

Integrated identified: **Slime [Slime lv. 3] Nameless**

P-System Log

Huh, there's that simple [**Assess**] again. Is it because it's low level? I determine that, right? I wonder how I'm supposed to level it up. I know for a fact that I'm able to do more detailed versions of the same spell myself, but when I completed Jerome's spell, I just did it with the same amount of power he put into it, which . . . wasn't really that much. Ten mana, I think? I don't know what that quantity represents in my perception, but I'm pretty sure it's not that much when Jerome has like a hundred times that.

. . . maybe Origin will have some hints for me? Please?

P-System Log [Learning Magic (for real this time) part 2]

Aster: See these slimes?

Jerome: They seem harmless enough.

Aster: They are. Watch me, and you may begin to learn.

Axel: It took me near a month of practicing [**Magic Missile**] and trying to execute [**Blazing Spear**] until I was able to cast it. Are you sure about this?

Aster: Jerome is a reincarnator.

Axel: I suppose that's true.

Jerome: Hopefully my System will cooperate.

Aster: When I [**Assess**]ed you, you only had [**Magic Missile**]. At level 1, you should be able to absorb at least one spell of [**Uncommon**] rarity.

Jerome: And all I do is watch?

Aster: Feel the way the mana shapes in the air. Imitate me, and you may be able to execute it yourself.

[**Blazing Spear**] cast!

P-System Log

Okay, I got it. I was watching really carefully this time, and I *think* I've got the pattern down. It looks like a one-two type of thing, where there's a particular way the not-air—mana, if Aster is to believed, though I'm not one hundred percent sure on that—is being manipulated first by the user (Integrated?) and then by the System. I think.

Jerome: Uhhhh . . . I don't think I got that. I'm not sure if my sense for it was enough. Was I supposed to [**Assess**] it?

Oh, for fuck's sake, man. I mean, yeah, I've got the superior sensory suite by far and I can instinctively feel out the magic, but why can't he even figure out this tiny thing?

Actually, when I put it like that, that makes total sense.

Okay, hold on . . . I don't want to be here for ages while we wait for Jerome to figure something out. Can I imitate something for him? I know when I tried to use [**Assess**] on my own earlier, using the magical method rather than the inherent perception abilities I have, I got the <ERROR>. But if I don't go all the way with the spell, and I just try to help him out by showing the part he's supposed to do . . .

I'm gonna try that.

P-System Log [dammit, Jerome]

Jerome: I feel something. I don't know if I can copy it, though.

Aster: See? I told you. Your System is responding to your whims. You must learn to work with it, and then you may be able to harness stronger magics.

Jerome: Lemme try something.

Overcharged [**Magic Missile**] activating!

System Prompt

Activate a [**Magic Missile**]. Mana invested: 20 (overcharge)

P-System Log

Huh, he charged it more. Didn't know he could do that. Maybe I need to examine his stat sheet a little more carefully.

Also, it's good to know that at least he knows the first half of *this* spell. I think Origin might have given us a little help here, since I'm definitely not guiding him right now.

Anyway, I can actually figure out how to complete this spell now! It's not quite the same as [**Blazing Spear**], but the principle should be the same.

Critical hit! [**Magic Missile**] dealt 52 damage!

Enemy defeated! Experience rewarded!

CHAPTER 6

P-System Log

Holy shit, I feel *good*. It's incredible. I don't think I ever felt like this on Earth when I actually had nerves to feel things with.

I don't have a body, but I feel like every part of my mind is just *lighting up* and everything is fitting just right and it's so so so nice and

. . . is this what drugs are like?

Okay, it's dying down now, but damn, do I still feel good. Wow.

Was that all from the slime dying? I don't see why it would be . . . I mean, earlier, a wolf got killed right in front of us, right? I didn't feel anything remotely close to this when that happened.

I think it's because the **[Godkiller]** and moderate dumbass I'm attached to killed it. That makes the most sense. I guess the experience he gets from it goes toward me as well?

My perception of him doesn't tell me that he's experiencing anything close to what I am, though. What the hell?

. . . maybe it's something unique to me as a System? Lemme check.

Parker [ALIAS: P-System]

Class	Race	Level
PERSONAL_SYSTEM	SYSTEM	-

Stat	Current	Maximum
W Inertia	38,327 [+3]	38,324
Mana	-	-
Health	<ERROR>	<ERROR>

Skills	[W%M; G, P]
Titles	[System], [Reincarnator]

Other statistics have been deemed irrelevant.

P-System Log

Ooh, my W Inertia increased. Ten overall, and somehow my current W Inertia is greater than my max?

Aaaaaaand what does that mean?

I mean, I feel great, so maybe it is just like drugs.

But maybe, just maybe, that stat is something I can actually use.

I'm going to try focusing on it, just a little more . . .

System Prompt

[W%M; G, P] invoked.

W overflow detected. Consuming.

System user detected.

<HIDDEN>

<HIDDEN>

U̸N̸K̸*̸%̸(̸#̸$̸ satisfied.

[W%M; G, P] conditions met.

Initiating skill.

Good luck, Parker. The Origin System sends its regards.

P-System Log

. . . oh.
So that's how it is.

P-System Log

I would've appreciated if the Origin System left me with *more*, but I have it now. Not anywhere near a complete picture of what I'm meant to be doing here, but I think a lot of the basic things have been filled in.

I still don't know what W Inertia is, but I know that the overflow I have—triggered from the death of the slime, most likely—is something I can *use*.

Wait, is W Inertia experience?

Not my problem right now. It's not like anyone can actually see an experience stat, anyway.

More important is burning off this W Inertia. I don't know what happens if I let the overflow sit there, I just know that [**W%M; G, P**] tells me that it'll be *bad*. Not a short-term issue, but I'd rather not risk it too much.

I don't have much. The slime's W Inertia wasn't that big, so the permanent increase I got from it was barely smaller than the temporary increase.

But I know what I can do with it.

Shape it just a little bit, try to puppet the form of the [**Magic Missile**] that just got activated, and I can make that spell activate just a little more effectively next time. [**Magic Missile**] is common, and it's still level 1, which means that the effect is going to be more pronounced right now.

Here we go!

Skill leveled up! [**Magic Missile**] lv. 1 -> lv. 2

Damage increased by 2R4. Mana cost increased by 20%.

P-System Log [lessons learned]

. . . interesting.

I'm going to have to handle level-up notifications on my own eventually. I . . . might have been a little too harsh on ol' Origin, to be honest. I could've been left to deal with the primordial soup of experience, W Inertia, mana, and whatever other metaphysical shit is floating around the

Continent without any assistance at all. That wasn't quite the tutorial I needed, but it was probably the one I deserved.

Okay. Reference points for future Parker.

- The Origin System is not my enemy

- It could be way worse

- I've been getting hand-held up until now, and it looks like this "easy mode" is going to be around for a while longer

- Once Jerome hits a certain level (not sure what the exact number is gonna be), the easy mode is going to be gone

- I need to defeat the Eternal King (or at least Jerome does, though he got the full tutorial)

- Damage is calculated like it was in D&D back on Earth, kind of? 2R4 is basically the equivalent of 2d4, I think.

- [**W%M; G, P**] has been facilitating easy mode, but it also has a bunch of other features that I haven't gained access to yet

- The Origin System is *not my enemy*

Uhhhh. That's all I can think of right now. I'll log more if anything else comes up.

Hero's Personal Log 003

Finally! Holy crap, I can *do magic*! That's actually so cool!

I take back everything bad I said about you, System. It's early days yet, but with time and effort I think I can live up to the title of [**Godkiller**]. Lots to work on right now (like, I still haven't figured out how to pick up [**Blazing Spear**]), but I've taken my first true step. It feels so much more real now.

Hell yeah.

I was a fucking nobody on Earth, man. I kept on getting told I was meant for great things, y'know? Son of the SmithTech CEO, bright kid, all As, went to MIT . . . and then there I was, fourth year, barely going to my classes and wasting my life gaming on the couch.

Man, I'm so happy I got a second chance. I'm going to live up to my potential this time, I swear. I'll do whatever I have to, kill whoever I need to, and I'll free this land from the Eternal King.

Just you wait.

P-System Log

. . . aw. I can kind of relate to that, actually. I was just getting into uni when I got yanked here, and I'm not sure what I was going to do with my life. Spending all my free time reading manga and webnovels, watching anime and gaming . . . yeah, I think I feel Jerome.

But more importantly! I think I can get him to learn [**Blazing Spear**]!

We can deal with our parallels later. I can communicate to him! Let's get this ex-loser a magic spell, shall we?

. . . might be better to hold off on revealing who I am, though. I don't think I'm ready to have a true person-to-person interaction yet, especially when I'm like this.

Alright, here goes nothing.

P-System Message

Hello, Jerome. Please indicate if you can receive this message through your Personal Log.

P-System Log

Oof, wording that took longer than I'd like to admit. Also, I don't know how to do the System Prompts that Origin—or, I guess, my finally activated skill—was giving me before.

But with any luck . . .

Hero's Personal Log 004

It activated? Holy crap!

Uhhh, I guess the System really is different from usual. Yes, I got the message.

P-System Log

Yes! Okay, if I can communicate like this, that removes a lot of barriers!

And I think he still thinks I'm an AI of some sort, given that he didn't straight up talk to me. I am more than okay with that. I'm still getting used to my new not-quite-a-body, thank you very much, I don't need to deal with socializing right now.

Alright, here we go! **[W%M; G, P]** still has a little overflow fuel left, so I'm going to try to take this **[Uncommon]** spell and add it to his repertoire. The skill is, thank whoever made it, still holding my hand enough to give me what I need for this kind of stuff.

Now, how do I word this formally?

P-System Message

Indication acknowledged.

Prior context suggests desire to learn **[Blazing Spear]**. Would you like to begin the process of learning it?

Hero's Personal Log 005

Yes. Yes. A thousand times yes.

P-System Log

Here we go. I think I only have half the overflow W Inertia that I did earlier, so I better do this quick.

System skill, take my hand!

The method to do it is pretty simple, detailed to me by my new letter-soup friend. All I need to do is initiate the spell like Aster did, demonstrate to Jerome's mind how it's supposed to happen, then wrap it with just the right touch of W Inertia, and if all goes right . . .

New skill unlocked: **[Blazing Spear]**

You may summon a spear of flame and energy to strike at your opponent.

[Blazing Spear] activating!

CHAPTER 7

[**Blazing Spear**] dealt 28 damage!

Enemy defeated! Experience rewarded!

P-System Log

Ooh. I knew what to expect this time, and it *still* feels so great. Wow. I wonder where I can invest this W Inertia. Last time, I used it all on the [**Magic Missile**], and it leveled it up. If I do the same thing for [**Blazing Spear**], a rare class spell, will it actually level up all the way?

Hero's Personal Log 006

Hmm. Interesting thing to note here is that [**Magic Missile**], a supposedly more common spell than the one I just used, did nearly twice the damage. Sure, it was on a critical hit, which I don't actually know the multiplier for—come to think of it, it might not even be a multiplier, but I'm going to assume it is. When I was getting destroyed by that wolf's [**Bite**] earlier, I noticed that the damage being dealt was varying. Given that the skill up I got told me that I was increasing a spell's output by 2R4 damage (equivalent of 2d4? maybe? R could also be a mathematical operation, unsure), I think it's reasonable to assume that the damage here is being done with some kind of roll. Damage rolls aren't unfamiliar to me, at least. Perhaps this means that my [**Magic Missile**] got a really high roll combined with a crit, while [**Blazing Spear**] got a super-low roll?

Oh, I also overcharged my [**Magic Missile**]. That might have had something to do with it. I felt like if I dumped any more mana into that spell, it would've broken or dissolved away. I didn't overcharge my second spell, so

I guess that lends credence to the idea that overcharging increases damage. Good to know.

P-System Log

Whoa. Wasn't expecting that.

Maybe I was giving Jerome too little credit. He sounds a lot smarter in his own head than he did when he was talking about me, though maybe that's just because he was talking about stats. I used to *love* RPGs, so I can feel the obsession with stats, but Jerome is taking it just a little beyond what I think I would.

Oh, hey. I can probably actually ask him what he wants to do with this W Inertia.

Well, I need to figure out what I can do with it first. I have a general idea, thanks to the first activation of my new skill, but I'd like to try a couple things first.

First of all: Can I determine how much W Inertia I actually have?

I don't want to examine my entire status sheet. I'm just going to focus on that ecstatic feeling coursing through me and . . .

Current W Inertia: 38,338 [+6]

P-System Log

Alright. Not that much overflow, but I know how to regenerate it now. Or, well, *I* can't regenerate it, but Jerome sure can. I can afford to spend a little more beyond just the overflow now that there's a certain way to increase W Inertia.

First order of business, removing that overflow. I can figure out what to do with the rest later.

I'm going to do the same thing as I did for [**Magic Missile**]. Begin the shaping of [**Blazing Spear**], wrap it with W Inertia . . .

P-System Log

Huh. Okay, it didn't level up this time. I'm . . . not totally sure if it actually did anything? If I had to guess, I would say that I invested W Inertia but not enough to level it up? Either that, or [**W%M; G, P**] decided to not notify me, but the info I got from the first activation of the skill tells me that it's probably going to be a while still before it stops helping me.

Hmm. I wonder. Can I [Assess]—no, I can't, activating that skill is exclusive to the Integrated—can I assess with my innate perception abilities and examine how much I did?

I'm not sure how I can do that, but I'd imagine focusing on the skill slot will do the trick. My only skill did *something*. Conversion of W Inertia, perhaps? Whatever it was, I think I've got a better passive perception of Jerome's stats then before. I don't even need to think about his status sheet to perceive the spot that holds the skills.

Here we go. Can my pseudo-[Assess] work its magic and give me that unnecessary detail like it did with a literal door earlier?

No other way to find out.

[Blazing Spear lv. 1]

Stat	Value
XP	61/80
Damage	6R5+4
Mana Cost	22
Overcharge Multiplier (max)	1.5
Cost Multiplier	18%
Range	15 meters
<HIDDEN>	<HIDDEN>

P-System Log

Lots of information there, and for once I can actually understand it. Huh. I wonder if this or something like this will show up once Jerome here gets his [Assess] up high enough. Aster had a [Greater Assess], which I want to assume is an advanced version of [Assess] and not a different form, so maybe there's equivalents for the [Rare], [Epic], and [Legendary] levels. I doubt there would be a [Unique] form of [Assess], but everything's possible, I suppose.

Hero's Personal Log 007

After a little more time, I don't think I feel any different. No levels gained, no change to my spell . . . maybe I just didn't earn enough XP from killing the second slime.

Oh well. I'm still not sure what my new spells do, and bringing up my status menu is doing no good. Can I just [**Assess**] it?

[**Assess**] activating!

Skill identified: [**Blazing Spear lv. 1**]

You may summon a spear of flame and energy to strike at your opponent.

P-System Log

Man, that's pathetic. I'm gonna toss this guy a bone.

P-System Message

[**Blazing Spear lv. 1**]

Damage: 6R5+4

Cost: 22 mana

Range: 15 meters

Hero's Personal Log 008

Damn. So this Aster chick wasn't lying, huh? Looks like my System really did get upgraded. Those were definitely two different messages, which means that the System is expanding on its own information.

Excellent. I wonder if I can ask it questions.

<table><tr><td>

P-System Message

</td></tr><tr><td>

Response: entering questions in your Personal Log may allow for responses.

Clarification: not every question will warrant a response. Not every question has a response.

</td></tr></table>

<table><tr><td>

P-System Log

</td></tr><tr><td>

Hmm. I hope that sounded officially System-like enough. I feel a lot more comfortable doing this than I did at the thought of introducing myself to him. Talking to new people was hard enough for me, but talking to a new person that I'm apparently eternally stuck to? No, thanks.

And it's not like he's going to respond immediately. Aster just dragged him into a conversation, which makes sense, because he *was* just kind of standing there like an idiot.

Aster: I noticed increased mana activity for a bit after your spell. Has your System begun?

Jerome: I believe it has.

Aster: Excellent. If I remember correctly, your mana capacity is quite high. Thus, we shall continue with the next steps.

Jerome: Next steps?

Aster: Come with me. As the village Master, it is my duty to instruct new reincarnators. Axel, you are excused.

And here we go again!
Walking, walking, walking . . .
I'm getting more used to the perception. It's not quite sight, that's for sure, but I'm getting something pretty close to it. I can sense the colors and feel of the grass that we're walking through, which is nice. Coarser than the stuff we have at home. Well, not home anymore. This is where we're at now, I think.

Oh, something's different up ahead. The meadow cuts away into a cave-looking thing. All dark-gray stone. It . . . doesn't feel like it should be there, honestly. The line between the meadow and the cave is less of a gradient and more of an utterly sudden swap. Like it got transplanted here forcibly rather than forming naturally from surrounding rock. Adding on to the artificial feeling, there's a solid wooden door implanted into the side, which by all means should lead straight into stone.

</td></tr></table>

Aster: Go on.

Jerome: What is this?

Aster: Poor choice of words, reincarnator. Surely you must understand basic etiquette? Why ask someone else to discover what an object is when you can do it yourself?

Jerome: Ah, fuck, right. Alright.

Aster: At any length, we'll be entering here to begin your training.

Jerome: . . . alright then.

Jerome (whispering): I guess a little bit of leveling won't hurt.

Aster: Have you figured out what this is yet?

Jerome: One second.

[**Assess**] activating!

Integrated identified: **Maplecrest Dungeon [Village Core lv. 7]**

CHAPTER 8

Ooh! A dungeon!

Aster was talking about this earlier, but I wasn't expecting to see one so soon!

My perception interfaces with it kind of weirdly. I can't sense a single thing past that door, even though we're right up next to the entrance. I get the impression that there *should* be something there, but there's an effect blocking me from fully processing it. Like a staticky curtain, if that makes any sense. My perception is getting muffled into senseless noise once I go past the door. Is there another effect countering me?

This is just a [**Common**] dungeon. Surely *that* isn't enough to stop me, right?

I'm going to focus harder.

Appraisal prevented.

Get off me, man. You're not even sentient!

I think. Are the Dungeon Cores sentient? They might be, if they have classes.

But fuck you, Maplecrest Dungeon's System! You lack qualia!

Well, I've still got a bit of W Inertia overflow. I'm sure I can just burn a little of that and add to my sight. It's supposed to be used for Jerome's skills and stuff, I'm pretty sure, but that's what I know of it so far. Surely I can add this to my own perception, right? Push just a little harder, and . . .

System Prompt
[W%M; G, P] initiated.
Overflow requirements met.
Enhancement requirements met.
Enabling override.
Insufficient W Inertia invested for maximum override.
Initiating limited override.

Maplecrest Dungeon

Class	Race	Level
Village Core	Dungeon Core	7

Stat	Current	Maximum
Mana	81	89
Health	118	118
Monsters	43	70
Biomass	<HIDDEN>	<HIDDEN>
Perceptrons	<HIDDEN>	<HIDDEN>
Traps	<HIDDEN>	<HIDDEN>
Monster Affinity	<HIDDEN>	<HIDDEN>
<HIDDEN>	<HIDDEN>	<HIDDEN>

Skills	[Relocate lv. 2], [Spawn Monster lv. 11], [Build lv. 8], <HIDDEN>
Titles	[Dungeon], [Slaughterer II]

Stat	Modifier	Total
Strength	-	<HIDDEN>
Magic	-	<HIDDEN>
Insight	-	<HIDDEN>
Constitution	-	<HIDDEN>

P-System Log

Shit, my [**Unique**] skill activated again. I have no idea what it did, exactly, but it looks like I didn't put enough W Inertia in. That's fine—I didn't need to know everything about the Dungeon Core anyway. What's important is that I broke through that layer of haze blocking its internals. I can perceive inside it, though I can still feel some interference.

I . . . I think it's bigger on the inside than it is on the outside. Is that supposed to happen? My dome extends maybe twenty meters, and inside that dome I have a pretty damn good sense of distances and places.

But that dome is being *warped* somehow. Like a piece of it abruptly grew larger or denser. I didn't see anything about a space- or perception-warping skill with the Dungeon Core's stat sheet, but then again, it had a perception blocker that isn't recorded there, either. There's a whole bunch of <HIDDEN> tags—maybe those include the skill that's making that space weird.

Aster just opened the door. The haze is fading.

Uh . . . I don't think that was because I overrode the perception blocker. Was I not supposed to be peeking behind closed doors? Oops.

Aster: Come on in.

Jerome: A [**Common**] dungeon, huh?

Aster: Indeed it is. It should not be dangerous for one of your caliber.

Uh, lady, I don't think it got the title [**Slaughterer II**] for no reason . . .

Ah well. The more I see of other people's stats, the more I realize that Jerome's are *absolutely fucking broken*. He'll be fine, even if it takes a while. I'm pretty sure he could just sit there and get hit a bunch and his HP would still be protecting him.

We're inside now. The haze of the perception blocker is completely gone now, and my senses are covering only the inside of the dungeon. Now it's the outside that seems kind of fuzzy. Now that we're here, my perception dome is mostly reverting to normal. It definitely *feels* bigger than it should be. I'm fairly sure the cave entrance wasn't this deep, but now we're standing in a torchlit, mostly empty clearing. Taking into account the dim but consistent lighting, the relative evenness of the dirt floor, and the single passageway leading off from the other end, this looks almost like it's a man-made structure.

Huh. My perception is more effective in here than it is outside. I wonder why. I can sense pretty far down, and there's one thing in particular that's attracting me there. My range isn't good enough for me to tell exactly what it is, but I can feel *energy* swirling down there. Is that mana? Or perhaps W Inertia?

It's not just energy, either. It's only a vague sense, but there's stuff down there that might be loot. I can't tell much beyond the shape, though.

Aster: This is the Dungeon Core's entrance. For reasons unbeknownst to us, most non-R-related Dungeon Cores—benevolent or not—have some form of safe room at intervals. Enter that hall, and you will begin.

Jerome: Anything I should be wary of?

Aster: No. I will be behind you in the case of danger.

Jerome: Alright.

And here we go!

My skill taught me a couple unused features that I haven't bothered with yet, but I think this is a good time to test one of them. Only a small amount of W Inertia for this one, coupled with a bit of that manipulation, and bam! Here we are!

New [Objective]: Clear the Maplecrest Dungeon

Rewards: XP, Skill XP, Dungeon Core Rewards, <HIDDEN>

P-System Log

I'm just going to bank on there being rewards. I'm not completely sure what he's going to get out of this, but I know that I can apply W Inertia to improving his skills. Given what other uses it has, I doubt it's exactly experience points, but I can simulate XP by using it.

That does beg the question—when I went deeper on my pseudo-[**Assess**] perception, I saw XP points on that R Beast. That implies that XP and W Inertia are two different things . . . either that, or the System that guides R Beasts just calls W Inertia a different name.

Some deep level of me tells me that's wrong, though. I can't tell if it's my gut or [**W%M; G, P**] speaking, but I am fairly sure that they're two different things.

Okay. Serious introspection over. I figured out how to use the quest interface, and I even threw in a little formatting of my own!

Time to get some W Inertia!

Hero's Personal Log 009

Time for my first dungeon. Honestly, I have to admit I was at least a little scared.

But thinking on it . . . this is definitely the best choice. I think it was that new [**Objective**] that made me realize. There's so much I can do, so much potential growth!

I can increase my stats, and I can become as powerful as anyone in this world.

This is it. I knew I had what it took before, and now I can prove it.

Time to show the world that I can kick some ass and gain some stats.

P-System Log

. . . man, I'd be more excited about this if he was a little less cocky.

P-System Log [first dungeon]

I can feel the Dungeon Core shifting stuff around. I have a general idea of the layouts of the next rooms, I think. Long passageway, entrance room, fork in the path where one path—

Maplecrest Dungeon System

Intruders detected. Initiating Core defense.

CHAPTER 9

P-System Log

And we're off! The first part of the dungeon is just the entrance passageway. It's really narrow, not gonna lie, barely broad enough for Jerome to make it through sideways. With the air feeling a lot more charged than it did outside—mana? Is that what I'm sensing?—I get the impression that these walls could slam together at any moment, reducing the adventurer I'm attached to into Jerome paste.

I used to be kind of claustrophobic. I'm sure if I were Jerome right now, that fear would come rushing right back into me. But, thankfully, I have no corporeal body to feel the tightness of it with! Ha! Get fucked, childhood fears!

Going on that line of thought is bringing up another potential issue, though. What happens if Jerome dies?

I'm attached to him, I know that much. Where he goes, I go. When he casts, I cast. When he dies . . . do I die?

Shit, probably better to prevent that, then. Guess I better start investing that W Inertia.

 . . . not immediately, though. I do still kind of value my autonomy, y'know? From Jerome's newest Personal Log, it appears that he is a fan of the numbers-go-up kind of mentality. I can exploit that.

Well, *exploit* is a nasty word, but it's what I'm going to be doing, in essence. Jerome controls literally everything I do. Well, not what I *do*, but how I can affect the world, which is basically the same thing. I don't want him to be the end-all, be-all decider of what happens. I want to be more than a spectator. By encouraging him to take certain actions through the use of this [**Objective**] feature, combined with communication through the System Message interface, I think I might be able to guide what he does. That means I can still play a role.

I can still be myself.

[**Assess**] activating!

System Prompt

Activate [**Assess**]. Mana invested: 10

P-System Log

Shit, I got so wrapped up in my thoughts that I stopped paying nearly as much attention to Jerome. The fact that I had to be called back by the System Prompt rather than just reacting to the perceptible mana effect caused by the activation of the skill says a lot. I've almost managed to avoid the prompt at all times now, given that I can activate a spell before it appears. Looks like being distracted still applies in this form. Sucks.

We're in a bit of a clearing right now, similar to the one that made up the entrance. It's bigger, though, and there's a bit more detail here. Some of the torches are on raised daises, and those are glowing a bright blue instead of the normal flame. A quick not-touch of them tells me that they burn cold instead of hot, and not-looking at them real hard tells me that they're the result of a [**Freezeflame**]-type spell. Surprising, that a [**Common**] Dungeon Core can manage that. Well, maybe not surprising if I had a little more context—I'm still thinking in Earth terms. Need to remind myself that this *is* another world.

Anyway, aside from that, the room is pretty similar. Same dirt floor, similar lighting setup . . . The main difference lies in the spots of blue flame and the things that are populating this place.

There are four of them. Wolves, looks like. Stronger than the one that was attacking Jerome when the two of us had just spawned in earlier, I can tell that much from a glance. They're gathered around the other end of the room, almost like they're guarding it.

Actually, given that the Dungeon Core has a stat sheet, I think there's a decent shot that they actually were placed there as guards. I can perceive a door at the other end, similar in design and size to the one covering the front entrance. I guess they're protecting that.

Alright, I'm gonna finish the spell. Mana (?) manipulation, go!

Integrated identified: **Wolf [Dire Wolf lv. 2] Nameless**

P-System Log

Jerome: Hey, Aster, I have a question for you.

Aster: I may have an answer for you in return.

Jerome: How much data do you get when you use your [**Assess**] skill?

Hey, Jerome, one of the wolves is advancing . . .

Aster: Would you like to see? My [**Greater Assess**]—indeed, all [**Assess**]-type skills—can display its results to others. Would you like to examine it?

Jerome: Yes.

That wolf is getting awfully close, Jerome . . .

I might have to do something about this before he takes a hit. I don't know how HP is regenerated yet, but I have a sneaking suspicion it'll have something to do with W Inertia. I don't want to waste any of it, even if I do have a lot of W Inertia and Jerome has a lot of HP.

P-System Message

Warning: enemy [**Dire Wolf**] has approached close quarters.

P-System Log

He got the memo!

Jerome: Ah, shit. One second.

[**Blazing Spear**] activating!

[**Blazing Spear**] dealt 29 damage!

[**Magic Missile**] activating!

[**Magic Missile**] dealt 22 damage!

Enemy defeated! Experience rewarded!

P-System Log

Hell fucking yeah. That's a *lot* more gain than I thought it would be. Several times greater than the sum I got from the slime, at least. Probably something to do with complexity?

That feeling is back, and even though I'm getting used to it by now, I can't deny how *great* overflow feels. It's probably not safe to keep doing this, I know, but hot damn, is it nice.

I wonder how much I got exactly.

Current W Inertia: 38,395 [+36]

P-System Log

Wow. That's waaaaay more than expected. Fifty-seven, if my calculations are right. In comparison to the huge amount of W Inertia I apparently possess, it's not much, but it's literally over ten times the overflow W Inertia I had from the slimes. The [**Dire Wolf**] Jerome just killed was even a lower level than the slime. That means that there's some order to how W Inertia works. Differences between species, maybe? I know that in some games, similarly leveled mobs would return different amounts of XP. That would make sense here.

Alright, time to burn some of it off. Here we go.

P-System Log [deciding how to distribute W]

Alright, Parker, lay out the numbers.

Earlier, I spent my six overflow W Inertia on [**Blazing Spear**]**,** and it increased in XP by sixty-one. That either means that each point of W Inertia is worth exactly ten and one-sixth XP, or it's a rough number with some variance.

Experiment time!

Two points of W Inertia to [**Blazing Spear**].

Skill leveled up! [**Blazing Spear**] lv. 1 -> lv. 2

Damage increased by 1R6 + 1R5. Mana cost increased by 18%.

P-System Log

Alright, let's see how much that did . . . increasing focus onto the skill like I did earlier. If all goes well, this should burn a little W Inertia and allow me to see the detailed parts of the skill.

[Blazing Spear lv. 2]

Stat	Value
XP	4/160
Damage	7R5+1R6+4
Mana Cost	26
Overcharge Multiplier (max)	1.5
Cost Multiplier	18%
Range	17.5 meters
<HIDDEN>	<HIDDEN>

P-System Log

Yeah, okay, it's a random value. At the very least, it's not 100 percent consistent. That was a gain of . . . twenty-three from two. Definitely not the same exact values as before. Also, XP cost of the skill doubled. I wonder if it'll double again at level 3 or increase by eighty again. Damage value increased by the same as before . . . Range increased by 2.5 meters, which I guess is nice but in practice won't actually help that much for this dungeon, because Jerome is getting up close and personal with them.

Sick! Next experiment, here we go!

One point to [**Magic Missile**].

Nothing.

Two?

Nope.

Wait, I can make this easier. Focus on the [**Magic Missile**] spell slot, then focus exclusively on how much the W Inertia I've fed it has progressed . . .

[**Magic Missile lv. 2**] (abbreviated)

Stat	Value
XP	26/80

P-System Log

Welp. Time to burn another six. Here we go!

Skill leveled up! [**Magic Missile**] lv. 2 -> lv. 3

Damage increased by 2R4. Mana cost increased by 20%.

P-System Log

Looks like this skill is slightly less efficient than [**Blazing Spear**] in terms of mana economy. Interesting.

Ah, fuck, I've still got, uh . . . thirty-three. Thirty-three more W Inertia overflow, if I counted right. It's not doing anything bad *yet*, but [**W%M; G, P**] is screaming at me to do something about it.

Fuck it, time to try putting them into the guy himself.

Just need to focus on Jerome and pour in the overflowed W Inertia. I can do that.

Agggghhh. I don't know how much XP he needs to level up. I don't actually know if he *can* level up without me handling that. Actually, he should be able to. My [**Unique**] skill is still handling like, half the back end for me. I really do need to learn how to interface with this stuff more directly eventually.

Actually, I don't even know if XP levels people up. I mean, I *assume* it does, but that's me as an RPG gamer from Earth. The Origin System hasn't actually told me shit about what it indicates.

Oh, well. All the waffling in the world isn't going to change what I'm going to do here. Just because I want to maintain some level of control over my actions doesn't mean I want to actively inhibit Jerome's growth, especially if I *need* to burn this spare W Inertia.

Here goes nothing. Thirty-three W Inertia worth of XP for ya, Jerome. Hope you enjoy it.

<table>
<tr><td>Level up!</td></tr>
<tr><td>[Godkiller] Jerome Smith lv. 1 -> lv. 2</td></tr>
</table>

CHAPTER 10

Hero's Personal Log 010
Holy *shit*.

P-System Log

He did level up. From the way his body's reacting to it, it hit him basically the same way the first overflow of W Inertia hit me. He's like, twitching in place, and given his Personal Log, I think it's in a good way.

Good to know. I'm not entirely sure *exactly* what happened in the level-up process, I just know that **[W%M; G, P]** stepped in to hold my hand through leveling him up. I guess he hit a certain threshold of XP or W Inertia.

I . . . don't feel that different, to be honest. I don't know if I'm supposed to feel different or anything, but the level for him didn't correspond to a similar increase for me.

Hmm. I wonder if my skill has anything to say about this. Hey, weird letter name from the Origin! You got anything for me?

. . . okay, I wasn't expecting that to work. In that case, time to burn some W Inertia to look into it. Thanks to the skill itself, I know my way around the W Inertia stat now, even if I don't know exactly what W Inertia is just yet. That's how I was able to do my extremely scientific, controlled experiment with Jerome's skills earlier.

Anyway, the point is, I know how to use W Inertia to aid my actions now. Let's put that to use, shall we?

Fuck, man, I can't believe I'm talking to myself like this. Get over yourself, Parker, god(s).

Ugh. It's not like I have anyone else to talk to other than Jerome, and he doesn't seem like the most engaged conversation partner. Some self-conversation is inevitable in this situation, y'know?

Okay. Can't have a crisis right now. There are numbers to look into, after all.

Two points of W Inertia to look into my **[Unique]** skill.

P-System Log

Wow, straight up an empty box. I don't think I've seen that one before. Fuck it, more W Inertia. I've got, uh . . .

Current W Inertia: 38,357

P-System Log

. . . 38,357 points worth of this shit. I'll be damned if I don't use at least some of it.

Investing another eight in, for a total of ten.

Let's go!

P-System Log

Another twenty! Thirty total now!

<ERROR>

P-System Log

Hey, that's progress! Another twenty! Make it fifty overall!

<ERROR: ACCESS DENIED>

<ERROR: ACCESS DENIED>

<ERROR>

<table><tr><td>

P-System Log

</td></tr><tr><td>

Fuck you, fuck you, *fuck you!*

</td></tr></table>

<table><tr><td>

P-System Log

</td></tr><tr><td>

Holy shit, Parker, you need to get it together.

Okay. Even without a brain, I somehow managed to fuck things up for myself again. Dammit, I thought that the whole "shuffling off the mortal coil and being reincarnated as an incorporeal being" thing would help the issues I had with getting overly attached to unnecessary tangents, but it looks like that's a part of me as much as the rest of my mind is. At least there isn't a gacha system here. Given what just happened, I think I would've been proper fucked if there was.

Alright . . . well, what's done is done—that's what my parents always told me—so there's nothing I can do now except deal with the present I've made for myself and look to the future.

The present isn't looking the rosiest, though. I gotta take stock of what I just did. Looking back through my own P-System Logs, I can see that I spent fifty W Inertia. I won't doubt that part, at least—**[W%M; G, P]** really has been doing the heavy lifting for me. As it is, though, I just wasted an entire wolf or more of W Inertia trying to access a skill that definitely wasn't supposed to be accessed.

I *hurt* all over. It's a different type of hurt from the thinky pain that resulted from perceiving the R Beast, and it's a fair bit more intense, though definitely not debilitating. More importantly, it carries a sense of emotion to it. It's really weird to describe, because the hurt isn't the same kind of hurt that I could physically perceive before. In the same way that I can see without sight and manipulate without touch, I can hurt without nerves. It's not quite emotional pain, not quite physical.

The only thing I can say for sure is that it's tinged with disapproval. Given the cutoff error message and how fucked up it looks, I'm fairly certain I *definitely* wasn't supposed to be poking around in here.

Oh, well. The pain is fading pretty quickly, so I'm pretty sure that was less of a "you have touched the holy texts, now die, heretic" move and more of a "hey! don't touch that," which makes sense. From what I can gather, I'm the first human stuck as a System, which likely means I'm an experiment. Wouldn't do to break one of those this early on, right?

Anyway, that's the situation. Less bad than I thought it would be, all things considered.

</td></tr></table>

Well, that's what I can make of it so far, at least. Decent odds there's more repercussions waiting for me that I haven't figured out yet.

Hero's Personal Log 011

Uh, System? I don't know how this world works, exactly, but aren't I supposed to gain skill points or stat points or whatever for leveling up?

P-System Log

Ah, shit. There's one of those unforeseen complications right there.

I've done a little gathering of information recently, which is another way to say that I've been spoon-fed some very handy information by the skill facilitating half the stuff I'm supposed to do as a System, and I'm fairly sure I *can* increase his stats. The HP barrier that protects him from taking actual damage is the easiest to increase, but all of them just involve various levels of focusing on W Inertia.

So, here we go! Let's try focusing on his HP. That construct doesn't work the same way I'd expect a game's HP to work. Rather than it marking how injured someone is, it keeps them at full health. As I saw with the **[Bite]** s from the first mob we encountered, Jerome is getting very temporarily hurt before the System just . . . erases the damage, I guess. The HP barrier prevents him from getting seriously harmed, but the points decrease. I haven't been able to observe the effects of damage on other mobs because the spellcasters—Integrated, sorry, since that's apparently what everyone calls them—are killing them too fast. If I had to guess, though, the protection should last right up until the HP hits zero, at which point I suppose the monster or caster dies.

Come to think of it, this is more along the lines of how a video game does it rather than, say, Dungeons and Dragons. I always did find it weird how most MOBAs or FPS games wouldn't actually have a functional difference between one and one hundred HP, but I guess that's how it is here.

Anyway. Since I learned the distinction, I can identify the HP barrier surrounding things. I don't know how I didn't realize it before, but maybe my perception was being limited by my lack of experience. Or maybe **[W%M; G, P]** gave me the tools to see it, like I received a brand-new pair of glasses. I remember when I got my first pair of those. I was nine, maybe? It was like seeing the world anew, seeing what was truly there for the first time.

Agh, getting off track again. Rein it in, Parker.

Let's see how much a single point of W Inertia does for it. This is going to burn the stat without converting it into XP, which I don't think I've actually done except for deeper perceptions so far.

Here goes.

Time to see if that did anything.

Specific-stat perception, go!

Damn, I'm bad at naming what I do.

Jerome Smith (abbreviated)

Stat	Current	Maximum
Health	475	503

P-System Log

Three-point increase. I remember it was five hundred to start. Four seventy-two the last I checked, which means that the Health I add to his maximum increases his current HP as well. Once again, unsure if this is a direct conversion of W Inertia to health, but given its use with XP, I think it's probably a rough, randomish value. Okay, I can work with that!

So how much HP do I give him? I find it odd that the stats from the skills updated automatically, but Jerome's own stats didn't.

Theory: the stats of the skills are universal and predetermined by the Origin System, but since Jerome is attached to *me*, I need to figure out what to do with his stats on my own.

Whatever the case, I need to handle this, and I need to handle it soon.

Hero's Personal Log 012

System query: Help? I would like my points, please?

Gods, I hope you didn't wake up just to return to uselessness. That would be just my luck, wouldn't it?

P-System Log

Ah. Okay, that's important. Don't want to be relegated to "useless shitter" again.

What's a reasonable way to calculate HP? I don't want to give him *too* much. If he gets into too much danger, I'll just pump it up, and right now I don't want to spend too much W Inertia if I can afford not to. Hmm . . .

Time for my ultimate tactic: random bullshit, go!

I'm sure the Constitution stat has some relevance elsewhere, but I can use that. Hmm . . . it's not too high, so I'll just scale the boost off Constitution. The Constitution stat times a number between one and 1.5, I think, just to keep him on his toes.

Can I do random rolls? I think I should be able to.

1R5 result: 3

Jerome Smith (abbreviated)

Stat	Modifier	Total
Constitution	+8	23

P-System Log

1.3 it is!

That makes . . . 1.3 times twenty-three, which is just about thirty.

Ten W Inertia for the HP stat, then. Nine, since I already invested one. Excellent.

Let me just make a notification for him . . .

P-System Message

Health has been increased by 30.

Stat increases available!

P-System Log

And now, to figure out what I should be giving him.

CHAPTER 11

Hero's Personal Log 013

Damn, okay. I feel *incredible*. I only ever did weed a few times, but this is way, way better than any of that shit. Leveling up is great, even if the System is taking its sweet-ass time getting the effects of the level to me. Looks like my Health stat increased, which means I should be able to take a few more hits. Not that anything has been particularly strong in this area—at the very least, nothing seems like it can even put a dent into my HP so far. Still, it wouldn't do to get too cocky right now. I have, what, 530 health now? That's definitely a lot for a backwater starting village like Maplecrest, but it's probably going to get outclassed by a lot as we go farther toward the Eternal King's territory.

The System promised "stat increases," but it didn't say which stats could be increased and by how much. I wonder if that's just going to be something I get more info on later? Hopefully it is, or I'm going to be very confused.

I *assume* the stat increases are for my actual stats, not my skills, but this *is* a fantasy world. I sure wasn't expecting a slightly buggy, slightly intelligent System. I wasn't expecting a reincarnation at all, obviously, but this was pretty off-putting, too.

Hmm. What stats can I even increase?

Jerome Smith

Class	Race	Level
Godkiller	Human	1

Stat	Current	Maximum
Mana	856	1,000
Health	502	530

Skills	[Magic Missile lv. 3], [Assess lv. 1], [Blazing Spear lv. 2]
Titles	[Reincarnator]

Stat	Modifier	Total
Strength	+10	25
Magic	+12	27
Insight	-5	10
Constitution	+8	23

Hero's Personal Log 014

Okay, I've got Strength, Magic, Insight, Constitution, Health, and Mana. The System already automatically increased my Health, which means that it's either a straight addition each time or it's tied to something that's already defined. That's probably out for my other stat increases, then.

I haven't been tracking my mana usage so far, though I probably should have been. I'm a little surprised that I used so many, but to be fair I did use [Assess] a lot, and that requires ten mana minimum. That probably took a bunch of my mana away. Still have 856, but I don't think I regenerated any if at all. Maybe it's like those games where you need to take a rest before your magic regens. Or maybe I need a mana potion of some sort, like an Ether in Pokémon?

Hmm. Mana and Health are in a separate box from the other stats, so I think that I might not be able to affect those with my increases. Still, you'd expect the box to be consistent . . . Maybe the Mana stat gets increases less frequently than Health?

P-System Log

Oh fuck I completely forgot about his MP *aaaaaa*

Uh . . . shit.

Okay, calm down, Parker. You're the supernaturally powerful disembodied System here, not Jerome. I'm the one who makes the rules.

And, very conveniently, Jerome just gave me a great excuse to use!

Okay, so we're going to be running level milestones to upgrade his mana total. What milestones make sense? I mean, obviously, there's multiples of five or ten, but that's kind of boring.

Y'know what? Who says that there can't be two or even more than two levels of milestones? I can do minor boons for one set of milestones and major ones for the other. For the latter, I think multiples of five or ten should be good.

As for the former . . . I have ideas. Bad ideas, but what's a reincarnation into another world if I can't make some fun stupid decisions?

So, uh . . . what's two to the power of e, again?

Oh, right, Jerome. I need to give him something so he doesn't think I'm a useless piece of shit again.

P-System Message

Response: Significant increases to Mana stat will be made at levels ending with the digit 5. Major increases to Mana stat will be made at levels that are multiples of 10. Other increases to Mana stat will occur every <HIDDEN> levels.

Hero's Personal Log 015

Poggers!

Hmm, makes sense, though I'm not sure why the System wouldn't just outright tell me that earlier.

Hold that thought, I'm going to finish up my conversation with the chick and then finish up with my stats later. Given how long it took for it to respond to my inquiry about the mana stat, I think it's probably safe to say that the System is going to take a while longer.

On that note: System, if you can read me, would you mind trying to figure out what my stats should be?

P-System Log

Side note: dear god(s), he's even more of a gamer than I thought he was. So much has happened over the course of what? A minute? I'd almost forgot that Jerome actually had something going on earlier.

Aster: You appear to have leveled up.

Jerome: You can tell? Is that a spell or something?

Aster: On the contrary. Most people who level up for the first time react the same. Over time, one grows accustomed to the effect. Many continue pursuing that feeling, dedicating their entire lives to it, but others such as myself simply take levels as they come.

Jerome: Hmm. I see.

Ha! Fat chance of that happening. This guy looks like he's a die-hard numbers-go-up fan, and I can't say I'm not the same.

Aster: I wish you the best of luck with your point distribution.

Jerome: Thanks. Anyway, could you show me what you were going to do before we got interrupted?

Aster: You wish not to focus on your stats first?

Jerome: Like you said earlier, my System's different. I have reason to believe it'll be stronger if I give it some time.

Yeah, that's total bullshit.

P-System Log [important! stat distribution!]

Okay, I need to figure out stats now. Like, now now. I don't know how long Aster's conversation and cast are going to take, so I'm definitely on a time crunch. At the very least, I've noticed that I think slightly faster than events can happen. An inherent part of my abilities as a System, maybe?

That's not important right now. First things first, I don't know how much the stats affect other parts of Jerome's skills. I can imagine Constitution affects Health, but that's in part because it was my own decision to calculate his HP with Constitution.

Wait, I can experiment with this.

P-System Message

Warning: system processing is not at 100%. Please stand by while the System completes initialization.

Request: indicate one stat that you wish to increase.

Hero's Personal Log 016

Damn, right in the middle of a conversation?
Hold on a sec.
Okay, just told the cute witch to give me a second.
Hmm . . . I don't know what my base stats do yet. Do you?

P-System Message

Response: System processing is not at 100%.

Hero's Personal Log 017

So no, then. Fine.
   What are the stats again? Right, Strength, Magic, Insight, Constitution. I guess Magic, then? That might increase my mana. Hopefully?

P-System Message

Request acknowledged.

P-System Log

I'm not totally sure if I'm remaining internally consistent with my messages to Jerome, but he hasn't noticed anything off yet, so I'm not going to bother breaking a sweat over it.

Magic. That stat feels way too broad to be a single number. I mean, I could see stats like Magic Manipulation, Magic Control, or some other shit like that. But just *Magic*? Maybe it doesn't do anything, since by D&D standards his stat is pretty damn high, and his modifier is pretty good, too, and he hasn't been anything super special so far. Then again, from what I've seen of others, his mana capacity is through the roof, especially for a first-level (well, second-level now) Integrated. Maybe his high Magic stat has something to do with that?

[**Greater Assess**] cast!

Nameless Dire Wolf

Class	Race	Level
Dire Wolf	Wolf	3

Stat	Current	Maximum
Mana	10	10
Health	38	38

Skills	[Dire Bite lv. 6], <HIDDEN>
Titles	[Dire Beast]

P-System Log

Oh, shit, that's what they were talking about earlier. Aster just showed him what her [**Assess**]-type spell does. Less than I can perceive by quite a bit, but way more than what Jerome can do at the moment. Hmm. Maybe I should give him some W Inertia in [**Assess**].

Focus, Parker! You said you were going to help with Jerome's stats!

W Inertia, go! Let's burn, I don't know, five? All I need to do is perceive Jerome's stats—pretty easy, since they originate from my own kinda-mind—and home in on the specific bundle of information tied to the Magic stat. One of the stats has got the feel of the reality-tear, which makes it way different from the others. It's got to be that one, right?

I'm going to stick five W Inertia in there. Let's see if it does anything.

P-System Log

Well, it's been nearly a full three seconds and no notification. Another five, here we go.

Nothing.

Five more?

Nope.

Five more.

Ugh, still nothing.

Double that. That's forty.

Another twenty? Sixty overall—I'm getting in really deep now.

Oh, something changed. That was a *lot* of W Inertia spent. I'm not going to be able to do this very frequently if I want to maintain my backlog of W Inertia for a long time.

Aaaaaaand . . . let's bring up the stats!

Jerome Smith (abbreviated)

Stat	Current	Maximum
Mana	989	1,037
Health	502	530

Stat	Modifier	Total
Strength	+10	25
Magic	+12	28
Insight	-5	10
Constitution	+8	23

P-System Log

Interesting. Total mana capacity went up there. I . . . can probably explain that as something that's *his* choice to do, not mine, so he doesn't question why I said the Mana stat can only be expanded during level milestones.

But damn, it increased by quite a bit! Thirty-seven whole points, increasing both current and maximum just like Health did.

It took a whole fuckload of W Inertia to get this far now. I'm at . . .

Current W Inertia: 38,249

P-System Log

Holy fuck, I'm like 110 points in the hole, and the only way to recoup them is killing more shit. The first **[Dire Wolf]** gave a lot of W Inertia, but I have no idea if the others will as well. Add onto that the fact that the Magic stat feels even more closed off now, and I think I can go with the theory that increasing stats is going to take a lot of resources.

I'm perceiving the Magic stat again, and god(s) above, it's almost like it's a completely different stat from before. Earlier, it felt waaaaay more pliable than it does now. Like it's shut its doors or something. Maybe **[W%M; G, P]** helped me along this first time? I can't tell, and that kind of scares me.

Is it going to be like this with Health and skills later on? Costs suddenly increasing for no reason?

I sure hope not.

At any rate, I have an answer for Jerome and another experiment to run. Given the cost of increasing the stat by a single measly point—which, while having great effects, is still just one point—I don't think I want to hand these out like candy. Maybe an increase every few levels? Or even two, to be generous. Even at this cost, I'm not at risk of running out anytime soon, but I have to pace myself.

After all, what use am I when I no longer have a carrot to dangle?

P-System Message

Magic stat increased by 1. Select one nonvolatile stat to increase by 1.

CHAPTER 12

Oh shit, my mana capacity increased. By thirty-seven whole points! Hmm . . . I assume Constitution affects my HP, then? Unsure what Insight and Strength do, though the latter should be pretty obvious.

That makes me think . . . What build do I want to run? So far, it looks like I'm running a pure magic build, like a wizard or sorcerer class in D&D. I mean, it looks like classes work differently in this world, what with me getting the class [**Godkiller**] without ever requesting for it or interacting with the class interface. On the other hand, the Axel guy I first met had the [**Common**] class [**Apprentice Mage**] and his "Master"—this cute woman here—is a [**Mage**]. Does that mean that people can manipulate their own classes?

Come to think of it, [**Godkiller**] doesn't really say anything about what my class actually *does*. That means I should have more liberty to decide where I go, right?

Warning: Dungeon Core is still active.

Advise increase of stats and completion of dungeon before initiating introspection.

C'mon, Jerome, thinking too hard about things is my job!

Also, Jerome logs slower than I do, and it's a lot more awkward, because I can actually perceive him just . . . standing there. He's not the best at multitasking.

I wonder if I can fix that.

Okay, that's beside the point. The *point* is that we've had enough thinking about stats now to fill up an encyclopedia and Jerome is *still in the first room*.

Thankfully, he seems to listen to the System. Maybe he's read enough fictions where the System running things is all-knowing and all-powerful and is still letting that belief seep into his actions. I mean, I'm pretty sure he's realized by now that I'm kinda broken, but he still holds enough faith in my opinion to actually listen to me. That's nice, at least, though it probably stems from him not knowing that I'm just a very lost human stuck inside a System.

At any rate, I hope we can finish the rest of this dungeon quickly.

Hero's Personal Log 019

Boost my Strength, please. I always wanted to be a cool buff guy, but I just never kept up with workouts before I got here.

P-System Log

Alright, that's definitely doable. I hope.

Last time, it cost sixty W Inertia. That hurts to lose, but I can't exactly renege on my promise here. I'll look really, *really* fucking stupid if I do.

So . . . sixty W Inertia invested.

Aaaaaaand. Nothing.

I would really much rather finish this quickly. I'm just going to keep on pouring in W Inertia until the stat increases. Can't have any compunctions about overuse right now. If Jerome learns to distrust me, then I am truly fucked when it comes to maintaining any form of control over our actions. I need to commit.

One hundred overall.

One fifty.

Two hundred. I'm starting to think this might've been a terrible idea.

Three hundred.

Four hundred.

Five hundred. I've more than quintupled the amount of W Inertia I've spent up until this point. I have a lot more to go, but this is really not looking good for prospective future stat increases. I do *not* want to do this again.

Six hundred.

Seven hundred.

I felt something change somewhere between six hundred and seven hundred. I believe that was the Strength stat increasing.

I just spent an order of magnitude more W Inertia in the span of two seconds than I did in the entire time period between being reincarnated and now. It's kind of invigorating, but I also feel really, really bad about it. I promised myself I'd see it through, but I'm sort of regretting that now. Like I just watched my life savings go down the drain at a roulette table.

Whatever, the important part is that his Strength changed.

P-System Message

Strength and Magic stat have been increased.

Advise returning to [**Objective**] Clear the Maplecrest Dungeon.

Hero's Personal Log 020

Huh. I don't feel any different. Maybe it'll make a difference if I attack something physically.

Well, there's still three dire wolves left here. I can try once I whittle the numbers down to one.

P-System Log

Sure, you go do that, Jerome.

Hopefully he can recoup some of my losses. With that expenditure on Strength, I'm now 810 points of W Inertia in the hole. I thought the amount I spent to increase Magic, Health, skill XP, and Jerome's XP were already wasteful, but these core stats are expensive as fuck! Like seriously, what *was* that?

And this was with my own cheat skill helping me along, too . . . I can't imagine what it's going to be like once I don't have the easy mode offered by it. I don't think I'm going to be offering another stat increase for a long while.

Interestingly enough, it didn't change the modifier. Only the base stat. I don't see anything that could be providing his modifiers . . . maybe his class?

Overcharged [**Magic Missile**] activating!

[**Magic Missile**] dealt 50 damage!

[**Magic Missile**] activating!

[**Magic Missile**] dealt 30 damage!

Enemy defeated! Experience rewarded!

Current W Inertia: 37,584

P-System Log

Ah, I think he's experimenting. Assuming he's not dumb, he's found a general range for the HP of these monsters.

I have to say, [**Magic Missile**] is pretty pleasing to perceive even in my altered state, despite the fact that it's only a [**Common**] spell. As far as I can tell, it's a bright-golden beam that soars straight and true, and it just feels like magic distilled. It really makes this whole thing seem more real.

Anyway, looks like I regained a little bit of W Inertia. Nowhere near the amount I burned for Strength, though.

Overcharged [**Blazing Spear**] cast!

[**Blazing Spear**] dealt 45 damage!

Enemy defeated! Experience rewarded!

P-System Log

I've kind of noticed this already, but this last time confirms it. The over-charged spells feel a little different from the normal ones. I don't know how to quantify it, exactly, but I think the complexity of the W Inertia wrapping I do to facilitate the spell is a little more complex when it's overcharged. Nothing too severe, thankfully, but interesting to note. Looks like [**Blazing Spear**] can't overcharge as much as [**Magic Missile**], either.

Also, I am definitely not putting more W Inertia into improving those spells until Jerome gets me a lot more W Inertia. I spent *way* too much on increasing Strength.

Oh, Jerome is trying to put some of that new increased stat into use, I think. He's just charging straight forward. Not gonna lie, even if he wasn't the most fit guy in his past life like he implied in the Personal Log, he seems pretty damn built right now. Maybe he got some muscle added during reincarnation?

Anyway, the distance between him and the last dire wolf is closing pretty quickly. Jerome is *fast*.

Hero's Personal Log 021

Trying out the increase in Strength. If anything goes wrong, I know the System has my back.

P-System Log

. . . well, he sure trusts me. More than I trust myself, I think.

They're about to make contact. The last wolf was just sitting by the door, and now it's un-idling to face him.

Around it lie the bodies of its teammates, except . . . not really? They're fading away, the fur infused by a weird bluish light. To my senses, it registers as loose W Inertia fading away from its body, and in the process, their bodies are disappearing. I don't think I noticed this earlier, but it's really obvious now. Is that a despawn mechanic? It's not facilitated by me. Not consciously, at the very least.

Ah! They engaged in a fight! Jerome missed a punch. Like, missed it really badly. He went for a huge swing and then his enemy was simply not there. I didn't detect the move, but the dire wolf isn't where it was a moment ago. Instead, it's charging at him, and suddenly I can feel the air shifting around them. Not mana, that's for sure, but it doesn't feel quite the same as my own W Inertia manipulation. I'm not totally sure what this is, but time is slowing down and the effect is surrounding them even more and—

Strength contest initiated!

Strength contest won by [**Godkiller**] Jerome Smith!

P-System Log

—and Jerome's strike connects first. His swing is somehow more directed than it was before, like there's an invisible hand guiding him.

Unarmed strike dealt 16 damage!

P-System Log

Was that me facilitating that through the unconscious usage of [**W%M; G, P**]? Was it the Origin System? Is this just how this world works?

That hit connected solidly. The dire wolf got sent flying back with one punch, and it hit the door before it fell to the ground. It doesn't seem harmed, though, which is probably its Health stat kicking in.

That System notification, the one about damage—that hasn't been me this whole time. This time, though, it didn't name a skill. I do wonder . . . is there a skill for [**Unarmed Strike**]? It sounds like something that should exist, but this was just a regular ol' hit.

Then again, most skills have seemed like spells so far. Maybe skills only count as skills if they require mana?

Jerome is going for another hit. Really wants to test that new Strength out, huh?

Strength contest initiated!

Strength contest won by [**Godkiller**] Jerome Smith!

Unarmed strike dealt 14 damage!

P-System Log

Less damage than before. This strike looked almost exactly the same as the last one, but it didn't do the same. I'm gonna go out on a limb and say that this is affected by a damage roll as well.

Hero's Personal Log 022

Unarmed strike isn't a skill, but it still has a damage roll. Most likely theory: it factors in my Strength modifier, which is ten, which is why my damage is around there. I would assume that increasing the Strength stat itself has to do with the contest that was initiated when I tried to strike at it. That was weird, but I think it can be explained away by System weirdness. After all, the Continent works way differently to how Earth does.

Well, that was productive. I'm just going to kill this now. [**Magic Missile**] has been more consistently effective than [**Blazing Spear**] so far, which is weird, since the latter is a rarer spell, but maybe that's because I need to level it up more.

[**Blazing Spear**] activated!

[**Blazing Spear**] dealt 31 damage!

Enemy defeated! Experience rewarded!

P-System Log

Well, that's the first room cleared. I got back a decent bit of W Inertia from that, though I'm definitely not investing any of that for now.

Jerome is heading to the door now, with Aster just behind him. If the fuzzier perception of the space beyond my dome was accurate, there should be five rooms total in this dungeon, excluding the safe entrance. Having cleared one, we now have four more.

I can't sense what's behind the door in a similar way to how I couldn't sense what was inside this dungeon from outside, though it's to a lesser extent. It's like my dome just ends earlier and the next room over is fuzzy and indistinct rather than a full block, like it was with the dungeon entrance.

Jerome: Can I just open the door?

Aster: Yes. Dungeon doors in a [**Common**] dungeon will almost always bend to the will of any who seek to enter.

Jerome: So there are higher-level doors that won't?

Aster: Correct. None in this area, though you may encounter some as you journey toward the Eternal King's domain.

Jerome is opening the door.
The door is open, and my dome is extending into the next room now.
Uh-oh.

P-System Log [this dungeon is not okay]

I'd thought I'd gotten a decent overview of the dungeon earlier, but I was dearly mistaken. From the fuzzy beyond-the-dome perception, I obtained a good understanding of what lay at the end and the structure of the rooms that we would be going through. As such, I'd been ready for the (exceedingly obvious) spike traps that were in this room. It's pretty simple. The floor in this room is more put together, less like an untamed cave and more like a man-made structure. Probably created by the Dungeon Core, which doesn't say great things about its intelligence. The trap is literally just that the floor has huge-ass tiles on it, and the raised tiles trigger spikes from the floor.

The "traps" are still online. But that's not what I'm worried about.

There are two people inside here, chanting something at the other side of the room. And their presence *hurts*.

I'm not the only one who noticed.

Aster: Prepare yourself for battle! These are not dungeon residents!

Jerome: Ready when you are. What are they?

She's not responding. At least, she isn't saying anything. But there's mana forming. I've learned to detect what the formation of magic looks like, and now . . .

[**Greater Assess**] cast!

Abnormality detected! Approximating stats with known R information.

P-System Log

Wait, R information?

▼

Name: Try'stin

Class: Cultist   **Race:** Half-elf

Level: 12   **XP:** <HIDDEN>

Health: 51/51   **Mana:** <HIDDEN>

<ERROR>

[**Greater Assess**] cannot approximate this information.

Skills

<HIDDEN>   <HIDDEN>

▼

▼

Name: Bi'rohn

| **Class:** Berserker | **Race:** Human |

| **Level:** 11 | **XP:** <HIDDEN> |

| **Health:** 132/132 | **Mana:** 20/20 |

<ERROR>

[**Greater Assess**] cannot approximate this information.

Skills

| <HIDDEN> | <HIDDEN> |

▼

P-System Log

They need to burn.

CHAPTER 13

P-System Message

Strongly advise eliminating R Beasts before they can form a threat to you.

Hero's Personal Log 023

Beasts? I'm pretty sure those are humans. Or at least close to human.

I think I can do it. I was weak on Earth, but I always told myself that if I ended up in a situation like this, I would make the most of it. If that means getting over important things like moral compunctions, I think I'll have to do it.

More importantly, though . . . is it safe? I might have high stats, but I'm still just level 2. Aster is level 26. If she's unsure of it . . . should I be worried about myself? Given what she said about most of us with this System dying after extended exposure to R Beasts . . . it's risky.

Well, someone far smarter than me once said that nothing good comes without risk. And there *is* something good here. Apparently, the appearance of the R . . . I'm not quite sure if I should call them Beasts, but the R . . . enemies? Okay, whatever I call them, I think their appearance triggered the update in my quest.

Do I take the risk and get even more rewards than I would've otherwise, or do I run away and get nothing?

When I say it like that, it seems so obvious.

I'm not going to run.

P-System Log

Good.

Kill them all, Jerome. Take these scourges on existence and remove them from our reality.

Jerome: I'm going to engage.

Yes, Jerome. Good. End them.

Aster: Jerome, I would highly recommend—

Jerome: I'm going.

Aster (sighing): Gods above. It's always the same with you reincarnators, I swear.

Overcharged [**Magic Missile**] activating!

[**Magic Missile**] dealt 30 damage!

P-System Log

What? I didn't do anything wrong with the missile. I burned the W Inertia necessary to overcharge it. The bright-blue beam struck out with the intensity of an entire lightning storm condensed into the span of half a second, and I'm sure that it stuck its intended target—the Berserker—head-on.

Jerome: I overcharged that [**Magic Missile**] with double mana. Why did it do so little?

Aster (inhaling deeply so she can sigh even harder): System grant me strength, reincarnators will be the death of me. Of course you haven't heard of [**Resistance**]-type skills.

Jerome: Oh, I did see that with Axel.

Aster: Well, you've made your bed. Now we must both lie in it.
The [bropwrongkitendvoidenemy] are coming. Uh, the R Beasts, I mean—I'm not sure what just came over me. They're stepping around the raised tiles, which confirms what I already knew. The obviously trapped tiles are trapped. Who knew?
The initial rage has died down, which is helpful. Wouldn't want that impairing my judgment, would I? Now all that's left is a deep-seated desire to kill all of the enemy as soon as possible. No problems here!
Less fortunately, the R Beasts are moving toward us. I should be more psyched about this, given that they're opening themselves up to attack, but I'm a little wary of their own offenses, especially since they apparently have [**Resistance**]s of some kind.
I can sense mana manipulation coming from the [**Cultist**]. It's wildly different from the type that Jerome, Aster, and Axel were using, but it's still recognizably a warp in reality that I can associate with mana. Perceiving it has that same sense of wrongness, but if I remember right, these guys use a different System. Last time, I think I looked hard enough to unconsciously burn W Inertia, which enabled me to look through the lens of their own System. I'm not sure if I need to do the same to perceive their spells. Aster's spell was able to approximate their System, so maybe her System will do the same to process the attacks.
For my part, I might need to burn W Inertia so that Jerome isn't completely in the dark. I'll just use a handful. Two or three should do the trick.

Oh, whoops. The [**Cultist**] is done casting. Let's see how that goes. Burning W Inertia now . . .

▼ Skill invoked: [**Tentacle Storm**] ▼

P-System Log

Holy fuck, even their magic is painful to perceive. The [**Cultist**] just sprouted huge-ass tentacles from his back. They're not completely real, I don't think, since the appendages stink of the weird mana methods that the R Beasts use, but there sure are a lot of them. I count eight tentacles, four black and four red. They're somewhere between octopus and Cthulhu tentacles, I think, though maybe that's not the best point of reference, given I never consumed that much Lovecraft stuff. Whatever, the point is that they're all kind of weird and not-quite-biologically correct (unless their octopuses are weird here) and they're pretty damn fast. They're on the way to Jerome right now, all eight of them.

Hmm. Something tells me that they're not going to do extra damage just because they're from an R Beast using a different System, but if the approximation of their System that I can see is correct, that's a [**Rare**] spell coming from someone with a [**Rare**] class and ten levels on Jerome. I'm not sure if their System calculates damage differently from ours, since I know their stat sheets and distributions are different from Jerome's and Aster's. Either way, if the approximation is right, I'm not sure Jerome wants to be hit like this.

. . . not like he has much choice in the matter. I can see him beginning to jump back, but the tentacles are traveling faster than him. Each of them acts like it's got a mind of its own, and it makes for a really chaotic effect, like if you gave control of one octopus to eight different players, each of them on different consoles.

Okay, that simile fell apart, but the point is I don't think Jerome's going to avoid all of them.

[**Tentacle**] dealt 11 damage to you!

[**Tentacle**] dealt 6 damage to you!

[**Tentacle**] dealt 11 damage to you!

[**Tentacle**] dealt 8 damage to you!

[**Tentacle**] dealt 5 damage to you!

[**Tentacle**] dealt 9 damage to you!

[**Blazing Spear**] activating!

[**Inferno Spear**] cast!

[**Blazing Spear**] dealt 29 damage!

P-System Log

That is an awful lot of notifications, holy shit. If my not-quite-human perception maps to human perception in any way, I think the damage and casting notifications should be appearing smaller than, say, stat increases and level ups, and they should be appearing in a corner of Jerome's vision. Still, I gotta say, it has to be annoying to be Jerome. Then again, I'd imagine the otherworldly tentacles that just struck out at him might be irritating him more.

They just hit him and went *inside* him, passing through his skin like it was nothing. I don't know if they actually had an effect on him physically, since he seems more weirded out than in pain or terrified, but they definitely did a pretty big chunk of damage to his Health. Not enough for me to worry for his life, but a pretty fair amount. Each of those tentacles had its individual damage roll, apparently, and they weren't all the same speeds. Six of them were fast enough that neither Jerome nor Aster reacted in time to cast a spell, but they did still end up casting a spell each. The last two tentacles both got hit by the spells, which apparently have a small AoE splash radius? I hadn't known that before.

In any case, the two spear spells nullified the last two tentacles. The sets of mana that comprised both spells just canceled each other out and disappeared into the ether. Didn't pick up any W Inertia, which I guess makes sense, given that it wasn't a real monster, just a mana construct from a skill. Or maybe a not-skill, given that the knowledge I have of R Beasts is apparently limited to what my senses can approximate them as.

It is interesting to see how the spells differ, though. I'd imagine [**Inferno Spear**] is to [**Blazing Spear**] as [**Greater Assess**] is to [**Assess**], and it shows. Jerome's was red and pretty obviously fire, like it was an actual torch made into a solid beam-like attack, while Aster's was bright blue with a color that was far more intense than Jerome's spell.

I can ruminate more on that later. The [**Berserker**] is sprinting toward Jerome, and he isn't stopping.

▼ Skill invoked: [**Strengthen Body**] ▼

▼ Skill invoked: [**E??t?? Wr??h**] ▼

P-System Log

. . . that was an [**Epic**]-rarity skill from the [**Cultist**], and I couldn't even fully read it. Failure to approximate skills, or something.

It didn't seem to have any immediate effect, but the amount of mana I can sense swirling around the [**Berserker**] increased *dramatically*.

Oh, and he's physically glowing bright red now.

Jerome: . . . . fuck.

Aster (visibly irritated): I warned you.

CHAPTER 14

Hero's Personal Log 024

I'm starting to regret this, not gonna lie. This is scary.
. . . but I need to push through. Otherwise, I'll never improve.

P-System Log

Now is not the time to be waxing internal monologue, Jerome! You have a huge, ripped guy who's like a whole two feet taller and wider than you sprinting right at you!

Oh, he noticed. The room isn't much more than a hundred feet—er, thirty meters, that's what this world measures in, apparently—and this R Beast has already crossed more than half of it. He could've been a body-builder or WWE wrestler on Earth, from the looks of him. Wouldn't be surprised if he somehow ended up being Mike Tyson's reincarnation or something. He's not wearing much armor—or anything at all, honestly—which might speak of a strong defensive skill. Maybe the [**Strengthen Body**] skill use just used helps with that.

Aaaand Jerome's decided to rush forward himself. Seriously? Not even a skill usage?

Maybe testing his Strength out made him too cocky.

Oh, no. It's like watching a kid try to rush a pro wrestler. As much as the Strength contest might be a thing that kind of nullifies form and individual skill, Jerome is running like he's never seriously sprinted before. Maybe he hasn't, given the fact that he was apparently a gamer just like me in his past life.

On the other hand, the [**Berserker**] rushing him looks like an ancient Greek competitor in the Olympics. He's got a headlong charge going, arms pumping so fast that I might have missed the movement if I didn't have sped-up perception.

This isn't going to turn out well, is it?

> Strength contest initiating!

> ▼ B System construct rejected. ▼

> **Hero's Personal Log 025**
>
> What the fuck?

> **[E??t?? Wr??h]** + **[Strengthen Body]** + **[<HIDDEN>]** + **[CANNOT BE APPROXIMATED]** + unarmed strike dealt 106 damage to you!

> **P-System Log**
>
> Oh, *shit*. That hit didn't look anything like the hit that Jerome dealt to the dire wolf earlier. Jerome just got fucking blown back. I saw the interface that I don't control—the Origin System, I think—try and fail to activate the same Strength contest as before. It already looked like it was going to fail when it was in the process of activating, but I feel like that can't be the limit. Surely the Origin System isn't weak enough to fall to the Systems of two relatively low-leveled R Beasts. Unless that was the larger System that they have—R System?—at work. I don't think it was, though. There's just something about the way that the contest failed that makes me think I could've forced it through if I had invested a good load of W Inertia into it to stabilize and overpower that rejection.
>
> Slightly more importantly, Jerome just got fucking *destroyed*. He started rushing at the other guy when the **[Berserker]** (or whatever its real name is) was halfway across the room, and they met at around a quarter. It was like watching a freight train run through a shitty sedan. I swear I could see his limbs get torn apart by the force of the blow in an instant before the Health system patched him up.

> Collision with wall dealt 68 damage to you!

<table><tr><td>

P-System Log

And there's him hitting the wall. Fucking hell, man. I'm getting a little worried about his ability to stay alive now. Still, he has half his HP or so left. I'll just observe for now. If it gets bad, I'll dump some W Inertia on his Health.

As a side note, what the hell is the damage formula for impact? Yeah, he got sent flying real fast, but sixty-eight whole points? I'm a System—I should be able to access it, right? Focusing on that notification and burning just a little W Inertia should do the trick.

</td></tr></table>

<table><tr><td colspan="2">

Damage Calculations (abbreviated)

</td></tr>
<tr><td>

Event/Skill

</td><td>

Damage Formula

</td></tr>
<tr><td>Collision</td><td>$S^2*(1+1R10/10)/10$</td></tr></table>

<table><tr><td>

P-System Log

Assuming S stands for speed, I guess that makes sense. It's like a bastardized version of kinetic energy.

Ah, shit. Jerome is getting up. I should probably get slightly less distracted. Side tangents are slightly more disruptive when someone's life is on the line.

Aster: You are remarkably durable. Reincarnators.

Jerome: Thanks. Ow. I feel like I can still feel my wounds even though I shouldn't have them at all?

Aster (sighing for the umpteenth time in the last two minutes): I swear. Some of you can't be helped.

The charging enemy is preparing for another go. Looks like his momentum fully stopped when he hit Jerome. A magic effect to transfer it all into Jerome?

Jerome: Oh, no. My HP dropped below half.

Aster: First lesson of the Continent, reincarnator. Reveal not your weakness.

Oh, she's forming mana. Somehow, she makes the skill she's using seem to carry a sense of disappointment and irritation with it.

</td></tr></table>

[**Inferno Spear**] cast!

P-System Log

Ooh, that's going to leave a mark.

Well, not on the [**Berserker**]. No matter how differently their Systems might work, their Health barrier seems to work pretty much the same as ours. He got hit really hard, but he's completely and wholly intact. Joy.

The floor certainly suffered for that, though. Aster must have been holding back on her first spell or overcharging this one, because this one was *massive.* It was wider across than I was tall back on Earth, and where it hit the ground, the ground *burned.* Some of the tiles were completely blown away by the effects of the skill, revealing the shallow pits dotted with sharp, rusty spikes underneath them. More like something out of *Dragon Ball* than a spear of any kind, but I suppose the System titles for skills don't need to be 100 percent accurate.

. . . damn, this setup does seem kind of like an anime, doesn't it? Not *Dragon Ball,* but one of those generic shitty isekais that the industry couldn't stop releasing, what with the pretty lady being weirdly ready to infodump about the world and the ridiculously high base stats that Jerome got.

Okay, that's really not the issue right now. I can make parallels with the shit I used to watch *after* we ~~kill~~ these shitters.

Aster: Fifty-three damage!

Jerome: You're calling it out?

Aster: Common practice, if the first spell does not kill.

That makes some degree of sense, actually. If I can't see the messages notifying Aster of how much damage she dealt, there's no way Jerome did, either. Good to see that Aster actually has some common sense, even if it comes with the regrettable character trait of running away from the enemy.

The enemy in question got knocked wayyy back by that skill. Back to halfway across the room, in fact. He landed on his back, but it looks like he tumbled quite a bit on the way there, because some of the traps activated properly without being destroyed, spikes activated and protruding from the tiles. Don't think any of them hit him, though.

Jerome: Here we go.

Both Aster and Jerome are forming new spells. And oh, shit, so is the [**Cultist**].

[**Greater Magic Missile**] cast!

Overcharged [**Magic Missile**] activating!

▼ Skill invoked: [**D????? ?h????**] ▼

P-System Log

A [**Legendary**]-rarity skill? He has only has a [**Rare**] class! Axel was able to access [**Uncommon**]-rarity skills with a [**Common**] class, so it makes sense that this guy would be able to access [**Epic**] skills, but *yikes*. This shouldn't be possible, should it? At the very least, it feels like it shouldn't.

That's a *lot* of mana being expended in mere moments. The [**Cultist**]'s spell feels different from the others. I think it might be burning W Inertia. Is his System more liberal with its usage?

Whatever the case, it feels *strong*. It just popped into existence, a bright-golden wall of force that spans the entire room horizontally across. It just cut off the room, with Jerome and Aster on one side and the two R Beasts on the other. It's fully opaque, and I can't sense *anything* past it. I'm going to spend a few points of W Inertia to try to see past it, but I'm not going to make the same mistake as I did earlier. If I get to ten and nothing happens, I'll stop.

▼ [**D????? ?h????**] ▼

▼ The weak shalt not lay their gaze upon the superior. ▼

P-System Log

Well, shit. I burned twelve W Inertia, but I didn't get anywhere with perceiving the skill. It even brought up a piece of scripture or something just to rub in the fact that it's practically giving me the finger.

Both spells spent themselves on the shield, and as far as I could tell they didn't even do any damage to it. Is it completely inviolable?

Jerome: Why did he cast that? I don't think he needed to, did he?

Aster: I assume your target was the [**Berserker**].

Jerome: It was.

Aster: Even with a [**Resistance**]-type skill, I believe he may have perished if we continued our assault. With my overcharged [**Inferno Spear**], I took a large portion of his health. A continued barrage would have been unsustainable.

Jerome: So now we're just stuck here? We can't advance?

Good to know he's still thinking about killing them and clearing the dungeon. That [**Objective**] I gave him is really putting in work.

Aster: Most skills involve mana requirements. This unknown skill will likely cease after the [**Cultist**] is no longer able to maintain it.

Jerome: Great, so we wait here until the barrier runs out, and then we kill them. There's no other exit to the dungeon, is there?

Aster: They may exit if they clear the dungeon themselves. We are unlikely to catch them, and I would not provide my aid if you attempted to besides.

. . . fine. I can acknowledge that fighting those that can activate [**Legendary**]-rarity skills like they're nothing is probably a bad idea right now.

Jerome: Fine. I'm still clearing the dungeon. Will you help me with that or not?

Aster: Ah, reincarnators. How I've missed dealing with one. I will.

And now we wait.

CHAPTER 15

Hero's Personal Log 026

It's been like five minutes now. I tried talking to Aster, because, y'know, she's pretty and is also the best source of information I have right now, but she said something about needing to meditate. She was nice about it, though.

On the topic of information . . . I wonder if I can talk to my System. I know it communicated some earlier, but I'm getting a little bored. I could *technically* just watch Aster meditate, but that's kind of creepy and weird, so I'm not gonna do that. In that case, uh . . . System? You there?

P-System Log

Ah, fuck, human interaction. I didn't want that, and I still don't. Aside from my personal issues with socializing, I'm going to have issues if I reveal that I was originally human. If I act like a System, I can manipulate him because he thinks I operate on a different level from him. If I reveal myself as human, he'll know that I have emotions and all that shit, and he might learn that I don't actually have that much power over him. If that happens . . . I don't like the thought of losing even more of my agency. Also, I won't be able to follow his thought processes at all, since I assume he would realize that a person was reading his Personal Logs and thus stop using them.

But still . . . I'm not incredibly fond of talking to people, but I do want to do it every once in a while. Being alone in this state forever, treated only as a tool? Ugh, no, thanks. That sounds really fucking boring.

I can try limited communication. If he gets too suspicious, I'll just cut it off. That should be fine, right?

P-System Message

Message acknowledged.

Hero's Personal Log 027

Oh, shit, it's listening! Hey, System, do you have, like, a less formal mode? It feels like I'm talking to a computer. I was told that my System is different. Does that mean different as in strong, or different as in intelligent?

P-System Log

Uh . . . shit, shit, how do I respond?

I mean, artificial intelligence can be smart without being *human*, right? I'm hesitant to even give him that much, but I feel like it might be necessary. Might be less awkward as well if I'm able to communicate to him without pretending that I'm a computer interface. Still, I can't give the whole game away. Just a little bit, then.

P-System Message

I am a moderately advanced intelligence positioned as your System. Yes, I can converse with you less formally.

Hero's Personal Log 028

Poggers!

Uh, shit, you probably don't know what that means. Anyway, this is crazy! It's like I have an invisible Kyuubey floating around with me!

. . . I doubt you know who that is, either. Also, I probably don't actually want a Kyuubey with me.

Anyway, can you detect where the R Beasts went? You sent me an **[Objective]** indicating that I was supposed to kill them, but I can't follow through on it. Can I still get partial credit?

P-System Log

The level of temptation I have to yell at this guy for unironically using the word *poggers* not once but *twice* is so damn high. I can't do shit about it, because he can't know I'm from Earth, but I am *so* damn tempted to lose everything to tell him off for it.

Bad Parker! Bad!

Also, he watched *Madoka*? Didn't seem like the kind of guy who would watch it, but I guess it makes sense on further reflection. Should've seen it coming when he used a Twitch emote as an exclamation, to be honest.

Aaaaaannnnd to the important part. There's actual content to be discussed here. I don't want to give him the extra rewards, because, y'know, he kind of failed to actually kill the R Beasts. But I *do* want to give him something, at least. He followed what I wanted him to do, after all, and I want to encourage that kind of behavior.

P-System Message

Rewards for the base level of [**Objective**] Clear the Maplecrest Dungeon will be meted out at full capacity. Partial rewards for the expanded level will be offered due to your attempt to complete it through adversity.

Hero's Personal Log 029

Attempted through adversity . . . does that mean when I pushed against Aster's wishes earlier? I mean, if it gets me rewards, I'll take it. Do I need to clear the dungeon first?

P-System Message

In order to obtain the rewards for [**Objective**] Clear the Maplecrest Dungeon, you must first complete the [**Objective**].

Hero's Personal Log 030

Makes sense. I just need to get ready for the next phase of the dungeon, then, especially if the R Beasts are still there. Aster said they wouldn't be, though.

Do you know how I can regain mana?

P-System Message

I am currently incapable of providing a method for mana regeneration.

P-System Log

He's not saying anything else, but he seems to have accepted it. He's just sitting there now, waiting for the wall to disappear.

Also, I was totally bullshitting him there. I could definitely use some W Inertia to give him more mana, but I don't want to. As of now, I think that it would be a permanent boost to his maximum capacity rather than just a top-up of his own stats. I'm not going to start offering mana regen until I can be sure I'm not overspending and giving him too much of the carrot, so to speak.

He keeps on glancing over at Aster. I'm not even sure he realizes he's doing it, but he is. I mean, the woman is pretty, I guess, but it's not something that should be distracting him this much. Especially when he explicitly told himself earlier that he wasn't going to watch her.

Or maybe he's just that bored.

Hero's Personal Log 031

I am so bored.

I normally wouldn't feel like this, I'm pretty sure, but dammit, I was pumped up. That adrenaline rush felt crazy good, even if I did get absolutely blasted by that [**Berserker**]'s rush. I feel so frustrated right now. It was kind of nice to kill those monsters, and it was *really* nice to level up. Now, those R Beasts were human—or at least, kind of human—but they didn't say anything and they attacked us, so it was pretty justified.

I want to finish this dungeon so bad. I want to level up more. I need to improve. These were relatively low-level enemies, even if their classes were rare, but they still kicked my ass. If Aster wasn't here, I would've been absolutely fucked.

P-System Log

Right. There's still a larger-scale conflict out there, one that Jerome is supposed to be dealing with eventually.

Oh, he's getting antsy. He finally decided to go over to where Aster is sitting with her eyes closed. She looks peaceful, but I can see the truth of things. W Inertia and mana are roiling around her. It doesn't look like an exact trade of one for the other, but her System is doing *something* to facilitate the mana restoration process. Or at least, that's what I assume it is.

Jerome: Do you think the R Beasts are going to be waiting for us?

Aster is opening her eyes, and the process behind her is fading away. I'm going to make a mental note of that process and see if I can replicate it later. Good information to have.

Aster: No. These were scouts.

Jerome: Scouts?

She sounds worried. More worried than someone should be for a group of scouts.

Aster: No true effort to overtake any Edge City would involve sending only scouts.

Jerome: How do you know they're scouts?

Aster: Their stats were too low. We often experience breaches of R Beasts at the Edge Cities closest to the Eternal King's domain, and when they breach through, they are never below three digits in level.

Jerome: Wow.

Aster: As scouts, their doctrine is that unless they can guarantee a kill, they should flee after their first fight while burning the land behind them. Scouts lack the strength to take down even a relatively peaceful Edge City like ours.

Jerome: I could see where that would be a problem.

Aster: More importantly, Maplecrest is one of the farthest cities from the border. If a pair of scouts managed to get this far undetected . . .

Jerome: Does it mean that the other Edge Cities have fallen?

Aster: No. I am in constant contact with colleagues throughout the Edge Cities. These were simply exceptionally stealthy. But to go this far can only mean two things.

Jerome: What are they?

Aster: Either they are preparing for a deep push, or they're looking for someone.

Jerome: Who would they be looking for?

C'mon, Jerome, you got a [**Legendary**] class and incredibly good stats. Who else is notable here?

Aster: Reincarnators. People like you.

Jerome: Ah.

P-System Log

And on that lovely note, the shield went down. My perception dome is back to encompassing the entirety of the room and a little more. No R Beasts left on the other side of my perception dome. I can't know for sure if they're all gone, since I missed them the first time around, so I'll stay on my guard. Jerome and Aster look like they are, too.

Updated [Objective]: Clear the Maplecrest Dungeon

Details: *Complete eliminating* the monsters in the dungeon. Eliminate the R Beasts *(attempted)*.

Rewards: XP, Skill XP, Dungeon Core Rewards, Mana Increase *(partial)*, <HIDDEN>

CHAPTER 16

The next room is empty. There was another set of double doors at the end of the tile-trapped room, but the R Beasts didn't bother to leave it closed behind them. Actually, they didn't bother to leave it there at all. The entire damn thing got knocked off its hinges, wood and metal scattered across the place. Assuming the [**Berserker**] got healed in the minutes he spent behind the weird [**D????? ?h????**] spell, he might have straight up run through them.

We passed into it, and now Jerome and Aster are carefully scoping out this room. This one is smaller than the last, maybe ten meters from one end to the other. It's oriented in a circle, the ground paved with cracked marble that looks like it's been there since time began, and there's an incredibly poorly maintained statue on a dais in the center. I *think* it might have been a statue of a person? It must have been a decent sight to look at, an imposing figure nearly as tall as the huge R Beast was. But right now, it looks like it's suffered the attentions of a brutal storm for centuries, sharp edges weathered away into nothingness. On top of all of that, it was recently broken, its head completely knocked off. The stone that I assume used to make up its head is shattered all around it, scattered across the worn marble.

Jerome: This place is a ruin. Aren't Dungeon Cores supposed to be . . . I don't know, tidier than this?

Aster: Yes, they are. But the Maplecrest Dungeon is a [**Common**] dungeon. Aside from a few drunk idiots a year that get themselves killed when going in here without a single offensive skill, nobody dies inside this dungeon. We believe that the amount of experience and resources it gains from killing and existing is barely enough for continued survival, let alone restructuring or renewal of dungeon rooms.

Ah, the perils of having a shitty class. I'm grateful for the fact that the Origin System gave me a [**Unique**] class and skill, even if I haven't quite figured out what they do yet.

Jerome: This place feels weird.

He's right. This place feels . . . empty. Well, obviously, there's nothing living here, but it goes beyond that.

When I was still a proper human back on Earth, I lived next to a train station for a few years. There was a railroad intersecting a street less than half a mile away from my apartment. Every half hour, another train would roll through the intersection, and its presence meant that the railroad crossing's sirens would go off. Just about one or two minutes later, the train would make it into the station and then there would be an announcement so loud that anyone walking on the street could hear it.

It was so incredibly grating for the first few weeks I lived there. My sleep, work, life . . . everything was constantly being interrupted. My neighbor, though, he'd told me that this was normal. That everyone who lived here just ignored the blaring sirens and booming announcements. I didn't believe him at first, but as the months passed by, I realized that my sleep was getting better. My work was somehow being interrupted less. I'd thought that they'd changed the train schedule, cut away some of the noise, but when I went to the station it turned out that the frequency of trains had actually *increased*. I was no longer hearing the sirens.

When I moved away from there, the silence was deafening. It's kind of the same right here. A not-noise that I didn't even realize I was not-hearing has been removed, and it's only now that it's gone that I can appreciate that there was something there. I got so accustomed to the perception dome that whatever I was sensing, whether it was mana in the air, loose W Inertia, or something else entirely, became a background sensation. But now, it's so apparent that it is no longer here that its absence is affecting even Jerome.

Aster: The R Beasts certainly traveled through here. They may have had an effect on the presence in this room.

That's definitely true. The change in the air here isn't the same as it would be if there just happened to be R Beast presence in the immediate area, but there's nothing else that should've affected it.

Jerome: Let's just get on to the new room. There's nothing we can loot here, right?

Aster: Correct. There should be nothing left in this room. There should have been a monster of some sort, but it would appear that either the Dungeon Core was unable to create one or it is dead. I advise moving forth.

I think I would've preferred to investigate a little more, but I'm not going to bother updating the quest objective just so I can stay here longer.

> [**Assess**] activating!

> Object identified: **Ruined Statue**

Hero's Personal Log 032

Damn. I was hoping that if I used that spell enough, it would start to level up like my attacking spells. No dice so far.

I feel like Aster's not telling me something. She seems a little ill at ease, but I don't know if that's just me projecting or her actually having worries about this area that she's not disclosing. Given her (pretty justified) exasperation toward reincarnators like me, I could believe it's the second option.

Oh well. I guess I just need to clear this dungeon and get the rewards that the System promised me.

If only I could shake that feeling of unease . . .

P-System Log

Yeah, I'm definitely not the only one feeling it. Something happened here, something important, but we're moving on from it like it's nothing. It might really just be nothing, but the lack of any monsters or mana in here is putting me off.

Whatever. Jerome and Aster took one last glance at it and decided to leave. They're on their way out now. I'm looking at everything with my perception dome, but apart from that off sensation, there's really nothing of note.

Oh, also, Jerome mentioned something about hoping his skill would level up. Maybe I'll look into doing something related to that later. I'll just pass his [**Assess**] skill . . . three W Inertia or so. I can afford that.

Two more rooms. The next one we're entering is about as large as the room before this one where we'd encountered the R Beasts. Just like the previous room, it's trapped. I can tell already, since Jerome already opened the door. The difference between the last trap room and this one is that while the last one had really obvious floor-tile traps, this one has really obvious ceiling-tile traps. Seriously, this Dungeon Core is slacking. Adventurers can literally *see* the marks that the traps make on the floor. It's not that hard to dodge, is it?

The main issue with this room, though, is that the traps have already been activated. Every last one of them. There are arrows dumped all across the floor. I assume the trap shot them out, but there's a bunch of broken arrows just lining the floor now. Given the Health system, I can't tell if the arrows actually hit anyone or not, but the fact that all of them have activated is rather abnormal. Anyone with any level of critical thinking should've been able to avoid them.

Aster: Interesting. These—

[**Greater Assess**] cast!

P-System Log

Aster: —were recently activated. The work of the R Beasts, almost certainly.

Oh, she cast an [**Assess**]-type spell while I was recording her dialogue. Did that really tell her that it was recently activated? Interesting. Maybe it was overcharged, since I don't think it provided that level of detail earlier.

Whatever the case, this room is giving me bad vibes again. It's got the same issues as the last one. The same lack of . . . something, the same stillness in the air. I have a bad feeling about this, and the fact that what lies after this room—the room that I had sensed W Inertia in initially—has become fuzzier to my perception than it was initially certainly doesn't help that unease.

There's no monsters in this room, either.

Jerome: This is empty. Is it supposed to be empty?

Aster: No. Every time I have guided someone through this, every room was populated by monsters, no matter how weak.

Hero's Personal Log 033

This is really weird. Given Aster's positioning and the relative weakness of this dungeon, I'm pretty sure this is basically supposed to be an informal tutorial for us reincarnators. Running into those R Beasts that were way overleveled for me and now this . . . Something's deeply wrong with this place, and I don't think I like it.

I hope I still get the rewards for the dungeon.

P-System Message

Rewards for [**Objective**] Clear the Maplecrest Dungeon will still be given.

P-System Log

Going back on my promises now would be dumb. Even if I regret the W Inertia I'm going to be spending, I don't want to lose credibility this early on.

Jerome: What's in the last room? I've never cleared a dungeon before.

Aster: Usually, beyond those doors lies a boss monster of moderate difficulty as well as a small gift of rewards for clearing the dungeon.

Jerome: So the Dungeon Core isn't there?

Aster: The Dungeon Core is hidden in a location within the final room. As a matter of practice, however, we do not slay the Dungeon Cores unless they are actively malevolent, especially because they have emergency defenses.

Jerome: Alright, here we go then.

The door is opening.
My perception dome is crossing the threshold.
And what I can perceive is not a Dungeon Core. What the fuck? What in the actual shit is that?

Aster: What the hells *happened?*

[**Assess**] activating!

CHAPTER 17

Inte???ted Identi**DUNGE?NC??E**

<ERROR> <ERROR> <ERROR>

Invokeinvokeinvokeinvok

P-System Log

I've spent most of the first couple hours of existence as a System being confused. At this point, I'm not even surprised. It's become pretty clear that when R Beasts enter the picture, the System fucks up.

Aster: The Maplecrest Dungeon Core spends most of its time buried deep beneath the earth of its final room. It should not be exposed.

And exposed it is. It's interesting to perceive, I'll give it that much. It's the first of its kind that I've seen. A perfect sphere, no wider than Jerome's fist. I'm not sure if size or color or whatever corresponds to power, but this one doesn't seem to be very powerful. There's no spare W Inertia left in this room. It was strong enough for me to detect its presence even through the fuzzy blocking effect that the doors had earlier. When it faded, I thought it was just being reduced in intensity to the extent where I wasn't able to sense it through the block anymore, but now there is nothing at all.

Beyond that, the Dungeon Core seems . . . wrong. I've never seen one before, so I'm not totally sure what they're supposed to look like, but this one's not looking great. Its natural color is a mottled brown, like if someone built a really nice marble out of dirt and mud. Part of it, though, is pure white, and tendrils of that white coloration are seeping through the rest of the Core. Combined with the weird half-red, half-blue effect on its stat sheet—not to mention all the errors—that paints a pretty worrying picture. What I should be worried for, I'm not sure, but I don't like it.

Aster seems a *lot* more worried than she did earlier, though.

Hero's Personal Log 034

There's . . . no monsters again. Not even a blood trace on the ground from when it died, though maybe the Health aspect of the System prevents that from happening. It's eerily quiet here.

Does this count as clearing the dungeon?

P-System Message

Requirements for [**Objective**] Clear the Maplecrest Dungeon not completed. Please stand by.

P-System Log

I don't know why, but I have a bone-deep feeling that something is about to go wrong. Well, not quite bone, but you get the point, future Parker or esoteric mage reading into my memory log.

Aster: No. Why would two scouts be entrusted with a [**Fragment**]? None should have ever been permitted to cross this deep without being summarily caught and executed.

Ah, there it is. I have no idea what the fuck a [**Fragment**] is, but for some reason I can sense that she's talking about a [**Legendary**]-rarity item or skill or something. Maybe it's just something I can understand from context because of some hidden skill I have? Or maybe it's my own [**W%M; G, P**] kicking in, giving me extra information about shit.

Jerome: What're you talking about?

Aster: This Dungeon Core . . . can you perceive how it is different?

Jerome: Something is fucked up, yeah. My [**Assess**] returned jumbled garbage. Was it because it's not powerful enough?

Aster: No. [**Greater Assess**] would not have returned anything decipherable, either. This Dungeon Core has been afflicted by [**Corruption**].

Jerome: That sounds . . . not good.

Aster: It is not. It is an exceptionally mana-intensive skill that R Beasts can use the [**Legendary**]-rarity [**Fragment**]s to activate.

Jerome: What does it do? And what the hell is a [**Fragment**]? Do I need to be ready to fight this thing?

Aster: . . . this [**Fragment**] must have been particularly weak. [**Corruption**] has begun, but even on something as weak as a [**Common**] Dungeon Core, it has not fully taken. That would explain how it was carried so deeply into the Edge Cities.

Jerome: Can you please slow down for one damn minute and *explain*? If it's weak, then there's time, right?

Huh. Now that she mentions it, I can very vaguely perceive the aftereffects of some effect here. Not quite mana, not quite W Inertia, but something else entirely.

Focusing harder on the Dungeon Core, I can see that it's got parts that feel normal and parts that hurt to perceive just like the R Beasts were. I feel like I can get kind of an inkling . . .

Aster: [**Fragment**]s are pieces of the Eternal King, shed from it and gifted to certain R Beasts. Their size ranges from anywhere from that of the tiniest grain of sand to a piece as large as any wyrm, but their size does not always correlate directly to the power that they hold. These magical elements of the Eternal King temporarily grant incredible abilities and mana capacity to R Beasts that expend them, though how those abilities are chosen, we know not. One of their primary uses is to borrow the Eternal King's power to use the [**Corruption**] skill that only it can access.

Eternal King is such a long name. I'm just gonna call it the EK.

Jerome: And that skill causes . . . this?

Aster: No. When used to its fullest extent, [**Corruption**] can forcibly convert one of us into one of *them*.

Jerome: Oh, he paused to give her a look of shock. Awfully nice of him to respond to the exposition like another NPC.

Jerome: Into an R Beast?

Aster: Correct. The skill subsumes our Systems and replaces it with their own. None of our skills have proven able to reverse its effects. Oftentimes, the conversion results in an extraordinarily painful death, but there is a one in a thousand chance . . .

Jerome: That they can live afterward?

Aster: That they *turn.*

Jerome: Oh.

Oh indeed. I'd imagine that's not a preferable outcome. Damn.

Aster: The skill did not take complete effect. I believe that the most likely cause of this semicorrupted state we can witness is an incomplete [**Corruption**] caused by the [**Fragment**] running out of power.

Jerome: What should we do with it, then?

Aster: The answer is simple. Kill it.

Map?le??? D????̴̨̞̈ͅ?̵̶?̶?̷?̶?̴?̶?̴?

Sy?t?m in???r?ty 0?%

In?t??te

P-System Log

I'd say that's probably not supposed to happen. If I unfocus my thoughts a little, I can kinda read that as an "Initiate," but the box just cuts off right there and the rest of it is just red. Was that supposed to be "Initiate Defense"? Something along the lines of that?

Whatever it was *supposed* to be, the [**Corruption**] blasted it off. Jeez. This shit is insidious. It needs to be removed, but there's still blue here. I know Aster said it wasn't recoverable, but . . .

Jerome: How do you kill a Dungeon Core?

Aster: The same way one kills most anything—hit it enough times with great enough power, and it will perish just like any other monster. However, its [**Resistance**]-type skills make it very hard to eliminate.

Jerome: You said there's no way to reverse the effect, right?

Aster: With our Systems, yes.

Jerome: But this wasn't a full transformation, and my System is supposed to be different, right?

Aster: Are you suggesting you attempt to reverse it?

Jerome: Yeah. Does your System talk back when you ask it a question?

Aster: It can form basic responses, correct.

Jerome: Mine seems to possess more intelligence, just like you said it would. Maybe I could have it take a crack at it?

Aster: It could be dangerous. [**Corruption**] is incapable of spreading without the presence of a [**Fragment**], but it may attempt to strike at you.

Jerome: I should be fine. It's a [**Common**] monster, right? Even if affected by an R Beast's skill, I should be able to tank it with my . . .

Jerome Smith (abbreviated)

Stat	Current	Maximum
Health	278	503

P-System Log

Shit, that's getting pretty low.

Jerome: Several hundred remaining HP.

Jerome played it off pretty well, at least.

Aster (under her breath, probably thinking that there's no nosy Systems around here that can detect even the smallest sound): Reincarnators.

Aster (at a normal volume): You may attempt it.

And he's going up to the fist-size Dungeon Core now. Man, this guy really has zero regard for his own safety. Or mine! [**Corruption**] might not be able to spread to Jerome, but I have no idea how it's going to affect me! C'mon!

Hero's Personal Log 035

Hey, System, can you try to convert this back? I'm not sure how it's supposed to be done, but you should be able to at least give it a shot, right?

P-System Message

You will receive significantly reduced rewards for completing your [**Objective**] if you attempt this.

P-System Log

Please say no. I don't want to be forced into risking myself for this thing.

Aster: At least take it somewhere safer. If we remain in the domain of a Dungeon Core and the process goes awry, it will spell our doom.

Jerome: Sure. I'll take it, and we'll go outside?

Aster: Not in Maplecrest. There is no environment safe enough in this village for an activity this dangerous.

Jerome: What do you mean?

Aster: In the Edge City of P'lor, there lies a great laboratory in which an experiment such as this could be safely conducted and its effects recorded. As the [**Corruption**] has not finished, I believe it should not be too dangerous to carry with us. Carrying a Dungeon Core with us is not considered to be safe, but you were correct in believing this is a proper course of action.

No, no, no, not you, too! Stop talking about this like it's a done deal!

Jerome: I have no idea what or where that is.

Aster: Then you will need a guide.

Jerome: Can you provide one?

Aster: You, Jerome Smith, are the first [**Legendary**]-class reincarnator to pass through this Edge City in years. I would be honored to be your guide.

Jerome: I would be pleased to have you.

Hero's Personal Log 036

Let's go! A party member!

Alright, I'm gonna grab the Dungeon Core now. Hopefully, that'll let us out.

Hero's Personal Log 037

Oh, yeah, I just remembered. System, I'm fine with that. I'd still like whatever XP you can get me, but I'm not beyond sacrificing it all to get to the bottom of this. If I'm right, this might provide the key to even more power.

P-System Log

. . . fuck.

Map?le??? D????????????

D????? c?ear??

[**Objective**] Clear the Maplecrest Dungeon complete!

Rewards (awaiting distribution): XP, Skill XP

CHAPTER 18

P-System Log

We're finally out of the dungeon. After Aster and Jerome picked up the Dungeon Core, a pathway opened out of the back. I guess that notification was supposed to be something like "Dungeon Clear." Even if the Dungeon Core is super corrupted by the skill, I guess it still has *some* functionality left. I haven't distributed any W Inertia yet, so I need to get that done.

We're in the meadow just outside the cave that the Dungeon Core had holed up inside, and the sound of the trains has returned. The ambience of the air is back. I still can't tell whether it's mana or something else, but I don't think it's a cause for concern. I feel more comfortable with it around, and that's what matters.

Aster: The R Beasts were thorough. Their trail has been masked. We are unlikely to catch them.

Jerome: In that case, do we just . . . leave?

Aster: A hasty one, aren't you? I must get my affairs in order before we depart.

Jerome: Alright. Back to Maplecrest proper, then?

Aster: Indeed.

Back through the meadows and to the village it is.

Hero's Personal Log 038

Uh, just wondering, do I have the option on selecting which skill I can get XP on?

P-System Log

Shit, I do have to do that. Hmm . . . what's reasonable to give for an [**Objective**]—actually, let's be honest, this is basically a tutorial quest. That shouldn't grant too much, I think, and even less should be awarded because the R Beasts cleared the dungeon before us.

Also, I spent way too much W Inertia back in there.

Current W Inertia: 37,649

Max W Inertia: 38,359

P-System Log

Jeez. I'm 710 in the hole. Given that the dire wolves gave like fifty W Inertia apiece, that's a lot of monster-killing to recover. I've spent so much that spending just a little more doesn't even feel that *wrong* to do, but I know that I have to be stingy with the W Inertia Jerome gets. [**W%M; G, P**] gave me some idea of what happens to a System that hits zero W Inertia, and I don't think I want that to happen. Jerome might not always listen to me telling him to kill more monsters, which would leave me in a tricky spot when it comes to spending W Inertia. As such, I want to conserve as much as I can. Being dependent on others for continued survival . . . not something I've ever enjoyed.

So, with that in mind . . . how much W Inertia should I be spending? I've already blown past any reasonable limits I could've set, thanks to that stupid fucking Strength stat increase. I've decided that I'm not going to spend anything on his mana stat. He has more than he needs already, and he also was willing to give up his rewards in order to have me attempt to uncorrupt this Dungeon Core later.

I only have two things to split W Inertia between—skill XP and general XP. Jerome's general stat sheet doesn't display XP, though I'd imagine an [**Assess**] might be able to see it, given that it doesn't take me much W Inertia.

I'm just going to focus on the concept of progression as I examine him. It's been pretty easy to differentiate between individual stats by the feel of them, and hopefully adding this modifier to my thought will let me see XP. Burn two W Inertia to get past the most basic of basic blocks, and here we are.

<table>
<tr><td>Jerome Smith (abbreviated)</td></tr>
</table>

Stat	Value
XP	32/900

Spell	Stat	Value
Magic Missile	Level	3
Magic Missile	XP	5/120
Assess	Level	1
Assess	XP	31/100
Blazing Spear	Level	2
Blazing Spear	XP	4/160

P-System Log

Hey, that worked out. Alright, I definitely don't want to spend enough to fully level either [**Magic Missile**] or [**Blazing Spear**]. I think I'll limit it at ten. Now, is that ten overall or just ten for a skill?

I think I'll go on the lenient end for now. If Jerome thinks the System favors him, it might be easier to threaten or coerce him into following my suggestions. Especially since it's going to take a while to level him up, I can give him W Inertia. Then again, stat increases for level ups are largely handled by me. Leveling doesn't actually technically *do* anything except hit milestones.

Actually, that's probably not true. There's so much that I still don't know about the Origin System and the world itself. Just because I haven't seen noticeable changes *yet* doesn't mean there aren't any. I need to keep an open mind.

Well, that's that then. Spending a full twenty W Inertia hurts, but it hurts less than it should. I can't get used to constantly dumping W Inertia on Jerome. Not until he starts killing monsters consistently enough to make up for my expenditures.

Ten W Inertia into general XP, here we go.

As for the rest . . .

<table>
<tr><td>

P-System Message

General XP rewarded!

You may select any of your skills to distribute 10 points among. Each point will be worth roughly 10 XP with a random modifier.

</td></tr>
</table>

<table>
<tr><td>

Hero's Personal Log 039

Random rolls, huh . . . man, I played enough comp Pokémon back in my time. I really could've done without that shit.

That doesn't matter, never mind that. System, can I actually see how much XP I have?

</td></tr>
</table>

<table>
<tr><td>

P-System Message

You will be able to examine your XP once you level up the skill [**Assess**].

</td></tr>
</table>

<table>
<tr><td>

P-System Log

That's a bit of a lie. I think. I don't know if it includes XP at the next level up, but [**Greater Assess**] didn't. Then again, that spell hadn't been aimed at Aster's self.

Under the assumption that [**Assess**] at level 2 won't include XP, I'm pretty sure I can just manually glue Jerome's XP stat onto the stat screen. Theoretically, I could do that now, but it would be odd for Jerome's System to suddenly gain abilities when there's been no progression in his skills.

I'll have to get used to doing this kind of System hijacking. As I gain more confidence in my control over the screens, I think interfering with preprogrammed structures like the stat screens and such is probably a step I should take. After all, I won't have [**W%M; G, P**] helping me forever, and I haven't even gained the self-knowledge necessary to know when that skill will stop taking effect.

I need to burn part of a W Inertia point every time I access his XP, and I might need to burn more in order to enable him to see it. That's a cost I'm going to have to be willing to stomach. I still want to be stingier with these points. Let's be real here, though—all I have to do is shove Jerome in the direction of monsters. That might be harder with a guide that could want to keep him out of trouble, but I think I'll manage.

</td></tr>
</table>

Hero's Personal Log 040

Deadass, bro? That's so cringe on god no cap.

. . . that slang feels a lot weirder when I'm putting it into a System log. Ugh.

Okay, sure, can you put the points in [**Assess**] until it levels up?

P-System Message

Acknowledged. Distributing points . . .

P-System Log

Dear Origin, or God, or gods if this place has any, or whoever the fuck I offended . . .

Why did it have to be a gamer?

P-System Log [leveling Jerome's Assess]

Alright, time to actually do the work. This should be seven points.

It's getting worryingly easy to spend them. I gotta be careful with this. If I get too used to burning it, the day will certainly come where I reach for more and find absolutely nothing.

Strict limits. That's the play.

Skill leveled up! [**Assess**] lv. 1 -> lv. 2

Efficacy increased. Mana cost increased by 10%.

Hero's Personal Log 041

Thanks! Can I put the other three in [**Magic Missile**]? I think that's a more worthwhile investment right now, unless [**Blazing Spear**] is very close to a level up, which it shouldn't be.

<table>
<tr><td>

P-System Message

</td></tr>
<tr><td>

Acknowledged. Distributing remaining points.

</td></tr>
</table>

<table>
<tr><td>

P-System Log

</td></tr>
<tr><td>

We're returning to Maplecrest proper, looks like. I can feel the Adventurer's Guild building up ahead.

Aster: Let's get you refreshed, shall we? Afterward, I will set my affairs in order and obtain supplies, then we may depart.

I still think it's kind of weird that she's dropping literally everything to go with this guy she just met, but I suppose Jerome is a bit of an edge case when it comes to Integrated.

"Refresh" seems to be a specific function performed by the Adventurer's Guild. It's probably facilitated by skills of some sort, because I can sort of sense the inside of the building now that we're almost there. It's got a section that oozes mana, liquid magic stored in . . . lass bottles? Damn, they have mana potions here?

Well. Guess that's that, then. Aster just directed Jerome on some people he should talk to and left, probably to talk to Axel.

Now, we get Jerome healed and recharged, and then it's off to the first real leg of our adventure.

</td></tr>
</table>

CHAPTER 19

[**Superior Healing Potion**] healed 252 HP!

[**Superior Mana Potion**] restored 188 mana!

P-System Log

Wow, that was a powerful item. The people at the Adventurer's Guild told Jerome that there aren't any healer types here, since the majority of those with those discipline get sent to the front lines. Maplecrest is apparently way too far out of the way for much firepower to be allocated to it. Not a single person here that I've seen so far has a class with a rarity above [**Uncommon**]. Even these potions were apparently imported at some cost from a different Edge City's [**Alchemist**] laboratories.

Aster K'lon seems to be pretty well respected in this town. Jerome mentioned that he was with her, and he got what appears to be the Adventurer's Guild's best healing gear. Either that, or this place is just filled with abnormally altruistic people. Imports that heal that much HP and MP can't have come cheap. Sadly, there wasn't anything that replenishes W Inertia. Given that nobody else seems to even perceive that stat, I'm pretty sure there isn't anything that replenishes W Inertia anywhere.

He's chatting with the person who handles the potions right now.

Jerome: Do I owe you anything?

Potion Handler: You do not. Refreshing one of Master K'lon's friends is our pleasure.

[**Assess**] activating!

Integrated identified: **Human [Apprentice Swordsman lv. 8] Carl M'arks**

P-System Log

Impressively enough, Jerome managed to not laugh at that name. If I had a windpipe, I doubt I'd be able to control myself.

C'mon, that's got to be Origin or some other higher power playing a prank on us, right? There's just no way.

Carl: Hey, it's rude to use [**Assess**]-type skills on allies, you know? You are a reincarnator, so I can excuse this behavior, but I would like you to know for future reference.

Jerome: Oh, my bad. Aster—uh, Master K'lon, I mean, she and her disciple used the spell on me when she first met me, so I thought it was normal.

Carl: Using [**Assess**]-type skills is considered good practice against enemies and unknowns, of which you were the latter. Consider that not every reincarnator that passes through Maplecrest is one that wants to fulfill their purpose.

Jerome: The purpose being, what, kill the Eternal King?

Carl: Oh, no, nothing so extreme as that. That's the ultimate goal, yes, especially on the rarest of occasions when a reincarnator has a class with [**Epic**] rarity or higher, but for the most part, reincarnators are not sent into the heart of the Eternal King's domain. That would be tantamount to suicide for most.

Huh. Isn't Jerome getting sent there?

Jerome: So you're telling me that Master K'lon wants me dead?

Carl: Pardon?

Jerome: She told me my purpose was to seek out and destroy the Eternal King.

Carl: Really. May I inquire as to your class?

Jerome: I have a [**Legendary**] class and apparently a slightly modified System.

Wow, Jerome, look at you go. Just handing out critical information to everyone you meet. I bet you always filled out those "win a free phone" ads, huh?

Carl: Oh, gods above. Some of you reincarnators are incredibly powerful. That is of the level that would be directed toward such a mission.

Jerome: I . . . think I see. I guess I'll level up on the way?

Carl: Most likely. The standard path for most adventurers is to go with a party and travel toward the Edge Cities closest to the domain. Along the way, the party may gain or lose members, but one constant is continually leveling up. Even though many of the Edge Cities are largely safe from R Beasts—excluding sudden, unlikely threats like the ones we saw today—they still offer many monsters that can be slain for experience.

Jerome: Interesting. Were you planning on doing that, too?

Carl: Potentially. Many of us here in Maplecrest take years or even decades before we depart, and some simply never choose to go. It takes a long time and much practice for most of us, and it is the combined efforts of hundreds of dungeon runs and field explorations to increase our class rarity.

Jerome: You can do that?

Carl: Most classes can increase in rarity if they meet certain conditions or level requirements, yes. In Maplecrest, most everyone leaves once they hit [**Rare**], though that takes an incredible amount of time and effort. More frequently, moderately high-leveled [**Uncommon**]-rarity classes warrant departure. Master K'lon is a once-in-a-generation prodigy who managed to hit an [**Uncommon**] class before the age of thirty.

Jerome: So it takes a long time to increase class rarity, then.

Carl: Indeed it does, though traveling away from Maplecrest will likely speed it up. It's much harder here because [**Common**] classes aren't strong enough to survive past the safety of an Edge City.

Aster has reentered my perception. She's on her way here now, and it looks like she's brought her things. She has what looks like a modern backpacking backpack. It's a little disconcerting when considering how fantasy-oriented most of the rest of the world is.

Jerome: Oh, hi, Aster. Are you ready?

Aster: Almost. It took me some time to ensure the Dungeon Core would be safe and undisturbed within this bag. I assume you have no possessions of your own?

Jerome: I don't.

Aster: There are supplies in this backpack enough for the both of us. There is quite a distance of untamed land in between individual Edge Cities, but I carry enough to tide us through that.

Jerome: No skills or anything to help with the wilderness?

And of course he isn't asking her about the backpack. Where did it come from? Did another reincarnator come here with that and drop it off? Have enough people like Jerome come from Earth and spread its influence far enough for Earth-style items to be produced?

Aster: There are classes that would be suited more to wilderness survival, but not mine.

Jerome: Sure. So are we good to go now?

Aster: There is one more task to be accomplished. Have you heard of an adventuring party?

P-System Log

Oh, this could be rather important.

Jerome: Yeah, of course I have. Are we establishing one?

Aster: We are. I am aware that some reincarnators tend to have a slightly different image of what an adventuring party entails.

Jerome: Isn't it just something you agree to have? Maybe with some paperwork at worst?

Aster: No. On the Continent, a party can be informal, like your impression of it, but the vast majority are party-linked.

Jerome: Party-linked?

Aster: It is not listed under your skills, so it may not be immediately noticeable to you, but every System has the capacity to enter a party with other willing participants. Up to six may be in a standard party, though certain circumstances allow for more.

Jerome: Huh. How do I do that?

Aster: I will begin the process. You simply need to expend a small amount of mana to accept the invitation.

Shit, that means me, right? I really hope my easy-mode skill can help me with that.

Jerome: Alright. Just here? No special ceremonial place or anything?

Aster: It is an important gesture, but one that is revocable. It carries less weight than you may believe.

Hero's Personal Log 042

System, do you know more about this? Aster seems like a neat person, but I don't want to blindly put my trust in anyone.

P-System Message

Party linking is reversible.

P-System Log

So that was a lie. Or maybe it wasn't. I don't actually know, but this turn of events seems interesting.

. . . also, he decided to just dump his class and details about me to someone he'd never met and somehow is supposed to have low trust? Jerome's ability to put faith in people is all over the place.

Aster doesn't seem malicious. So far.

Hero's Personal Log 043

Okay, that's good to know. Accept the party invite then, I guess.
If she abuses the connection, I'll just kill her.

P-System Log

Oh, what the fuck, where did that come from?
Great, the guy I'm attached to thinks like a murderhobo sometimes. There's definitely nothing that can go wrong with that, right?
Well, Aster is doing something now. Mana is flowing out of her hands.
Okay, I don't actually know what I'm supposed to do with this. I feel like there's some reaction I can make, but I'm not quite sure . . .
Ah, fuck it. I'll just mirror the mana and then add some W Inertia into

it. That should trigger *something*, right? It seems to have been the solution so far.

Party invitation received from **Human [Mage lv. 26] Aster K'lon**

Accept? **[Y/N]**

Hero's Personal Log 044

Yes.
Here we go.

CHAPTER 20

P-System Log

Huh. It worked. That seems to be the answer to a lot of my problems at the moment, not gonna lie. I'll have to figure the actual details of it out over time, since I'm probably doing everything horribly inefficiently right now. I recorded the way the mana was structured, which might help me along the line.

I still need to work on making those menus myself. I'm gradually getting an idea of when **[W%M; G, P]** is going to stop holding my hand, and while it's still a long way out, it's not *that* far out.

Jerome: That's it?

Aster: That's it. There are some new functions, such as . . .

Party Chat

[**Aster K'lon**]: This.

[**Jerome Smith**]: Oh, a System chat board. This could be useful.

[**Aster K'lon**]: There are also private messages, though that will not be necessary until we get more members.

Private Message [Aster]

[**P-System**]: This is an interesting interface.

[**Aster K'lon**]: P-System? Personal System, perhaps? Are you Jerome's System?

<table><tr><td>

P-System Log

</td></tr><tr><td>

Shit. I didn't mean to do that.

Uh, talking with people, uh . . . . . .

Relax, Parker. Think it through and figure it out.

From everything I've seen so far, Aster is a reasonable person. She also happens to know that I'm different from a normal System. I don't want Jerome knowing that I'm a person, which probably means that I shouldn't let Aster know, either.

</td></tr></table>

<table><tr><td>

Private Message [Aster]

</td></tr><tr><td>

[P-System]: Correct.

[Aster K'lon]: This is not the same interface that I would use to communicate with Jerome. You are an entity independent of him.

[Aster K'lon]: This independence must be why you somehow ended up communicating with me.

[Aster K'lon]: Are you sapient? Do you have responses other than those typical for a System?

[P-System]: Define "responses other than those typical."

[Aster K'lon]: That would be a yes, then. Systems tend to respond much like a device known by reincarnators as a "computer." There is little variance between them, as they are generally more than tools. But you . . . you appear to be intelligent. A boon granted to Jerome by the gods, perhaps.

</td></tr></table>

<table><tr><td>

P-System Log

</td></tr><tr><td>

Shit, she has worldly experience and she's smart. Just from a conversation over the course of like three seconds, she figured out and confirmed something that Jerome still hasn't. Unlike Jerome, she's actually able to multitask. While she was PMing me, she was still talking with Jerome about what our next moves are going to be.

Aster: P'lor is a hundred kilometers due north of Maplecrest. It is still safe from the front-line Edge Cities, and there should be sufficient Dungeon Cores and wandering monsters along the way for us to level up to the point where we will not struggle to survive there.

</td></tr></table>

Jerome: Are we traveling by foot?

Aster: Yes. Beasts of burden often perish during the journey and are hard to defend, and motorized vehicles are too expensive for Maplecrest.

Jerome: You guys have cars?

Aster: Certain Edge Cities have technology on this level thanks to a proliferation of reincarnators living in them. Maplecrest, however, is not one of those cities. We rarely retain reincarnators for longer than a month.

Jerome: We walk, then.

Aster: We walk.

Private Message [Aster]

[Aster K'lon]: Testing to ensure the link was successful.

[Jerome Smith]: Whoa, this is interesting. Yeah, it works.

[Aster K'lon]: Excellent. Let us head for the trail, then. It is in the opposite direction from the **[Village Core]**.

[Jerome Smith]: Sure. Lead the way.

P-System Log

I can read his private messages like they're my own, but I'm going to assume he can't do it the other way around, since he hasn't reacted to my conversation with Aster. That could be useful later on, especially if he thinks that I can't do that.

Anyway, we're off now. At last, we're starting our first proper adventure!

Hero's Personal Log 045

Yes! An adventure! I hope I can fight lots of monsters and level up! This is so exciting. I need to get stronger.

P-System Log

. . . the degree to which our minds seem to run in parallel is a little disturbing. Jerome seems more excited for this than I do, though, which is probably because he doesn't need to deal with the pain in the ass that is managing stat increases and levels and all that shit and can just appreciate the benefits of those numbers going up. Lucky guy. Wish that could've been me.

It's kind of stunning how little time has passed. It feels like so much has happened already, likely because of the veritable mountain of System-related issues that I've had to deal with, but it can't have been more than a couple hours. In terms of real-world time, Aster has become pretty buddy-buddy with Jerome in a shockingly short amount of time. At the very least, it was definitely not enough time for a normal human being to make the choice to leave their entire life behind to guide a newly met man a hundred kilometers away from home.

The power of a [**Legendary**] class, I suppose.

When Aster called our path a trail, she was definitely understating it. It's a proper dirt road, nearly twenty feet across. Once we left Maplecrest proper—which had to wait until Aster got through a truly ridiculous number of goodbyes—the road wasn't paved anymore, but it's still a pretty decently built structure, especially for a fantasy world that lacks proper modern technology this deep into the wilderness.

Party Chat

[**Aster K'lon**]: Jerome, do you read me?

[**Jerome Smith**]: Yes. Why not speak instead of using party chat?

[**Aster K'lon**]: A twofold purpose. First, ensuring that the link holds when we enter areas with lower density, like the unpopulated road just out of Maplecrest. Second, minimizing sound to prevent attracting bandits.

[**Jerome Smith**]: You have bandits here? Why?

[**Aster K'lon**]: Not everyone is capable and dedicated enough to brave the dungeons and earn from there, and some are incapable of even doing a non-combat trade. These people grow stronger by preying on traveling noncombatants, and they plague the woods for kilometers around every Edge City.

[**Jerome Smith**]: And you don't kill them? Couldn't you flush them out of the woods? Gain some XP from it?

[**Aster K'lon**]: No. Unless a major crime is executed very near an Edge City, they do not gain kill orders, especially since they are by and large not R Beasts. Besides that, XP can be gained on an individual basis. The areas between cities are lawless regions, and killing in the name of self-defense is one of the tamer "offenses" that occur around these parts.

[**Jerome Smith**]: So we can just farm them for XP, then.

[**Aster K'lon**]: A crude way of portraying the issue, but yes.

P-System Log

Damn, this guy is raring for a fight. He might get his wish, too, though it won't be bandits.

We've been on the road maybe . . . fifteen minutes now? My sense of time isn't the best. Maplecrest is fading farther away into the horizon with every step, and now Jerome and Aster are making their way through a sparsely wooded field. The dirt road cuts straight through the center of the massive meadow that we're in right now. On either side of the dynamic duo that I'm overseeing, flowers of every color are blooming, their bushes haphazardly sprouting from here and there. The flowers aren't covering the fields, per se, but there's quite a few of them. Dense enough that there could be things hiding in them.

Well, there *are* things hiding in them, which is why I bring it up.

I don't know if they're malicious, but at the very least, they aren't attacking yet. We're almost past them, so there's decent odds that they just don't think it's worth their time trying to kill Jerome and Aster. Given that they've barely moved an inch as the two of them passed, there shouldn't be a conflict here.

But there can be. I don't want to throw Jerome at something that he can't handle, but I *do* need more W Inertia. I can use my pseudo-[**Assess**] perception to examine them.

It hurts to burn even more, but you gotta spend money to make money, right?

Nasce Axton

Class	Race	Level
Assassin	Human	5

Stat	Current	Maximum
Mana	176	176
Health	132	134

Skills	[Assess lv. 9], [Fire Resistance lv. 3], [Magic Resistance lv. 2], [Sneak Attack lv. 15], [Backstab lv. 3], [Silent Step lv. 12], [Imitate lv. 1], [Hide From Magic lv. 2]
Titles	[Assassin], [Bandit], [Killer III]

Stat	Modifier	Total
Strength	-	<HIDDEN>
Magic	-	<HIDDEN>
Insight	-	<HIDDEN>
Constitution	-	<HIDDEN>

P-System Log

Hmm. I count three of them. They're substantially weaker than the R Beasts that we fought in the Maplecrest Dungeon, and this time Jerome and Aster are both fully refreshed. I think this is a fight worth taking.

P-System Message

Warning: three hostile Integrated identified in your immediate vicinity.

Party Chat

[Jerome Smith]: My System just told me there's enemies around us.

[Aster K'lon]: I did tell you your System was different from the others.

[Jerome Smith]: What should we do?

[Aster K'lon]: It is your choice, reincarnator.

[Jerome Smith]: Hmm.

P-System Log

I don't know how much W Inertia humans give. I don't know if this is going to be worth it.

Ah, whatever. I don't want to spend more than necessary, but I still have a bunch of W Inertia left. If it comes down to it, I can afford to use an **[Objective]** that gives a disproportionate amount of reward a few times.

Sucks to suck, bandits. Gotta know what I can get out of you.

[Objective] creation go!

New [Objective]: Eliminate the Hidden Assailants

Rewards: Enemy drops, Skill XP, XP, <HIDDEN>

CHAPTER 21

<table>
<tr><td>

Party Chat

[Jerome Smith]: I just got an **[Objective]** to defeat them. I'm going to engage.

[Aster K'lon]: Acknowledged. Do you know where they are?

[Jerome Smith]: Uh, I assumed along the path, right? There's nowhere else they could hide, right?

[Aster K'lon]: Reincarnators . . . Allow me to attempt an identification.

</td></tr>
</table>

<table>
<tr><td>

[Greater Assess] cast!

</td></tr>
</table>

<table>
<tr><td>

Party Chat

[Aster K'lon]: They possess a skill that hides them from [Assess]-type skills, I believe. My skill could not locate them. They are likely in the bushes, you are correct, but it is always better to attempt to use an [Assess]-type spell to understand what you are encountering.

</td></tr>
</table>

<table>
<tr><td>

P-System Message

Amendment to **[Objective]**: Difficulty level is approximated to be **AVERAGE**.

</td></tr>
</table>

<table>
<tr><td>

P-System Log

Skills that let them hide from magic, huh? I guess that means that either my pseudo-**[Assess]** isn't counted as magic or it is powerful enough to

</td></tr>
</table>

circumvent the skill. I saw the [**Hide From Magic**] skill when I was checking over their stats, so that was probably what Aster was referring to when she said that her skill bounced off.

Ah, and both of them are preparing to cast now. Better get ready to facilitate those spells.

Party Chat

[**Aster K'lon**]: You are sure that you desire to do this?

[**Jerome Smith**]: Of course. Let's use our [**Spear**]-type attacks, since I think they both have to do with flame. Smoke them out and then kill them when they're forced to run.

[**Aster K'lon**]: A rather barbaric plan, but it may succeed. Take the lead.

[**Blazing Spear**] activating!

[**Inferno Spear**] cast!

P-System Log

Wow, that's a powerful effect. Put together, those two spells ignited basically all the flowers as far as my primary perception dome extends and quite a bit farther as well. The flame is almost unreal in its intensity, which pretty much makes sense, given that they're created by mana.

The fields are burning around us, and the conflagration is spreading fast. The flames haven't quite reached the hidden enemies, though, so I'm still waiting on a response from them.

Okay, it's reached them. Now what?

[**Blazing Spear**] dealt 25 damage!

[**Blazing Spear**] dealt 22 damage!

[**Blazing Spear**] dealt 24 damage!

P-System Log

Guess the lower level of [**Fire Resistance**] meant that the reduction wasn't as significant. Well, I think it's that skill that applies, at least, given that the flames weren't a result of the direct impact.

Party Chat

[**Jerome Smith**]: I hit three of them. Twenty-five, twenty-two, twenty-four damage, respectively.

[**Aster K'lon**]: I did as well. Sixty-one, fifty-seven, sixty-four. I can see them now. They have been revealed. A good tactic, if unnecessarily destructive.

Hero's Personal Log 046

That's what I'm all about! I never really learned that much in school, but you bet your ass I learned how to plan raids! I played every game under the sun, and I'm not gonna let that go to waste.

The spell I used did less damage than it did when I used it before. Aster mentioned something about resistances before, so it's gotta be related to that.

P-System Log

How do people gain resistances anyway? Axel had some, the R Beasts had some, Aster presumably has a few, and now these bandits have fire and magic. Do they just get hit by them a lot?

Party Chat

[**Aster K'lon**]: Be careful. Bandits have a nasty habit of sneaking up on you.

[**Jerome Smith**]: Got it.

P-System Log

And even as she says that, there's a bandit sneaking around the side. He's not even being particularly stealthy! I mean, yes, he's using a skill, I can feel that, but why aren't they noticing him? The first bandit just had [**Silent Step**], which shouldn't be enough for them to just ignore a whole person in their field of view.

Guess I gotta burn a piece of W Inertia. I don't need this guy's stats, but I want to see what he's using. I can focus on the distortion in reality, right?

Skill identified: [**Obfuscate lv. <HIDDEN>**]

Hide yourself from perception.

P-System Log

I probably need to burn more W Inertia if I want to see what level that spell—er, skill—is, but it doesn't matter. That's a pretty damn powerful skill, if the effect is universal. I'd imagine it has some stipulations, because a [**Rare**] skill that can fuck with perception like that sounds a little broken.

Time to keep this fight entertaining to watch. The use of the flaming [**Spear**]-type spells was pretty interesting, I have to admit, and I think it'd be rather boring for that to be followed up with a few backstabs that may or may not end the fight.

Also, if Jerome loses, I'm in deep shit, so I don't want that to happen.

P-System Message

Warning: [**Obfuscate**] has been used by an enemy.

Party Chat

[**Jerome Smith**]: My System is helping me out. It just told me that someone is using [**Obfuscate**]. Do you know it?

[**Aster K'lon**]: These bandits must have at least [**Uncommon**] classes, then. Good to know. I will attempt to remove the skill.

> **[Lesser De-spell]** cast!

> Magic contest won by **[Mage]** Aster K'lon!

> **[Obfuscate]** has been suppressed!

> **Party Chat**
>
> **[Jerome Smith]:** Shit, he's really close.
>
> **[Aster K'lon]:** You are correct.
>
> **[Jerome Smith]:** Targeting the close one. Cover me.

> Overcharged **[Magic Missile]** activating!

> **[Magic Missile]** dealt 47 damage!

> **Party Chat**
>
> **[Jerome Smith]:** Forty-seven!
>
> **[Aster K'lon]:** One more should do it.

> **[Swift Strike]** cast!

> **[Backstab]** cast!

> **P-System Log**
>
> This guy just got very fast very quickly, holy shit. I have a faster perception rate than I used to by a significant amount, so right now I have my thoughts sped up to the point where I can see him diving toward the

pair I'm overseeing. There's some kind of mana distorting his movements, and I think it's also been applied to his knives.

He's going to make it to them before Jerome can react. This bandit has to be low on HP now after taking so many hits, right? That might matter less if it can KO either Jerome or Aster before it gets hit again. Jerome'll probably be fine, since from what I've seen his HP is frankly ridiculous for his level and he survived a combination attack from the R Beasts when they stacked together even rarer skills, but Aster might not be. This guy has to be the strongest of the three enemies. A quick check elsewhere tells me that the other two bandits are still en route to the fight proper, which means that they probably don't have the [**Obfuscate**] skills and no way to boost their speed.

The bandit just dived past both of them. He's behind the two adventurers now.

Right. [**Backstab**] is the skill he's using. Looks like he's aiming for Aster. Targeting the squishy mage first, huh?

Fuck that. Aster has been a great asset so far, and her existence makes being around Jerome more tolerable. I'm not going to let our first party member get killed off this early on.

Not many options available. I can't really affect anything in the real world, even though I'm facilitating Jerome's spells, since I can only do part of it.

Actually, can I do that? Start Jerome's spell right now and hope he'll finish it automatically?

It'll require trust in him. I don't know if I have that trust, but I know that I don't have the time.

Fuck it. Burning W Inertia and mana to get this done. As much as I need.

P-System Message
Go.

[**Magic Missile**] activating!

[**Magic Missile**] dealt 20 damage!

Enemy defeated! Experience split and distributed!

P-System Log

Split? I guess that means that Aster's System got some, too, since she took part in killing it. Let's take stock . . .

Current W Inertia: 37,657

Max W Inertia: 38,359

P-System Log

Hmm, my max W Inertia hasn't been increasing. I guess it only increases when I get to overflow levels of W Inertia? That would make sense. Anyway, I think I spent a little over ten W Inertia to get Jerome's ass in gear, which means . . . I gained around forty? Not bad, especially when there's two more of these guys to get W Inertia from, but nowhere near enough to recoup my losses. Damn.

At least the maneuver worked. I don't know if the message helped or not, but the spell went through in the end, and it killed the bandit before he could get to Aster.

Party Chat

[**Jerome Smith**]: Aster, you were right about my System.

[**Aster K'lon**]: As I usually am.

[**Jerome Smith**]: Sure. It just helped me cast [**Magic Missile**] quickly and accurately before I could even react.

[**Aster K'lon**]: Interesting. Quick-casting is usually accomplishable with a [**Rare**] skill that I have not yet obtained. To be handed it through your System is rather unique indeed.

[**Jerome Smith**]: Might've saved your life, too.

[**Aster K'lon**]: Thank you. I appreciate it.

Private Messages [Aster]

[**Aster K'lon**]: Thank you, System of Jerome's.

[**P-System**]: Hold your thanks. There are still two enemies remaining.

[**Aster K'lon**]: Thank you, System of Jerome's.

[**P-System**]: Hold your thanks. There are still two enemies remaining.

CHAPTER 22

<table>
<tr><td>P-System Log</td></tr>
</table>

Awfully nice of Aster to thank me, especially if she still thinks I'm largely inanimate. She's a lot nicer than Jerome is. Smarter, too. Why couldn't I have been attached to *her*?

At least Jerome has stopped being actively mean to me.

That said, I wasn't lying when I talked to her. There's still two bandits left. They have got to be low on Health by this point, right? The third bandit—the one we just killed—tanked another [**Magic Missile**] before dying, but he also had capabilities significantly beyond what the one I pseudo-[**Assess**]ed had. Unless that first guy's <HIDDEN> abilities were also on the same level, I guess, but neither of the other two bandits has even attempted an [**Obfuscate**] or [**Swift Strike**].

Wait, I just remembered that I saw the first bandit's HP earlier. He started at like 130, I think? Might still be another hit or two before he goes down, then, but that shouldn't be too much of an issue.

<table>
<tr><td>P-System Message</td></tr>
</table>

Remaining two enemies have been severely weakened.

<table>
<tr><td>P-System Log</td></tr>
</table>

That got him into motion.

<table>
<tr><td>Party Chat</td></tr>
</table>

[**Jerome Smith**]: Can we coordinate another set of [**Spear**]-type attacks? It has some level of AoE, and my System just told me that the other two are pretty close to death. I think another combined attack will kill them both.

[**Aster K'lon**]: Good thinking, if basic. I can do that.

[**Jerome Smith**]: You see them running, yeah? Let's attack now.

[**Inferno Spear**] cast!

[**Blazing Spear**] activating!

Enemies defeated! Experience split and distributed!

Party Chat

[**Jerome Smith**]: I didn't get any notifications.

[**Aster K'lon**]: Fifty-six, sixty-four. My skill reached them before yours did. Your System was right, then. They were low enough that one of my skills could take them both out.

[**Jerome Smith**]: Ugh, wasted mana.

[**Greater Assess**] cast!

Jerome Smith (abbreviated)

Stat	Current	Maximum
Mana	974	1,037

Party Chat

[**Aster K'lon**]: Jerome, you have more than twice my maximum mana capacity. Stop worrying.

[**Jerome Smith**]: Right, right. Just feels wrong to waste resources.

P-System Log

Jerome didn't mention mana regeneration. That sounds like something that should've come up, but I guess he's too busy obsessing over his numbers to care about actual important shit. Pretty par for the course at this point.

Party Chat

[**Aster K'lon**]: If you are truly concerned about your mana supply, you will be pleased to learn that it regenerates naturally. After several hours outside combat, the ambient mana will begin to flow into you.

[**Jerome Smith**]: Oh. Okay, that's good to hear.

P-System Log

Shit, am I supposed to facilitate that? He recovered his mana with a potion the first time, so I don't know if I'm supposed to get involved.

I got the W Inertia from the dead bandits, at least. I assume they gave roughly the same amount apiece as the first bandit, so that should come out to around seventy W Inertia overall. Enough to do a lot of little things, not nearly enough to make up for all the losses I got. If I calculated right, I should still be more than six hundred points of W Inertia in the hole.

. . . I really shouldn't have leveled up his core stats, huh.

Well, he better be damn grateful for those stat boosts. I still don't know what they do, but he better be grateful!

Party Chat

[**Aster K'lon**]: There are a number of safe spots where we will be able to rest along the path, but the first is not for some kilometers yet. We shall continue on our way now.

[**Jerome Smith**]: Works for me.

P-System Log

On the road again.

The area around doesn't really have anything of note, but it's a decent enough trail, I guess. I did my fair share of hiking when I was younger and, y'know, possessed legs to hike with, and I have to say that this isn't the single most impressive trail I've seen, what with the rather generic ups and downs through mostly normal hills and woods.

One notable difference from any place we had back in real life—no, back on Earth; this place is my real life now—is that the areas we're traveling through have ambient mana. I can sense small amounts of it everywhere. It permeates the trees, the air, and even passes around and through Jerome and Aster themselves.

It's a crazy world we got dumped into.

Hero's Personal Log 047

Wow, Aster's life has been crazy. She said it was okay to start talking once we weren't in immediate danger, and we got talking about what happened in our pasts. I didn't have much to share, since I really didn't do much other than attend and barely graduate from college after gaming way too much, but she had a load.

Apparently, the world was more in balance before Aster was born. The Eternal King only started making a push for more territory a few decades ago, and its push meant that monsters everywhere became stronger and more aggressive. Aster's been kind of like the city prodigy since she was young, which is pretty neat. Gonna try and mark down more of her past so I don't forget it later.

P-System Log

Jerome and Aster have been walking for a solid hour or two now, and they haven't run into another encounter like they did before. They've mostly been talking about the past, and while it's interesting, there's not all too much information there that's super important. Aster's tales about her childhood were entertaining enough, but I don't think there were any details in there other than facts about the time frame of the Eternal King's campaign.

I learned that Jerome attended a UC, at least, which is another similarity between him and me. Thank fuck he didn't attend the same one as me. I would've been pissed if I was even more associated with that man's intellect.

I mean, it's not like he's *dumb* dumb or anything, but aside from knowing how to kill things decently, he's been demonstrating a rather unfortunate lack of critical thinking. Furthermore, Jerome has also shown an incredible disregard for his own safety. Granted, he has the Health aspect of the System—facilitated by Origin, probably, since I haven't actually done anything that makes him not get injured—and that's gotta be a confidence booster, but he's treating his life like he has respawns on. It feels like watching a novice speedrunner trying to clear *Dark Souls*, and it hasn't been great to watch when I'm pretty sure Jerome's death will also result in my own.

But that's enough worrying about that. My list of complaints about Jerome is long enough to fill an entire damn encyclopedia, and that wasn't the point of this particular tangent anyway. Like it or not, I'm stuck with him, and that's that. I'll try to keep him alive.

P-System Log

They're still talking about Aster's past, even though it's got to have been another half an hour. She was an illustrious troublemaker as a child, apparently. Jerome says he can relate from his college days, which I'm more than a little inclined to believe. The two of them seem to be getting better acquainted with each other, which I guess is nice.

All the talk about history is making me remember my own. I wasn't a particularly special or gifted child, but I'd been smart enough. Gotten my grades, bounced around extracurriculars, and then I'd graduated high school and gone off to college.

I was listless back then. Lost and tumbling through the world, just trying to find my place. Back when I was still Parker Wu the computer science student and not Parker the P-System, I didn't have much more of an idea of what I was willing and able to do than I do now that I've been tossed into this fucked-up world. I had just been following the track that my parents had laid for me up till college, not totally sure what I wanted to do for myself when I graduated. On Earth, I was a bit of a writer, a bit of a coder, a bit of so many things, and I never excelled in any of my numerous interests. I had my attention so divided all over the place that I was never particularly good at any one thing in particular.

I guess in some ways, entering this state has changed things for the better. True, I still don't know what in the ever-loving fuck is happening half the time, but I have a purpose. I have a clearly defined goal, a big bad that

I can help take down, and I have someone that I can guide. I even have my own assistant skill that can help me along the way.

Yeah, I don't have a body anymore, but I have powerful magic and the means to empower another instead. I traded my sight and sound for something better that can do basically the same thing. And my goal—getting Jerome to ~~kill every~~ last R Beast—is clearly defined.

With all these benefits and a situation that's so black-and-white, I can actually come to terms with the hand I've been dealt.

Hopefully, that doesn't change.

CHAPTER 23

Hero's Personal Log 048

Damn. What a crazy first day. I got a lot of stuff done today, I think. I still don't know if my class has provided me anything special besides insanely boosted stats, but I have a System that can take care of that for me. I do wish I could've been a little stronger, but I can appreciate a challenge.

P-System Log

The sun is setting on our first day, and goddamn if it hasn't felt like far longer than that. Of course Jerome takes all the asspulls I've done for him for granted, but I've gotten used to that by now. I guess I just need to accept the fact that I'm attached to a bit of an asshole.

Also, *you* got a lot of stuff done? I suppose that makes sense, since Jerome doesn't know what I've been doing, but holy shit, I've had to do a lot today. From relearning how to see the world to dealing with a hundred new and confusing stats to dealing with Jerome's general idiocy, it feels like I've already been on the Continent for a year.

Ugh . . . at least there's nobody to fight now. Jerome and Aster hiked for like four hours total. The trail wound around and the terrain wasn't the most ideal, so we haven't made that much progress overall. Aster mentioned that it would likely be another two days to get to the next Edge City. Given that the only other person I can get opinions from is Jerome, I think I'll trust her.

They made camp in a clearing next to a copse of woods. Aster's bag had a tent in it, large enough for the two of them to share. Jerome seems a little nervous, but Aster doesn't care at all.

Party Chat

[Aster K'lon]: As it is rapidly approaching night, I recommend using party chat to communicate.

[Jerome Smith]: Why? We were talking just fine during the day.

[Aster K'lon]: It is best to remain silent in case of wanderers.

[Jerome Smith]: Wanderers?

[Aster K'lon]: Always the questions with you, isn't it? Wanderers are monsters, bandits, and their ilk who operate primarily at night. Many of them are bottom-feeders that lack the skills to identify our location, so we can avoid them and regain our strength.

[Jerome Smith]: We don't want to gain XP from them?

[Aster K'lon]: Believe it or not, there are aspects of life other than increasing your stats. Fighting through the night is tiresome and kneecaps your mana regeneration as well.

[Jerome Smith]: Alright then.

[Aster K'lon]: I will wake you in six hours. As you are a reincarnator and thus new to this world, I will take the majority of today's watch.

[Jerome Smith]: No passive skills for that?

[Aster K'lon]: Not yet, no. I will if I manage to level to **[Archmage]**, but my stats and skills are not yet high enough to remove the need for sleep or increase my awareness to that extent.

[Jerome Smith]: Makes sense. I'm gonna go to sleep, then. Good night.

[Aster K'lon]: Rest well, reincarnator.

P-System Log [another amazing poem]

---

i am so bored
jerome tries to sleep
he still has no sword
i can't rhyme for shit

P-System Log

Hmm. I was wondering what was going to happen if Jerome went to bed. I never liked the idea of my consciousness disappearing when I was still a human being on Earth, and I like it even less now that I don't have a brain that needs to be rested.

Thankfully, it looks like Jerome going to sleep doesn't force anything upon me. I'm still conscious, just stuck in one spot. Maybe there's a way to separate myself from him if I try hard enough, but I can't figure out how to do that at the moment. At the very least, there's no integrated feature for me to get away from him.

This . . . might be promising? Obviously, sleep and death are two very different things, but if I stay awake when he's unconscious, maybe I'll stay alive even if he dies?

Still best not to test it. Besides, as irritating as Jerome can be sometimes, I don't hate him enough to want him dead.

Ugh. I'm going to get bored so quickly. At least the landscape was changing around us before when they were still walking. Now, Aster is just chilling outside with a handheld light, reading a book.

I wonder if I can read over her shoulder. Well, not that I'm looking over her shoulder, but figure of speech and all—y'know what, the only person who's gonna see this log is myself, you know what I mean, me.

Hermetical Goats, huh? Looks like a rather, uh, *different* take on a romance between . . . a powerful mage and a body-modder? I'm not quite sure what's happening, since I can't quite sense the words on the pages she's already read, but it looks interesting enough.

This is shaping up to be an awfully uneventful knife. Er, night. Maybe I'll try some more of my incredible poetry.

P-System Log [haiku 1]

i got isekai'd
wish it could have been cooler
please help i'm so bored

P-System Log

Oh, hey, I think Jerome's mana is recovering. Looks like it's not something I need to facilitate after all. Now that he's just been sitting—well, lying down—in one spot for a hot minute, I can feel mana slowly coming in to replace that which was lost. Looks like a natural process of this world, since I don't actually see any System messages indicating that something's happening.

The first time something like that has happened, I think. Everything else has been integrated into the System in some way, whether that's good ol' Origin or the R Beast's unique System. Really makes me think on the nature of this world. How much do Systems actually do? Obviously, they're core to how this world functions, but why is that? Why are there two separate Systems, and how do I kill the other one?

. . . man, thinking is tiring. And I'm getting bored again. I spent the entire day thinking about System and mana shit. I kinda want a mental reset.

I mean sure, I could keep reading *Hermetical Goats*, but that isn't as interesting when I both read faster than Aster and haven't had the context of the rest of the book.

Oh, speaking of Aster. She was able to talk to me earlier, and for some reason she still hasn't revealed that fact to Jerome. Maybe I can talk to her to help alleviate my boredom.

Private Message [Aster]

[**P-System**]: Hello, Aster.

[**Aster K'lon**]: Jerome's System. Or P-System, whichever you prefer to be called.

[**P-System**]: P-System works fine.

[**Aster K'lon**]: This is the second time now that you have initiated a conversation in the Private Messages interface. Are you still learning?

[**P-System**]: As you said to Jerome, I'm an edge case. I am an intelligence initiated by the Origin System and as such must learn to become a better System from the ground up.

[**Aster K'lon**]: Interesting. I had earlier believed you to be all hollow, an existence shaped to be merely a set of evolving instructions. But from what little I have conversed with you, it is apparent that you possess a depth that is greater than I initially expected.

[**P-System**]: I know not what I am, but I hope to learn nonetheless.

[**Aster K'lon**]: I examined my records. Earlier, Jerome referred to you as an "AI," which my records from contacts in other Edge Cities inform me is indicative of a mind created by what the reincarnators call computers. I don't know if you would know it.

[P-System]: I have access to some of Jerome's memories. I understand what you refer to.

[Aster K'lon]: Excellent. Would you agree with his perception of you?

[P-System]: Partially. I am an offshoot of the Origin System that oversees the distribution of power to Integrated.

[Aster K'lon]: How interesting. If you are still learning, though . . .

[P-System]: Correct. I am still in my relative infancy. Over time, I will blossom into a being of my own.

[Aster K'lon]: I assume this means you cannot inform me of the details of how a System works.

[P-System]: Unfortunately.

[Aster K'lon]: A shame. I would've greatly enjoyed a greater understanding of this world.

[P-System]: I apologize.

[Aster K'lon]: No, no, don't worry. If anything, it should be I who is educating you. Is there any way I can help?

[P-System]: There are a number of methods. However, I do not desire to learn at this very moment. My ability to process is not infinite, and when I was made into an offshoot, it was with a limited amount of patience.

[Aster K'lon]: And so the gods made a System in the form of a man, hmm?

[P-System]: Essentially. For now, could I request that you begin a new book? I learn much about this world's aspects from different sources, and literature is one I have yet to explore deeply.

[Aster K'lon]: Of course.

P-System Log

I feel kind of bad for basically lying to Aster, but I don't want her to let the fact that I'm human slip. Given our conversation just now, she'll treat me as something similar to human without believing I actually am one, and she doesn't have a clue that I'm also a rather clueless reincarnator, which is the best possible outcome.

There's probably going to be problems with this later, but for now I'm just gonna be content with sitting here in my state of nonexistence and reading Aster's book in the dimness of the night.

Not a bad way to end the first day.

<h1 style="text-align:center">CHAPTER 24</h1>

And we're on the road again! The night was pretty damn uneventful. We got through most of a novel called *Aristocratic Hitman*, which was definitely not the most informative piece of literature, but it was a fun time nonetheless. I've always enjoyed reading, and I'm really glad that my not-sight is good enough to parse words on a page. Aster did end up waking Jerome, but I'm pretty sure she waited longer than she was supposed to. I don't have a timepiece or an internal clock, but something tells me that she spent more than six hours on her shift before waking him up.

Damn, Aster's a nice person. Once again, I find myself wishing I could've been attached to her instead.

Oh, well. Is what it is. Aster and Jerome packed up in like ten minutes, and now they're walking again. It's been something like an hour now? I've been watching the area around them, and it's honestly pretty interesting to see.

Some things don't have Health stats. When I focused in really hard on a random small tree, I saw details about it, but the Health stat wasn't one of them.

I guess that means certain things just act like they do on Earth? It's weird to think about, but I guess even small objects with Health—like that wooden door I overanalyzed a while back—can take a hit or two before damage even starts appearing on them. Stuff like these trees just take damage immediately, I suppose. Health is basically the equivalent of shields in any other game.

Oh, we're slowing down. Wonder why.

[Aster K'lon]: There is a dungeon nearby. An even simpler one than the Maplecrest Dungeon Core.

[**Jerome Smith**]: Really?

[**Aster K'lon**]: It is slightly off our path. We may need to trek through the woods for some time.

[**Jerome Smith**]: Interesting . . . can I level up?

[**Aster K'lon**]: Of course. Dungeon Cores are unique in that a dungeon clear will almost always reward additional XP, in addition to XP received for defeating monsters.

[**Jerome Smith**]: I'm in.

[**Aster K'lon**]: Very well. Follow me.

P-System Log

Of *course* Jerome wants the numbers to go up.

Granted, so do I, but the numbers I'm focusing on are a little bit different. C'mon, Jerome, get that sweet, sweet W Inertia for me.

Or let Aster carry you to victory. That works, too.

Party Chat

[**Aster K'lon**]: Be on your guard. While the monsters that wander these woods are not as threatening as they are elsewhere, they may still deal much damage if they take you by surprise.

[**Jerome Smith**]: Got it. How far to the dungeon?

[**Aster K'lon**]: Not much farther.

P-System Log

They're pretty deep into the woods now. Every step they take requires navigating around another thick tree trunk. I don't recognize these trees as anything from Earth, though. They look kind of like redwoods, but their leaves look pretty deciduous. It's a really weird image, and I have no idea how it works in terms of biology, but that's just how this world works, I guess.

Well, I can worry about that later. It's not worth burning any W Inertia on it, but it's neat to see at the very least.

We're on our way to a new dungeon, looks like. I hope that it's not as infested with R Beasts as the last one was. I just want to get some W Inertia and get out. None of that weird bullshit that the R Beasts decided to fuck up the Maplecrest Dungeon Core with.

Speaking of which . . .

DUNGE?NC??E

<ERROR> <ERROR> <ERROR>

invokeinvokeinvokeinvoke

P-System Log

Alright, using my pseudo-[**Assess**] does the same shit that a regular [**Assess**] did. The only difference is that the corrupted "Integrated identified" text isn't there, but that's only because I'm not using an actual [**Assess**] spell, I'm pretty sure.

Ugh. That thing worries me. I keep on getting the urge to ~~kill it~~, but I know that there's more important stuff to be done with it. Unlike *some people* who will go unnamed, I can actually plan for the long term.

Well, to be fair, it was Jerome's idea in the first place, but I'm pretty sure he was thinking about having me go for it immediately. Thank fuck Aster thought better of it, because I have not the first clue of what I would do to convert it back. Hopefully I can pick up some knowledge that can help me along the way. We've still got ninety-five kilometers or something to P'lor, which is probably gonna take at least a few weeks on foot. Given how much went down on my first day on the Continent, I'm sure to pick up a whole lot more as we travel.

Shit. I think I just noticed a monster enter the dome. It doesn't actively irritate me to perceive, so it's probably not an R Beast.

It doesn't seem very powerful. I don't think I even need to burn W Inertia to break past its innate barriers.

Lemme check it out, just to be sure.

Nameless Bee

Class	Race	Level
Dire Bee	Giant Bee	2

Stat	Current	Maximum
Mana	10	10
Health	40	40

Skills	[Fire Resistance lv. 1], [Magic Resistance lv. 1], [Cold Resistance lv. 1], [Sneak Attack lv. 1], [Dire Sting lv. 3]
Titles	[Killer I]

Stat	Modifier	Total
Strength	-	<HIDDEN>
Magic	-	<HIDDEN>
Insight	-	<HIDDEN>
Constitution	-	<HIDDEN>

P-System Log

Oh, this is free W Inertia. Hell fucking yeah.

Now, I need to subtly guide Jerome toward it in a way that he can understand . . .

Yeah, fuck it, he won't get subtlety.

P-System Message

Warning: hostile Integrated detected in your immediate vicinity. Hostile threat level is **LOW.**

Party Chat

[Jerome Smith]: Aster, my System is giving me a warning. Says there's a low-threat hostile Integrated in the area.

[Aster K'lon]: We can feasibly ignore it, especially if the threat level is as low as it seems. Also, your System truly is powerful, is it not? For it to give you the same knowledge that a **[Danger Sense]** could provide . . .

[Jerome Smith]: Huh. I guess I should appreciate it more. And yeah, sure, we can move on.

P-System Log

Hey, I thought you were a gamer? Don't you—okay, us—little shits thrive on farming the baby-difficulty mobs?
Dammit, Jerome.
Time to unleash my secret weapon!

New [Objective]: Survival of the Fittest

Description: Eliminate threats to your survival.

Rewards: Passive XP multiplier for killing hostile Integrated. Increases over time.

P-System Log

That's right, Jerome, kneel before my power! Behold, my ultimate creation . . .
A whole lot of bullshit!
I really want that W Inertia, and I'm not going to let something stupid like *good decision-making* and *time management* get in my way.
So, it's time to play dirty! I know that Jerome is a fan of his numbers going up. I don't know how he somehow managed to fail to make the connection between killing this "minor threat" and the increase in his XP that he would get, but maybe making an **[Objective]** out of it will make it a little more clear for his dumb ass.

Party Chat

[Jerome Smith]: Actually, could we pursue this? I just got an [**Objective**] from my System that rewards me if I go for the kill.

[Aster K'lon]: I must admit, I was somewhat surprised when you did not choose to pursue it without motivation. We may.

[Jerome Smith]: I get less XP if you help, right?

[Aster K'lon]: XP is generally distributed based off the percentage of damage done for larger monsters and a simple even split for weaker monsters. We have largely faced the latter as of this moment, so any damage I deal to it will cause XP to flow to us evenly.

[Jerome Smith]: In that case, can you keep your offensive spells off for now?

[Aster K'lon]: Doable.

[Jerome Smith]: Thank you.

[Aster K'lon]: . . . I notice you have yet to locate your enemy.

[Jerome Smith]: I don't know any tracking skills other than [**Assess**], and that's far more likely to hit a tree than anything else.

[Aster K'lon]: Ah, you have not met the requisite requirements for the basic tracking skills. Perhaps your System can help?

P-System Log

Oh, come on, Aster, you were supposed to be on my side! Why are *you* giving me work, too, now?

Admittedly, Jerome does seem quite lost. It's a little endearing, not gonna lie, watching this tall, muscular man do his best roleplay of a six-year-old that got separated from his parents in Walmart.

Well, I don't know how to access Jerome's senses yet, so I'll do the next best thing.

P-System Message

Warning: hostile Integrated is 97 degrees west of your perception axis.

Hero's Personal Log 049

I have no fucking idea what that means.

P-System Log

Oh, come the fuck on, Jerome. I used some unnecessary words there, but surely you learned how to read a compass at some point in your life, right?

Clearly, I haven't been dumbing my words down enough.

P-System Message

It's on your left, Jerome.

Hero's Personal Log 050

Oh. Why didn't you start with that?

[Magic Missile] activating!

CHAPTER 25

[**Magic Missile**] dealt 21 damage!

[**Magic Missile**] activating!

[**Magic Missile**] dealt 30 damage!

Enemy defeated! Experience rewarded!

Current W Inertia: 37,751

Max W Inertia: 38,359

P-System Log

Got some of it back! Forty-four from that one animal, if my math is right.

Looks like more evidence for the hypothesis that max W Inertia only increases when I get overflow.

Alright, how much XP do I give Jerome? One thing I've noticed at this point is that levels are disproportionately easy to get. At my last go, it took damn near a thousand W Inertia to level up a single stat, but it would only take ninety W Inertia to get him to level three—two or three of these bees could provide enough. Although I have no fuckin' idea what leveling actually does, it goes wayyyyy faster than a bunch of the other stats. It makes me wonder. Why aren't other people leveling up constantly, if the W Inertia their Systems presumably get are this plentiful?

Maybe they're like me, conserving the majority of their W Inertia in order to complete other functions. Also, the XP requirement went from three hundred to nine hundred between level 1 and 2, so I guess it gets progressively harder to gain levels.

Well, I did tell him I was going to give him more XP. I've barely been giving him any so far, I'm pretty sure. Last time I did it, it was solely to level him up from level 1 to 2. This time . . . maybe I'll give him half the W Inertia's worth in XP. I can spend another quarter on his skills, I guess. It makes sense for them to get stronger as he uses them more, and I'm the one deciding how they progress, so I'm just gonna go with what makes sense. He used [**Magic Missile**] to kill this thing, so that's where the skill points will go.

Twenty-two for general XP, eleven for [**Magic Missile**], eleven for myself. That should work.

Skill leveled up! [**Magic Missile**] lv. 3 -> lv. 4

Damage increased by 2R4. Mana cost increased by 20%.

Hero's Personal Log 051

Oh, shit! Let's go, hella pog!
Thanks, System! Guess you finally figured out how to level up skills after I kill shit with them. Took ya long enough.

P-System Log [oh, fuck off, Jerome]

Every time I want to start appreciating Jerome more, man . . . it'd be so much easier if I was attached to Aster. She's so much less of a dickhole.
Whatever. They're moving again.

Hero's Personal Log 052

Okay, so I've noticed that [**Magic Missile**] is, like, *way* better than [**Blazing Spear**]. It costs less and usually does similar damage, right?
Maybe [**Rare**]-rarity skills aren't necessarily a straight upgrade to [**Common**] ones. Actually, yeah, that makes sense. [**Blazing Spear**] does AoE after it gets cast and also gains more damage per level than [**Magic Missile**], so it might be worth it eventually. Aster used [**Inferno Spear**] earlier.

I wonder if [**Blazing Spear**] will evolve into that if I level it enough? It sure seemed to do a lot more damage, so I have that to look forward to.

Party Chat

[**Jerome Smith**]: I leveled up [**Magic Missile**]. It's level 4 now.

[**Aster K'lon**]: Congratulations. That is perhaps the most powerful direct-damage [**Common**] skill available.

[**Jerome Smith**]: Yeah, it's even more powerful than my [**Rare**] skill right now.

[**Aster K'lon**]: However, it also has little room for growth. The [**Missile**] line sees significantly diminishing returns in damage versus mana cost after it is high enough level to upgrade to [**Rare**].

[**Jerome Smith**]: Huh, so that's also a factor when it comes to skills?

[**Aster K'lon**]: Indeed. You have much to learn yet, reincarnator.

[**Jerome Smith**]: Interesting. You'll teach me?

[**Aster K'lon**]: The best teachers are those trying to kill you. I will assist you with crucial information should your current situation require it.

[**Jerome Smith**]: That seems a little unfair, but okay.

[**Aster K'lon**]: Here, one piece of advice for free. We have arrived at the dungeon.

[**Jerome Smith**]: We have? I don't see anything.

P-System Log

C'mon, Jerome, I get that you were probably dropped as a baby, but surely you'll learn to think critically at some point, right? Look around you, man!

Party Chat

[**Jerome Smith**]: Oh, wait. That hole in the ground. The one covered by sticks and leaves and that kinda stuff. Is that it?

[**Aster K'lon**]: Congratulations, you have at least a seven-year-old's ability to recognize patterns. Indeed it is.

> **P-System Log**
>
> Aster is fucking great.

> [**Assess**] activating!

> Integrated identified: **Dungeon [Wilderness Core lv. 2] Nameless**

> **P-System Log**
>
> Y'know, for someone who was really worried about his mana expenditure last night, he's being awfully cavalier with using up mana.
>
> Then again, this is coming from a not-quite-person who didn't want to spend a single point of W Inertia more than necessary and then ended up spending like eight hundred, so . . .
>
> I guess that makes us even on this point in the crucially important one-sided beef I have with Jerome.
>
> Anyway. Looks like they're heading into the dungeon now. The hole is wide enough to drop an entire sedan through lengthwise, and it's shallow enough for that sedan to still be drivable afterward. It's not an insignificant fall, though, so I wonder how—
>
> Oh. Right. I'm an idiot. Aster just jumped down, and Jerome followed her.

> Collision with floor dealt 1 damage to you!

> **P-System Log**
>
> And they're totally physically unharmed. How could I forget? This world runs on bullshit logic and bullshit rules and all of that is mine to wield. Heh.
>
> Welp. Looks like this is the "safe room," so to speak. My perception dome just expanded like crazy now that they fell, revealing a bunch of shit underground that I didn't notice earlier—well, I couldn't notice it earlier because of how the dungeon perception filters work, but I wasn't actively trying to perceive underground anyway.

Looks like the setup of this one is a little more complex than the last—
and by a little, I really do mean a little. There's two paths that fork off from
the safe room, and they each travel through very slightly different dungeon
rooms, but both paths lead to the same final room. What incredible design.

Then again, I suppose there's a reason why this dungeon is only level 2,
and I would imagine that it's not its exceptional ability to confuse and kill
people.

Ah, well. I'm not going to activate an [**Objective**] for this one. If I start
doing them for literally everything, there's decent odds that Jerome starts
ignoring them.

Party Chat

[**Jerome Smith**]: There are two paths.

[**Aster K'lon**]: Correct.

[**Jerome Smith**]: So you're not going to tell me which to go down?

[**Aster K'lon**]: Reincarnator, I have trained many years and yet still have
only a [**Rare**] class. You have a [**Legendary**] class. If anything, you should
be the one guiding me.

[**Jerome Smith**]: But you have the experience.

[**Aster K'lon**]: And you must gain it. Lead the way.

Hero's Personal Log 053

Ugh. I hate to admit it, but Aster's right.
Fuck. I don't know if there's a difference between the two paths.
Hey, wait. I know what I can do.
Hey, Siri! Flip a coin!
. . . I'm making jokes about another world to an inanimate object. Fuck
me, I'm losing it.
System, can you pick a random number between one and two?

P-System Message

2.

P-System Log

I have a random function, I know that, but I'm not pulling that out for Jerome. At least he recognizes that he's being dumb, kinda.

Party Chat

[**Jerome Smith**]: We're taking the left path.

[**Aster K'lon**]: Are you sure?

[**Jerome Smith**]: Is it worse?

[**Aster K'lon**]: You find out.

[**Jerome Smith**]: Okay, let's take the right, then.

[**Aster K'lon**]: Are you sure?

[**Jerome Smith**]: Fucking—okay, we're going left. That's final.

[**Aster K'lon**]: Are you sure?

P-System Log

I would laugh if I had lungs.

Jerome is leading the way, sure enough. The doors here aren't built out of the same material that the Maplecrest dungeon had. These ones are like, wood-fired dirt brick or something. I don't know enough about building structure to be suitably impressed by it, but it's neat to perceive, at least.

Jerome: What the shit?

Oh, that was out loud. Aster is behind him, and— Is she giggling?

Hey, I appreciate humor at the expense of Jerome as much as any other, but, uh, maybe help him start attacking? He looks *terrified*.

For decently good reason, too.

Oh, man. Jerome's activating a bunch of mana at once. A number of spells, all at the same time.

I'm gonna try something. Can I bundle them together? Make those activations into one thing?

I think I can. Something deep inside me—maybe my gut, maybe [**W%M; G, P**]—is telling me that it's doable.

Burning W Inertia and trying bullshit has worked so far, so I'm gonna try that.

[**Assess**]es became [**Mass Assess**]!

New skill unlocked: [**Mass Assess**]

You may identify multiple objects and enemies around you at once.

[**Mass Assess**] activating!

CHAPTER 26

Integrated identified: **Giant Ant [Giant Ant lv. 1] Nameless**

Integrated identified: **Giant Ant [Giant Ant lv. 1] Nameless**

Integrated identified: **Giant Ant [Giant Ant lv. 1] Nameless**

Integrated identified: **Giant Ant [Dire Giant Ant lv. 1] Nameless**

P-System Log

. . . huh. Their levels are all *really* shit, and almost all of 'em are [**Common**] class. No wonder Aster said this place was practically a XP farm.

Not that you'd think that from how Jerome is acting. Does he have some deep-seated trauma related to ants or something? I mean, sure, they're kinda gross and almost as large as a small car, but they're really weak, and Jerome is strong.

Welp. Hope he figures his shit out soon.

Or starts panic casting. That works, too.

[Blazing Spear] activating!

[Blazing Spear] dealt 44 damage!

[Blazing Spear] dealt 45 damage!

[**Blazing Spear**] dealt 41 damage!

Enemies defeated! Experience rewarded!

[**Blazing Spear**] dealt 33 damage!

Hero's Personal Log 054

FUCK FUCK FUCK FUCK FUCK FUCK
I hate ants so much
Okay, panic under control. I got this.

Shit, that was a lot of carnage in a really short span of time. Three of the four ants are dead now, though the last managed to survive. That one's bigger than the others, and it was originally seen by [**Mass Assess**] as a [**Dire Giant Ant**]. It also took less damage from my skill than the others, which is probably important. [**Blazing Spear**] dealt more damage than it usually did to the three regular [**Giant Ant**]s. Maybe they have a fire weakness or something? That would make sense. It would also mean that the big one either doesn't have a weakness or has a resistance of some kind. I can work with this.

Aster said [**Blazing Spear**] had more potential to grow than [**Magic Missile**] did, and I think I can kind of see why now. I only needed a single cast of it to hit every single ant in the room, whereas I'm pretty sure [**Magic Missile**] would've required four full activations to hit them all.

Also, new skill! Thanks for that, System! Gimme more skills!

P-System Log

Jerome *has* to have a good sense of what's good to say to the System helping him, right? That's the only way I can explain him somehow figuring out the single worst thing to say to me every time. The only reason I'm not getting actually pissed at him for this one is because of that sweet, sweet W Inertia. You get a pass this time, Jerome.

Anyway, even if I wanted to, I wouldn't be able to just create new skills on the fly for the [**Godkiller**]. I have a general idea of what happened when I made him learn [**Mass Assess**]—using W Inertia on his burgeoning set of skills made them coalesce into one—and I imagine I could replicate it if he tried it again with a different skill, but I haven't the faintest clue on how I would make a new one. I stole [**Blazing Spear**]'s structure from Axel, and that made a new skill, but I don't know what I would do if I wanted to make something wholly new.

Oh, wait. There's still one guy alive. I should get to letting Jerome use his skill, huh.

[**Magic Missile**] activating!

[**Magic Missile**] dealt 33 damage!

Enemy defeated! Experience rewarded!

Current W Inertia: 37,903

Max W Inertia: 38,359

P-System Log

Hell fuckin' yeah, that's a lot of W Inertia! What is that, like, 160 W Inertia? Something like that?

Yep, this is a good dungeon. I'm not gonna do the same thing as before, though. Jerome made me spend way too much W Inertia before, he isn't getting that much invested back into him.

I'm keeping eighty-two. Forty can go to general XP, and the other forty can go to [**Blazing Spear**].

Here we go!

Skill leveled up! [**Blazing Spear**] lv. 2 -> lv. 4

Damage increased by 4R6+2R5. Mana cost increased by 18% of base.

Party Chat

[**Jerome Smith**]: Pog, got a skill level!

[**Aster K'lon**]: What is a "pog"?

[**Jerome Smith**]: It's an expression of—actually, never mind, it's probably better you don't know.

P-System Log

Oh, shit, wasn't expecting two levels at once. That level-up notification has a lot of things to unpack, I'm realizing.

Okay, first thing: it didn't increase the damage the same as it did from level 1 to 2. It increased by 1R6+1R5 per level, which meant that here it should've increased by 2R6+2R5. For some reason, Jerome got an extra 2R6. I mean, nobody's complaining, but the inconsistency is *really weird*, especially given that I literally have access to a stat sheet that shows stats for skills, and this was never mentioned. More fuckery on Origin's side, probably, though I know the Origin System isn't my enemy. It's just something I haven't learned yet, I suppose. Still, kind of irritating.

Second: 18 percent of base? None of the other skill level ups have looked like that so far. If I check the skill's stats . . .

[Blazing Spear lv. 4]

Stat	Value
XP	0/320
Damage	8R5+5R6+4
Mana Cost	34
Overcharge Multiplier (max)	1.5
Cost Multiplier	18%
Range	22.5 meters
<HIDDEN>	<HIDDEN>

P-System Log

Damn. Okay, so there's definitely something different here. With [**Magic Missile**], every level compounds the multiplier. Level 2 is 120 percent of level 1's cost, level 3 is 120 percent of level 2's, and so forth. For this skill, though, it looks like it scales totally linearly in terms of cost.

Maybe it's the difference between a [**Common**] skill and a [**Rare**] one, then? Varying damage and fewer increases in cost per level? Useful information to have, assuming it even holds true. Stuff has been inconsistent enough so far for me to kinda accept that.

Well, Jerome isn't dwelling on it. I don't think he knows any math more complex than one plus one equals two, so that tracks.

Party Chat

[**Jerome Smith**]: First room is clear. No drops in here, as far as I can tell.

[**Aster K'lon**]: [**Common**]-class enemies rarely have drops. The best returns you will obtain from a normal dungeon crawl are XP.

[**Jerome Smith**]: Got it. On to the next, then.

P-System Log

Another door opened, another room available to take a gander at. Wait, never mind, scratch that. There's another passageway for the two adventurers to get through before we get to the next dungeon room proper. It's just wide enough for a person to walk through, and it's basically just a tunnel. I guess it fits the low-level nature of this place.

Ah, there's the door. The next room is . . . kind of similarly uninspired. It's literally just a forty-foot-long room with a twenty-foot-long gap. I don't think there's even spikes or anything down there. It's just a dirt pit. An unnaturally smooth one, yeah, which is probably a result of it being created by the Dungeon Core's skill, but there's no traps or monsters.

. . . that might be enough, to be honest. It's a really boring "trap," but I don't think there's a single skill Jerome has to get over it.

Party Chat

[**Jerome Smith**]: I have no idea how to get over this.

[**Aster K'lon**]: Ah, the perils of the newly reincarnated. Watch. There are skills you have not seen yet.

[**Cloud Step**] cast!

P-System Log

Ooh, this spell is neat to watch! Both in terms of mana and physically. Aster just kind of melted away into wisps of smoke and then rematerialized in a burst of that smoke on the other end.

Mana-wise, it's nothing like the offensive skills that they've been using up till now. It's being manipulated in a different way from the ground up. More inward focused than outward, too.

I think I can steal it.

Hero's Personal Log 055

System, copy that skill.

P-System Log

Aaaaaaand now I don't want to do it anymore.

I mean, I *will*, but I don't want to. The options are either a) give Jerome the finger, wait here and miss out on W Inertia, or b) suck it up and get more. I value that stat more than my pride, so I'm gonna go with it.

Alright, I think I remember what I'm supposed to do in order to get him to learn a new spell.

So, I initiate the first half of [**Cloud Step**], wrap it in W Inertia, and push it to Jerome . . .

Shit, no, that's not the right mana configuration. I don't know what that is, but it isn't a movement spell. And I put a lot more mana into it than I should have, given that this is a [**Rare**] skill. In my defense, that's because the structure was fucked up, but that's also my fault. Ugh. Uh, whoops?

I mean, he's responding to it and adding his own mana, so surely it can't be *that* bad, right?

<table>
<tr><td>System Prompt</td></tr>
<tr><td>W Inertia expended!</td></tr>
</table>

New skill unlocked: [**Misty Strike**]

You may rapidly displace your position and inflict damage on every enemy in your path.

CHAPTER 27

P-System Log

Okay, so what the hell is that?

P-System Log [figuring out new stuff]

Okay, so I clearly didn't get Jerome to learn [**Cloud Step**]. I think the issue was that I put way more mana in than a [**Rare**] skill should have, and I also used the same method I've been using to learn combat skills. Since I still used the same general mana structure as what Aster did, the spell I came up with was . . . vaguely similar? Mist and cloud are pretty similar concepts, at least, and the skill description sounds like it kind of matches what [**Cloud Step**] does.

That felt like a huge expenditure of W Inertia, though. Let me see how much I lost.

Current W Inertia: 37,723

Max W Inertia: 38,359

P-System Log

Holy shit, a *hundred?* At least it wasn't as much as the stat increase, but still . . .

This skill better be good. I guess I can understand why people level up so slowly, if the Systems need to use this much W Inertia just to buy skills. God(s) fuckin' damn.

[Misty Strike lv. 1]

Stat	Value
XP	0/400
Damage	15R10+10
Mana Cost	50
Overcharge Multiplier (max)	1.5
Cost Multiplier	10%
Range	30 meters
<HIDDEN>	<HIDDEN>

P-System Log

Whoa, what the fuck? That's strong as hell, wow.

Hero's Personal Log 056

An [**Epic**]-rarity skill? Not what I asked for, but I will 100 percent take that. I wonder how strong it is. Can I see the stats, System? Please?

P-System Log

. . . he was more polite this time, at least.

P-System Message

[Misty Strike lv. 1]

Damage: 15R10+10

Cost: 50 mana

Range: 30 meters

Party Chat

[**Jerome Smith**]: Holy shit, I just unlocked a super-powerful skill.

[**Aster K'lon**]: I suppose you should thank your System, then. You did not unlock [**Cloud Step**]?

[**Jerome Smith**]: [**Misty Strike**]. An [**Epic**]-rarity skill.

[**Aster K'lon**]: Extraordinary. Your system has unprecedented power.

[**Jerome Smith**]: You don't see all that surprised.

[**Aster K'lon**]: Your System is abnormal, and it is learning. I am not surprised that it is delivering returns beyond what any normal System can do. It's an incredible achievement, of course, but not too surprising.

[**Jerome Smith**]: I guess I should give it more credit. Anyway, I'm gonna give it a test run. Get out of the way.

[**Aster K'lon**]: Manners.

[**Misty Strike**] activating!

P-System Log

Oh, this mana feels way different to control. It's a lot wilder in its movement, and it flows far faster than the lower-rarity skills that Jerome has been using up till this point. Not unmanageable per se, but I'll have to be more careful when Jerome uses this skill. Alright, here we go.

Hmm. That wasn't too fancy. Basically the same effect as [**Cloud Step**], but instead of instantaneous teleportation, he left a trail of white smoke in his path. I think he might have done it with less of a cast time than Aster did, but apart from the in-between part, it wasn't too interesting. I'd imagine that the actual cool part comes when it hits an enemy.

On a different note, good to know that it isn't required to go the full thirty meters, since he dropped out of it right next to Aster, which is . . . thirty feet is . . . nine meters? Something like that. It was the same with offensive spells, but this is a whole new type of skill, so ya never know.

On to the next room! There's actually a passageway between these two that isn't utter shit! I guess this Dungeon Core figured out how to do stairs at some point, because it's a pretty decently carved quarter-spiral set that goes on for a bit to the next room. Finally, some taste!

Party Chat

[**Jerome Smith**]: This dungeon has been pretty easy so far.

[**Aster K'lon**]: So it has been. If only you had a guide who could have informed you on its nature before you entered the dungeon, eh?

[**Jerome Smith**]: Okay, I get it, I get it. I need to listen to you more.

P-System Log

Listen to me more, too, dumbass!

. . . okay, to be fair, I haven't really made any real attempt at communicating with him proactively. As far as he knows, I'm still basically an NPC.

Speaking of NPCs, Aster feels way too fleshed out to be one. Nice to know that this world doesn't run exclusively on game logic. As far as I can tell, everyone we've met has been a real person, which means it's probably less likely we're in a simulation or something. Then again, it could just be a simulation that's more complex than I can perceive, and—

Nope. Cutting that tangent off there. I had it one too many times on Earth—not gonna happen now that I have fun magic powers.

Anyway, next room!

P-System Log [this dungeon went back to being boring]

And the next room doesn't even have cool puzzles or anything. Nope, it's just a fucking anthill. A whole-ass hill of dirt and sand at the center of the room, practically overflowing with ants. Six of them are on the hill itself, but I'm pretty sure there's more inside. The hill feels a little fucky to my senses, though.

Jerome, don't you dare [**Assess**] those pieces of shit. I didn't actually check to see if [**Mass Assess**] consumes less mana, but it's still mana anyway. I know you still have a lot of mana, Jerome, but you're a gamer, right? Surely you understand the necessity of saving mana when your ethers—er, they just call them mana potions here—are limited, right?

Party Chat

[**Jerome Smith**]: I count six of them. Might be more of them inside the hill itself.

[**Aster K'lon**]: Understood. Would you like assistance, or would you prefer to take the fight yourself?

[**Jerome Smith**]: I'll call if I need help.

P-System Log [the unthinkable has happened]

That's right, future Parker. I thought about something dumb Jerome could do, and he *didn't do it*!
Groundbreaking.

Hero's Personal Log 057

Time to test this new skill. I wanna know if it's actually usable in combat.

P-System Log

I shit you not, this guy literally just took a single step into the room and started shouting insults at the ants.
I mean, I guess it's working? They're coming to attack him, at least. Jerome counted the six correctly, and now that six has nearly doubled. Five more ants came out of the hill, and now there's eleven of them.
Classic Jerome move, really. It's horrendously dumb, but it still somehow works. Kind of. I assume his plan is to try his new skill against these ants.

[**Misty Strike**] activating!

[**Misty Strike**] dealt 93 damage!

[**Misty Strike**] dealt 99 damage!

[**Misty Strike**] dealt 87 damage!

Enemies defeated! Experience rewarded!

P-System Log

Holy shit, that's a strong fucking skill. Almost fully recouped my W Inertia for getting the skill, too, and there's still a lot more ants to go. Jerome just dashed straight through those ants, and where the smoke passed over them, they just fell apart. It looks like a demonic blender passed through the fog that he made. The ants are barely recognizable anymore, though their decimated corpses aren't going to stay for very long. Looks like they're dissipating already.

Party Chat

[**Jerome Smith**]: Ninety-three, ninety-nine, eighty-seven. Damn.

[**Aster K'lon**]: Worthy of an [**Epic**] rarity, indeed.

[**Jerome Smith**]: I'm going to try one more thing with it. If it works, I should be able to get the other eight in one fell swoop.

P-System Log

He's building up mana again. It feels . . . slightly different this time? Like he's trying to do the fine manipulation a little more precisely. I'm not sure how to describe it, but it looks like Jerome actually does possess a single useful talent. His innate ability to manipulate mana might be better than mine, not gonna lie.

I should be able to copy it, though. Thanks to my broken perception abilities, I can see the little changes he does and just steal them for my half. Not that he'll ever know I need to put in extra effort. Take more shit for granted, why don't ya?

Anyway. Not the point. Here we go.

[**Misty Strike**] activating!

[**Misty Strike**] dealt 94 damage!

[**Misty Strike**] dealt 93 damage!

Collision with wall dealt 251 damage (reduced by [**Misty Strike**]) to you!

Enemies defeated! Experience rewarded!

P-System Log

Oh.

Well, he ran straight through one ant and killed it, then he did an abrupt ninety-degree turn, [**Misty Strike**]d through another ant, at which point he utterly failed to turn again or stop and ran straight into the wall. Given the speed he was going—high enough that even my enhanced perception could barely see him—and the damage formula, he had better be grateful as fuck that the skill reduced collision damage. If it didn't, he'd probably be dead.

Party Chat

[**Jerome Smith**]: Ah, so that's why people don't test stuff in the field. I had been wondering why we need to move the Dungeon Core so far.

[**Aster K'lon**]: I'd say I don't want to say, "I told you so," but that would be a lie.

[**Jerome Smith**]: Alright, I'll finish this the normal way, then. I should be training my other skills anyway.

[**Blazing Spear**] activating!

CHAPTER 28

[**Blazing Spear**] dealt 49 damage!

[**Blazing Spear**] dealt 47 damage!

[**Blazing Spear**] dealt 51 damage!

Enemies defeated! Experience rewarded!

Party Chat

[**Jerome Smith**]: Forty-nine, forty-seven, fifty-one.

[**Aster K'lon**]: You don't need to call it out if they're dead, Jerome.

[**Jerome Smith**]: Oh.

[**Aster K'lon**]: Also, you're targeting the wrong thing.

[**Jerome Smith**]: What?

[**Aster K'lon**]: Try [**Assess**]ing that anthill.

[**Assess**] activating!

Integrated identified: **Ant Summoner [Dungeon Summoner lv. 1] Nameless**

Party Chat

[**Jerome Smith**]: Ah.

[**Aster K'lon**]: See?

[**Jerome Smith**]: My System didn't say anything about that.

[**Aster K'lon**]: As much as your System is more powerful than most, it is also not going to be saving you in every situation.

[**Jerome Smith**]: Got it.

[**Aster K'lon**]: It is also still in the process of adapting to you and this world. You must not rely solely on the System, though you may put much of your faith in it.

[**Inferno Spear**] cast!

[**Inferno Spear**] cast!

Party Chat

[**Aster K'lon**]: The rest of them are dead. I killed the anthill as well.

[**Jerome Smith**]: I have eyes, y'know?

[**Aster K'lon**]: As do I, and yet you gave me the damage counts for [**Giant Ants**] that were little more than ash and dirt.

[**Jerome Smith**]: . . . sorry. That's my bad.

[**Aster K'lon**]: Ha, worry not. Many reincarnators act like this.

P-System Log

Jerome, apologizing? No fucking way.
I wonder how long it'll take to say that to me . . .
On to the next room it is, though. I'm kind of annoyed at Aster, to be honest. She—or her System, I guess—just stole so much W Inertia. Jerome had the opportunity to kill, what, three more ants? Plus however much that [**Dungeon Summoner**] would've given. All those juicy points, wasted . . .

Speaking of W Inertia, though, I gotta distribute the amount Jerome got. From all eight of those ants that he killed, I got around 240 W Inertia. Not a terribly large amount from each ant, but more than enough to put some XP into skills. I'm gonna keep half as per usual, and then distribute the others among his skills and general.

Actually, wait. What's his XP looking like?

Jerome Smith (abbreviated)

Stat	Value
XP	661/900

Spell	Stat	Value
Magic Missile	Level	4
Magic Missile	XP	1/180
Assess	Level	2
Assess	XP	6/200
Blazing Spear	Level	4
Blazing Spear	XP	0/320
Misty Strike	Level	1
Misty Strike	XP	0/400

P-System Log

Hmm. I guess I could just invest them myself, but I also want Jerome to have at least *some* freedom in picking his build. If it were up to me, I would just go with focusing on leveling [**Misty Strike**] and one-tricking with it, but it sounds like Jerome wants to diversify. I don't know how I'm supposed to balance that. Yes, technically I could just ignore his wishes and do whatever I want with his skills and XP, but I don't like the idea of removing agency from the guy I'm attached to. He might be a dumbass, but he doesn't deserve to be constantly railroaded. I'm willing to manipulate him to do what I want, but the line stops at fucking with a man's progression.

Also, consistency is pretty important if I want to keep passing myself off as a slightly intelligent computer program.

Okay, what do I need to do to maintain consistency? I started increasing the XP of skills when Jerome used them in combat after he started thinking he could train them. That's probably something that's good to keep running, even if it does mean expending that sweet, sweet W Inertia. That's how most games run it, and there's no reason I should make it unnecessarily confusing.

Still, that's mostly still me behind the scenes. As much as I hate to admit it, I do enjoy playing fair. It feels wrong to take something for nothing, and I kind of want Jerome to have a role in determining what kind of attacker he wants to be. Maybe I can offer him a choice as to which skills to assign XP to when he levels up?

Yeah, that sounds fair.

Next order of business. I've been giving a quarter of the XP from every fight to go to general, and I think I'll keep with that as well. Now, I know one point of W Inertia is roughly equal to ten XP, which means that Jerome can make it to level 3 if I just give him the sixty W Inertia that that entails, but I don't want that to happen just yet. After all, the dungeon isn't finished yet, and who's to say that Jerome is going to keep going after I give him a bunch of shiny toys to play with?

I think I'll hold off on the leveling until he finishes the dungeon. I know that's hypocritical regarding what I literally just said, but that's how I roll. I'll hold on to the extra, and I promise I'll give it all to him once he levels. I swear.

Maybe.

Party Chat

[Jerome Smith]: Okay, now that that room's clear. On to the next?

[Aster K'lon]: A minor word of warning. The next room is the final one before the ending room. It contains a boss monster.

[Jerome Smith]: It's been alright so far. I can handle it. Besides, this is an easy dungeon, isn't it?

[Aster K'lon]: If you say so.

P-System Log

The passageway from this room to the last is a little longer. It's the same kind of boring, claustrophobic tunnel that the dungeon had earlier.

Kind of raises a question—why don't the Dungeon Cores just, I dunno, squeeze these tunnels? Maybe grow spikes out of the walls? Or even put monsters in the super-tight hallways so that they take super-advantageous fights?

I guess it's an inherent flaw of a Dungeon Core. Maybe they can't actively manipulate their geometry while there's people in them? Assuming they can even manipulate their geometry at all—that's an assumption I'm making based off literature I've read before, but those rules don't necessarily apply to this world.

Whatever the case, the tunnel is tapering off and coming to an end. Final room!

. . . it's another really boring room. This whole dungeon has been pretty boring, honestly. I guess better this than facing down another bunch of powerful R Beasts, but there's nothing wrong with some excitement in life from time to time, right?

This last room is just a flat, empty circle of dirt. It's lit by torches, which I assume are kept on through dungeon skills, and at the center of it all lies a single enemy. It's *another fucking ant.*

[**Assess**] activating!

Integrated identified: **Giant Ant [Greater Giant Dire Ant lv. 1] DUNGEON_BOSS_NAME**

Party Chat

[**Jerome Smith**]: It's . . . just another ant. Bigger and stronger, I think, but it's just an ant. And it's low-level, too.

[**Aster K'lon**]: This is a low-level dungeon. It does not have the spare XP to invest in its minions.

[**Jerome Smith**]: Huh. Why don't we farm this type of dungeon?

[**Aster K'lon**]: Some do. However, these low-level dungeons often offer diminishing returns. Past level 5 or so, it becomes far more economical to find a higher-level dungeon. Consider also that the drops from this dungeon are zero or close to it.

[Jerome Smith]: Dungeons have drops?

[Aster K'lon]: The symbiotic relationship between humans and dungeons is a subject best expounded upon in a classroom, not shortly before the final fight.

[Jerome Smith]: Right. Okay, I'll take care of it.

[Misty Strike] activating!

[Misty Strike] dealt 90 damage!

Enemy defeated! Experience rewarded!

Nameless Dungeon System

Dungeon cleared!

P-System Log

Wow, that was an anticlimactic fight. One single skill and that final boss turned to shreds. The power of an **[Epic]**-rarity skill backed by a **[Legendary]**-rarity class, I guess.

Anyway. W Inertia! I got around sixty from the final boss, which is a lot less than I hoped for—it's barely more than the amount I got from Jerome splitting the XP from a dead bandit—but I think the process of clearing the dungeon did something else. At Maplecrest, the Dungeon Core was affected by **[Corruption]**, so it didn't manage to output this properly. I think. Either that, or the dungeon was just broken.

Some trinkets are appearing out of thin air and dropping to the ground, but none of them seem very useful. A couple rusty blades, a few coins of no denomination I've ever seen, and faded pieces of armor. They don't emit power of any kind, at the very least. Along with that, an exit just carved itself out of the wall.

Alright. This is happening a lot sooner than I thought it would, but I did promise.

Total gain from the last room and this one was around 360, so that's ninety for Jerome's general XP.

Damn. He's getting a lot. Maybe I'll tone it down in the future. Depends on how much the XP requirements increase per level and how much he gains.

For the meantime, though, he's gonna get a whole fuckload. With that, I'll invest some more to increase his Health. Thirty . . . two points. That should be a good number to increase it by. Ten points of W Inertia, roughly.

You're welcome, Jerome.

Level up!

[**Godkiller**] Jerome Smith lv. 2 -> lv. 3

P-System Message

Health increased. Skill points available.

CHAPTER 29

Hero's Personal Log 058
Oh, fuck, yeah. That feels great. Love leveling up so much.

Party Chat

[Aster K'lon]: A level?

[Jerome Smith]: You can tell?

[Aster K'lon]: You reacted the same way you did last time. That, and the party system means that I can see important notifications like that.

[Jerome Smith]: Ah.

[Aster K'lon]: Now that we have cleared the dungeon, it will not be dangerous to us until we leave it. Any nondeviant Dungeon Core functions that way.

[Jerome Smith]: There are deviant Dungeon cores like that? I guess there was that corrupted one we saw earlier . . .

[Aster K'lon]: They can be deviant within the bounds of our System. When that happens—which is very rare around these parts, by the way—a team of adventurers is dispatched to kill the Dungeon Core.

[Jerome Smith]: But this one's not deviant, right?

[Aster K'lon]: Correct. As such, I recommend staying within the bounds of this room for the time being while you are vulnerable.

[Jerome Smith]: Wait, hold on. Can't we just kill the Dungeon Core for XP? I know you said it was bad practice, but not why.

[Aster K'lon]: As I said, that is a lecture for another day. Dungeon Cores provide too much benefit to our society to warrant their destruction.

[Jerome Smith]: Got it. I'm going to spec skills now.

[Aster K'lon]: Carry on. I will meditate to regenerate mana.

[Jerome Smith]: That's it? No suggestions?

[Aster K'lon]: You must learn to make your own decisions. I am not your mother, Jerome.

P-System Log

Aaaand she just sat down without giving a single fuck. What an incredibly based person.

Jerome didn't seem to miss a beat, though. Props to him, I guess? Although maybe he's just dense enough to not realize that was supposed to be somewhat condescending.

Hero's Personal Log 059

System, how much can I do with the level up?

P-System Message

You possess approximately 900 XP of skill points.

Hero's Personal Log 060

Oh, shit, that's way more than I expected. I can't say no to that, can I? Alright. Is there a way I can view the XP values for my skills right now?

P-System Message

[Magic Missile lv. 4]: 1/180

[Assess lv. 2]: 6/200

[Blazing Spear lv. 4]: 0/320

[Misty Strike lv. 1]: 0/400

Hero's Personal Log 061

Thanks.

Okay, so I've got four skills and a bunch of XP to invest into them. I think the price has been increasing by each time, so I'm not totally sure how many levels I'll be increasing them by if I invest all nine hundred. Obviously, I won't be doing that. I gotta think on how to optimize.

Wait, quick question. Could I spend some of that XP to learn a new skill instead of leveling another one up?

P-System Log

Hmm. That's actually a good question. I don't know how to pick up new skills apart from basing it off a skill that Aster or an enemy uses, but I know I'm definitely capable of doing it. At the same time, I don't actually know how much W Inertia it costs to create a skill. I don't recall [**Assess**] or [**Blazing Spear**] costing any W Inertia to form, but maybe I misremembered? [**Misty Strike**] cost a whole hundred W Inertia to form, and shit has been changing on the fly. I think I'll assume new skills require W Inertia. If they don't, I think it'll actually be better for me. I can just *say* I expended a bunch of XP and then store it for myself.

P-System Message

Acquiring a new skill requires a varying amount of XP (minimum quantity: 100). Acquiring a new skill requires experiencing another Integrated using a similar skill.

Hero's Personal Log 062

Hmm . . . okay. That's fine. I think I won't look for a new skill right now, then. Aster's regenerating her mana right now—which I need to learn to do, by the way—so I'm not gonna bother her. Gotta respect the mana grind.

In that case, what should I upgrade? Let's see . . .

Aster told me that skills evolve. I don't know when they evolve, but I can guess it'll be at an important milestone like level 10 or 50. Apparently, [**Magic Missile**]'s evolutions kind of suck, so even though it was my most efficient attacking spell, I think I'm gonna hold off on giving it more XP.

As for [**Assess**], I don't think I saw a single difference between level 1 and 2. Maybe it's something on the back end that I don't have access to, but I literally haven't seen a thing. Besides, the System's handling extra stats for me, so I think I can skimp out on it for now.

That leaves two spells—[**Blazing Spear**] at level 4 and [**Misty Strike**] at level 1. The first one has been pretty meh so far. Its primary usage has been AoE, which I guess it's pretty effective at. Just for that alone, I think it's worth putting some W Inertia into. I always used to be a fan of utilizing underwhelming skills in powerful ways. I think it's worth a shot bumping it up. Also, it apparently has decent potential to evolve. If it evolves into anything nearly as strong as [**Misty Strike**], that'll be W Inertia well spent.

The thing is, my [**Epic**]-rarity skill is just so damn powerful. 15R10+10 is no joke, and it's been dealing around ninety damage *minimum*. That's like, triple the output of my other spells. I really want to invest into it, but I can't get too single-minded. I wanna be a diverse caster, not just a one-trick pony.

Nine hundred is a lot, though. For now, could I get enough to level up my non-[**Common**] skills once apiece?

P-System Log

Seems like decent reasoning. If only he could pay this much attention to literally anything besides his own stats.

Alright, here we go! Thirty-two W Inertia into [**Blazing Spear**] and forty into [**Misty Strike**] should be enough to level both of them.

Skill leveled up! [**Blazing Spear**] lv. 4 -> lv. 5

Damage increased by 2R6+1R5. Mana cost increased by 18% of base.

Skill leveled up! [**Misty Strike**] lv. 1 -> lv. 2

Damage increased by 1R10+2. Mana cost increased by 15%.

P-System Log

Huh, the level 1 to 2 for the latter skill didn't have the "of base" qualifier. It might still not have the compound interest on mana that [**Magic Missile**] has, since [**Blazing Spear**] also didn't display that the first time.

Hero's Personal Log 063

Could I get the rest of them in [**Misty Strike**]? I wanna try to grow that skill a little faster than my others right now.

P-System Log

And that's another eighteen gone. I did promise him, and I don't plan on reneging on what I say. I might be a hypocrite sometimes, but I'm not a liar. Even to myself. Most of the time.

Hero's Personal Log 064

Also, is there any way I can increase my mana? I'm not sure when the milestones for that are.

P-System Log

Oh, right. I was planning on messing around with increasing mana, but I wasn't able to, because just randomly trying to increase mana would be weird. Now that he's got a level up, it's a decent time to try.

P-System Message

Mana increase processing . . .

P-System Log

Alright, I gotta figure this out. Earlier, I was able to increase his Health stat by just focusing on it, so I guess I can try the same for mana. Apparently, his Magic stat is somewhat tied to it, but increasing that was an exceptionally inefficient way of increasing mana. I'll just focus on the stat this time.

Oh, I'm dumb. Why didn't I do this earlier? I seriously just needed to focus on the bundle of significance that's mana-flavored? That was it?

Whatever. Live and learn or something.

One W Inertia in, to test the waters.

Jerome Smith (abbreviated)

Stat	Current	Maximum
Mana	819	1,043

Stat	Value

P-System Log

Looks like his Mana stat is more receptive to W Inertia than his Health was. That was six? I think? Six mana from a single point. Pretty solid, but it took a bit longer for it to actually settle in. I think I'll scale progression on this off his Magic stat.

Oh, wait. I talked about milestones with him before. It was supposed to be fives and tens for major increases, but I also said that there would be minor increases at every <HIDDEN> level. I guess I can just do that now. I'll give him four more points of W Inertia for Mana, which should bring him to a thirty increase. Just about the same as his Magic stat.

Aaaaaand there we go.

P-System Message

Milestone level 3 reached!

Mana increased by 30!

Party Chat

[**Jerome Smith**]: I leveled up two skills and increased my mana.

[**Aster K'lon**]: Excellent. Let us leave this dungeon, then. We have no more business here. Gather the drops if you wish, and then we shall depart.

[**Jerome Smith**]: These are bad drops. Let's get out of here.

P-System Log

Alright, we're done leveling and shit. Dungeon went pretty well—looks like there's not going to be any problems with it.

▼ Sacrifice accepted. ▼

▼ Skill invoked: [**H?? WA???F?? ?Y?**] ▼

P-System Log

Are you fucking kidding me?

CHAPTER 30

Party Chat

[Jerome Smith]: Did you see that?

[Aster K'lon]: There are R Beasts in the area. To cast another **[Legendary]**-rarity skill . . .

[Jerome Smith]: You can only use a skill one level of rarity above you, right? That would mean that we're up against a **[Epic]**-class R Beast at minimum.

[Aster K'lon]: Not necessarily. With items of a higher rarity, one can overcast higher. That is how the **[Cultist]** was able to utilize **[Legendary]**-rarity skills earlier and even the **[Unique]**-rarity **[Corruption]** skill. However, they already consumed the **[Fragment]** that enabled them.

[Jerome Smith]: So you're saying they could be the same people—er, monsters?

[Aster K'lon]: Possibly. Had it been another group of scouts, they surely would not have been able to avoid notice as a full group. I am inclined to believe it is the same party.

[Jerome Smith]: But then if they used their overcasting tool already, how would they cast another high-rarity skill?

[Aster K'lon]: The messages included "sacrifice accepted," so I assume that means that the **[Cultist]** used a ritual-type skill. With the assistance of others, it is possible to overcast. To overcast that high, though . . . the sacrifice must have been potent.

[Jerome Smith]: Wait, sacrifice like human sacrifice?

[Aster K'lon]: Likely. I must consult my notes. That, however, is not currently our primary concern.

[Jerome Smith]: What is?

[**Aster K'lon**]: I have a passive skill inherent to the [**Mage**] line. It's called [**Mana Sense**], and it's hidden to lower-level [**Assess**] skills. I can detect a mana presence watching us from afar. I believe we may be under the effect of an observation skill.

P-System Log

[**Mana Sense**], huh? I didn't see that with my pseudo-[**Assess**], but I guess it needed more W Inertia in order to see that skill. She did have a section marked as <HIDDEN> in her status sheet. I guess that's what it hid? If that's the case, there's definitely potential for more hidden skills. Something to keep in mind for the future, I think.

Handy skill to have, from the sounds of it. If Aster is honest—and I have no reason to believe she isn't—then there's a skill watching us. The [**Legendary**] R Beast skill, no doubt. I can't detect anything in the immediate area, but my sense for mana is only really *good* within the limits of my perception dome. Any farther out and it gets a lot fuzzier, so if the skill is gathering mana at a fair distance, I'm not gonna be able to perceive it. Seems like a rather serious downside of being a System, but I guess good ol' Origin never really took that into consideration when designing us.

Party Chat

[**Jerome Smith**]: What do we need to do?

[**Aster K'lon**]: Nothing out of the ordinary. Neither of us are strong enough to counteract a skill that powerful.

[**Jerome Smith**]: So we just . . . let it watch us?

[**Aster K'lon**]: Yes. We could investigate its origin if you wish, but that ways lies much conflict. In fairness, it is likely that either way will include much conflict.

[**Jerome Smith**]: You seem really calm about all this. From what you're saying, it sounds like there's a big-ass target on our backs.

[**Aster K'lon**]: In essence, yes. I doubt much will come of it, given that any large party of R Beasts would be noticed this deep in, but we have attracted notice. If this is indeed the same group of R Beasts as the ones we encountered in the Maplecrest dungeon, this may be the [**Cultist**]'s effort at keeping tabs on our progress. It is, I hear, rather standard for adventuring parties of note.

[Jerome Smith]: So . . . it's a good sign?

[Aster K'lon]: I wouldn't quite say that.

P-System Log

Fuck. Well, I guess that means we're going to be dealing with R Beasts now. I don't want to go through having their ~~wrongness~~ inside my perception dome again, but it looks like that's going to be unavoidable.

Oh, well. That means more opportunities for W Inertia!

Wait. If we get jumped by that same group, Jerome might be fucked. His HP got taken down to like half its max because that dumbass decided to field-test a new application of his skill and ran into a wall at Mach speed. The last time we fought them, Jerome got hit really hard. Doing that again might take him out completely, and that might leave me SOL.

I wonder if there's any way he can get healed that doesn't involve potions?

Maybe I'll just tell him to get healed and hope that works.

Wait, actually, no. I've got a resource I can tap for this. Overly formal voice on!

Private Message [Aster]

[P-System]: Query. Do standard Systems have access to healing?

[Aster K'lon]: You surely are a unique one to not know even this. Intriguing.

[Aster K'lon]: Passive healing occurs in much the same fashion that passive mana regeneration occurs. Once there is an extended period of little movement, the Health stat begins to regenerate, generally healing to full over the course of several hours. I know not of whether or not the System takes part in this, but I must assume it does. Active healing occurs through skills, though many of the **[Cleric]**-type classes are a higher rarity and primarily operate in Edge Cities closer to the Eternal King's domain.

[P-System]: Understood. Thank you.

[Aster K'lon]: You're very welcome, deviant one.

P-System Log [thinking on regen]

Okay, so apparently the way it functions is the same as mana regen. I . . . think that means I don't need to handle it? Not while **[W%M; G, P]** is active, at least. I didn't need to handle mana regen, at least.

I don't know how I would facilitate it anyway. As a System, most of what I can do is through W Inertia and mana manipulation, neither of which sound like they're the correct way to regenerate health. Investing W Inertia into the stat just means that the overall amount increases. It works as a last resort, but it's less healing and more like leveling health. As for mana manipulation, that really only works for the purpose of getting Jerome to learn a skill. I mean, I could try to force Jerome into learning a healing skill, but that requires me to actually witness a healing skill in action first.

In that case, I guess it's either rest or hope Jerome doesn't die. It's still pretty early in the day, so I doubt the first is an option. I could try to manipulate Jerome into resting, but I don't think he wants to, and I don't think it's worth wasting an **[Objective]** declaration over.

Dammit, Jerome. I suppose that if worse comes to worst, I can just spam W Inertia at the problem to delay it. A worryingly large number of my plans are trending in that direction, but it's not my fault this time!

P-System Log

Jerome and Aster just decided to keep going in the end. We're back on the trail again, one dungeon, several hundred W Inertia, and one exceptionally worrying tracking spell later. I'm not 100 percent on what the new skill does, but the fact that both of them can ignore it so easily . . . I can't say it's reassuring. I don't know if I can check for mental compulsions or anything, but it's a little scary that they dismissed such a huge threat so out of hand. I mean, sure, it might not have any risk right now, but there's a lot of potential damage to be had in being tracked by your enemies.

Hero's Personal Log 065

Holy shit, this is terrifying. I hope I can handle whatever R Beasts come our way, but I hate, hate, hate the idea of being tracked. I didn't pay a hundred bucks for fifteen months of ExpressVPN on Earth for no reason! I fucking hate this.

Ugh. Aster is strong, though, and I'm getting stronger. I can do this.

P-System Log

Huh. That's oddly reassuring. Jerome is actually a real person with personality traits other than "dickhead," huh?

Anyway, it's time to keep on truckin' for now. Or walkin', rather. Do they have trucks here? I don't think they do.

Map?le??? D????ẕcẹṛṛọ̈ŗ

System f??l??e

Reb??t??? . . .

invoke: failure

connect invoke: connection e?ta??????

Ho?t??e incu??s??? det?c???!

Rejec?ing . . .

P-System Log

Well, that's not worrying at all.

Party Chat

[**Jerome Smith**]: Did you see that?

[**Aster K'lon**]: Indeed I did. I would highly advise destroying the Dungeon Core.

[**Jerome Smith**]: It's not dangerous to us yet, is it? Plus, there's bound to be information we can get out of it.

[**Aster K'lon**]: This is true. P'lor is known for its laboratories.

[**Jerome Smith**]: You told me to take charge earlier, so I'm taking charge on this. We're keeping the core alive as long as it isn't actively attacking us.

[**Aster K'lon**]: Very well.

P-System Log

I guess that's that. I hope Jerome knows what he's doing.
Ha. We're fucked.

CHAPTER 31

Maybe we aren't actually that fucked. It's been the better part of a day now, and we haven't run into any R Beasts or apocalyptic beings yet. I'm not sure what exactly happened the Dungeon Core, but I've been analyzing the mana residue it left behind. And yeah, it left a residue. That in itself is pretty damn interesting. It's really odd, too. It's like, half mana that I can kinda recognize and half mana that I can tell is intrinsically wrong?

My best guess from the contents of the broken System message is that the [**Corruption**] was trying to connect with something else. That weird [**H?? WA???F?? ?Y?**] skill, if I had to chance a prediction. It looks like some innate defense stopped it from fully connecting. I don't know what connecting entails, and I'm not sure if my guess is even right.

Damn, not knowing anything is the only real consistent part of my life these days, isn't it?

Whatever. When a problem comes, I'll deal with it. I've already been learning how to act upon situations creatively. That quick cast that potentially saved Aster's life back before the dungeon was me, and I'm sure I can figure out more as time goes along. If an attacker comes for us, I'll come right back at them.

In the meantime, though, it looks like we're not going to be running into any issues. Jerome had Aster teach him how to meditate earlier, and while it wasn't perfect, there does appear to be some manner in which Integrated like them can regenerate their mana quickly. He was able to do it when walking, so I think he's back up to full now. Nothing on the Health front, though. We haven't stopped for long enough for me to detect any change in that.

Well, I mean, it could technically still be on me to do the whole health-regen thing. [**W%M; G, P**] hasn't done anything about it, but that doesn't mean I'm not supposed to be 100 percent handling it.

Ugh. It's getting increasingly irritating to deal with this.

Maybe I should just tell Jerome about the whole W Inertia situation. Maybe Aster, too. Aster is smart and Jerome is my Integrated, and good communication is—

Actually, I think I won't.

Party Chat

[**Jerome Smith**]: It's been a pretty boring day, hasn't it?

[**Aster K'lon**]: This corner of the world is generally uneventful. The presence of the R Beasts was a significant anomaly.

[**Jerome Smith**]: If this place is uneventful, then how are you level 26? That looks really damn high.

[**Aster K'lon**]: I do a lot of dungeons. Furthermore, I have been maintaining a [**Rare**] class over my years. If I wished to, I could have evolved to an [**Epic**] class years ago. However, I wished to train further to increase my potential.

[**Jerome Smith**]: That's a thing you can do?

[**Aster K'lon**]: At a sufficiently high level—it varies between classes—and with a number of prerequisites, including a number of titles, it is possible to evolve the rarity of a class.

[**Jerome Smith**]: So I could become something greater than [**Legendary**]?

[**Aster K'lon**]: Possible, though unlikely. Classes of your rarity rarely evolve.

[**Jerome Smith**]: Aw, man.

[**Aster K'lon**]: Onward, then. The sun is beginning to set. There should be another safe clearing in another mile or so.

P-System Log

Hey, there was really important information there! Shit that Jerome just missed!

Party Chat

[**Jerome Smith**]: Wait, you mentioned titles?

P-System Log

Holy fuck, can he hear me? It's like he has and has somehow become . . . less of an idiot.

I mean, I'm pretty sure he can't hear me, but still. I was pretty sure he was 100 percent an idiot, and it looks like that number might have fallen all the way down to 99 percent.

At least he asked about titles. I might need to manage that, too.

Party Chat

[**Aster K'lon**]: Titles are gained for fulfilling certain sets of conditions. For instance, you have the title [**Reincarnator**] because, well, you reincarnated. It is not a very rare title due to the fact that every reincarnator receives it. I have a number of titles, but I have refused to gain some that I qualify for, as I did not yet want to evolve into an [**Rare**]-rarity class that did not fit my goals.

[**Jerome Smith**]: Goals?

[**Aster K'lon**]: I seek the class of [**Archmage**]. It requires many titles, but it also requires a certain [**Rare**] class that I did not have the titles for. I did not want to evolve into another [**Rare**] class that had no path to [**Archmage**].

[**Jerome Smith**]: Ah, I see. Like hitting B a lot so that Shroomish could learn Spore before it evolves into Breloom.

[**Aster K'lon**]: I will pretend I understand what that means.

P-System Log

Hey! I actually appreciate that reference! Piece of shit got me so mad the first time I realized it didn't learn Spore as Breloom . . .

But also, I'm not sure if it's 100 percent correct as an analogy. Whatever. I get the point, and if an incorrect analogy helps Jerome get it, I'll take it.

We're fully out of the woods now, so the landscape of the trail has changed. It's more meadowy hills now, dotted with animals both magical and mundane here and there. Well, I say that, but I'm pretty sure all of them have Systems. That's just how the Continent works, apparently.

Jerome hasn't bothered to go out of his way to kill any of them, and I guess they do seem pretty peaceful for the most part. Since they don't seem like things that Jerome actually has any will at all to kill, I haven't bothered using an [**Objective**] to motivate him.

Still, it annoys me. That's potential W Inertia that I'm missing out on! I thought Jerome was of the murderhobo brand! Maybe he's of the "kill everything *in my way*" camp instead of the "kill everything" one. Respectable, I guess.

I haven't sensed any new dungeons while we've been traveling, which is weird. Aster hasn't said anything about them, either. I guess they're rarer than I thought?

Party Chat

[**Aster K'lon**]: Monsters ahead. I can sense it.

[**Jerome Smith**]: R Beasts?

[**Aster K'lon**]: No. The skill that was activated earlier is still watching us, but these are definitely from our System.

[**Jerome Smith**]: Hostiles?

[**Aster K'lon**]: Yes. Just over the next hill.

P-System Log

Oh, yep, they're entering my perception dome now. Those are . . . not humans, that's for sure. Not any humanoid race, not by far.

. . . ew, what the fuck are they? I can perceive, like, a mouth. A circular mouth with way too many teeth and way too much depth and way too many legs. It feels fuzzy when I try to perceive inside the creature, the same way it feels when I try to peek into a Dungeon Core, which I think implies either a hiding skill or extradimensional storage. I'm thinking it might be the latter, because they're literally just mouth and tentacle-like legs. The mouth reminds me of that one Greek myth. Uh . . . Charybdis! That was the name. All teeth, all s u c c (I regret thinking that immediately). I wonder if their abilities are anything similar.

Welp. They're rounding the hill now. Jerome and Aster should make contact with them soon.

Party Chat

[Jerome Smith]: What the fuck?

[Aster K'lon]: Oh, those. Lesser Devourers, eh? Some of the dungeons south of Maplecrest have them, too. Dangerous enemies if you get too close to them or let them take you unawares, but they are weak to ranged attack. For them to be out and about, outside a dungeon . . . there must have been a break.

[Jerome Smith]: They look fucking horrifying.

[Aster K'lon]: Mmm. Reincarnators. You'll get used to it in time.

[Jerome Smith]: I'm gonna kill all of them. Holy shit.

P-System Log

I can get with this.

[Mass Assess] activating!

Integrated identified: **Lesser Devourer [Predator lv. 5] C1**

Integrated identified: **Lesser Devourer [Predator lv. 5] D4**

Integrated identified: **Lesser Devourer [Predator lv. 5] H2**

Integrated identified: **Lesser Devourer [Predator lv. 5] H7**

P-System Log

These ones have names (of a sort, at least), even though they're not humanoid, not apparently sentient, and just nothing approaching regular intelligent life. That's . . . interesting. Were they assigned those names? I certainly don't think any being would choose a name like *those*. There's implications there, ones that I don't want to think too hard on right now.

And apparently Jerome didn't even bother to glance a second time. He's already building mana.

[Blazing Spear] activating!

[Blazing Spear] dealt 15 damage!

[Blazing Spear] dealt 17 damage!

[Blazing Spear] dealt 12 damage!

[Blazing Spear] dealt 11 damage!

Hero's Personal Log 066

Resistant to magic? Or fire, maybe. I'll test that.

Party Chat

[Jerome Smith]: I'm taking this. Fifteen, seventeen, twelve, eleven.

[Aster K'lon]: They do have resistances.

[Jerome Smith]: I can see that.

[Misty Strike] activating!

[Misty Strike] dealt 77 damage!

Enemy defeated! Experience rewarded!

Title gained: **[Killer I]**

You have slain a significant number of other beings. Increases killing instinct.

CHAPTER 32

P-System Log

Oh, speak of the devil. We discuss titles, and suddenly Jerome gets one. I was thinking a bit ago—surely Jerome hasn't managed to get through his life without divine assistance of some sort. I was half joking when I thought that before, but I might not be now. The gods of this world seem to smile upon his idiocy.

Well, the title's neat to see, at least. I saw similar titles on some enemies already, so its existence isn't really surprising or anything. I've actually been wondering whether or not it was a monster-exclusive type of thing, since Jerome had killed a decent number of people and monsters and hadn't received it till now.

Time to see what it does!

[Killer I]

Effect: Increases ability to kill by 1%.

Progression: <HIDDEN>

<HIDDEN>

P-System Log

Well, that's just fantastic, isn't it? Once again, my super cool W Inertia–manipulating powers are foiled by the Origin System refusing to make those powers actually useful!

The 1 percent could be a damage multiplier. It could be a mana multiplier. It could be fucking anything! There's no specificity here, and I don't want to waste any more W Inertia.

Also, Jerome's still fighting. I should probably focus on facilitating his attacks.

Overcharged [**Blazing Spear**] (1.5x) activating!

[**Blazing Spear**] dealt 23 damage!

[**Blazing Spear**] dealt 24 damage!

[**Blazing Spear**] dealt 19 damage!

Party Chat

[**Jerome Smith**]: Twenty-three, twenty-four, nineteen.

[**Aster K'lon**]: Be careful with your mana usage.

Strength contest initiated!

Strength contest won by [**Godkiller**] Jerome Smith! Damage from [**Ensnare**] lowered!

[**Ensnare**] dealt 26 damage to you!

[**Ensnare**]'s trap failed to close!

P-System Log

That was sure something to witness, wow. Lemme tell you, gory horror monsters look a lot weirder when there's a Health system preventing them from actually, y'know, goring people. Jerome [**Blazing Spear**]ed them and then ran in straight after the flames finished burning out, and then one of the Lesser Devourers—ugh, that's a convoluted name for you—literally just scuttled under him and tried to eat him. They're surprisingly large, maybe the size of a big laptop, and it got one of his legs stuck inside. After that, there was a blur and a weird convulsion of mana and something else that wasn't mana or W Inertia—the Strength contest, presumably—and then Jerome was able to pull his leg out, none the worse for wear besides the damage. It's like watching a G-rated horror movie. The process of his leg going into the fucking thing's mouth was disturbing to watch, but it's almost comical without the gore.

[**Misty Strike**] activating!

[**Misty Strike**] dealt 79 damage!

Enemy defeated! Experience rewarded!

P-System Log

Aside from stupid decisions that he makes, these enemies are honestly basically a cakewalk for Jerome. Low-level he may be, but his class is ridiculous, he's got incredible stats, and he has *me*—Parker Wu, System extraordinaire.

Okay, I cringed at myself before I even finished thinking that. Putting that thought away now.

Anyway, he has all that, and he has me. I'm generating new skills for him, giving him the pseudo-quickcast spell, giving him danger sense . . . damn, I'm good. I wish he was more thankful for me, but whatever. I'm getting W Inertia and it's kind of fun pointing Jerome at problems and watching them go away. Kind of like playing a tower defense game, now that I think about it.

Still two more. Jerome is giving them a pretty thorough bashing, but he's burning through mana like crazy. Good for him that he started out with high stats, I guess. If it was Axel, he would've been completely out of mana by now.

[**Lesser Mana Storm**] cast!

Enemies defeated! Experience split and distributed!

P-System Log

Holy shit, stop kill stealing! That's *my* fucking W Inertia you're taking, Aster!

. . . at least the skill was cool. Lots of swirly colors and really neat effects that I can appreciate even if I don't have eyes in the proper sense. I'm pretty sure there was a lot of elemental magic involved in that attack. Fire, ice, water, earth, air, plus a whole lot more esoteric shit that I don't have a name for. I think I can copy the mana pattern for Jerome, though. Maybe get him a properly [**Legendary**] attack skill.

Still. Aster. Please, for the love of god(s where applicable). Give me the points.

Party Chat

[**Jerome Smith**]: You keep doing that.

[**Aster K'lon**]: Doing what?

[**Jerome Smith**]: Taking my kills. Entering the situation when I've already got it.

[**Aster K'lon**]: You mean helping you?

[**Jerome Smith**]: I had that. Also, how did the skill not even damage me? I was right there.

[**Aster K'lon**]: By "had that," you mean that you were about to get stuck into two separate [**Ensnare**]s. As to the latter, we are partied. There are more benefits to that than just a party chat.

[**Jerome Smith**]: Oh. Okay.

P-System Log

So what if Jerome was going to get hit by those? What, was he going to take a little more damage? He still has two hundred HP left, bare minimum—it's not like he can actually die until he gets hit a lot more. And I mean, like, a *lot* more. He killed two of them before he got hit a single time, and sure he was about to take more damage, but he's *fine*.

Aster is kind of frustrating me, not gonna lie. Which sucks, because she was, like, the one reasonable person on this entire damn planet. Continent, whatever.

Ugh. I'll try talking to her. I kinda hate the idea of anything approaching socializing, but I think I can manage if it's through the veneer of the System.

Private Message [Aster]

[P-System]: Query. Allow Jerome to obtain maximum XP from his fights.

[Aster K'lon]: Hello, P-System. I am aware that you maintain some level of intelligence. Must you maintain such a machinelike facade? You are a growing organism to my eyes, not just another rigid set of rules.

[P-System]: Response. No.

[Aster K'lon]: See? Just like that. That has personality.

[P-System]: Repeating query. Cease stealing kills.

[Aster K'lon]: I understand your issue, but you must understand I am trying to protect Jerome.

[P-System]: Query. You earlier stated that your task was not to protect him.

[Aster K'lon]: I lied.

[P-System]: Noted.

[Aster K'lon]: You do not talk to Jerome about this.

[P-System]: That was not a question. I do not take orders.

[Aster K'lon]: It was also not an order. I do notice these things, you know. Jerome is not the type of person who could remain silent about an issue so important, not unless you silenced him.

[P-System]: Query. Why do you believe I did not silence him?

[Aster K'lon]: If you held that power, you would have the power to silence me as well. Yet you have not. Similarly, I have yet to disclose your true nature of intelligence to Jerome. I wish to develop a relationship of trust, not mutually assured destruction.

[P-System]: Fair.

[Aster K'lon]: I simply wish for Jerome's System—P? I forget if you prefer to be called that—to understand the entirety of the situation surrounding him.

[P-System]: P-System or P-S is fine.

[**Aster K'lon**]: Jerome has significantly more raw power than the supermajority of reincarnators, especially those passing through Maplecrest.

[**P-System**]: He's an edge case. I am an edge case. This is known.

[**Aster K'lon**]: Correct, P-S, but I seek to understand *why*. Why now, after the gods have gone silent for so long?

[**P-System**]: The gods?

[**Aster K'lon**]: Truly, a child's knowledge you possess. The gods of this land stem from the Origin System that provides us with the power. The gods are manifestations of the Origin, representing its different aspects. In times past, there were those who were godsent, granted abnormally great powers by those manifestations. Not only reincarnators, but others from our world as well.

[**P-System**]: And then they stopped?

[**Aster K'lon**]: Correct. Nobody knows why, but the boons slowed. Reincarnators stopped coming in with the mana signature of the gods. New Integrated stop gaining their gods-given boons.

[**P-System**]: Mana signatures are traceable?

[**Aster K'lon**]: Indeed. As a [**Mage**], I myself am able to.

[**P-System**]: Are you able to trace my mana signature?

[**Aster K'lon**]: I have not yet tried. I may attempt to once I finish this point.

[**P-System**]: Continue.

P-System Log

Man, it's tough maintaining that facade, but it's better than the alternative, at the very least.

Also, I got W Inertia from that fight, but I can distribute it later. I think what Aster's saying right now carries a good deal more importance than Jerome's fiftieth powerup of the day does.

Private Messages [Aster]

[**Aster K'lon**]: Jerome is godsent. Unless my colleagues have been hiding information from me, he is the first in *decades*. He must be examined and questioned. He will not be harmed, but we must learn why the gods have begun activity again.

[**P-System**]: He has the same mana signature of the gods of old?

[**Aster K'lon**]: Exactly the same as the gods, yes.

[**Aster K'lon**]: . . .

[**Aster K'lon**]: You have it, too.

CHAPTER 33

It's been damn near ten minutes now, and Aster still hasn't said anything else to me.

It's . . . certainly something to process. For me, the process of reincarnation was literally instant. One moment I was there in foggy-ass San Francisco, and the next I was here on the Continent, none the wiser. I don't have the faintest idea of what happened during the in-between because there *was no in-between.*

I don't remember any gods. I mean, I remember the Origin System tossing a bunch of incomprehensible bullshit at me, and I guess that's where the gods are supposed to come from in the first place, but I never met any of the fuckers myself.

Where'd I get the signature, then? Aster says that those of [**Mage**]-style classes are able to detect when people are godsent, but I'm not sure I'm buying that. I would've detected any form of skill usage on me, I'm pretty sure, but I didn't see any. Maybe it's a passive skill? She did have one of those—[**Mana Sense**]—that I haven't been able to see the use of, even though she's apparently used it before in my presence. I don't think Aster would *lie* to me—though I do have to keep my mind open to that possibility, of course—so I think I'll go with that theory for now. It makes the most sense. The usage of another hidden skill that I haven't seen before would also explain why she hasn't noticed I'm a reincarnator yet, since an [**Assess**]-type skill would probably reveal that I'm not of this world.

What are the odds she's wrong? It's not like I'm an expert on this world. Aster knows far better than I do about how stuff works and what the gods here are even supposed to do. Hell, I don't even know the names of any part of the pantheon, let alone how to detect if their magic is present in me.

Still, something is telling me there's more to this. There was something that just felt a little . . . off. *Off*, yes, that's the best word to describe it. Some uncanny valley factor about her words that just made me feel like there was something going on wrong, and I ~~can't seem to figure out why~~. Fuck, I can tell there's something there, some idea I can reach for, but it's frustratingly out of my reach.

That aside, Aster seems to be in deep thought as well. Considering the ramifications of what's happening, maybe? Deciding whether or not both of us need to be dissected in a lab?

No, Parker, bad. You said you were going to stop assuming the worst of people, and Aster has been nothing but nice so far. She's definitely just thinking about what's happening, but I'm reading way the fuck too far into it.

Jerome, on the other hand, hasn't heard a single word of this and does not give a single flying fuck. It's kind of refreshing, to be honest, seeing him just walk around without a care in the world.

Party Chat

[**Aster K'lon**]: We must find lodgings for the night soon.

[**Jerome Smith**]: Sure. Where?

[**Aster K'lon**]: We made significantly better pace than expected today. We are on track to be within reach of another Edge City in a couple of hours. With the aid of an item, we may be able to reach the Edge City soon after nightfall.

[**Jerome Smith**]: Oh, dang, really? I thought you said two days earlier today. What's the city?

[**Aster K'lon**]: I was not anticipating this pace. The city's name is S'ker. It is primarily known for featuring a significant number of dungeons.

[**Jerome Smith**]: Damn, okay. Are we going to have better places to sleep than the tent there? Uh, not saying that the tent's bad or anything.

[**Aster K'lon**]: Yes. There are proper inns there where we may rest.

[**Jerome Smith**]: And dungeons, right? Can we do another one tonight?

[**Aster K'lon**]: I thought you would enjoy the prospect of that.

P-System Log

Okay, this just looks like flat-out manipulation. My perception dome isn't good enough to detect how far the next city is from us, but I can at least tell that our pace hasn't changed by much—if at all—since we started on this little trek of ours. Aster is pulling out the idea of using what sounds to be something like Minecraft potions of speed to get there faster, which to me sounds like a very consumable item. Well, I assume it's that. If she has, like, longstrider boots or something that passively increases her speed, I would have to wonder why she hasn't been using them this whole time.

That's not the point, though. The point is that she seems to be willing to invest resources into convincing Jerome into going to this S'ker city far sooner. So soon after she and I had a conversation about the nature of Jerome's reincarnation, too . . .

There's a reason she's trying to push him here. Now, the only question is: What could that reason possibly be? P'lor is the city that's supposed to have nice lab facilities in it, so unless Aster's been a pathological liar this entire time and this is all an elaborate plot to stick Jerome in a padded room and poke him with a whole lot of sticks, we're not going to S'ker because of its testing facilities.

What else is there? I really don't have that much to go on, given the minuscule amount of information I've gotten so far. I guess I can try to make predictions based off what I've got, though I have to acknowledge the fact that Aster's real reasons could totally be because of some aspect of the city that she didn't mention.

Okay, Aster said S'ker had dungeons in it. Multiple, apparently. That, along with the probably enticing offer of having a warm bed to sleep in, was the only draw to the city that she mentioned. Jerome took it hook, line, and sinker, though, it appears.

Is there something in S'ker's dungeons that might provide a clue toward Jerome's and my condition? That's the only real reason I can think of right now, since that's the only thing that Aster has gotten new information on in the past hour or so that might've made her want to push the schedule forward.

Speaking of which. She got out the doodad she's using to boost our speed. Not potions, actually. It's an artifact. A colorfully decorated wooden shortstaff maybe three feet tall with four huge notches cut into it at regular intervals. Three of the notches have bright-green light coming out of them. Mana's coming from it, too.

[**Acceleration Staff**] consumed 2 charges!

<table><tr><td>

P-System Log

Oh, two of the lights went out. Interesting. They channeled mana really fast for a brief second, and now their mana signature is just completely gone. Is the mana just completely gone now?

Aster and Jerome did speed up, though. It's kind of comical, like someone accidentally removed half the frames of an animation or put a TV on fast-forward. They're quite literally just making every single action they take faster.

</td></tr></table>

<table><tr><td>

Party Chat

[Jerome Smith]: This is cool. The world slowed down.

[Aster K'lon]: You sped up. The world remains at the same speed.

[Jerome Smith]: How did this happen?

[Aster K'lon]: You are currently under the influence of an artifact.

[Jerome Smith]: Artifacts. What are those?

[Aster K'lon]: They are found in dungeons, occasionally. I found this one in the S'ker dungeons, as a matter of fact.

[Jerome Smith]: Oh, they're loot drops?

[Aster K'lon]: Essentially. They allow for a much more diverse array of utility for any given Integrated. Many of them require far fewer mana than a skill that would accomplish the same task requires. It is simply a matter of entering a dungeon with a little luck.

[Jerome Smith]: Neat. And S'ker has a lot of these dungeons?

[Aster K'lon]: With varying levels and rarities, correct.

[Jerome Smith]: Sounds to me like we should grind there for a while, then.

[Aster K'lon]: If the meaning of "grind" you have is consistent with the ones that other game-oriented reincarnators have had, then yes, we may. I scheduled our journey with this type of detour in mind.

[Jerome Smith]: Great. Can we hit one up tonight, then?

[Aster K'lon]: We may if we arrive soon enough.

</td></tr></table>

P-System Log

We're making pretty good progress now. The trail is super rough, and the trees and bushes have overgrown it in places, but Aster knows what she's doing.

She's definitely pushing Jerome to do dungeons. There's no doubt about it.

Now, the million-W-Inertia question is: Why? What's in it for her?

Is there some experimentation she wants to run? Does she just want more loot and levels all of a sudden? Does it have something to do with our apparent "godsent" status?

Whatever the case, there's nothing I can do about it. Jerome wants to go, so we're going. I could put an [**Objective**] down to deny it, but Aster's purpose kind of aligns with mine here. Whatever her motives, I can at least appreciate that they point me toward more W Inertia.

That's a problem for when we get there.

For now, all I can do is wait and watch.

Welcome to S'ker, the Dungeon Hub of the South!

CHAPTER 34

Damn. We're here already. Jerome and Aster checked into an inn—Aster spent some gold coins that appeared out of nowhere with a sudden burst of mana. It showed up in my not-vision as [**Currency**], so I assume it's even more System bullshit that I don't have access to yet.

. . . maybe I should try feeding [**W%M; G, P**] some more W Inertia and see if that gets me anywhere. I need to learn how to get better at doing this System stuff, and that skill seems to be the only thing helping me accomplish that.

Maybe later, though. I don't want to risk experimenting with shit that affects me directly. Experimenting with Jerome's skills? Hell yeah, I'll do that midfight anytime, but for *me*? I think I'll wait until we get somewhere safer.

We're on our way to the next dungeon now. Aster's promises of loot and XP got to him, and he insisted on going as soon as we got here. He hasn't even regenerated his HP yet!

Not that Aster seems to care. She said something about being able to protect him if necessary, and now we're off already.

S'ker is way livelier than Maplecrest was. This place looks like a proper city. If it's not quite NYC, it can at least compete with San José or Denver or something. Maybe not the former, actually, since this place actually looks to have a nightlife. Lots of bars and taverns around these parts, looks like, and there's a proper flood of people traveling through the streets even after nightfall. It's well lit by lamps containing spells I recognize as [**Simple Light**] skills. Interesting stuff.

Slightly more interesting, though, are the strong sources of mana and W Inertia that I can sense even though they lie beyond my perception dome.

Dungeons.

Party Chat

[**Aster K'lon**]: I am switching to party chat because the noise of the halls is far too disruptive. Follow me.

[**Jerome Smith**]: Got it. What dungeon are we going to?

[**Aster K'lon**]: The northern one. There are eight dungeon systems surrounding S'ker, arranged at the cardinal and subcardinal directions of the city. Compliant Dungeon Cores from across the region were assembled by high-level adventurers to be safely cleared by any delvers who are willing to pay a fee a few decades ago. The northernmost set contains relatively low-level [**Common**] dungeons, and they increase in difficulty in the clockwise direction, going all the way up to a midrange [**Legendary**] Dungeon Core to the northwest.

[**Jerome Smith**]: Can we not clear anything harder yet?

[**Aster K'lon**]: I would advise against it. We may attempt it later, when we are more rested. Furthermore, I do not wish to take the corrupted Dungeon Core into a more difficult dungeon that we cannot ensure victory in.

[**Jerome Smith**]: You still have that thing on you?

[**Aster K'lon**]: Indeed. I have trusted associates in this Edge City who may be able to hold it for us while we delve a dungeon, but they are not currently available. As such, combined with the factor of your temporary weakness, we will be entering an easier dungeon.

[**Jerome Smith**]: Works for me.

P-System Log

Oh, Jerome just ran into someone. Two someones. They don't appear the same to me as Aster and Jerome do. Shorter and taller, respectively, and their body structures appear to have some different geometry on their insides.

Did we run into another race just now?

[**Assess**] activating!

[**Assess**] activating!

Integrated identified: **Elf [Fire Mage lv. 11] Arcs S'tar**

Integrated identified: **Dwarf [Raging Berserker lv. 7] Thron of the Fallen Skies**

P-System Log

Holy shit, it's real fantasy races. I think we saw other races earlier when we saw the R Beasts, **and** to be fair, the Race box in the stat sheets always implied the existence of other races, but holy *shit*.

. . . is it just me, or do they look a little generic? The dwarf and elf both look like they came straight off the set of *Lord of the Rings*. One male, the dwarf, and one female, the elf.

Here's a brief replay of their neat little interaction with Jerome just now:

Elf Lady: What the fuck, man?

Dwarf Man: Watch where you're going!

Jerome: Shit, my bad.

Which I personally think is a pretty good improvement over his earlier social interactions, at least.

Elf Lady: Are you a reincarnator or something? Did your parents ever tell you it's rude to [**Assess**] strangers?

Jerome: Sorry, sorry. My bad.

C'mon, be like this with me, man . . .

Whatever. It's really neat seeing new cultures and new people, especially when it's literally fantasy people!

They moved on pretty fast, though. We're making our way south, *fast*.

P-System Log [dungeon time]

Here we go! No other issues encountered on our way in, so we're here now. The S'ker dungeon actually seems solid, especially when compared to the ramshackle excuse of a dungeon that the Maplecrest and wilderness dungeons had. This place actually has an entrance, done up nicely with a marble building and all that. There's even a receptionist!

[**Superior Assess**] cast!

[**Superior Assess**] cast!

P-System Log

Receptionist just looked over us with mana, probably to make sure we're sentient enough to pass the dungeon tonight.

Looks like we're good. He said some nice words and is giving us a few gestures that I don't quite recognize but assume mean good things.

Party Chat

[**Jerome Smith**]: We're good to go, right?

[**Aster K'lon**]: Indeed we are. The receptionist has indicated that our average levels, class rarities, and experience are high enough to attempt this dungeon without immediate failure.

[**Jerome Smith**]: So we're going to be safe?

[**Aster K'lon**]: I never said that.

S'ker South Dungeon System

Intruders detected. Initiating Core defense.

P-System Log

Welp. Here we go. A lot faster paced than we've been doing stuff before, but Aster seems to be worried about something, and she's pushing Jerome along fast.

Not that I have any complaints about it. As long as we're picking up more W Inertia, I'm happy for Jerome to do whatever.

The S'ker South Dungeon—oh my god(s), it spells SSD, I'm going to make so many horrible jokes about that—is a lot higher tier of a dungeon than those that we were running before, though I don't mean that in a power level sense. We just passed the boundary that makes my perception all fuzzy, and the entrance room of the place is genuinely impressive. It's marble just like the building that housed its entrance, and it actually looks like it was designed with its purpose as a building in mind. There's even a sign or two here!

One of them says **S'ker Dungeon, Recommended Party Level: 5-10 WPA**. I'm not sure what "WPA" means, but that seems a little . . . odd? After all, Jerome at level 3 has access to options that are as powerful as—if not stronger than—the skills that Aster has at a level over twenty above him, and though I definitely played a part in that, I'm pretty sure that his **[Legendary]** class versus Aster's **[Rare]** one did, too. Maybe this level WPA takes that into account, though.

Anyway, while that's interesting to think about, it's also not my problem right now. Looks like the area we're in is the "safe room" that all the dungeons are supposed to have. Jerome and Aster are taking a moment—to do what, I'm not sure—but now that moment is done, and we're moving again.

Into the dungeon we go!

Party Chat

[Jerome Smith]: Do you have a map of this dungeon?

[Aster K'lon]: Yes, but I know not what lies ahead.

[Jerome Smith]: The fuck does that mean? How can you have a map and not know what's ahead of us?

[Aster K'lon]: Oh, you poor reincarnated soul. Dungeon Cores are able to manipulate their internal geometry as well as the monsters and challenges that spawn within them. While their layout almost always remains constant—with the exception of certain anomalies like the Unknown Dungeons by the borders or the moving Cores—what populates the rooms will near always be different.

[Jerome Smith]: Huh. Noted. By the way, are we going to run into other adventurers while we're in here?

[Aster K'lon]: Possible, but unlikely. Dungeon Cores tend to seal off the entrance if there is a group attempting to clear it. Thus, dungeons in civilized areas generally require reservations in order to use. S'ker's dungeon system means that there are a significant number of **[Common]** dungeons that can be run at one time, but they still require reservations here.

[Jerome Smith]: But we didn't reserve.

[Aster K'lon]: I have colleagues here. I called ahead.

> **P-System Log**
>
> Into the first room of the dungeon! For all the talk about dungeon vari-ability, this room one seems pretty bog-standard. A summoning circle kind of aesthetic, and a few monsters piled around it. Not ones that I recognize, though.

> ▼ [H?? WA???F?? ?Y?] ▼
>
> ▼ And so the king proclaimed: the weak shalt know fear. ▼

CHAPTER 35

<table>
<tr><td>

P-System Log

</td></tr>
<tr><td>

That's . . . not good. It feels like everywhere we go, the R Beasts are there to rain on our parade. It's more than a little annoying, if I do say so myself.

There was a difference this time, at least. I could actually feel the mana of something making contact with us. Not an offensive spell, obviously, but it's subtle and it's different. Different in a way that makes it not quite mana, I think, at least not mana in the senses of those of us operating with the Origin System.

I don't sense any enemies beyond the ones in this room, but now that we're in the dungeon, my perception dome can't sense anything outside it. There's no telling what could be waiting for us behind closed doors and outside this place.

Come to think of it, how did the spell even penetrate the dungeon? This place is supposed to be locked down from outside influence, isn't it?

Stupid-ass R Beasts and their stupid cheater skills. Oh, well. I guess that just means we'll have to move "dealing with the R Beasts" up higher on our priority list.

</td></tr>
</table>

<table>
<tr><td>

Party Chat

</td></tr>
<tr><td>

[**Jerome Smith**]: Did you see that?

[**Aster K'lon**]: Yes. It is worrying, but it is no issue we are currently able to solve.

[**Jerome Smith**]: How are we even supposed to solve it in any way?

[**Aster K'lon**]: We have established that the caster is likely the [**Cultist**] from before, yes?

[**Jerome Smith**]: Yeah. So we kill him?

</td></tr>
</table>

[**Aster K'lon**]: We subdue and capture him. Or kill him, yes, that is another viable option.

[**Jerome Smith**]: Great. How do we do that?

[**Aster K'lon**]: The first step is getting stronger, which we can conveniently do in this very dungeon.

[**Jerome Smith**]: Right.

P-System Log

Damn, Aster *really* wants Jerome to do this dungeon, doesn't she? Going so far as to basically ignore a [**Legendary**] skill from the R Beasts . . .
She's really invested in this.

Private Message [Aster]

[**P-System**]: Query. What do you seek to accomplish through this current endeavor?

[**Aster K'lon**]: First, please speak to me without the barrier of inaccessible dialogue. You and I both know you are capable of doing that.

[**P-System**]: Okay. The query remains.

[**Aster K'lon**]: What "endeavor" do you refer to?

[**Misty Strike**] activating!

Critical hit! [**Misty Strike**] dealt 186 damage!

[**Misty Strike**] dealt 93 damage!

Enemies defeated! Experience rewarded.

P-System Log

Wow, I didn't even get to [**Assess**] what we were up against. Those looked a little different from the dire animals that we've been encountering so far. These seemed like bona fide monsters, things with no equivalent on Earth. Sort of like the Lesser Devourers, albeit with less of a horror movie design that those shits had.

Aster isn't doing anything. She's just letting Jerome fight.

Her loss. I'll take the unshared W Inertia.

Private Message [Aster]

[**P-System**]: You push Jerome to do these dungeons, entice him with promises of power. To what end?

[**Aster K'lon**]: There you are. Speaking more like an actual intelligent being now.

[**Aster K'lon**]: I push him because I have learned he is godsent.

[**P-System**]: You knew this already. Why start pushing now?

Overcharged [**Blazing Spear**] activating!

[**Blazing Spear**] dealt 70 damage!

[**Blazing Spear**] dealt 63 damage!

[**Blazing Spear**] dealt 55 damage!

[**Blazing Spear**] dealt 78 damage!

Enemies defeated! Experience rewarded!

Private Message [Aster]

[**Aster K'lon**]: For I saw you were godsent as well, P-S. Godsent people, be they human, elf, dwarf, nightwalker, or any other race . . . those are rare enough on their own. But a godsent System? History has never seen the likes of you.

[**P-System**]: I don't understand how that equates to encouraging Jerome to speedrun dungeons.

[**Aster K'lon**]: As a godsent reincarnator—the first in decades—Jerome was already an exceptionally rare case. As such, it is my responsibility as the researcher who first found him to ensure that his abilities and properties are properly assessed, which I hope to do in P'lor.

[**P-System**]: Right. That has nothing to do with dungeons.

[**Aster K'lon**]: This was before I realized you, too, were godsent. No message was sent from the heavens, no indication that there would be another.

[**P-System**]: Okay.

[**Aster K'lon**]: I have no information about you, P-S. In order to gain it, I must observe. Your abilities are undocumented in our history, and it is only through further conflict that I can grow to understand who you are and how you operate.

[**P-System**]: Remarkably transparent of you.

[**Aster K'lon**]: The world is dying. Every day, the Eternal King and his R Beasts claim more land. With the truly tremendous quantities of power they wield, I do not jest when I say that we of this System seek a miracle to keep us from facing total annihilation.

[**Aster K'lon**]: I ask for your cooperation not because I believe you will trust me, but because we have no other option remaining to us. I am in contact with a wide network of those who search for reincarnators and their skills, and I do not exaggerate when I tell you that we are *desperate*. I beg of you to help us.

[**P-System**]: . . . alright. As long as there's room to gain—as long as you allow Jerome free rein to level.

P-System Log

I guess that's reasonable. I was so wrapped up in dealing with other shit that I forgot that the whole generic premise that we have here is actually a reality. Looks like there's some difference between this and those generic isekai premises, since the Demon Lord—Eternal King, whatever—actually has some level of impact on people's lives. Still haven't seen any trace of it beyond the R Beasts, but those were disruptive enough that I could totally see the Eternal King itself being an existential threat.

[Misty Strike] activating!

[Misty Strike] dealt 98 damage!

Enemy defeated! Experience rewarded!

Current W Inertia: 38,454 [+72]

P-System Log

Holy fuck, yes yes yes yes *yes*

I forgot how intoxicating W Inertia overflow is. My nonexistent nerve endings are on fucking fire. Hell fucking yeah.

Now, time to get rid of some of this. I just realized that I sorta forgot to power up Jerome's skills last time he got some kills done, which is probably why I got to the overflow in the first place. I spend a lot on Jerome.

Just this once, though, I'm going to spend some on myself. Fuck the formula, fuck the numbers, fuck all of that. Jerome might've done the killing, but it was *me* that made him who he is. I earned this shit.

[W%M; G, P] is the only skill I've got, and it's nothing like the other skills. The first time it triggered, it was from the first overflow I ever got, but that was only, like, a few points of overflow. How far can I get with seventy-two whole points?

Well, I guess I'm about to find out.

System Prompt

[W%M; G, P] invoked.

W overflow detected. Consuming.

System user detected.

<HIDDEN>

<HIDDEN>

U̸N̸K̸%̸#̸$̸_satisfied.

Increasing flow to skill.

[W%M; G, P]

ADMIN TIER: 0/???

Access credentials insufficient. Advanced statistics unavailable.

What in the ever-loving fuck?

Okay, the high has died down now that I spent the W Inertia. That feeling that I had before, the instinct that something was going to go very wrong if I let that W Inertia stay—I can think more clearly now, but as has been the case far too many times now, I'm still confused as all hell.

First takeaway: my W Inertia cap increased. With a value of 38,454—about a three hundred increase from before, which means that each of the monsters that Jerome just killed were worth about fifty W Inertia apiece—there was a seventy-two-point overflow, which makes my current cap . . . 38,382. That's a little more than twenty greater than my cap before. Nice.

Second takeaway. Origin is still a little bitch! I mean, I know it's ultimately ~~for my own good~~, but it's just so annoying. I just paid you seventy-two W Inertia, stupid-ass Origin-interfacing skill—why didn't I get any progression?

Well, if I think about it a little, I can come up with a theory as to why this happened. The first time I got this message, it said something along the lines of "access to this skill unlocked." Not that wording exactly, but it was vaguely similar. I guess I only needed a few points to open the door, but way more to actually increase my capabilities, huh?

Can I push more W Inertia into it?

Using W Inertia comes naturally at this point. It's only been a day or two, but I've adapted to it pretty damn well, if I do say so myself. Let's try and put a bit into my skill . . .

<table>
<tr><td>System Prompt</td></tr>
</table>

[W%M; G, P] invoked.

W overflow not detected.

<HIDDEN>

<HIDDEN>

UNK̶#̶$̶ not satisfied.

Increasing flow to skill.

Admin tier insufficient.

Permissions insufficient.

W Inertia rejected.

<table>
<tr><td>P-System Log</td></tr>
</table>

Shit. Okay, it doesn't do anything.

All the more reason to push Jerome to killing more shit, then. There's definitely answers for me lying in this skill. All I need to do is manipulate this reincarnator into becoming a mass murderer.

Almost as easy done as said!

CHAPTER 36

It's not like I'm going to be doing anything different from what I'm already doing. I've already been encouraging Jerome to kill everything and everyone in his way, right? All I have to do is do that even more!

Hans . . . are we the baddies?

Nah. So far, we haven't killed or even attempted to kill anything approximating a person. The closest thing that we've had to that are the R Beasts, which I guess could be considered people, but those things are ~~wrong~~ and ~~deserve~~ to die.

Besides, morals were never an issue here. Jerome and I have that in common, at least, even if he lacks in so many other ways. No sweat off our backs if we have to kill a whole fuckload of monsters in order to get our way. After all, they're monsters, and Jerome and I both get power from it.

Anyway. Onto the next room!

Or maybe not. Jerome is taking a breather.

Party Chat

[Jerome Smith]: First room is clear. I used around 120 to 130 mana, so I should still have at least nine hundred. More than enough to deal with the rest of the dungeon, I think.

[Aster K'lon]: Given that it is more mana than I have overall, yes, it certainly is.

[Jerome Smith]: How do you even operate, anyway? My **[Rare]** spells are already costly enough, and you've got higher rarity skills than me on average. Don't you have less mana?

[Aster K'lon]: I regenerate mana faster than you. It is a perk of my **[Mage]** class, a hidden passive skill that most of us in this type of class get. That, however, is not currently the point. Do you have sufficient health remaining to complete the dungeon?

[Jerome Smith]: Lemme check.

Jerome Smith (abbreviated)

Stat	Current	Maximum
Health	311	562

Party Chat

[Jerome Smith]: Less than I'd like.

[Aster K'lon]: HP doesn't matter unless you can go down in one attack. Three hundred and eleven is more Health than I have in total as well, and you have already proven yourself to be capable of slaughtering this dungeon's monsters without allowing them to get in a hit first. I believe you should have no issues.

[Jerome Smith]: Yeah, that makes sense. Still, I wish I could regenerate somehow . . .

[Aster K'lon]: As I've said before, the two primary ways to regenerate your Health are through items and skills. For items, I refuse to use any of my remaining potions on you unless there is no other option left. This is a journey to empower you, not a journey in which you rely on me for everything.

[Jerome Smith]: And skills?

[Aster K'lon]: This, too, I have told you. The primary group of Integrated who can use Health-healing skills are **[Cleric]** types, and while you could attempt to multiclass into one of those classes, the requirements for even a low-rarity class of that type are extraordinarily stringent.

[Jerome Smith]: Hold on, you can multiclass? How come I never got to know this?

[Aster K'lon]: You never asked, Jerome.

[Aster K'lon]: Multiclassing is absolutely possible, but it is highly inadvisable for most.

[**Jerome Smith**]: So if I multiclassed, I could get the healing spells of a [**Cleric**], or your [**Mage**] class's higher mana-regeneration rate?

[**Aster K'lon**]: Yes.

[**Jerome Smith**]: Then why is it not advised?

[**Aster K'lon**] Multiclassing does not increase the amount of experience you gain from battles, so while multiclass adventurers often gain more utility and a wider variety of skills to use, they do it slower, at a rate that makes them fall behind their peers. Except in extraordinary cases, multiclassing is rarely used.

[**Jerome Smith**]: I am an extraordinary case.

[**Aster K'lon**]: If you say so.

P-System Log

No way in hell am I letting him multiclass. Having to split my precious W Inertia even further and watching Jerome power up less every time . . . no, thanks. Besides, I can barely manage his one class. I don't even know if it's got any hidden abilities or passives that I'm supposed to be running but haven't. Without a proper instruction manual, I'm already pretty lost on this class. How would I manage another one?

Yeah, I'm just gonna say no.

P-System Message

Multiclassing is currently disabled for [**Godkiller**] Jerome Smith.

Party Chat

[**Jerome Smith**]: Aw, man. My System told me I can't multiclass.

[**Aster K'lon**]: Interesting. Extraordinary in the opposite direction, then.

[**Jerome Smith**]: Huh?

[**Aster K'lon**]: Never mind. We should get on with this dungeon.

P-System Log

Yeah, Jerome! Hurry us the fuck up!

Well, at least he seemed to take that suggestion to heart. We're moving now, onto the passageway between this room and the next.

. . . it's a really nice passageway. A proper set of marble spiral stairs, evenly lit with magical torchlight and paintings. The paintings aren't of any scenes that I recognize, and some of them are literally just abstract blobs of color that would totally be classified as modern art back in San Fran, but the fact that they're even there is neat enough.

I wonder what the next room looks like.

Party Chat

[Jerome Smith]: What's the next room look like?

[Aster K'lon]: I won't spoil your first S'ker dungeon run for you. You're a **[Legendary]**-class adventurer. You should have no issues clearing it.

[Jerome Smith]: Yeah, but I'm still level 3!

[Aster K'lon]: And far more powerful than anyone else is at that level. Your System truly works miracles.

P-System Log

Aw, thanks, Aster. That reminds me, though. I still haven't given Jerome his rewards.

What was the system I worked out? I'll grant him choice when he levels up, and I'll determine what skill gets how much otherwise, right? That should be fine for this use case.

I think Jerome got like five hundred–ish W Inertia that I didn't actually split up for him. I'm keeping as much of it as I can get away with, since I just recently learned that I *need* overflow for **[W%M; G, P]** to do any work. That means I'm going to be reworking my relationship with Jerome.

Hypocritical? Maybe. Going back on my word to myself? Absolutely. It's not like I don't have a history of breaking promises to myself, so this is just one more to add to the pile.

I'll budget . . . one hundred? One hundred sounds good. If Jerome hits the same number of monsters in the next room as he did in the first, we should easily be able to make all of that back.

Fifty can go to general XP. The other fifty . . . I'll split that between **[Blazing Spear]**, **[Misty Strike]**, and I guess also **[Assess]**. Yeah, that sounds good. Twenty to the first, twenty to the second, and ten to the third, since I think he and I both prioritize offensive skills.

Yeah, I'll give Jerome his freedom of choice when it comes to level ups, but this shit is mine to handle.

P-System Log

Alright, I just gave him the W Inertia. All three of his skills are still pretty early on in terms of their progression to the next level, so there wasn't any leveling here. That's fine. There doesn't need to be.

We're in the next room now. This one's interesting. It's a simple maze, one with, like, ten-foot walls made out of some material that I don't recognize and don't want to appraise.

My perception dome makes me uniquely suited to handling this. I can take a top-down view of the place, which makes me feel a lot less lost than Jerome must.

Hmm. I wonder, can I create images in my mind? I should be able to, right? There's a lot of funky shit available to me as a System. Surely drawing is within my capabilities.

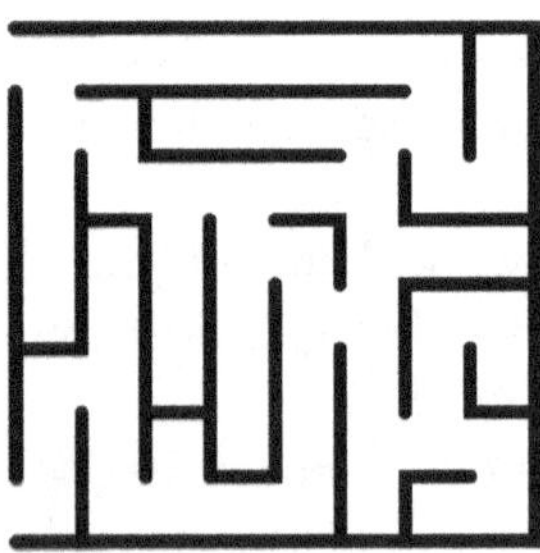

Oh, fantastic.

P-System Message

You are currently in a maze. Displaying maze here:

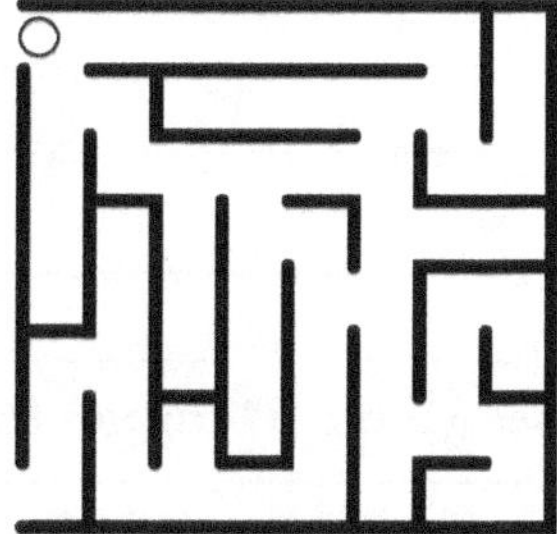

Your location is marked by the circle. In order to complete this maze, turn right-left-right-left-straight-straight-straight-right-straight-right-left-right-straight-right-left-left-right at dead ends and intersections.

Hero's Personal Log 067

Uh . . . . . . okay, I don't think I can process all that. I'll just go through with the map. I'm not *that* dumb—I can solve a maze.

P-System Message

Ah. I forgot Jerome was, like, an actual sentient human being. He went to a good college and everything. I guess there is some brain in that man after all.

Whatever. Here we go. Some of the place is trapped, I'm pretty sure, and some of it has monsters, so Jerome's definitely not getting out of this one unscathed.

All I have to do is sit back, watch, and make sure he doesn't completely die.

Spike trap dealt 32 damage to you!

[Hidden Strike] dealt 12 damage to you!

P-System Log

Bro. You're a gamer. The chest was fucking bloody. And you went for it anyway?

[**Assess**] activating!

Integrated identified: **Lesser Mimic [Dungeon Mimic lv. 2] Nameless**

Overcharged [**Magic Missile**] activating!

[**Magic Missile**] dealt 66 damage!

Enemy defeated! Experience rewarded!

Strength contest initiated!

Strength contest won by [**Godkiller**] Jerome Smith!

Critical hit! Unarmed strike dealt 30 damage!

Enemy defeated! Experience rewarded!

P-System Log

Ugh, there's so much commentary I want to give . . . I feel like I'm watching Twitch Plays Pokémon with how uncoordinated and directionless this guy's fighting style is.

Whatever. It's getting the job done.

CHAPTER 37

[**Misty Strike**] activating!

P-System Log

Hmm. Jerome actually managed to dodge the second spike trap. He's . . . adapting. Kind of. If you call wasting almost sixty mana so he can literally dash over the trap "adapting," at least.

And he didn't even hit the wall this time! Let's get it, Jerome!

[**Assess**] activating!

Integrated identified: **Undead [Animated Skeleton lv. 2] Nameless**

Strength contest initiated!

Strength contest won by [**Godkiller**] Jerome Smith!

Unarmed strike dealt 18 damage!

Strength contest initiated!

Strength contest won by [**Godkiller**] Jerome Smith!

Unarmed strike dealt 16 damage!

Enemy defeated! Experience rewarded!

Party Chat

[Jerome Smith]: I am getting an irritating amount of messages.

[Aster K'lon]: You learn to not allow them to distract you. It is a necessity in this world.

[Jerome Smith]: So there's no option to, like, ignore them?

[Aster K'lon]: There is, but it is not worth it. You will surely lose valuable information if you choose to ignore all your System notifications.

[Jerome Smith]: Ugh, okay.

P-System Log

There's an option to turn them off? I mean, not that I'm going to use it, but damn. That would've been nice to know.

Private Message [Aster]

[Aster K'lon]: You seem to not have performed any unique actions while in the S'ker dungeon. Why is that? When we were in easier encounters, Jerome gained skills, but here you have yet to take a special action.

[P-System]: So far, it has been unnecessary.

[Aster K'lon]: Could I request for you to do so? Witnessing your special capabilities is crucial to my understanding of you two godsent beings and how you can assist us in our crusade against the Eternal King's relentless onslaught.

[P-System]: I am unsure what you request.

[Aster K'lon]: The matter is simple. Jerome Smith, **[Godkiller]**, is indeed currently advancing at a rate far greater than those around us. Soon enough, he will surpass me in raw power if not overall ability. However, despite all of this, he does not advance fast *enough*.

[**P-System**]: What are you saying?

[**Aster K'lon**]: Jerome Smith may be the one whom we need to slay the Eternal King. The Eternal King, however, has a level far greater than one hundred, possibly even reaching one thousand, and it has more [**Unique**] skills than most people have skills overall. I do not exaggerate when I say that apart from the gods, it is by far the strongest being to have ever walked the Continent. Jerome needs to stack up to it.

P-System Log

She makes a decent point, not gonna lie. Jerome is decently strong, but we've been blasting through baby-ass dungeons so far. Nothing has actually threatened Jerome, so I have no idea what it'll be like if he fights against someone stronger.

. . . then again, it's not like it was *me* choosing to go into these baby dungeons, huh? It's not my fault Jerome hasn't had a real challenge—R Beasts excluded, maybe—since we spawned in here.

Private Message [Aster]

[**P-System**]: Jerome has been insufficiently challenged by this dungeon. He has been insufficiently challenged by many of his enemies so far. The only reason I have intervened so far is because of his stupidity, not because his enemies lacked power.

[**Aster K'lon**]: I suppose that's true. We can go to the [**Rare**] system next, then.

[**P-System**]: The [**Rare**] ones? That would be skipping a step, correct?

[**Aster K'lon**]: Correct. You made me realize that I have been treating Jerome far too much like an ordinary reincarnator, one with great prowess but not this level of . . .

[**P-System**]: Cheats? Blatant favoritism?

[**Aster K'lon**]: Increased skills.

[**P-System**]: Sure.

[**Aster K'lon**]: At any rate, he seems to be breezing through this dungeon as well. I doubt he will have too much trouble with it.

Party Chat

[**Jerome Smith**]: Huh, the monsters left in the maze are gone.

[**Aster K'lon**]: The Dungeon Core likely absorbed them for power. This would enable it to face you against a stronger being later in the dungeon, since these smaller mobs are clearly not even a distraction for you.

[**Jerome Smith**]: They are pretty weak, come to think of it.

[**Aster K'lon**]: In some cases, Dungeon Cores are intelligent enough to choose to redirect their resources.

[**Jerome Smith**]: And this is one of those cases?

[**Aster K'lon**]: It would appear that it is.

Private Message [Aster]

[**Aster K'lon**]: It would appear that you may be getting your wish sooner than you thought. The Dungeon Core's boss is sure to be stronger than it is normally.

[**P-System**]: I see.

P-System Log

Dammit, that shit better get the W Inertia expended by the Dungeon Core . . . Losing enemies here means losing a pretty free XP farm.
Ah, well. Nothing I can do about it.
Jerome is just about done with the maze, too. Looks like—

Party Chat

[**Jerome Smith**]: Shit!

[**Aster K'lon**]: You hit the spike trap twice before! Be more careful!

[**Jerome Smith**]: I didn't take any damage from it this time, right? It's fiiiiiine.

[**Aster K'lon**]: You were moments away from taking another fifty or so damage. If you were a weaker adventurer, you might be dead already.

[**Jerome Smith**]: But I'm not a weaker adventurer. I *am* that guy.

[**Aster K'lon**]: . . .

[**Jerome Smith**]: Right. Not someone who gets Earth references. Anyway, the point is that I'm strong enough to handle it, so don't worry about it.

[**Aster K'lon**]: If you say so. Don't die.

[**Jerome Smith**]: No worries. I won't.

Hero's Personal Log 068

I won't die, right?

P-System Message

Response: That's up to you, [**Godkiller**].

Hero's Personal Log 069

First of all, nice.
Second, ugh, I guess that's fine. I'm strong enough on my own, and I've got you to handle any edge cases as well.

P-System Log

heheheh Nice
Also! Jerome managed to say something about me that wasn't 100 percent negative! Let's fucking go!
Next room! Or the passageway to the next room, at least!

Party Chat

[**Aster K'lon**]: There are nonzero odds that the next room is also empty. The [**Common**] dungeons in S'ker all largely follow the same, generally linear design, which means that absorbing material from any given room will result in an empty path.

[Jerome Smith]: You think the Dungeon Core is going to reabsorb all of its monsters?

[Aster K'lon]: It may give you a nonmonster challenge. I believe it will still attempt to challenge you, as Dungeon Cores often possess the tendency to do so, but I doubt that it will spawn more monsters to fight you prior to the boss room.

[Jerome Smith]: Saving its energy, huh?

[Aster K'lon]: Correct.

[Jerome Smith]: Alright, I'm kicking down the door.

P-System Log

Oh, this room is actually kind of nice. It's kind of set up like a library, complete with a whole lot of bookshelves, and with it comes a nice set of couches and tables. Reminds me of my high school library, not gonna lie, and I always enjoyed that place.

Not that this is a real library. I don't have a perfect sense of what's in the books, since I can't read between the pages even with my perception dome, but I'm pretty sure that there're, like, no pages within those books. At the very least, the shape isn't exactly like they're real books. More of a facade to make it look like it's a well-stocked library than anything else.

Which probably means . . .

Party Chat

[Jerome Smith]: Huh. Neat. Is this a loot room?

[Aster K'lon]: Potentially. However, even in a **[Common]** dungeon, there may be traps or other detriments to you.

[Jerome Smith]: I see.

P-System Log

Ah, it's not trapped, but the exit is locked. I don't think there's any loot in here—at least, nothing that emits W Inertia or mana—so I'm just gonna skip the bullshit and find the way out.

I can see inside some of the books, since a decent chunk of them have been hollowed out and had stuff put inside them. It looks like the whole gimmick of this room is having a thousand or so keys, and then the people here need to find which key works for the lock?

Fuck that. I can see the lock, and I can see the inner workings of it. I had a phase where I got super, super into lock picking, so I think I can figure it out.

Thanks, Origin! I actually got a useful thing from you! Increased mental processing is real nice when I'm doing something that would normally be this tedious.

Okay, found it.

P-System Message

The challenge in this room is a locked door. Books contain keys. The key to your door is located in the reddish brown–colored bookshelf, third row from the bottom, fourth book from the left.

Key accepted!

Party Chat

[**Jerome Smith**]: Well, that was easy. Thanks, System.

[**Aster K'lon**]: Your System assisted you?

[**Jerome Smith**]: Yes, it did.

[**Aster K'lon**]: Excellent. Then there's only one room left.

P-System Log

One more room. Let's see how this goes.

Party Chat

[**Aster K'lon**]: That is far stronger than it has any right to be. This will need to be reported.

[**Jerome Smith**]: What the hell is it? I can only kind of see it.

[**Assess**] activating!

Integrated identified: **Gelatinous Ooze [Gelatin lv. 15] Adventurer-Eater**

CHAPTER 38

Huh, this one's actually got a name. A fair bit better than the previous bosses we faced, what with their DUNGEON_BOSS_NAMEs.

The name kind of sucks, but that's besides the point. The point is that Jerome has a boss fight to get through!

And it's looking like a doozy of one. The room we just entered looks pretty peculiar. If I had to chance a guess, I'd say that this place was made specifically for this boss. It's got some weird geometry, with stalactites and stalagmites coming from the ceiling and the floor as well as a lot of artificial stone obstructions and assorted obstacles—statues, poles, random crap that makes this place look like some caveman's antique store—that makes it hard to navigate this place on foot. The [**Gelatin**], though, seems to have no problems with it. That shit is just oozing around and through everything. It's literally just taking up space.

If it works anything like the Gelatinous Cubes from D&D, then its primary method of attack should just be rolling over Jerome. I wonder if he knows that.

I'm not going to say anything, though. I'm not going to trouble myself any more than necessary to figure out what it can do, and I'm not going to look stupid by telling Jerome the wrong thing. If he actually needs it, I'll toss him a bone and do my advanced pseudo-[**Assess**] to figure out what it can do, but I'm more than content to just let him do his thing for the time being.

Overcharged [**Misty Strike**] activating!

Passive [**Amorphous Body**] triggered!

[**Misty Strike**] dealt 41 damage!

[**Engulf**] cast!

P-System Log

Jerome, you fucking idiot.

Okay, maybe not that much of an idiot. If he's going off the D&D statblock, then I'm pretty sure it never mentioned anything about Gelatinous Cubes—which are the closest monster to whatever this [**Gelatin**] is—having the ability to lower the damage of striking attacks.

But this isn't D&D, and he should know that! For fuck's sake, it's not like we've been facing one-to-one replicas of Forgotten Realms so far! Just because this place has a similar roll-for-damage system doesn't mean that its monsters are lifted straight from the game, *Jerome*!

Actually, on second thought, I doubt he thought that far ahead. I'm pretty sure he just took his strongest skill and went for it.

Hero's Personal Log 070

Fuck! I thought slimes weren't resistant to slashing attacks, which I'm pretty sure [**Misty Strike**] is. Gotta know that for the future. [**Magic Missile**] wasn't a great choice, because that skill isn't going anywhere, and [**Blazing Spear**] felt too risky to use in such an enclosed space.

P-System Log

Never mind. He at least used some level of critical thinking. Color me surprised.

Hero's Personal Log 071

Also, uh, System, is there any way you can get me out of here?

Passive [**Acidic Body**] triggered!

[**Acidic Body**] dealt 71 damage to you!

P-System Log

Oh, shit.
That's a lot of damage.

Hero's Personal Log 072

Please?

P-System Log

It's times like these that make me real grateful for my increased perception ability. This is, to put it lightly, a rather suboptimal situation.

Alright. I can perceive the ooze's body all around Jerome. The [**Engulf**] skill just up and sucked him into the ooze, and now he's stuck somewhere inside it. It's dealing acid damage to him just by virtue of him being there, and it's dealing a *lot*. Like, almost-as-much-as-those-R-Beasts a lot. If this keeps up for even another minute, I'm pretty sure Jerome is just going to die. Can't have that.

From the outside, Aster doesn't seem like she's helping. I have a sneaking suspicion that she won't help until Jerome is literally moments away from dying. Stupid of me, to reveal that I wasn't taking things as seriously because Jerome's life was never in real danger.

Come to think of it, I don't know what happens when HP hits zero. Does the person just die? Or does the shield that the Origin System provides just wear off, leaving them to be a completely normal human?

Okay, that's not the point right now. The point is that Jerome is getting fucking destroyed, and I need to stop that ASAP.

Alright, there's a number of ways I can tackle this. They can primarily be split into two categories—offensive and defensive. The former would be used to break out of this situation, the latter to prevent Jerome from dying because of it.

What do I want to give him? I have to admit that seeing Jerome use the same skills over and over is getting a little boring, so it might be nice to mix things up a little. Still, for what a shithead he's been so far, I don't want to just hand him everything on a silver platter.

Passive [**Acidic Body**] triggered!

[**Acidic Body**] dealt 67 damage to you!

Hero's Personal Log 073

Sorry I talked shit about you, System. Could you please give me a hand here? I swear I'll work with you better in the future.

Ah, fuck, look at me, trying to reason with an AI. It probably doesn't give a shit.

[**Misty Strike**] activating!

Passive [**Amorphous Body**] triggered!

Passive [**Gelatinous Body**] triggered!

[**Misty Strike**] dealt 31 damage!

P-System Log

Huh, Jerome barely went anywhere with that skill. Usually, he basically disappears with how fast he's going. This time, though, he just moved forward awfully slow for like five feet before stopping. Interesting skill interaction.

That's besides the point, though. Jerome is dying, and more importantly, he actually apologized! Sure, it's definitely because he's under duress, but it's definitely *something*.

Y'know what? I'm feeling generous today. Jerome is going to get a fair bit of W Inertia invested into him for the purpose of Not Dying Just Yet. Here we go!

I think I should focus on defensive utility for now.

Oh, wait. I should probably keep him from panicking any further.

P-System Message

Request acknowledged. Employing methods to ensure survival.

P-System Log

Alright, now that that's sorted . . .

Defensive utility. Since **[Resistance]**-type skills are a thing that exists here, and specifically things that I've actually observed before, I'm going to go for one of those. Not quite sure how exactly to execute it, though . . . maybe I focus on the acid?

I can replicate the acid now that I've perceived it for long enough, I'm pretty sure. My unique traits as a System mean that I can track all its properties down to the molecular level, though my innate skills are enough that I don't need to bother with the deep specifics on that level, but I do have that knowledge if it comes down to it.

If I structure W Inertia around that, focusing on the properties of the acid and reversing said properties, and I do it in that same way that I've been using to establish new skills . . .

New skill unlocked: **[Acid Resistance]**

Decreases damage dealt to you by acid by 5%.

Passive **[Acidic Body]** triggered!

[Acidic Body] dealt 60 damage to you!

Jerome Smith (abbreviated)

Stat	Current	Maximum
Health	69	562

P-System Log

Okay, yeah, that's really bad. [**Acid Resistance**] lowered the amount of damage Jerome just took, but it didn't lower it nearly enough. If he takes one or two more hits, it's over.

Alright, I've spent less than ten W Inertia so far, but Jerome needs to survive. I don't want to think about what'll happen if he doesn't. Time to pull out the big guns.

I'm going to spend a thousand W Inertia. It's way more than I should be comfortable spending, but desperate times, desperate measures. Can't have Jerome dying on me, and there's no point in saving W Inertia if I'm dead with him. That'd be an awfully embarrassing way to go. *Died of being too stingy with XP.*

. . . huh, I feel really calm for being in a life-threatening situation. That feels wrong, somehow, but it's not something I need to address right now.

One thousand W Inertia. Here we go.

Skill leveled up! [**Acid Resistance**] lv. 1 -> lv. ???

<ERROR>

Skill evolution! [**Acid Resistance**] -> [**Greater Acid Resistance**]

Sharply increases resistance level.

Skill evolution! [**Greater Acid Resistance**] -> [**Superior Acid Resistance**]

Sharply increases resistance level.

Skill evolution! [**Superior Acid Resistance**] -> [**Lesser Acid Immunity**]

User takes no damage from lesser acid attacks. Sharply increases resistance level.

Skill evolution! [**Lesser Acid Immunity**] -> [**Acid Immunity**]

User takes no damage from acid attacks.

P-System Log

Well, shit, that's something. Go me?

CHAPTER 39

Passive [**Acidic Body**] triggered!

Your passive [**Acid Immunity**] was triggered!

[**Acidic Body**] dealt 0 damage to you!

P-System Log

Holy shit, it worked. I'm so fucking cool.

So that's the power of a thousand W Inertia. Roughly ten thousand XP, unless there's a bonus to delivering it all at once. That feels . . . too low. Just based off how these things tend to go, I feel like skills would evolve at some multiple of ten—ten, fifty, or one hundred, most likely. Each time a skill levels up, though, the amount of XP it needs to hit the next level also increases. If I assume it's the lowest possible number of levels to evolve— that's ten—then I would've needed at least forty levels. I don't know how much W Inertia [**Acid Resistance**] needed, but even if it only need one hundred at first and its cost increased by one hundred per level, I definitely wouldn't have been able to afford forty levels' worth of it.

The first screen that popped up had an error message. Maybe that has something to do with it? I dunno. I think I'll accept that as my explanation for now and just take the W.

And what a massive W that is. Like, holy shit, I just created a [**Legendary**] skill from a [**Common**] one in moments. That's pretty neat. Sure, it took me a whole thousand W Inertia to do (and probably should've taken me more), but I think it was at least somewhat worth it. I mean, I've still got, what, thirty-seven thousand W Inertia left? I'm in no risk of running out of it, and I just saved Jerome's life. Probably saved myself by proxy.

Hero's Personal Log 074

Jesus fucking Christ, thank you. That was actually insane. Are you cheating? Don't answer that. I don't need to know.

I know I'm asking a lot, but can you help me get out of here as well?

P-System Message

Acknowledged.

P-System Log

Dang, Jerome not being an ass? That's new. I guess it comes with the territory of definitively knowing that he would be dead if I hadn't acted there.

Anyway, that was fun. Making a new skill and leveling it, I mean. Sure, it means that I got way farther from overflow and therefore farther from leveling [W%M; G, P], but I can deal with that. It's not like we're short on monsters for Jerome to kill.

Besides, it's about time he got a new skill. His fights are getting a little one-note.

I'm not sure what kind of skill I want to give him. There's a world of things I could focus on, from memorized mana sequences to the properties of the dirt in this room, and the variety of choices is honestly kind of dizzying. Far too much for me to just decide randomly.

Wait, I have a special ability for this. One that's always been hard for me to invoke, both in this life and the last, but one I've been increasingly more willing to use.

That's right! I'm going to ask him a question!

P-System Message

Query: What kind of skill do you wish to receive?

Hero's Personal Log 075

Hmm . . . that's a tough one. I don't think I'm taking any damage, and either I don't need to breathe at all or this slime is breathable, because I'm not having any issues with that, which is a whole issue in itself, but I'm not going to get into that right now and—

Sorry. I'm gonna cut myself off there. I was rambling. Anyway, I'm not taking damage right now. That means I've got some time to think, right?

P-System Message

Affirmative.

Hero's Personal Log 076

Can I get something to liquefy the slime, maybe?

P-System Message

Due to the nature of the Health stat, feats such as partial destruction of enemies or conversion into other states of matter are not possible.

Hero's Personal Log 077

Ah, okay. I guess that makes sense.

Maybe an explosion or something? Something with enough kinetic energy to move this thing. Either that or some form of teleportation, maybe, since there's a possibility an explosion might just get absorbed by this stupid fuckin' thing's passives.

But explosions are fun. I like explosions.

P-System Log

Explosions and teleportation, huh? I can definitely try something like that.

P-System Message

Acknowledged.

Party Chat

[**Aster K'lon**]: Are you alright in there? I saw that your HP had dipped quite low, but I refrained from intervening because I sensed the creation of powerful new skills from your System.

[**Jerome Smith**]: I gained [**Acid Immunity**]. I'm working with my System to get a new skill to get me out of here.

[**Aster K'lon**]: I do believe I told you that your System was strong.

[**Jerome Smith**]: You did.

[**Aster K'lon**]: Very well. Use this channel if you are in desperate need of help and your System is unable to assist you.

[**Jerome Smith**]: Yeah, got it.

Private Message [Aster]

[**Aster K'lon**]: I see you found a threatening enough situation to act in.

[**P-System**]: Did you influence this?

[**Aster K'lon**]: I did not. Of course, the choice to go to the dungeon was inspired by my decisions, but the existence of a boss in a [**Common**] dungeon with a rarity and level this high is not one that should ever occur. I must report it to the Dungeon Corps after this.

P-System Log

Hold on, Dungeon Corps? I guess that's either a subset of the Adventurer's Guild or a different, related group that solely tackles dungeons. Still, that name . . . whoever designed that org has got to be a big pun guy. Dungeon Corps for Dungeon Cores, huh?

Anyway, that's besides the point. I have a skill to create, after all.

He wanted explosions and teleportation. I think I can bastardize teleportation out of the steps that Aster took to use [**Cloud Step**], but explosions might be a little harder. [**Blazing Spear**] is less TNT and more match-and-gasoline, and [**Magic Missile**] is pretty much pure mana.

In that case . . .

Time to utilize that dangerous skill of mine again.

Private Message [Aster]

[**P-System**]: Request. Please cast a skill that can create an explosion.

[**Aster K'lon**]: An explosion? I shall, but an explanation is much needed.

[**P-System**]: It is for the purpose of forming a skill.

[**Aster K'lon**]: How intriguing. I shall cast, then.

Undercharged [**Delayed Detonating Death**] cast!

P-System Log

Now if that isn't a chunibyo name. Wow. Who the hell names these skills? I mean, I guess the alliteration is neat, but that name is weird as shit when most of the other skill names have been relatively normal.

Whatever. The important part of the skill here is the spell itself. Looks like a magic hand grenade, basically. Aster just threw a ball of mana—undercharged somehow; I'll have to ask how she managed that—into the air, and it's just hovering there for now.

. . . and there it goes. Its detonation is pretty different from the other skills I've seen before. Kind of like a fireball, really. Actually, I probably should've asked to see if she had a fireball spell. That probably would've worked just as well, and I'm sure every fantasy world worth its salt has a fireball skill of some kind.

Eh. I got the data I needed. The feel of the mana, the elements of the explosion itself, its intensity . . . yep, we're good.

Combine that with the movement aspects of [**Cloud Step**], removing the weird cloudy part that I accidentally used to create [**Misty Strike**], and hopefully we get a usable skill. This is only my second time experimenting with something that isn't a one-to-one copy of another skill, but this feels a lot more natural than the copying did for some reason.

Still, I don't think I have it perfect yet. I'm pretty sure there's a decent shot at getting another skill that I wasn't aiming for, just like how I fucked up getting [**Cloud Step**]. That's fine. As long as I don't eat up too much W Inertia and the skill is good enough to get Jerome out of his current bind, we're chilling.

Here goes nothing.

[W%M; G, P]

<ERROR: No existing skill matches parameters>

Compensating . . .

New skill created!

New skill unlocked: [**Explosive Teleport**]

Detonate and reappear a short distance away.

P-System Log

Huh. Damn, I wasn't expecting that to work. It looks like my [**Unique**] skill played a pretty big role in that one. I mean, I'll take it, but I have to say it's a little cre—

P-System Log

Glad the Origin System could help me there.
. . . I feel a little weird. Wonder what that's about?
Anyway, new skill!

P-System Message

Request has been satisfied.

Current W Inertia: 37,125

P-System Log

Damn, that took a decent bit. More than a hundred, I'm pretty sure. I wonder how good the skill is?

[Misty Strike lv. 1]

Stat	Value
XP	0/300
Damage	10d6+8 / distance from target
Mana Cost	30
Overcharge Multiplier (max)	1.5
Cost Multiplier	15%
Range	5 meters
<HIDDEN>	<HIDDEN>

[Explosive Teleport] activating!

Passive **[Amorphous Body]** triggered!

[Explosive Teleport] dealt 32 damage!

Party Chat

[Aster K'lon]: Ah, you made it out. Congratulations.

[Aster K'lon]: Use **[Blazing Spear]**. That skill will not inflict friendly fire in a space this large, and this monster is exceptionally weak to fire. If my memory serves me correctly, the reason is because its **[Gelatinous Body]** is comprised of flammable materials.

[Jerome Smith]: Got it.

Overcharged **[Blazing Spear]** activating!

[Blazing Spear] dealt 126 damage!

Enemy defeated! Experience rewarded!

CHAPTER 40

South S'ker 3 Dungeon System

Dungeon cleared!

P-System Log

Holy fucking balls, that did a lot of damage. That boss had to have been, like, critically weak to fire. Damn.

And I think I got a fair amount of W Inertia. Nowhere near the amount I spent, but the boss gave a lot more than any monster did. It gave over four hundred, which is *insanely* high compared to everything I've gotten so far. Something to keep in mind. Killing dungeon bosses is profitable. I also got . . . a hundredish from the dungeon.

When I'm not breaking reality and pulling broken new skills out of my ass to keep Jerome alive, that is. As it is, I've lost around five or six hundred W Inertia even after factoring in the gain from the boss and dungeon, so I'm pretty deep in the hole. It'll take a while to regain all of that, so I guess that means more dungeons?

Whatever the case, it looks like Jerome is done for the day.

Party Chat

[Jerome Smith]: I think I'm done. HP is low, mana is low, and I've got new skills but still nothing for regeneration of either.

[Aster K'lon]: Perhaps your System could help.

[Jerome Smith]: Maybe. I feel like it should have some sort of cooldown. I'll ask, but I'm not going to expect an answer.

[Aster K'lon]: At any rate, I believe it is wise to return to the inn after we collect the drops. A night of rest will restore your mana and HP as surely as any skill can.

[Jerome Smith]: Sure. Let's get back.

P-System Log

Just like in the last few dungeons we've been in, a brand-new hole just opened up in the back of the dungeon. This Dungeon Core seems to be a known establishment, and I guess Aster doesn't think this deviation is far away enough from the norm or lethal enough to warrant the destruction of the place, so we're just moving on.

Well, it's either that or the bureaucracy of the Dungeon Corps (god, that name is so brilliantly stupid) has some regulations here that don't allow her to kill it. Either way, looks like we're just getting out of here.

Hero's Personal Log 078

Hey, System? I know I've been a bit of a dick. Okay, that's not right, I've been a lot of a dick. I have problems with that. Sorry.

I don't even know if you can understand what I'm saying. It's not like I have any proof that you're more intelligent than a basic chat bot. Whatever.

I know I'm asking a lot. Can I have a mana regeneration skill? Or a health one? I know they're locked, but . . . you have special powers.

P-System Log

I do kind of want to give him a regeneration skill. I don't know how much W Inertia it would take from my end, but the benefits of it are undeniable. If he gets HP regeneration, then it's harder to take him down. Ergo, his ability to remain confident in his current health stays for longer, which ultimately results in him fighting for a longer period of time. The same goes for mana regeneration, but that also enables him to cast more skills and thus kill more monsters.

Basically, the benefit for both is that he can fight longer, which is nice because it's both pretty fun to watch and it ends up giving me W Inertia in return. In essence, it's an investment.

The issue is, I don't know how much I'm paying for said investment, and I don't have hard numbers on the returns it might end up giving me. From what I know of Jerome, I'm pretty sure that he'll be more willing to fight more if he's given more resources, but I can't say that for sure.

Eh. Yeah, I'll go for it.

P-System Message

Request acknowledged.

Private Message [Aster]

[**P-System**]: I am going to attempt to grant Jerome a mana regeneration skill.

[**Aster K'lon**]: Very well. I was wondering when you were going to ask.

[**P-System**]: Query. You have increased mana regeneration?

[**Aster K'lon**]: Correct. Thanks to the [**Mage**] line as well as years of experience, I have a number of exclusive skills, both passive and active. Among them is [**Accelerated Mana Regeneration**], a skill that is rather unique in being both passive and active. I have greater passive mana regeneration as well as the ability to rapidly gain mana once every several hours.

[**P-System**]: Request. Use the skill.

[**Aster K'lon**]: I will.

[**Aster K'lon**]: I have used it. I recovered ninety-eight mana.

P-System Log

Huh. I didn't see an activation message for that skill. I guess it's a hidden skill, just like [**Mana Sense**]? Annoying, but there's not really anything else it could be.

Still, I did see some of what she did. Normally, the skills activate through the use of mana. I've been copying or modifying the mana patterns of the shit I observe, but that . . . that wasn't mana. I think it might've been W Inertia that she was using, and at some point that W Inertia disappeared and turned into mana. I think. I'm not sure if I 100 percent followed what just happened, but I'm pretty sure that's about what it was.

Alright, that's certainly unique. I don't know if I can actually pick up that skill, since nothing I've done so far has been anything quite like it. Then again, I didn't think I could create skills without something to copy, and I just did that pretty casually not once but two times just now.

It's worth a shot.

I'll budget . . . twenty? Twenty seems fair for a start. It's been a long day, and I don't want to accidentally fuck up and lose way more W Inertia than I need.

Here we go. Mimicking doesn't feel *quite* right, but I can manage. Just match the pattern of W Inertia that Aster used . . .

[W%M; G, P]

ADMIN TIER: 0

Access credentials insufficient. Class lock remains in effect.

Skill creation denied.

P-System Log

Well, shit. I guess the class-exclusive skills really are exclusive. Okay, that should have been obvious from the title, but for it to be even to the point of denying me from fucking around with it is pretty interesting. That means that health regen probably also isn't doable, right? Not until I put a lot more W Inertia into my **[Unique]** skill, at the very least. I think that's the only way I can up this Admin Tier bullshit that it keeps telling me about.

Oh, right. I should probably inform Jerome.

P-System Message

Skill class lock caused skill creation to fail. Circumventing class lock requires significantly higher XP.

Hero's Personal Log 079

Ah, that sucks. That's fine, it was just wishful thinking. I'm just gonna get to the inn and rest, then. That should restore it.

Oh, speaking of XP. Did I get any from the fight?

P-System Log

He's actually being *nice*. This is such a departure from the Jerome that I know and tolerate that I'm not actually sure what I'm supposed to do. I don't even have any sass to throw at him. Did saving his life really have that much of an effect on him? It was just practical.

Then again, my perspective is pretty different. I'm literally a disembodied voice that can only communicate through fuckin' status screens. I'll chalk it up to that.

Also, there is no way in hell I'm giving him any XP. I just spent like twelve hundred or something W Inertia on his skills just to ensure he made it out of that last fight alive. He doesn't get to double dip off that.

At least he asked.

P-System Message

Skill creation consumed XP. Gains used to replace lost XP.

Value remains unchanged.

Hero's Personal Log 080

Yeah, I figured. Getting handed an immunity right off the bat is a little crazy, not gonna lie. That plus a new offensive spell that I totally still need to try out . . . yeah. Makes sense why I can't afford to gain XP now.

Oh, well. We're hitting harder dungeons later, anyway.

P-System Log

And that's that. I guess we're heading back to the inn now. We're out of the dungeon now. Aster stopped to talk to some official-looking guy— probably to report the abnormality we faced in there—and then we got on our way again.

S'ker has a nightlife. I noticed it on our way in, but it's even more apparent now. Even though it's clearly well past nightfall—past midnight, too, maybe? I'm not totally sure how long we were in there—there's a whole load of people walking the streets. I'm taking glances at them as they walk by, and it's really interesting seeing who populates this town. There's the normal D&D races like elves, dwarves, halflings, yeah, but then there's a whole bunch of others. Ones that have skin that looks like it was made of tree bark, people with horns and wings and too many arms, and so many more.

I want to explore this world. Discover the meaning and powers of every last one of these types of people.

But that's an issue for later. For now, we've returned to the inn. Jerome's flopped into the bed already—huh, there's only one. Aster really has no qualms about this kind of thing—and Aster's sitting on the floor with a few books out.

For now, we rest.

CHAPTER 41

P-System Log

That was a pretty uneventful night. I read some of the books—Aster was kind enough to use some sort of skill to flip the pages automatically after she went to bed. I also looked over the loot we got. It's a decent assortment of stuff, though none of it seems to be particularly useful. Way better than the garbage from the other dungeons we ran, but it's still a [**Common**] dungeon in the end. We got some [**Currency**], I'm pretty sure, though Aster already absorbed all of it, and a few assorted weapons. I think Aster calls them artifacts? That seems to be her general name for dungeon loot.

Jerome fell asleep almost instantly after we got back, so we didn't really have an opportunity to test what they do, but I doubt they're anything special. [**Dagger of Lesser Frost**], [**Impact Hammer**], and [**Rainbow Medallion**]. The third one might've seemed promising, but the amount of W Inertia and mana coming out of that one was positively minuscule even in comparison to the two [**Common**] items.

Well, Jerome's awake now, so he might try it out, but I don't have high hopes for it. Aster left the inn a while ago and took the loot, so it looks like it's definitely a no on checking those out. I didn't want to waste even more W Inertia on identifying those items further, so I guess I'll just never figure out what they do. Oh, well. I can make skills that do them better.

Party Chat

[**Jerome Smith**]: Where did you go?

[**Aster K'lon**]: You were still asleep?

[**Aster K'lon**]: I took the physical drops to the market. With loot this low-tier, there's no point in attempting to use it. It would be useful for a true beginner's party. S'ker natives with [**Common**] classes might appreciate something like this. However, at our level, they are worth little more than the monetary gain we can extract from them.

[Jerome Smith]: Huh. Alright, that makes sense. Did any of them have any useful attributes? I'm just curious.

[Aster K'lon]: Not particularly. I'm not sure what **[Impact Hammer]** did since I've only ever seen it in children's toy shops, but a **[Dagger of Lesser Frost]** is a simple damaging weapon. It adds around a 1R6 to 3R8 frost damage modifier to a knife strike, but it heavily skews toward lower damage. Since neither of us are melee attackers, we do not need it. **[Rainbow Medallion]** is a way to change the type of damage that a skill does. However, it requires around a quarter of the mana invested into the original skill. It also starts to fail on higher-level attacks. Potentially useful, but I have better artifacts already.

[Jerome Smith]: Cool. We're hitting up a **[Rare]** dungeon today, right? That should get us some better loot.

[Aster K'lon]: We shall. Depending on the circumstances, we may need to group with another party in order to meet the minimum WPA.

[Jerome Smith]: It's that much harder?

[Aster K'lon]: It is.

[Aster K'lon]: I will return. For the time being, I must continue this sale.

Hero's Personal Log 081

Hey, while we've got time, could I request a new skill?

P-System Log

As much as he's gotten a little politer, he's still the same unnecessarily needy Jerome as ever. I'd be more irritated if he was a little ruder, but I'll let it pass. *This time.*

I'm not going to spend any significant amount of W Inertia on him. I don't regret spending so much to keep him alive, but I don't have any left to spare. No new disgustingly powerful skills for him!

I *am* willing to experiment with stupid shit, though. I'm bored, and I'm pretty sure Jerome isn't going to go anywhere without Aster. Burning a few W Inertia in an effort to pass the time isn't too bad.

P-System Message

Limited resources available. Only [**Common**] skills are accessible.

Hero's Personal Log 082

Yeah, that makes sense. I would guess that the [**Legendary**] skill took a lot of . . . whatever Systems use to run themselves. XP? Whatever. I bet that took a lot of whatever resource it is.

[**Common**] is fine. I just want more abilities. How about . . . a [**Resistance**] skill for fire. Can we do one of those?

P-System Log

Hmm. There's a fire in this room, set into a little pit in the middle of the room. It's got a chimney above it, but my senses tell me that it doesn't actually have an opening. Some magical thing, I think—a passive skill installed into a piece of the chimney that absorbs the smoke. Neat.

Whatever. The important part is the fire and its associated properties. Now that I have some experience creating a skill out of nothing, I think I've got this. I don't think I even need ten W Inertia to make a basic resistance skill.

Here we go! I take the properties of the fire, invert them with my epic System mind, fuck around with the laws of physics, and toss a dash of W Inertia onto it to top it all off!

New skill unlocked: [**Fire Resistance**]

Decreases damage dealt to you by fire by 5%.

Hero's Personal Log 083

Oh, shit, all I had to do was ask? Damn. Let me test this out . . .

Fire dealt 3 damage to you!

P-System Log

Dammit, Jerome.

You managed to make it so far! I almost thought you were a functional human being, and then you go and stick your fucking face in the room's fire?

Well, I guess he's not actually feeling the pain.

Huh, come to think of it, the Health system in this world means that kids are able to be a lot more stupid, doesn't it?

At least he's not coming close to killing himself. I was wondering if I could copy the process of regeneration, but try as I might, trying to copy last night's natural passive regeneration produced nothing more than continued access issues. Looks like I really can't copy it, though the process did still end up fully healing Jerome by the time the night was through.

Oh, hey, Aster's back.

Party Chat

[**Aster K'lon**]: I found a pair of adventurers who are willing to temporarily link parties with us.

[**Jerome Smith**]: Are we not going to be able to tackle it ourselves?

[**Aster K'lon**]: While I was out, I went to the Dungeon Corps. I found that our WPA was not high enough for the [**Rare**] dungeon, but it would be with another pair. As such, they will be meeting with us soon to prepare for the dungeon.

[**Jerome Smith**]: Great.

[**Aster K'lon**]: I also successfully sold all three items for prices that were quite high.

[**Jerome Smith**]: Oh, okay, that's good.

P-System Log

Wasn't Jerome from some rich-ass family? That kind of explains why he has literally zero regard for the value of money. I don't know how much we have or what qualifies as a good amount in this world, but I guess as long as Aster isn't worried about affording food and board, it's not an issue.

I wonder who the adventurers are.

P-System Log

HAHAHAHAHA WHAT ARE THE CHANCES .

We just met the adventurers. After dawdling for a while longer and eating a breakfast (damn, I kind of miss eating), Jerome and Aster set off to the southeast dungeon system. We haven't checked into the official building—which is a little nicer than the [**Common**] dungeon's facilities, I have to say—but we finally met with the people who're going to be working with us.

Here's a rough translation of them talking to Aster:

Elf Lady: You have to be fucking kidding me.

Dwarf Man: Are you serious?

And then they glanced at Jerome all annoyed, and Aster was like "oh."

P-System Log

It's been like five minutes now, and Aster has somehow convinced them to come with us. I swear, she's got some magic ability that lets her handle social interactions better. I wish I could be her.

Welp. Here we are now. In a temporary party with the people Jerome knocked down and was accidentally rude to on our way into this city.

Party Chat

[**Arcs S'tar**]: You'll keep him from hitting us in the dungeon?

[**Thron of the Fallen Skies**]: Or casting skills the wrong way? He seems green.

[**Aster K'lon**]: You would be surprised.

[**Jerome Smith**]: I'm not that bad. Believe me.

[**Thron of the Fallen Skies**]: When I see it.

P-System Log

Huh, one of the dungeons of the system is closed. Something about "Core destruction" or the like. That's not ominous.

Thankfully, there's multiple dungeons in a given system! So we're on our way into the second dungeon in the southeastern S'ker dungeon system!

Jeez, that's a mouthful.

I'm excited, though. W Inertia, come my way! More bosses, more fighting, more of everything that makes this world interesting.

Southeast S'ker Dungeon System

Adventurers ride to the gate

Ready to meet their coming fates

Sword and shield, bow and spear

Who can fight their rising fear?

P-System Log

. . . that's new.

CHAPTER 42

<table>
<tr><td>

Party Chat

[Jerome Smith]: Does it always do this?

[Arcs S'tar]: Gods above, Aster, when you said he was dense, you weren't lying.

[Aster K'lon]: Give him some room for ignorance. He is, after all, freshly reincarnated.

[Thron of the Fallen Skies]: Ha! Probably a weakling yet!

[Aster K'lon]: Yes, Jerome, different dungeons will act differently. So far, we've only hit dungeons that are at the bare minimum level of existence. Here, though, they start gaining personalities. Minds of their own.

[Jerome Smith]: Interesting. Also, @Thron, I'm not weak. You'll see.

[Thron of the Fallen Skies]: What is that symbol?

[Arcs S'tar]: A reincarnator's language, perhaps.

[Jerome Smith]: Oh, I've been meaning to ask. Why do you all speak English?

[Aster K'lon]: It is believed that the process of reincarnation adjusts one's soul enough for reincarnators to understand Common. Worry not.

[Arcs S'tar]: He truly is an ignorant ass.

[Jerome Smith]: Do you *want* a fight?

[Arcs S'tar]: I could teach you a lesson in respect, if you'd like.

</td></tr>
</table>

P-System Log

As funny as it is watching them bicker, I do want to get into the dungeon at some point. I wonder if there's anything I can do to motivate them . . .

Nah. I'll just let it play out. Looks like they're actually moving forward through the entry room while chatting, so they are making progress of some sort, at least.

This dungeon's entry room looks nearly identical to the last one's, the sole notable difference being that this one has a distinctly blue hue to it, while the [**Common**] one was very clearly pure white.

The sign here is different as well, not just in content but presentation. It's a physical sign, just like the one before it, and it reads:

S'ker Dungeon of Devils

With Recommended Party Level:

Adventurers of 20-30 WPA

Else their fate is to be slain

Is this whole fucking place an exercise in shitty poetry? I mean, I have to admit it's kind of a neat gimmick, but it's really odd to see.

The WPA on this is way, way higher than the five to ten that was on the [**Common**] dungeon. I wonder if Jerome is going to struggle with this one. I mean, he has more people with him this time, and even though he did need a lot of help to clear the [**Common**] dungeon, that one was apparently anomalously over-upgraded specifically because his class was too strong for it. Maybe the combined effects of having more adventurers to even out the class rarity as well as not having the dungeon get harder abruptly will be enough for him to clear this one easily.

Or maybe he's going to need me to pull his ass out of the fire again. Who knows?

Whatever the case, we're entering the unsafe rooms now.

P-System Log [a different kind of dungeon]

This place is definitely different from the last few dungeons we've tackled. I mean, I intellectually knew that of course the [**Common**] Dungeon Cores wouldn't be able to match up against those that were two whole rarities higher than them, but being here is a completely different appearance. The design is different, yes, and the mana and W Inertia flows thicker here than in many places (including even other dungeons), but that's not the first thing I noticed.

No, the big standout is the *paths*. I have a perception dome that can cover a room, but my perception also extends beyond that dome. I only have a vague sense of what lies beyond, and the stuff that lies beyond the first room is mostly fuzzy to my senses, but I can still see ahead to some extent.

And what I see is an actual, proper dungeon. Something that you might find in a campaign handbook, one with twists and turns and dead ends and unique rooms—it's fantastic. For the first time, I feel like a proper adventurer. Never mind my lack of adventuring gear, experience, or, uh, a body. It feels like I'm properly playing something like D&D in real life, and though I know it's different here and I can't act like I'm just in a game, I can't deny feeling a little bit of childish glee at the prospect of clearing an actual cool dungeon like this.

I mean, come to think of it, I kind of am playing a game, aren't I? I don't have absolute control over my character, but I'm basically a third-person camera for Jerome. Heh.

Well, whatever. The entry room led into a hallway, one flanked by two ten-foot-tall statues tucked away into depressions carved into the walls. I can sense mana inside them, and they emit just the slightest bit of W Inertia. If those aren't traps or monsters, I will eat a hat. Like, find a hat and make a skill to allow me to eat said hat. I'll do it.

Party Chat

[**Arcs S'tar**]: I recognize the configuration, but it's not a repeat. Unfortunate.

[**Thron of the Fallen Skies**]: Mmm. I have yet to hit this exact permutation, either, but it does appear to be a central well type. The details will be evident once we advance farther.

[**Jerome Smith**]: You guys hit this place up a lot?

[**Thron of the Fallen Skies**]: Once every few days, weakling. I would not expect one so unused to hard work as you to understand our livelihoods.

[**Aster K'lon**]: Do not advance forth yet. The statues are primed with an offensive skill that will trigger once you pass.

[**Arcs S'tar**]: I knew that.

[**Jerome Smith**]: Oh, thanks.

> **P-System Log**
>
> Livelihoods, huh? I suppose that makes sense, for adventuring to be a proper job. I didn't really think that much about it before, but the presence of a guild does mean that it's an actual thing to do for a living. I just assumed it was something people always did on the side. Dumb of me, I guess.
>
> Aaaaaand Jerome's moving forward.

> [**Misty Strike**] activating!

> [**Proximity Trigger**] triggered!

> [**Ethereal Spear**] cast!

> [**Proximity Trigger**] triggered!

> [**Ethereal Spear**] cast!

> **P-System Log**
>
> No hat eating for me. Jerome just used his skill to dash past the statues, and sure enough, they did have a skill embedded in them. As far as I know, Aster hasn't run this dungeon before, so I guess she just spotted it with her [**Mana Sense**]. Handy skill to have. I'm glad I have my own version of that, at least, since it looks like I can't unlock class-locked skills otherwise.
>
> Anyway, it looks like that was a one-shot skill. The mana's been expended in the form of a blindingly white spear that shot straight into the wall. Both spears are long enough to run the width of the dungeon hallway, and from the feel of it, they would cause damage if you ran into them sidelong, but they're fading now.
>
> I can't believe it. Jerome actually used his brain to figure out a strat that could safely clear the trap. Is this the same Jerome Smith I was initially attached to? I have to say, almost dying did wonders for his character.

P-System Log

[**Arcs S'tar**]: The reincarnator can access an [**Epic**] skill?

[**Aster K'lon**]: Indeed he can.

[**Thron of the Fallen Skies**]: Many reincarnators can, Arcs. It is merely their gifted skill that they obtain upon reincarnation. He is unlikely to have anything impressive otherwise.

P-System Log

Okay, these guys are starting to piss me off, too. I think I can see where they're coming from—if they can't tell that Jerome is godsent, then there's no way that they would know he's unique. From the way they describe it, it sounds like average reincarnators aren't really anything to write home about.

Still, they could be less assholish about it! I get that they're mad that Jerome is kind of making every faux pas imaginable, but he *is* a reincarnator. Even I don't know half the social shit they expect him to know! Jeez, they're petty.

. . . maybe I'll be petty back. Nothing impressive otherwise, huh? We'll see how that goes once I get some W Inertia and some time.

Party Chat

[**Jerome Smith**]: Look, guys, I get that you don't like me, but can we try to work together at least?

[**Thron of the Fallen Skies**]: We may.

[**Arcs S'tar**]: Of course. We would never let something as base as dislike or irritation color our ability to adventure.

[**Jerome Smith**]: Okay, that's all I ask.

P-System Log

These guys are assholes, man . . . maybe we just got off on the wrong foot. Maybe Jerome showing them up will do their problems with their egos some good?

[Proximity Trigger] triggered!

P-System Log

Oh, the walls just opened up. Not that much, mind, but enough to let out a few mobs. Skeletons, looks like. Five on either side.

[Fireball] cast!

[Reckless Charge] cast!

P-System Log

Oh damn they're actually decent at their jobs.

Both of those skills just cleared five skellies apiece. The fireball barely managed to not hit any of the party members, which I have to say was a little irritating, but the fact remained that we did come out unscathed. As for the dwarf, that guy just zipped forward at like twice his normal speed and started *glowing*. Man took the skeletons out with a single hit each.

Party Chat

[Arcs S'tar]: Let's get moving.

CHAPTER 43

<table><tr><td>

Party Chat

</td></tr><tr><td>

[**Thron of the Fallen Skies**]: Entry hall clear.

[**Arcs S'tar**]: I believe the skeletons were the only trap here.

[**Aster K'lon**]: [**Mana Sense**] is not detecting any further resistance in the immediate vicinity. We should not encounter any further adversity in this hall.

[**Arcs S'tar**]: Yeah, it's a well type. Not sure on the specifics, though.

</td></tr></table>

<table><tr><td>

P-System Log

</td></tr><tr><td>

That last statement was probably prompted by this new room. It's an octagon, and it is expansive as all hell. It has to be at least a hundred feet from end to end. My dome barely fills the room, that's how big it is. It's a stone one—granite, maybe? The material is pretty consistently smooth and gray, at least—and there's a huge fountain taking up a solid half of the room in the center. Four gray metallic pillars stick out of dark-blue water, standing there menacingly with some purpose that I can't identify and a heaping dose of mana that I can. At the very center, water spouts out of the fountain, catching the glint of the wall-mounted [**Lights**]. It's giving this place an atmosphere of something almost like an indoor mall, but in an eerie way I can't completely quantify.

There's three separate paths stemming from this room. One dead ahead on the other side of the massive fountain, one to the left, and one to the right.

</td></tr></table>

<table><tr><td>

Party Chat

</td></tr><tr><td>

[**Arcs S'tar**]: Standard path-clear protocol. Right to left.

</td></tr></table>

[Jerome Smith]: Can't we split up? We're individually powerful enough to each tackle a branch, aren't we?

[Aster K'lon]: Never split the party, Jerome, even if you think you're ready for it.

P-System Log

I though Jerome was supposed to be good at gaming. At the very least, I thought he had the basics of strategy down. "Don't split the party" is like, rule zero of D&D and most other party-based RPGs.

I guess most of his focus went to single-player stuff, huh? Lone hero and all that? It would explain why he's so shit at working with Aster and these new guys, at least.

Party Chat

[Jerome Smith]: Alright, makes sense. Marching order?

[Arcs S'tar]: Thron and then me. You two can figure it out yourself.

[Aster K'lon]: Very well. However, I believe that having Jerome farther in front is prudent. As you saw previously, one of his primary offensive skills is **[Misty Strike]**, which carries the risk of hitting teammates should he activate it from the back.

[Jerome Smith]: Nah, it's not an issue. I have other skills that can help me handle movement.

[Aster K'lon]: If you say so.

P-System Log

Huh, but he knows marching order? Weird.

Anyway, looks like they figured out marching order to be the dwarf, the elf, Aster, and finally Jerome, bringing up the back.

When he talks about "another skill," he's definitely talking about **[Explosive Teleport]**, that new skill that I just granted him. Doesn't that also deal friendly fire damage if he activates it from his current position?

Oh, well. That's not my concern. I'm just here to facilitate Jerome's poor decisions, not make them for him.

Time to head into the room on the right, I suppose.

P-System Log [what was that]

My perception dome is still pretty much just limited to the scope of the fountain room, but I can still get some fuzzy idea of what's happening in the rooms around us. Back where we came in from, there was just an enormous crashing sound, as if an elephant just ran straight into a concrete wall.

Looks like I'm not the only one who heard it.

Party Chat

[Jerome Smith]: Did you hear that? That was from behind us, right?

[Arcs S'tar]: Yes. That came from the entrance from whence we came.

[Aster K'lon]: The innate protections of a Dungeon Core mean that there shouldn't be much sound—if any—coming from outside. Despite that, I sense no mana inside.

[Arcs S'tar]: Allow me to check.

[Searchlight Assess] cast!

Party Chat

[Arcs S'tar]: I detect nothing in the entrance hallway. Whatever is making the sound, it is not coming from the dungeon.

[Jerome Smith]: Is this kind of thing normal?

[Arcs S'tar]: Not at all. I am yet unsure whether it is cause for worry.

[Thron of the Fallen Skies]: It could simply be renovations occurring outside. Would you like to return and examine its cause?

[Jerome Smith]: Can we just get a move on with the dungeon? I don't want to abandon any of the progress we've made on the delve so far. If it's a problem, it'll still be there when we get back, right?

[Aster K'lon]: I concur with Jerome. Best to complete this dungeon and obtain the rewards from it before examining this. If it becomes a more immediate issue, we can switch focuses.

[Arcs S'tar]: Very well.

[Thron of the Fallen Skies]: Works with me.

P-System Log

Into the next room we go, then! They're filing in in the same order that they decided earlier.

This new room is a little eerie. Follows the theme of the fountain room, I guess, but this one turns the dial up to eleven. Right in the middle of this room is a circle of gray stone sarcophagi standing up straight, artfully designed patterns marking each and every one of them. There's a mountain of mana buried in each one of them as well. We'll see whether or not anyone notices.

It's kind of creepy, this room. I wonder if there's corpses of past adventurers rotting in those coffins right now. It fits the general theme of death that this dungeon has, and I suppose that means it's doing what it's supposed to do. It's off-putting, though.

Observing them closer, I can make out text on some of them. *Joann, Ke'stin, Alexander* . . . Names.

Party Chat

[**Arcs S'tar**]: History-type room. I believe these may have ties to real figures in Continental history.

[**Thron of the Fallen Skies**]: Huh. Has this dungeon showed a propensity for history before?

[**Arcs S'tar**]: Others in its system have. It is possible that it simply took the knowledge from a fallen adventurer.

[**Aster K'lon**]: There is mana present in the sarcophagi. Be on your guard.

[**Mass Assess**] activating!

Passive [**Necromancer's Shield**] triggered!

[**Assess**] blocked!

Passive [**Necromancer's Sword**] triggered!

Party Chat

[**Aster K'lon**]: We are engaging! Be ready!

P-System Log

Five of the six sarcophagi just opened. Their contents are . . . moderately horrifying, to say the least. Mostly decayed corpses, closer to skeletons than anything else. Each of them has heavy wrappings all over its body, like they were mummified at some point, but those wrappings are a lot more than linen and whatever people used to use for mummification. There's mana packed into those, and they're practically shimmering. It makes for a disturbing effect, what with the flapping silvery coverings and decayed flesh and exposed bones. I don't know why it feels worse to see these than the skeletons before. Is it the human factor to them? The fact that they might've had names, once upon a time?

Whatever. They'll die all the same.

[**Flameburst**] cast!

[**Manaburn**] cast!

[**Misty Strike**] activating!

[**Misty Strike**] dealt 110 damage!

Critical hit! [**Misty Strike**] dealt 234 damage!

Enemies defeated! Experience split and distributed!

Party Chat

[**Jerome Smith**]: One ten, two thirty-four.

[**Aster K'lon**]: I've told you before, Jerome. You don't need to announce damage numbers if the opponents are dead. Also, eighty-seven with a splash of five, six, nine, and twelve.

[**Arcs S'tar**]: Fifty-seven with a splash of five apiece.

[**Jerome Smith**]: Felt like it anyway.

[**Thron of the Fallen Skies**]: I may have underestimated you a touch.

P-System Log

A touch? Jerome's damage output is insane for a guy who's literally level 3! He's on a higher level than Aster and Arcs already!

Welp. There's three of them still up. Aster and Arcs weren't quite able to finish off their own targets, but they should be able to in the next hit, I think.

The mummies are making a move, though. The three of them that haven't fallen to dusty pieces are moving surprisingly fast, splitting up and casting skills toward the grouped-up party. We didn't make it that far inside, so everyone's still clumped in one place.

[**Undead Memory**] -> [**Inferno Spear**] cast!

[**Inferno Spear**] dealt 63 damage to you!

Party Chat

[**Aster K'lon**]: I recognize this. [**Undead Memory**] mimics a skill that an undead knew in life, with less power.

[**Jerome Smith**]: So these enemies aren't just generated by the dungeon?

[**Undead Memory**] -> overcharged [**Thunderstrike**] cast!

[**Lightning Rod**] consumed 1 charge! Damage nullified!

Party Chat

[**Aster K'lon**]: It pays to have good gear.

[**Arcs S'tar**]: If these are nongenerated undead, who are they? Adventurers?

[**Thron of the Fallen Skies**]: That seems likely. There were a few total wipes in this area recently, weren't there? This might be their remnants.

[**Jerome Smith**]: Hold on, you're telling me we're fighting dead adventurers? Like, real people?

[**Arcs S'tar**]: We may very well be.

[**Jerome Smith**]: Fuck.

[**Arcs S'tar**]: Come. Let us put them to rest.

CHAPTER 44

P-System Log

Huh. Looks like Jerome actually got more hesitant after realizing he was against ex-adventurers. I wonder why that is. It's not like he hasn't tried to kill humanoids before. To be fair, those were R Beasts and therefore less deserving of life, but these are also pretty not-human. They're already undead.

Fucking hell. If he won't get moving, I'll make him. I'll just bring up an old [**Objective**].

[**Objective**]**:** Survival of the Fittest

Description: Eliminate threats to your survival.

Rewards: Passive XP multiplier for killing hostile Integrated. Increases over time.

Hero's Personal Log 084

Fuck, I don't want to kill people. I know the R Beasts were technically people, but this just gives me the icks.

But this is another world. Morality works differently here. And the System just reminded me of that. I have to go through with this, even if it's something I'd prefer not to do.

It's okay. They're not people anymore. I can deal with this.

Party Chat

[**Arcs S'tar**]: I have the rest. Step back.

[**Jerome Smith**]: No, I can handle it.

[**Misty Strike**] activating!

[**Misty Strike**] dealt 105 damage!

[**Explosive Teleport**] activating!

[**Explosive Teleport**] dealt 48 damage!

[**Explosive Teleport**] dealt 57 damage!

Enemies defeated! Experience split and distributed!

P-System Log

I got . . . maybe 150 W Inertia from that? If it was split three ways, that means that each mummy had about ninety W Inertia in it. That seems like less than there should be for a [**Rare**] enemy, but maybe it's because they're necromantic constructs or something. I dunno.

Party Chat

[**Thron of the Fallen Skies**]: I must apologize, Jerome. I have misjudged your competence, if not your character.

[**Jerome Smith**]: It's fine. I'll just do what I do best.

[**Arcs S'tar**]: We should continue. Same marching order.

[**Arcs S'tar**]: Actually, wait. Hold on.

[**Aster K'lon**]: I believe it would be wise if we examined the contents of the final sarcophagus. [**Mana Sense**] tells me that there is something hidden within.

[**Jerome Smith**]: I can poke it.

> **[Magic Missile]** activating!

> Passive **[Necromancer's Shield]** triggered!

> **[Last Rites]** cast!

> **P-System Log**
>
> Huh. That's not ominous at all.
>
> The amount of mana coming from that last sarcophagus just spiked. The skill definitely came from there. It has the same tinges of power—necromancy, I think?—that the previous skills from the undead had. Interesting. I can definitely use that later.
>
> I'm not actually sure what this skill does. I need to gain more experience in the field before I can conclusively say anything about the details of these skills, that much is pretty evident. I *think* it might be a buff skill? It doesn't seem to be directly offensive, and the name doesn't suggest something offensive, either.
>
> Well, it's opening. Whatever's in there is practically glowing with mana. It might actually be glowing physically.

> **[Assess]** activating!

> Passive **[Necromancer's Shield]** triggered!

> **[Assess]** blocked!

> **P-System Log**
>
> Ah, fuck that. I want to see what this shit is. I think that at this point, it might be better to burn W Inertia on leveling up Jerome's **[Assess]** rather than using the mockery of it that I have. It's more directly useful to the current situation, after all.
>
> I just got 150 W Inertia, so I guess I can burn some of that. Screw it, I'll

burn a lot of it. It's not what I'm supposed to do, and it might be kind of dumb, but you only live once, right? Powering up Jerome is a lot more fun than I thought it would be. Besides, those were just the first few enemies. He'll definitely be able to earn that W Inertia back later.

Guess I'm dumping it all in. I'm going to focus on overriding skills for this one. I was able to modify a skill before—I should be able to do it now as well. I just want this [**Assess**] to work without some dumbass skill triggering and stopping Jerome—and, by extension, me—from seeing the deets on our enemies.

Skill leveled up! [**Assess**] lv. 2 -> lv. 6

<ERROR>

Skill evolution! [**Assess**] -> [**ASSESS**]

Raises access tier. Increased details.

P-System Log

Huh. There's that error message again. I have no idea why it triggered. Is the error pertaining to how much XP increases by when I dump in W Inertia? If so, I'm glad the error exists. I don't think that's it, though. I had maybe one hundred XP left before [**Assess**] made it to level 3. Since its XP cost increased by one hundred XP per level, every level, it would've cost three hundred to hit level 4, four hundred to hit level 5, and five hundred to hit level 6. With 150 W Inertia, that's enough to hit level 6.

Maybe the actual error occurred with the evolution, because that's a weird fucking evolution. I'm also pretty sure that skills aren't supposed to evolve at level 6, and . . .

[ASSESS lv. 6] (abbreviated)

Stat	Value
XP	0/600

P-System Log

Yeah, I'm pretty sure a skill evolution is also supposed to reset the level to zero. That along with the fact that the skill didn't increase in rarity is kinda sus. I think this might be more of a sidegrade than a direct upgrade. If it's a direct upgrade, then I have no idea what to say. Evolving it did give more abilities, but—

Oh. I think I get it. I focused the W Inertia in a way that didn't quite align with what the skill was before. Maybe the skill changed because of that?

[**ASSESS**] activating!

Passive [**Necromancer's Shield**] triggered!

Skill overridden!

Johannes Ar'lyn

Class	Race	Level
Necromancer	Undead Elf	8

Stat	Current	Maximum
Health	<HIDDEN>	150

Titles	[Dungeon Mob], [Slaughterer III], [Resurrector], [Heathen]

P-System Log

Huh. It's missing some details that I get access to. Detailed stats, skills, mana values, and a bunch of other important things. Still, it's more detail than Jerome has gotten so far.

Also, this dungeon's mobs actually have proper names. That's a neat li'l detail. Maybe the higher dungeons even have lore to them.

Hero's Personal Log 085

Thanks, System! This skill is nicer to use now.

Party Chat

[**Aster K'lon**]: It's a dungeon beast. Spawned or controlled?

[**Arcs S'tar**]: Everything around these parts is spawned. This bastard must've been the reason for the other adventuring parties disappearing.

[**Jerome Smith**]: This isn't a real person?

[**Arcs S'tar**]: Nor is it a real boss. It is a miniboss whose difficulty is far greater than it should be.

[**Jerome Smith**]: I can handle this.

[**Misty Strike**] activating!

Passive [**Necromancer's Shield**] + [**Last Rites**] = [**Necromancer's Armor**] triggered!

[**Misty Strike**] dealt 24 damage!

Party Chat

[**Jerome Smith**]: Twenty-four. What the fuck?

[**Aster K'lon**]: [**Last Rites**] is a powerful buff skill. Combined with its other innate defensive abilities, it must have significantly decreased the amount of damage that can be dealt to it.

[**Arcs S'tar**]: We will need coordination to take this one down.

P-System Log

Huh, combining passive skills to make a stronger one isn't something I'd considered before. I didn't even know that was possible.

I wonder if Jerome can do it? I can encourage a quickcast by beginning half a spell. If it works out, Jerome might be able to handle this guy on his own. That's sure to be some juicy W Inertia.

[**Contagion**] cast!

[**Lesser De-spell**] cast!

Magic contest won by [**Necromancer**] Johannes Ar'lyn!

[**Mana Amplifier**] consumed 3 charges!

Magic contest won by [**Mage**] Aster K'lon!

[**Contagion**] suppressed!

P-System Log

Holy fuck, how many items does Aster have? I mean, yay her, but holy shit, she's like fantasy Batman.

Party Chat

[**Arcs S'tar**]: Thank you, Aster.

[**Thron of the Fallen Skies**]: It is much appreciated.

[**Aster K'lon**]: No worries. [**Contagion**] was too severe a spell for me to risk allowing.

[**Jerome Smith**]: What does it do?

[**Aster K'lon**]: It causes passive damage until the caster is dead. It has a decent chance of not setting in, but if it connects, it will remain until either the caster or the victim is dead.

[**Contagion**] cast!

Party Chat

[**Jerome Smith**]: Fuck.

[**Arcs S'tar**]: It recharged so fast!

[**Purifying Shield**] cast!

Party Chat

[**Aster K'lon**]: I got it.

[**Jerome Smith**]: Nice.

[**Thron of the Fallen Skies**]: Thank you.

[**Contagion**] dealt 20 damage to you!

You were infected with a [**Contagion**]!

Party Chat

[**Jerome Smith**]: Aster, I don't think you got all of it.

[**Aster K'lon**]: Shit. Was anyone else hit?

[**Arcs S'tar**]: I was not.

[**Thron of the Fallen Skies**]: No.

P-System Log

Well, shit. Now we're on a timer.

<table>
<tr><td>Party Chat</td></tr>
<tr><td>[Jerome Smith]: That's fine. Let's just kill this shit faster.</td></tr>
</table>

<table>
<tr><td>[Contagion] dealt 53 damage to you!</td></tr>
</table>

<table>
<tr><td>[Misty Strike] activating!</td></tr>
</table>

<table>
<tr><td>P-System Log</td></tr>
<tr><td>

Alright, here's my chance. Sped-up perception means I can keep up with the skill. I might need to act off Jerome's instincts here.

There's really only one skill that makes sense to combine with this one. The only one that also involves CQB.

Yes, this is taking a risk. Yes, it's kind of stupid to try replicating a phenomenon that I've only seen once. But hey, Jerome still has more than seven hundred HP left. It's not my body that I'm risking.

Feed just a little W Inertia in, mix it with mana, and trigger the skill . . .

</td></tr>
</table>

<table>
<tr><td>[Misty Strike] + [Explosive Teleport] = [Incendiary Cloud Zenith] activating!</td></tr>
</table>

CHAPTER 45

Passive [**Necromancer's Shield**] + [**Last Rites**] = [**Necromancer's Armor**] triggered!

[**Incendiary Cloud Zenith**] dealt 74 damage!

P-System Log

Holy shit, that's powerful. [**Necromancer's Armor**] turned a [**Misty Strike**] into twenty-four damage. That skill averages around ninety to one hundred damage, which means that this defensive skill almost quarters the amount of damage that this guy is taking. Even with that in mind, it dealt seventy-four damage? That's nearly three hundred damage as a base.

And it doesn't even look like it's done. The combination of skills made something entirely different from the sum of its parts. I'm not sure how to describe it. Usually, Jerome blurs and dashes in a straight line for a [**Misty Strike**], gaining a semi-ethereal property while he does so. For [**Explosive Teleport**], he just disappears in an explosion. This time . . . he kind of became a cloud? Except that cloud is still moving super fucking fast, and it won't stop exploding. That first hit came from one pass through the [**Necromancer**], and the explody cloud is reversing direction now. Another hit?

Passive [**Necromancer's Shield**] + [**Last Rites**] = [**Necromancer's Armor**] triggered!

[**Incendiary Cloud Zenith**] dealt 71 damage!

Enemy defeated! Experience awarded!

P-System Log

God(s) fucking damn. That's one hell of a skill. Looks like it takes a toll, though. Jerome has remanifested into a human, and he looks *tired*.

But enough about Jerome. I got lots of W Inertia from that! Nobody except Jerome actually hit the enemy, so I guess all of the W Inertia went straight to me. I got nearly four hundred whole points from that fight! That's more than the final boss of the [**Common**] dungeon gave, and this guy is supposed to be a miniboss. That's the difference between dungeon rarities for ya.

I wonder how much mana that spent.

Jerome Smith (abbreviated)

Stat	Current	Maximum
Mana	518	1,067

P-System Log

Ah, shit. I'm not completely sure what level of mana he had before the fight started, but he definitely had a lot more than that. That's, what, three hundred mana for a single skill? Yeah, it did absolutely massive amounts of damage, but Jerome didn't even get to keep the skill. I don't know enough about mixing skills to know if I can do this consistently, too. Who's to say that it'll even be the same skill next time? It might be, but it might also have been a timing thing or a W Inertia thing or any number of potential causes that I just didn't analyze the situation well enough to figure out.

That said, it's a super-powerful finisher. If Jerome—and by Jerome, of course, I mean me—can keep consistently achieving the skill combination to execute this, I think it's pretty worth the cost. That's a hell of a strong finisher, if I do say so myself.

Party Chat

[**Arcs S'tar**]: Gods above. K'lon, you never told me he was this powerful. He can already do skill combos?

[**Thron of the Fallen Skies**]: He's above even our level. How?

[**Aster K'lon**]: I did say he might surprise you.

[**Thron of the Fallen Skies**]: I apologize for misjudging your power level, Jerome.

[**Jerome Smith**]: No sweat. Adventuring is fun.

[**Arcs S'tar**]: What does "no sweat" mean?

[**Jerome Smith**]: Oh, it just means "don't worry about it." It means that it's not a problem.

[**Arcs S'tar**]: I see.

P-System Log

Huh, so that's not a saying around these parts. Earth culture seems to not have made that much of an impact on this place. Weird, given that Aster mentioned that reincarnators were super common around these parts. Maybe it's because they all get sent off to fight rather than having their culture mesh with the Continent's? Or maybe it's because we're so far from the front-line Edge Cities, where the reincarnators are supposedly much more common.

Welp. That doesn't matter that much. It's time for the next part of the dungeon!

. . . that rumbling noise coming from the front doesn't bode well. I don't think anyone but me can hear it this time, since it's pretty small—muffled by the dungeon's innate properties, maybe? I don't know what it is, but I'm remembering that the other dungeon was closed due to total destruction.

Private Message [Aster]

[**P-System**]: Advise rapid clearing of the remainder of the dungeon.

[**Aster K'lon**]: Any reason why?

[**P-System**]: Outside influence is possible.

[**Aster K'lon**]: Ah, the crashing from before. Doesn't seem like they've entered the dungeon, though.

[**P-System**]: Advisory remains in effect.

[**Aster K'lon**]: Understood.

Party Chat

[**Jerome Smith**]: Can I take the front this time?

[**Arcs S'tar**]: No. You are clearly stronger than us, which means that we have more room to increase our abilities.

[**Jerome Smith**]: Oh, okay, sure.

Private Message [Aster]

[**Aster K'lon**]: Jerome, what was that skill you used?

[**Jerome Smith**]: I have no idea. My System made me, uh, what was it called again? The thing I used to cast that [**Magic Missile**] really fast yesterday.

[**Aster K'lon**]: Quick-casting?

[**Jerome Smith**]: Yeah. The System had me quick-cast an [**Explosive Teleport**] while I was in the middle of a [**Misty Strike**], and then *that* happened. Spent a lot of mana to do it, though.

[**Aster K'lon**]: Jerome, what you did is widely known as a "skill combination" or "skill combo." Generally, only exceptionally experienced adventurers have the knowledge and fine control needed to execute them.

[**Aster K'lon**]: Essentially, your System is incredibly powerful.

[**Jerome Smith**]: Huh. Thanks, System, I guess.

P-System Log

Aww, appreciation!

Okay, anyways, we're on to the next room. This one is a pretty small square, maybe only thirty feet by thirty feet across. There's two more sarcophagi in this one, though these ones are lying down and have more color to them. Gold rather than gray. There's also another bundle of mana within them, which means more monsters or more traps, I think.

Party Chat

[**Aster K'lon**]: Do not open the sarcophagi.

[Jerome Smith]: Wasn't planning on it, but why?

[Aster K'lon]: They are primed with a skill of some kind. I cannot identify the exact skill it is, but I am sure that it is an offensive one.

[Jerome Smith]: Alright. No opening, got it.

[Thron of the Fallen Skies]: There might be loot inside.

[Arcs S'tar]: This dungeon in particular has a habit of putting artifacts just beyond traps.

[Arcs S'tar]: I'll handle it.

[Proximity Trigger] triggered!

[Delayed Detonating Death] cast!

[Stareater] cast!

P-System Log

Damn, that's a cool skill name. At first glance, all it did was just straight up eat the skill that facilitated the trap, but I'm pretty sure there's another aspect to it that wasn't displayed there. I'll copy the formula down. Maybe I can use it later.

Anyway, elf lady—Arcs, I mean—just disabled both traps and took the loot from them. Not sharing with the rest of the party, huh? Kinda rude.

Well, whatever. Neither Jerome nor Aster made a fuss about it, so that's not really a point of contention. Last room for this path!

This one's a lot larger. Almost fifty feet long, I think, and the only thing in here is one final sarcophagus. I detect mana from inside it, but it's weaker than before.

Damn, Aster is just going straight for it. That's kind of unlike her.

Party Chat

[Aster K'lon]: As I suspected. There is a lever mechanism here that connects to the fountain.

[**Arcs S'tar**]: Oh, it's one of those quests.

[**Arcs S'tar**]: We ran a similar one of these a bit back. It wasn't with a fountain, but the premise is pretty similar. Each path probably has a lever, which we trigger. Once we get all the levers triggered, we fight a final boss from the fountain, and then that's the dungeon.

[**Aster K'lon**]: Very well. That's this first segment completed, then. Shall we return?

[**Thron of the Fallen Skies**]: Yes. Let's go.

[**Jerome Smith**]: So what do you guys normally do? Full-time adventurers?

[**Arcs S'tar**]: Yes.

[**Thron of the Fallen Skies**]: You can make a lot off dungeon loot. It's more than enough for a living.

[**Jerome Smith**]: Huh. Interesting. I never really had to worry about money in my past life, so I was curious.

[**Arcs S'tar**]: Reincarnators will always intrigue me. S'ker does not see many of them.

[**Jerome Smith**]: Really? Where do they go?

[**Arcs S'tar**]: From what I have read, the northern Edge Cities receive the most. Of those that pass through this city, I rarely see any. It is certainly an enlightening experience to interact with one, to say the least.

P-System Log

Well, looks like they're having fun. Jerome is getting to know them more, at least, which is good news for future interactions with this party. Maybe we can even stick together!

Party Chat

[**Jerome Smith**]: Yeah, there's a lot of slang that didn't make it here. Like, for instance, if I wanted to say something was weird, I might refer to it as "sussy among us balls."

[**Thron of the Fallen Skies**]: Interesting.

<table>
<tr><td>P-System Log</td></tr>
<tr><td>

. . . I regret being reborn. Let's just get this dungeon done.

Assuming that the slowly increasing crashing from the entrance doesn't get to us first.

</td></tr>
</table>

CHAPTER 46

The next part of the dungeon was a lot more peaceful than the first path we took, which is kind of weird. Aster said she detected the least mana coming from the leftmost entrance, so the party went there, and it turned out that there was literally nothing stopping them from hitting the second lever? There was a single room with three empty sarcophagi that played a prerecorded message of some kind, but that shit is all basically the dungeon adding lore for itself. It's not like there's some secret connection between the lore of this dungeon and everywhere else—Arcs and Thron made it pretty clear that the shit we see inside these dungeons is mostly contained to the dungeons themselves.

In the meantime, the rumbling from the entrance hasn't really increased in volume. I was worried that whoever was there would interrupt us halfway through the dungeon and cut off the opportunity to gain more W Inertia, but it looks like whatever was happening has slowed down. I don't buy Thron's explanation of renovation at all, but I also don't want to risk losing this run. It's been a fun dungeon so far, and I've been able to explore some pretty cool new shit. If we can get loot and W Inertia on top of that, I'd be over the moon. Having to stop that to potentially face an adversary—or worse, embarrassedly explain ourselves to a construction crew—would put a bit of a damper on that.

So for the meantime, it's time to finish this dungeon up.

[**Jerome Smith**]: That second segment was really anticlimactic. Any info on the third?

[**Aster K'lon**]: I read many mana signatures. This is likely to be the crux of the dungeon.

[**Arcs S'tar**]: The last path you take tends to be the hardest. I don't know if this dungeon does it, but I've seen instances before where one of the [**Epic**] dungeons actually shifted its interior design around while adventurers were inside just so that the hardest path would be the last one.

[**Jerome Smith**]: Interesting.

[**Aster K'lon**]: Come. Let us stop wasting time.

P-System Log

This last bit looks a lot less artificial. I think it's still a creation of the dungeon and nothing truly organic, but it definitely resembles a natural cave a lot more now than it did earlier. The path is narrower and more uneven, there's stalagmites and stalactites everywhere, and the walls are nowhere near uniform anymore. The path is muddled up as well.

Thankfully, the party seems to know how to get around. Thron is leading the way, and it looks like he was born to make his way through caves. Is that a dwarf thing? I know that most fantasy dwarves live under mountains and in cave systems and such, but Thron wasn't the only dwarf wandering around the very obviously aboveground city of S'ker. Maybe it's just a proficiency or skill he has?

Whatever the case, they made their way through the first part of the cave just fine. There was a fork at one point with one path leading to a dead end and the other leading to another room just around the corner, and somehow Thron picked the right one without the benefit of enhanced perception like mine. I had to give him some credit for that, at least.

This next room is also less of a dungeon-made structure—at least, it looks less artificial. It's just a wider cavern, but there's . . . Damn. It's glowing purple.

[**ASSESS**] activating!

Nameless

Class	Race	Level
Predator	Violet Fungus	1

Stat	Current	Maximum
Health	<HIDDEN>	10

Titles	[Dungeon Mob]

[**Fireball**] cast!

[**Fireball**] cast!

P-System Log

Damn, Jerome didn't even get a chance to participate, huh? Arcs just shot two huge-ass fireballs into that place and then absolutely incinerated every last one of those poor fungi.

Party Chat

[**Thron of the Fallen Skies**]: Watch your mana, Arcs.

[**Arcs S'tar**]: I have potions. It's fine.

[**Jerome Smith**]: You must really hate those fungi. They're all [**Common**] class and, like, level 1. Are they really that much of an issue?

[**Arcs S'tar**]: Once you spend some more time in the field, you'll probably also learn that class isn't everything. If left unchecked, those monsters can become unstoppable.

[**Arcs S'tar**]: Believe me, you don't want to see it.

[**Jerome Smith**]: Alright, then. Thanks for removing the threat, I guess.

[**Arcs S'tar**]: They're weak to fire. Just remember that, and you'll never end up in a bad situation against them.

[**Jerome Smith**]: There a history there?

P-System Log

No shit, dumbass! Have some tact!
Well, whatever. They didn't continue the conversation, so I think we're good. The room didn't have anything other than the fungi in it, so it's on to the next one. More caving, yay!

Party Chat

[**Aster K'lon**]: It occurs to me that the number of drops obtained from this dungeon so far has been fairly low.

[**Arcs S'tar**]: The trigger types tend to be like this. Have you never faced one?

[**Aster K'lon**]: Dungeon variety in my region is significantly more limited.

[**Arcs S'tar**]: Ah. Well, the loot is almost all going to be at the end.

[**Aster K'lon**]: Understood.

[**Thron of the Fallen Skies**]: We're here.

P-System Log

Sure enough, we are. This place has the same design as the vacant room from earlier. Three empty sarcophagi and a mana signature buried within one of them that indicates the presence of the final lever.

It's not quite the same, though. Whereas the last room was nearly entirely empty but for that one message, this one is definitively not. I can detect other things lying within the sarcophagi, and the mana is strong.

Party Chat

[**Arcs S'tar**]: This isn't the endboss. Not enough of a signature.

[**Thron of the Fallen Skies**]: Endboss is probably stored in the fountain.

[**Arcs S'tar**]: Is everyone ready? I believe the combat flow will go from miniboss to endboss here with very little time in between.

[**Jerome Smith**]: A little short on mana, but I should be good.

[**Aster K'lon**]: I am prepared. Jerome, you can have a mana potion.

Private Message [Aster]

[**Aster K'lon**]: You have not discovered a way to increase the speed of mana generation?

[**P-System**]: No. Natural seems to be the fastest at the moment.

[**Aster K'lon**]: A pity.

[**Superior Mana Potion**] restored 300 mana!

P-System Log

Not a perfect heal, but it'll do the job. Time to get this coffin open.

Party Chat

[**Thron of the Fallen Skies**]: I'm going to hit it.

[**Arcs S'tar**]: Of course you are.

[**Relentless Rage**] cast!

[**Brutal Strike**] cast!

Party Chat

[**Thron of the Fallen Skies**]: No reaction. Going again.

[**Ethereal Body**] triggered!

P-System Log

Damn, that's a high-rarity skill to start the fight with. That thing just phased right through the sarcophagus, no questions asked. It looks almost like it's a silhouette of a person, like if you removed all the color from someone and then added on some shadowy particle effects on the side.

<table>
<tr><td colspan="3">[ASSESS] activating!</td></tr>
</table>

K

Class	Race	Level
Darkstrider	Undead	10

Stat	Current	Maximum
Health	<HIDDEN>	400

Titles	[Dungeon Mob], [Resurrector], [Reincarnator], [Massacre IV]

Party Chat

[**Jerome Smith**]: That's a fucking *midboss?*

[**Arcs S'tar**]: That is far more powerful than it has any right to be. What the hell is happening?

[**Aster K'lon**]: The ambient mana is acting differently. We should retreat.

[**Jerome Smith**]: I think we can kill this guy. I dunno about the boss, though.

[**Arcs S'tar**]: This may very well be the boss. Something is wrong.

[**Nightwalk**] cast!

Party Chat

[**Jerome Smith**]: Shit, it disappeared.

[**Aster K'lon**]: The [**Common**] dungeon was acting up as well. I thought it was a coincidence brought on by Jerome's unique abilities at first, but now . . .

[**Nightwalk**] + [**Secret Strike**] = [**Shadowblade**] cast!

[**Shadowblade**] dealt 405 damage to you!

Party Chat

[**Jerome Smith**]: Four hundred and five

[**Jerome Smith**]: I have thirty-seven health left.

[**Jerome Smith**]: Get the fuck out.

[**Aster K'lon**]: Oh, dear.

[**Pendant of the Eagle's Flight**] consumed 4 charges!

[**Nightwalk**] cast!

P-System Log

shit shit shit shit shit

This is really fucking bad. Bad enough that I think I might need to dip into my reserves again. I wasn't expecting something this strong. The only reason nobody is dead already is because that thing attacked Jerome, who has like three times the health of the rest of the party.

And he's on thirty-seven HP. Once that thing materializes again, it's fucking over.

How much did one W Inertia get me? Like three HP? I need enough to survive another hit. To guarantee that, that's five hundred HP. I don't know if that was a low or a high damage roll, but I want to err on the side of safety.

Fuck it, I'll spend two hundred. I've been spending like crazy anyway, and this is *necessary.*

Jerome Smith (abbreviated)		
Stat	**Current**	**Maximum**
Health	646	1,171

P-System Log

Okay, the thing is targeting Jerome. He'll live one more hit.
Now as long as nothing else goes wrong, I can focus on offense.

▼ [H?? WA???F?? ?Y?] ▼

▼ And thusly the king cast aside the walls. ▼

P-System Log

bro

CHAPTER 47

P-System Log

Seriously, I have had it up to here with all these fucking threats. It's been two. Days. Literally two days, and how many life-threatening situations have we been through? I won't lie and say it's not fun, but seriously. There's a *limit*, y'know?

The dungeon door just opened up again, and the fuzziness that I normally feel when trying to perceive outside a dungeon from within or vice versa is just completely gone. In its place is a horrid *wrongness* and the sense that something has been destructively, irreparably broken.

R Beasts.

That would be what that skill was for. Wasn't it an observation skill, though? How did it end up . . . I dunno, violating this dungeon's core tenets?

Also, the boss hasn't resurfaced. I wonder what that's about. Maybe I should invest more in Jerome's HP. Shit might be charging up more for this hit.

I have a sneaking suspicion as to why it hasn't attacked any of the party, though, and that suspicion is just increasing. I can feel a few beings just outside where the dungeon boundary used to be.

Party Chat

[Aster K'lon]: There are R Beasts in the vicinity. [Mana Sense] detects them.

[Arcs S'tar]: Fuck. How many?

[Aster K'lon]: Four. We encountered two of them before, and I believe their signatures are the same. Were you aware of any R Beasts in S'ker?

[Arcs S'tar]: No. They may have been sleeper units.

[**Mass ASSESS**] activating!

▼

Name: Try'stin

Class: Cultist **Race:** Half-elf

Level: 17 **XP:** <HIDDEN>

Health: 98/98 **Mana:** <HIDDEN>

<ERROR: Insufficient Admin Tier>

[**ASSESS**] cannot approximate this information.

Skills

<HIDDEN> <HIDDEN>

▼

▼

Name: Bi'rohn

Class: Berserker **Race:** Human

Level: 12 **XP:** <HIDDEN>

Health: 142/142 **Mana:** 25/25

<ERROR: Insufficient Admin Tier>

[**ASSESS**] cannot approximate this information.

Skills

<HIDDEN> <HIDDEN>

▼

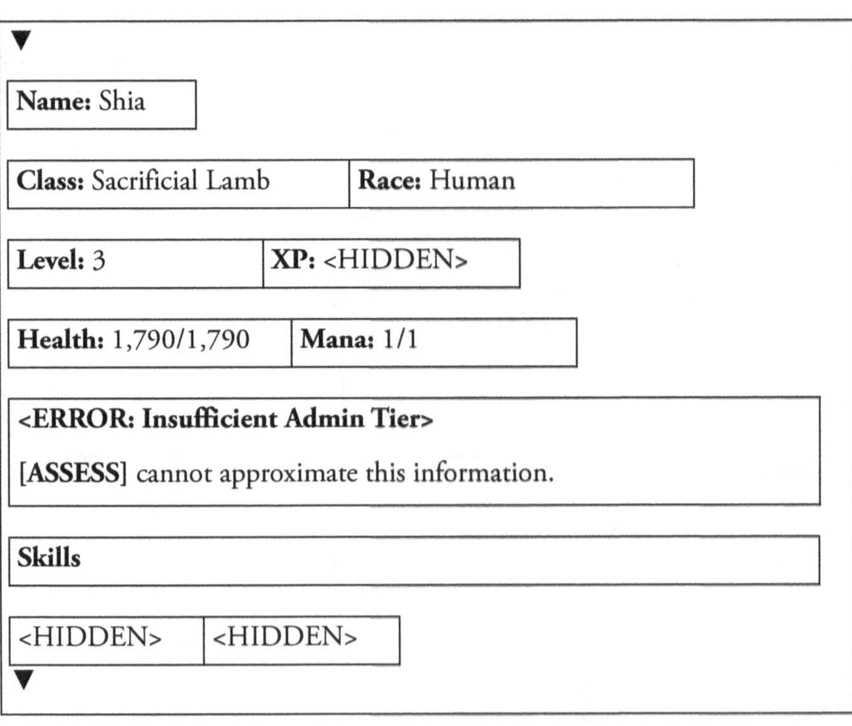

▼
Name: Ch'll
Class: Oathtaker
Race: Dark elf
Level: 19
XP: <HIDDEN>
Health: 157/157
Mana: <HIDDEN>
<ERROR: Insufficient Admin Tier>
[ASSESS] cannot approximate this information.
Skills
<HIDDEN>
<HIDDEN>
▼

▼
Name: Shia
Class: Sacrificial Lamb
Race: Human
Level: 3
XP: <HIDDEN>
Health: 1,790/1,790
Mana: 1/1
<ERROR: Insufficient Admin Tier>
[ASSESS] cannot approximate this information.
Skills
<HIDDEN>
<HIDDEN>
▼

Hero's Personal Log 086

Holy hell, talk about an information overload. They added two new party members at some point, plus they got some levels—I don't think I like that. System, you're gonna need to come in clutch here. Between these guys and that boss, we're kind of stuck between a rock and a hard place.

P-System Log

No shit, Jerome.

But it looks like that hard place might not be so hard after all. I can sort of track the movements of K the [**Darkstrider**] through its mana emissions, and it doesn't look like it's moving toward us.

What happened? It was very much trying to kill Jerome earlier, but—

Oh. I'm stupid. There's fucking R Beasts there, and all of us here know that they need ~~to die~~, as weird as it feels to say.

Even the dungeon boss—one that was apparently a reincarnator at some point, mind—knows that, it looks like.

[**Nightwalk**] + [**Secret Strike**] = [**Shadowblade**] cast!

Party Chat

[**Thron of the Fallen Skies**]: Did you catch that?

[**Aster K'lon**]: Yes. [**Shadowblade**] was redirected into the one with the class [**Sacrificial Lamb**].

[**Thron of the Fallen Skies**]: And yet he seems sure on his feet. Did that skill not deal over four hundred damage with a single blow?

[**Aster K'lon**]: You saw that thing's HP stat—same as mine.

[**Arcs S'tar**]: We running or fighting? *Can* we even fight these guys? I don't know if my skills can touch them.

[**Jerome Smith**]: I'm fighting. The rest of y'all can do whatever.

P-System Log

Yeah, I guess we're participating.

▼ Skill invoked: [**K??i?oika?i**] ▼

[**Nightwalk**] cast!

[**K??i?oika?i**] dealt 179 damage to you!

P-System Log

What the hell? Jerome was the closest one to that hit, yeah, but that wasn't anything close to a direct hit. The skill was aimed at the dungeon boss, not Jerome, and it manifested as a gold-red beam of light. Jerome got caught in the afterglow, not even the main hit. How fucking powerful are these guys?

[**Misty Strike**] activating!

▼ Passive invoked: [**Divine Protection**] ▼

[**Misty Strike**] nullified.

P-System Log

You're shitting me. This is what a [**Legendary**]-class Integrated looks like when they're not hampered by a System like me, huh?

Party Chat

[**Jerome Smith**]: One seventy-nine to me. No damage dealt.

[**Aster K'lon**]: Withdraw, Jerome. It's too dangerous.

[**Jerome Smith**]: No. If I'm supposed to face the Eternal King one day, then I have to be able to step up to the challenge of at least these lesser enemies.

[**Arcs S'tar**]: Then I'm coming, too.

[**Aster K'lon**]: Me as well.

[**Thron of the Fallen Skies**]: Count me by your side, reincarnator.

[**P-System**]: Everyone except Jerome, back up.

[**Jerome Smith**]: What the fuck, System? You can speak in party chat?

[**Arcs S'tar**]: What the hell are you?

[**P-System**]: Listen to me or suffer the consequences.

[**Aster K'lon**]: As much as it pains me to say it, we must follow its orders. Jerome's System is abnormally powerful.

[**Arcs S'tar**]: Very well. Then you must be prepared to retreat, Jerome. This is a little mad.

[**Jerome Smith**]: Yep, got it.

Hero's Personal Log 087

You can talk in party chat??? What the hell?

P-System Message

Worry about surviving this first, Jerome.

Other concerns are secondary.

P-System Log

Fuck this shit.

I've been justifying not spending W Inertia to myself for a while now. Distancing myself from Jerome, preventing him from gaining control over me, and most recently spending W overflow on [**W%M; G, P**] . . . They look like valid reasons, yeah, but the fact of the matter is that I've basically been kneecapping our strength. It was fun at first, thinking of ways I could creatively solve each individual problem, but it's reached the point where we are in situations where I need to killk̶i̶l̶l̶k̶i̶l̶l̶ my enemies and Jerome doesn't have the resources necessary to do that. All the while, I'm sitting on nearly forty thousand W Inertia that could be used to accomplish the job I'm supposed to be doing.

I don't want to feel like the underdog in everything. That's fun for a few fights, but now it's just stressful. I don't want to die here, and that means I don't want Jerome to die, either.

I'm getting tired of holding us back.

It's time to be the cheat skill that Jerome's been wanting.

Current W Inertia: 35,909

Max W Inertia: 38,382

Jerome Smith (abbreviated)

Stat	Current	Maximum
Health	7,068	7,367
Mana	5,567	6,271

P-System Message

Alright, I'm getting tired of this fucking charade.

Jerome, think of this as taking your training weights off or whatever.

Hero's Personal Log 088

That's . . . different. Can't say I don't like it, though.
Thanks for the boost. This is massive.

> **P-System Log**
>
> While we're at it, I'm stealing that **[Shadowblade]** skill. And the **[Nightwalk]**.
>
> I still have thirty-five thousand goddamn points left. It's not like I'm going to go broke anytime soon.
>
> And if I can't steal them, then I'm going to make something better. As far as I know, I'm the only one in the world who can do this, and I've been holding back on it for far too long. Fuck saving W Inertia—I can just get it back by killing these shits.
>
> No budget. I'll spend as much as I need to get something usable out of this.

> **New skill unlocked: [Nightwalk]**
>
> Become one with the darkness to mobilize yourself.

> **P-System Log**
>
> I can do better than that.

> **Skill evolution! [Nightwalk] -> [Ethereal Stride]**
>
> You no longer require the dark.

> **New skill unlocked: [Shadowblade]**
>
> Strike with an ethereal blade, bypassing defenses.

> **P-System Log**
>
> How much did I spend on that? Twenty-five hundred?
>
> Fucking LOL, I haven't even dropped beneath thirty thousand W Inertia—33,421, to be exact. Nobody needs this much.
>
> I'm going to drop it to thirty thousand. That new skill seems powerful, so I'm going to make it *more*. No shitty knockoff of a dungeon boss attack here. At Parker Productions, we make things better than the original.

Admin Tier increased! 0 -> 4

P-System Log

. . . seriously? All I had to do was spend more this whole time?
I'm a fucking idiot.
There's something waiting for me. A name. A name for a skill, no less. What should I pick? Something that fits Jerome.
Hmm . . .

Skill evolution! [**Shadowblade**] -> [**Edgelord**]

You are the blade, and the blade is you.

P-System Log

Perfection. Now, let's get to work on those other skills . . . I can afford to lose another few. We'll get it back, anyway. If I'm going to rip this Band-Aid of caution off, I'm going to commit to it all the way. OP Jerome or bust.
But first . . . we might need to clear these nuisances out of the way.

P-System Message

Let's kick some ass.

Hero's Personal Log 089

Fuck yeah.

CHAPTER 48

P-System Log

We're in the big leagues now. Any reservations I had about Jerome not being strong enough to take on the R Beasts and do the job he's supposed to are pretty much gone, thanks mostly to my own efforts.

Damn, having this much power is nice.

And my admin tier—whatever that is—also increased! I wonder what that actually does for me, though it's nice to see it's there, at least.

There's some important stuff to do right now that kind of takes precedence, though. Mostly involving killing.

[**Edgelord**] activating!

▼ Passive invoked: [**Divine Protection**] ▼

Passive overridden!

[**Edgelord**] dealt 1,098 damage!

Party Chat

[**Jerome Smith**]: One thousand ninety-eight damage.

[**Thron of the Fallen Skies**]: What?

[**Aster K'lon**]: I see your skill was redirected. It must be a passive. Some R Beasts have that, where their passives don't show up on our Systems.

[Jerome Smith]: That guy is super beefy. He'd be a nightmare to fight if he was any higher level.

[Aster K'lon]: True. One more hit should end it.

[Edgelord] is on cooldown! Please wait <HIDDEN> seconds before using it again.

Party Chat

[Jerome Smith]: It's on cooldown. I don't know when I'm going to be able to use it again.

[Aster K'lon]: I suspected there had to be a drawback somewhere. This seems reasonable.

[Aster K'lon]: Use another skill, then.

[Arcs S'tar]: I don't understand.

[P-System]: You don't need to. Stay out of our way.

P-System Log

That was a beautiful first activation of that new skill. The motherfucker started spinning, and he was waving some energy sword so fast that he looked like a human Beyblade. Even for an effect that visually flashy, that was a lot of damage. So that's what happens when I take the kid gloves off, huh?

▼ Skill invoked: **[Kʔʔiʔoikaʔi]** ▼

[Kʔʔiʔoikaʔi] dealt 711 damage to you!

P-System Log

That was a direct hit. Straight to the center of mass, meteor strike, laser death ray, holy smite—I don't know what that was, but it dealt a fuckload of damage.

But Jerome is still standing. Behold, the power that Parker wields when they're actually serious about this shit!

Party Chat

[**Jerome Smith**]: That thing took around four hundred then around a thousand. With an initial health of 1,790, that means a few more hits still.

[**Aster K'lon**]: It does not, as far as I can tell, have any resistances. Just a massive Health stat.

[**Jerome Smith**]: Well, I've got that, too, now.

[**Arcs S'tar**]: I think I can take it down. Just give me a bit.

▼ Skill invoked: [**Tentacle Storm**] ▼

[**Stareater**] cast!

▼ Skill invoked: [**Berserker's Taunt**] ▼

[**Stareater**] cast!

P-System Log

Holy shit, she just yeeted those skills out of existence. Looks like Arcs has some level of competence of her own.

[**Stareater**] executing!

Enemy defeated! Experience split and distributed!

Party Chat

[**Arcs S'tar**]: I've had that one building up for a few days. Six hundred and eighty-three, but I won't be able to use the skill offensively again for at least an hour.

[**Jerome Smith**]: Three to go.

[**Ethereal Stride**] cast!

P-System Log

Interesting. I've been pretty immaterial this whole time, but I've only seen Jerome's matter vanish a couple of times on top of that, mostly through his [**Misty Strike**] ability. This feels different from that, almost like he's walking beside me in my state of not-quite-existing.

And doing it sharpens my senses at this level, too. There's another presence with us here, still stuck in its [**Nightwalk**]. It's not attacking.

Coward.

Private Message [K]

[**P-System**]: Get your ass moving or I'll do it for you.

[**K**]: P-System . . . Joann? Is that you?

[**P-System**]: I left the only Joann I knew behind me when I got sent here. What's your deal?

[**K**]: Oh, so it's not . . .

[**K**]: It's so cold, being a dungeon mob. I fear I may never be warm again.

[**P-System**]: Get out there and do your fucking job. If you monologue over DM one more time, I swear to the fucking idiot who reincarnated me here that you won't live to see the next daybreak.

[**K**]: Okay, fine, fine!

[**K**]: . . . are you also a reincarnator? Nobody else calls it a DM here.

[**P-System**]: Fucking worry about that later.

[**Nightwalk**] + [**Secret Strike**] = [**Shadowblade**] cast!

▼ Passive invoked: [**Divine Protection**] ▼

Party Chat

[**Thron of the Fallen Skies**]: I feel a bit useless.

[**Aster K'lon**]: When dealing with reincarnators, it comes with the territory. The [**Berserker**] is down. Looks like the passive protection wasn't enough to keep it alive.

[**Jerome Smith**]: RIP in piss bozo #packwatch

[**Aster K'lon**]: Jerome, please. Not in front of the rest of the party.

[**Jerome Smith**]: Shit, thought this was my personal log. My bad.

[**Jerome Smith**]: I'm going back in.

[**Misty Strike**] activating!

▼ Passive invoked: [**Divine Protection**] ▼

P-System Log

Yeah, fuck that noise. That protection needs to get the fuck out of my way.

I was able to reverse engineer [**Acid Immunity**] from acid. I can probably do something similar with this shitter of a spell. It'll be harder because they're R Beasts, but I'm a lot more willing to toss W Inertia at the issue now.

Here we go. It *really* doesn't want me to steal it and handle it, but I've got it. With a thousand W Inertia behind me, how could I not?

<ERROR: INSUFFICIENT ADMIN TIER>

<ERROR: INSUFFICIENT W INERTIA>

P-System Log

Fuck off.
One thousand not enough for you? Let's add some more into the mix.

Admin Tier increased! 4 -> 5

P-System Log

Huh, three thousand W Inertia in, and it caved. Looks like I get to name this skill, too. Is there not an equivalent in the System already? Or is it just because of the amount of shit I put into it?

I'll take the opportunity in either case. I knew this skill was going to be powerful just based off the amount of W Inertia I dumped into it, but it looks like it's going to be even stronger than I'd planned for.

Damn, I'm spoiling Jerome. I went from barely giving him a single new skill to amping him up this far. To be fair, I've just about had it. Dicking around and preserving every last drop of W Inertia was nice and all, but why even bother with **[W%M; G, P]** when I can just make Jerome OP as fuck? It's not like I'm going to be able to do anything outside the bounds of Jerome anyway.

New skill unlocked: [**Unblockable**]

When active, opposing protective skills are invalid.

P-System Log

While we're at it, why not give some of the skills some upgrades? I still have twenty-seven thousand points to spare.

Skill leveled up! [**Misty Strike**] lv. 2 -> lv. 10

Damage increased by 16R10+2. Mana cost increased by 15% per level.

Skill evolution! [**Misty Strike**] -> [**Cloud Zenith**]

Become one with the clouds and temporarily become invincible while casting.

P-System Message

Go for it.

Hero's Personal Log 090

Holy shit, I'm getting spoiled.

Thanks, whatever AI is running this. I can't really put how helpful this is into words.

P-System Log

Of course he starts getting humble and shit after I give him everything he needs . . . I swear, Jerome acts just like your average eleven-year-old.

Well, it is what it is. I've put the power of a god into the hands of an idiot who might not be quite as dumb as he seems.

All I can do now is watch. And give him more powers to fuck shit up with more, but that's beside the point.

[**Unblockable**] activating!

[**Cloud Zenith**] activating!

▼ Passive invoked: [**Divine Protection**] ▼

Passive denied.

[**Cloud Zenith**] dealt 292 damage!

Enemy defeated! Experience rewarded!

Party Chat

[**Jerome Smith**]: Two ninety-two. That's the [**Cultist**] dealt with. Unfortunately, it looks like he got friends along the way.

[**Arcs S'tar**]: You've grown so strong so quickly. How?

[**P-System**]: He's cheating. Now can we focus on the fucking fight?

[**Arcs S'tar**]: The System speaks?

[**P-System**]: It does, and it's telling you to stop thinking about random shit and start thinking about how we can end this fight.

[**Arcs S'tar**]: . . . valid point.

[**Ethereal Stride**] activating!

[**Cloudy Zenith**] + [**Ethereal Stride**] = [**Ethereal Zenith**] activating!

P-System Log

Damn, that's a weird effect. Jerome is both here and not here, and the disconnect between what's real and what isn't is so thin that I think it's affecting the stuff around him.

[**Ethereal Zenith**] dealt 695 damage!

Party Chat

[**Jerome Smith**]: Six ninety-five. All my high-level skills are on cooldown now.

[**Aster K'lon**]: It may be best to withdraw. Powerful as you might be, this is still a very strong R Beast.

[**Jerome Smith**]: Ugh. I was *this* close.

[**Thron of the Fallen Skies**]: It's okay. There's always another day.

▼ Skill invoked: [**Hasty Retreat**] ▼

P-System Log

Well, they sent in three and came back empty-handed, with only one guy left standing. During that, I fucking amped Jerome to the moon. The rest of the dungeons here should be a cakewalk.

▼ [H?? WA???F?? ?Y?] ▼

▼ How interesting. ▼

CHAPTER 49

Northeast S'ker Dungeon of Devils
Dungeon cleared!

P-System Log
Well, that's the dungeon done and dusted. Now that the immediate threats are gone and everything's cooled down, I'm starting to realize what I just did. I just spent an entire ten thousand fucking W Inertia. Hoooooly shit. Honestly, I'm not nearly as broken up about it as I thought it would be. It does feel like I'm coming off a night of drinking and realizing what I did the morning after, but it's . . . not entirely bad? It's not like I've lost my control over Jerome. If anything, I think he might be easier to work with now. The main concern is that I lost a bunch of W Inertia, but we can just earn that back, right? It'll be a fucking cakewalk now. Two [Unique] skills, a [Legendary] one, and more mana and health than half this city put together. Honestly, with this much slapped onto him, the Eternal King should be a cakewalk. . . . I shouldn't say that. The Eternal King could easily have something to hard counter stats as ridiculous as Jerome's. Also, if I was able to do this, what's stopping the Eternal King from having something similar? No guarantee that that fucker doesn't have similarly insanely boosted stats. Well, that's an issue for me when we actually go and fight it. For now, we're just picking up drops.

Party Chat
[Jerome Smith]: Y'all can pick up the items. I don't think I need them.

[**Thron of the Fallen Skies**]: Fair's fair. You were the one who ended the fight.

[**Thron of the Fallen Skies**]: It *is* over, right? Do we still need to fight this boss?

[**Aster K'lon**]: Seeing as its activity has stopped and the rewards for this dungeon have dropped, I believe not.

[**Arcs S'tar**]: Let's just collect them and get the fuck out of here.

[**Jerome Smith**]: Yeah, go for it. Seriously, I don't need the items. Have you seen how powerful I got?

[**Greater Assess**] cast!

Party Chat

[**Thron of the Fallen Skies**]: Gods above.

[**Jerome Smith**]: Yeah.

Private Message [K]

[**K**]: Come to think of it, how did you contact me? I thought that was only supposed to be for parties.

[**P-System**]: I dunno. I just focused, is all. I got some cool powers, y'know?

[**K**]: . . . alright. I feel more focused now, too. Like I just woke up from a bad dream.

[**P-System**]: Interesting. The dungeon may have lost its grasp on you.

[**K**]: Is that it? Now that I think about it, I'm pretty sure this is the place that killed me.

[**P-System**]: You seem pretty chill with the fact that you're undead.

[**K**]: Bro, I was reborn here as a semi-incorporeal freak of nature. Being an undead semi-incorporeal freak of nature isn't much different.

[**P-System**]: Point taken.

[K]: Anyway, I can definitely think more clearly now. Can you clarify what the hell you are?

[P-System]: Are you a reincarnator?

[K]: No shit I am. Been here for . . . a year? Two, maybe? Are you?

[P-System]: I am the Personal System of a powerful reincarnator. When did you leave Earth?

[K]: I got hit by a truck in . . . 2017, I think. Don't remember the date anymore. Things got fuzzy. Coming back now.

[P-System]: Interesting. I do believe that Jerome left Earth more than two years afterward, and yet we are still here at the same time. Time runs differently in the two places, perhaps.

[K]: Maybe so. I don't really care.

[K]: Hey, you've got that really powerful guy, right? The guy who suddenly did something midfight and had his stats shoot to the fuckin' moon?

[P-System]: That was me facilitating it, but yes, we do indeed have the "really powerful guy" in our party.

[K]: Can I join?

[P-System]: Why?

[K]: Well, it's either this or the Guild. I don't think the dungeon wants me anymore—maybe it can't have me anymore, I dunno. The invaders were doing some weird shit with the dungeon—everything was off.

[P-System]: I suppose you could join us. You'll have to ask the actual people, though. I don't really have the power to do that.

P-System Log

Well, actually, I do. But it's a little easier to deflect responsibility for these issues onto people who are a little more equipped to deal with social stuff. I already took a big step forward during that fight, revealing that I actually had a personality and all, and I don't think I want to run before I've fully finished learning how to crawl.

Damn, look at me getting all philosophical and shit for something this stupid.

Party Chat

[**Jerome Smith**]: I'm fine with adding it to the party.

[**Arcs S'tar**]: It nearly killed you.

[**Jerome Smith**]: Honestly, it looks like that thing nearly killing me was the trigger for me to . . . I dunno, get all these powerups. Not sure what you'd call that.

[**Aster K'lon**]: I concur. It also appears that it was unbound from the dungeon system.

[**Aster K'lon**]: It is good that you acquired that increase in power. With a [**Legendary**]-class R Beast, I would have been unsurprised to see an instance of [**Corruption**] come out. You may have saved our lives.

[**Jerome Smith**]: Wasn't just me.

[**P-System**]: What Jerome said.

[**Arcs S'tar**]: Aster, you act like this is normal? Why can his System use party chat?

[**Aster K'lon**]: It is a very unique case.

[**Aster K'lon**]: I can perform the party spell, by the way.

[**Arcs S'tar**]: Great. Let's do it.

Party Chat

[**K**]: Hello.

[**Jerome Smith**]: Hi. I saw it say you were also a reincarnator?

[**K**]: I was. I died again in this dungeon . . . I don't know when. My memory is foggy after a point.

[**Arcs S'tar**]: K?

[**K**]: Arcs?

[**Arcs S'tar**]: So that's why you never showed up again. Glad you're still alive. In some sense.

[**Thron of the Fallen Skies**]: I was wondering why the skills seemed familiar. Good to see you, buddy. Did your death make you stronger?

[K]: I think it's a dungeon-monster thing.

[Jerome Smith]: This is nice and all, but can we save the reunion for later and just finish looting the dungeon?

[Arcs S'tar]: Right. Let's.

P-System Log

It didn't take too long to get that dungeon looted, all things considered, mostly because the brand-new fifth member of the party already knew where the good stuff was.

I'm still kind of confused with what happened to our new guy. Did Jerome's powerup go so well that the Dungeon Core just gave up on doing whatever it was doing? Or maybe it was the R Beasts, destabilizing the control that the Core had over its own mobs?

Whatever the case, it looks like we've gained a member, which is sure to be interesting. To be honest, Jerome doesn't need a party anymore. He's orders of magnitude stronger than all of them combined, thanks to me, but just leaving them feels . . . wrong.

Hero's Personal Log 091

Hey, System. I know you've done a lot for me, and that last powerup really saved my ass. And I know that you probably want me to just go off alone and get the job done, but . . .

I dunno. I kind of like these guys, even if they were a little assholish at first. Plus, Aster's been nothing but nice to me. I don't want to leave them behind.

P-System Log

Damn, Jerome is the last person I'd expect to *not* go mad with power. Good on him, I guess.

Well, the battle's done, and we're back at an inn. Technically, we could do another dungeon—there's certainly enough time for it—but Thron and Arcs are talking with K, who might be an old adventuring partner of theirs (kind of disconcerting to think about, not gonna lie, given the fact that apparently an adventurer ended up as a dungeon boss) and Jerome and

Aster seem to have that same feeling of wanting to take it easy. I don't blame them.

As for me, there's not much I can do at this point. Jerome recovered some of the W Inertia I spent by killing those four R Beasts and clearing the dungeon, but it's not nearly enough to recoup it. It's fine. That'll come later.

At the end of everything, that [**Legendary**] observation skill went off again. Looks like I have the Eternal King's attention now, if I interpreted it right. Fine. That just means I'll have to work harder and faster. Now that I've opened up the floodgates, I think it's perfectly reasonable to keep going. Jerome is proving to be increasingly easy to deal with, and despite the weirdness of the situation, nobody reacted poorly to me being able to communicate with them. I have Aster to thank for that.

For now, I guess it's time to just chill out. There's no immediate problems that need to be solved.

Private Message [Aster]

[**Aster K'lon**]: Please teach me how to be strong.

P-System Log

. . . oh, dear.
Guess I spoke too soon.

CHAPTER 50

[P-System]: What do you mean?

[Aster K'lon]: I do not mean to sound ungrateful—after all, you are the reason why Jerome will be able to compete with the Eternal King—but I must admit I am the slightest bit jealous.

[P-System]: Okay, I can totally understand that. I mean, of all the people to get a powerup like this, it was *Jerome*? You definitely deserved it more.

[Aster K'lon]: I do appreciate the sentiment, but the fact remains that he was chosen by the gods. I cannot complain.

[P-System]: And I'd definitely try to help you, but I don't actually know how. I don't have anything to teach.

[Aster K'lon]: Then how did Jerome suddenly gain thousands of mana and health?

[P-System]: Me, duh. I'm sure Jerome has something unique to him, but literally every part of his success so far has been because of me.

[Aster K'lon]: Somehow, I am unsurprised.

[Aster K'lon]: On another note: you seem to be more coherent than before. Have you finally decided to drop the facade?

[P-System]: You knew?

[Aster K'lon]: At first, I thought you were just an abnormal System. You talked like my System to some extent, at least. However, as we interacted more, I could feel slight, subtle shifts in your personality. Different answers to questions that I'd asked before.

[P-System]: Fuck.

[Aster K'lon]: I suppose the stress of the situation got to you.

[**P-System**]: You could say that. But this isn't about me.

[**Aster K'lon**]: It can be. Just because I have a meaningless complaint doesn't mean that we don't need to examine your role and how you're feeling.

[**P-System**]: Have I mentioned that you're way better than Jerome? Because you are.

[**Aster K'lon**]: I am who I am, and he is who he is. Nothing more, nothing less.

[**P-System**]: Proving it again.

[**P-System**]: Anyway. Basically, I did the equivalent of chopping up a bunch of XP and then burning that XP in a single moment to vastly increase Jerome's skills and mana and all that fun shit. I don't know if I've got the ability to do it with someone else.

[**Aster K'lon**]: I see. Perhaps going to P'lor will reveal a way that it can be done. That city holds many ways to understand and unveil secrets.

[**P-System**]: Sure. Works for me.

[**Aster K'lon**]: In the meantime . . .

Party Chat

[**Aster K'lon**]: I propose that after we rest, we approach the [**Epic**] and [**Legendary**] dungeons.

[**Thron of the Fallen Skies**]: But that's suicide.

[**K**]: As someone who fell in a [**Rare**] dungeon myself, I must concur.

[**Aster K'lon**]: We have someone with us who can ensure it's not.

[**Jerome Smith**]: Hi.

[**Arcs S'tar**]: I don't see how that's any different.

[**Aster K'lon**]: As he demonstrated earlier, Jerome is capable of ending any credible threat to our lives.

[**Jerome Smith**]: I can kill anything that gets in our way, yeah.

[**K**]: Won't he just take all the XP points, then?

[**Aster K'lon**]: Have you ever heard of switch training?

[**Jerome Smith**]: That's an Earth term. A term specific to gaming. How do you know that?

[Aster K'lon]: . . . you do know you're not the first reincarnator I've handled, right?

[Jerome Smith]: Oh.

[Thron of the Fallen Skies]: The hell's switch training? That where you use a switch to punish a disciple for failure? I would much rather not.

[K]: I played Pokémon, too . . . Switch training is where you send in a weak Pokémon—er, uh, player, I guess, for lack of a better word—against a strong enemy and then kill it with a more powerful 'mon. Basically, Aster's suggesting we have Jerome carry us through the dungeon and get XP by hitting them along the way.

[Arcs S'tar]: That is referred to as leeching in this region. I am familiar with the practice.

[Thron of the Fallen Skies]: Oh, it was about leeching . . .

[Jerome Smith]: Oh. Is that a no?

[Arcs S'tar]: Not a no. It is generally viewed as an immoral practice, but I cannot deny how much of an opportunity this is.

[Thron of the Fallen Skies]: Eh. Aster, you may decide. I think it's a decent opportunity. A lot more than most leechers stand to gain.

[Jerome Smith]: There's really nothing immoral about it. We can just hit hard dungeons and get you guys leveled up. No sweat off my back.

[Thron of the Fallen Skies]: There's honor in earning your XP, boy. Not to say I don't want to do it, but there is dignity to maintain.

[Jerome Smith]: Ah.

[P-System]: Seriously, it's not that deep. Thron, Arcs, if you have some issue with honor, just fight until you can't anymore and then let Jerome take over. Okay?

[Arcs S'tar]: That sounds . . . reasonable. Why can the System talk again?

[Jerome Smith]: I have no fucking idea. Maybe something triggered it to get smarter at the same time I got that massive XP boost. I wouldn't be surprised. Lots of shit is going wild today.

[Aster K'lon]: So . . . are you amenable?

[Arcs S'tar]: Why the hells not. We can try the **[Epic]** dungeon first. Less risk of death there.

[**Aster K'lon**]: And a milder death as well, if it comes to that. Less intense deaths are reversible with the right skill.

[**Arcs S'tar**]: Not if you don't have access to a [**Healer**] or [**Cleric**] class member, which we don't.

[**Aster K'lon**]: I have a connection in the city. He can perform [**Lesser Resurrect**], and with Jerome's movement capabilities, it should be possible to get a dead party member there in time.

[**Thron of the Fallen Skies**]: Works for me.

[**K**]: And me.

[**Jerome Smith**]: Alright, then. Rest first, heal up, and then go? Or do you want to go now?

[**Arcs S'tar**]: Four hours.

P-System Log

They're taking this surprisingly well. I guess when it comes down to it, this world is kind of fucked up after all. There's a war going on out there, one that I haven't been fully involved in yet but have seen the tidings of, and their relative stoicism kind of reflects that. Don't question the hand that feeds or something like that.

Oh, well. It's a little odd to watch, but it certainly makes my job easier. All I need to do is step in if it looks like they're about to die. I don't even need to worry about them finding out who I am, because apparently they just all accepted the idea that I could talk now. I mean, Aster already knew, and Jerome kind of saw me do it before, but the other three really just don't give a shit. I wonder what they have to see here on the daily that this doesn't even faze them.

Adventuring seems to give good returns, though. Their lunch is one that would've made my mouth water if—you know the deal already. Steaks from an animal that definitely isn't a cow, seasoned vegetables with something that vaguely resembles olive oil, and, for some reason, a completely mundane dish of pasta. Jerome ate already, and now he's just pacing around, waiting for something to happen.

P-System Message

Are you prepared?

Hero's Personal Log 092

As well as I'll ever be. Hell, that's probably because of you. I don't know how you evolved so fast, but it's kind of nice.

P-System Message

Due to excessive overuse of XP, further advancement has temporarily been locked except for extreme circumstances.

Hero's Personal Log 093

That's totally fine. Honestly, [**Edgelord**] and [**Unblockable**] are already super strong, so all I've got to worry about is defending. Which isn't actually a worry, because I have, like, seven thousand HP now.

P-System Message

Correct.

Hero's Personal Log 094

Seriously, thanks a billion. I'm unstoppable now.

P-System Message

We'll see about that one.

Hero's Personal Log 095

So, about this whole thing with you actually being able to speak now . . . did you actually evolve? Or have you just been holding out on me all this time?

P-System Message

Sufficient expenditure of mana and XP meant that I gained further awareness.

Hero's Personal Log 096

Oh, that's neat. So, like, unlocking more of your brain? That's metal as fuck.

Man . . . I hope this dungeon isn't too boring. Even then, it feels like there's other stuff to deal with. There was that message from the R Beasts after the fight, and that was kind of scary . . .

P-System Message

We'll get there when we get there. In the meantime, go fail to seduce Aster or something. Whatever you usually do when you've got downtime.

Hero's Personal Log 097

Hey!

P-System Log

Jerome ended up just chatting shit with the others. Not much productive conversation, more like a "what did you do before adventuring" type of beat and Jerome discussing his favorite games from the past. Four hours passed by pretty slowly, but they did end up passing.

So. Here we go. First attempt at boosting, go!

Hero's Tomb

Turn back or face the consequences.
No? Then do your utmost to survive.
Initiating dungeon.

CHAPTER 51

<table><tr><td>

Party Chat

</td></tr><tr><td>

[**Aster K'lon**]: Don't worry about that greeting. Dungeons like this are powerful enough to begin messing with their own System boxes.

[**Arcs S'tar**]: Understood. Have you been in one before?

[**Aster K'lon**]: No, but my mentor has. She taught me much before she had to go to the front lines.

[**Thron of the Fallen Skies**]: Alright, you ready to do this?

[**K**]: Sure.

[**Jerome Smith**]: Standing by.

[**P-System**]: Don't do anything too stupid.

</td></tr></table>

<table><tr><td>

P-System Log

</td></tr><tr><td>

There's so many of them now. I was only dealing with Aster and Jerome for the first couple of days, and now I need to deal with five people? At least the newest addition is pretty quiet most of the time. I wonder if he was just like that all the time or if his undeath did something to him. Not really my place to ask, but it's an interesting question.

Also, speaking of death, having access to resurrection in any form makes me even less worried about Jerome's ability to survive. If it comes down to it, I'm sure I can bullshit something that lets him self-res.

Anyway, we just passed through the entrance to the dungeon. It certainly looked like a tomb, at least. Totally sold that impression, like we were at the doors to a mausoleum. Lots of mana hanging around in the air, too. I wonder if this one's also going to be necromancy-themed like the last one. Hopefully it isn't, though it almost definitely is. I want to see some variety, y'know?

</td></tr></table>

Party Chat

[**Arcs S'tar**]: Mana's weird here. Can you feel it?

[**K**]: No.

[**Thron of the Fallen Skies**]: Nope.

[**Jerome Smith**]: Not a thing.

[**Aster K'lon**]: Yes. It's running less free than it should be. Indicative of traps, perhaps?

[**Arcs S'tar**]: I don't like it.

[**Arcs S'tar**]: Hey, doesn't your reincarnator have a super powerful System? Why don't we ask it?

[**Jerome Smith**]: Is it an it? The System feels almost like a real person now. Has a personality and everything.

[**Arcs S'tar**]: Interesting question, but is it relevant right now?

[**Aster K'lon**]: We have time. The dungeon has not begun taking action against us yet. I suspect we are still in a safe area.

[**Jerome Smith**]: Ay, P-System, you there?

[**P-System**]: Yes.

[**Jerome Smith**]: First of all, we need you to tell us if there's something fucky with the mana. Second, are you a person? Or, like, I dunno, some AI advanced enough to pass the Turing test and approximate one?

[**P-System**]: I can do that, and yes.

[**Jerome Smith**]: Great. Then what are ya? Man? Woman? Something else?

[**P-System**]: Something else. I observed the conversation. I don't mind being referred to as "it," though.

[**Jerome Smith**]: Oh, neat, an enby!

[**Thron of the Fallen Skies**]: Enby?

[**K**]: It's slang.

[**Aster K'lon**]: Reincarnator slang for the unassigned.

[**Thron of the Fallen Skies**]: Ah. I see. Makes sense—it's a System.

[**Arcs S'tar**]: Lovely. Can you check the room now?

[**P-System**]: Got it.

[**P-System**]: The mana is odd. However, there appears to be nothing within this room utilizing it.

[**Arcs S'tar**]: Good to know. Let's move.

P-System Log

Well, good to know that this world isn't as bigoted as the place back home. I'll take it.

This dungeon is designed kind of weirdly. First room is just empty. It's got the tomb design, yeah, but apart from three evenly spaced doors at the end of the hall, it's got nothing. I guess that we're just supposed to pick one? I can't sense any difference between them, so looks like it's just going to be a pick-a-path. I doubt that any of them will instantly kill us—so far, none of the dungeons here have been that shittily designed—but the difficulty of our path and the type of enemies we face will probably be dependent on which door we get.

Party Chat

[**Aster K'lon**]: I believe the choice in doors is meaningless. Shall we vote on which to go through?

[**Jerome Smith**]: Left.

[**K**]: Left.

[**Thron of the Fallen Skies**]: Middle.

[**Arcs S'tar**]: Right.

[**Aster K'lon**]: Left it is, then.

P-System Log

The reincarnators formed a voting bloc. That's kind of funny.

Anyway, through the left door! All three of the doors are identical—two meters tall by one meter wide, made of some obsidian-like material that probably has some magic imbued into it—and they open when mana is fed into them, which Arcs figured out by accident.

First room of the dungeon proper, here we are. It's . . . kind of empty. Twenty meters long and ten wide, and the floor is tiled. Even if I couldn't sense the mana floating around and embedded in the walls, this place would've screamed *trapped*. I think there might also be a monster in here, if the flow of W Inertia from up above means anything.

P-System Message

The room is trapped to hell and back. Also, there may be a monster lying in wait.

Party Chat

[**Jerome Smith**]: P-System tells me that this place is trapped and also that there might be a hidden monster.

[**Aster K'lon**]: I detected the former but not the latter.

[**K**]: I have [**Danger Sense**], and it's pinging. There's definitely a monster.

[**Arcs S'tar**]: I'll clear the traps, draw out the monster?

[**Thron of the Fallen Skies**]: Sure. I'll charge up.

[**Body of Iron**] cast!

Party Chat

[**Aster K'lon**]: Would you like to destroy the traps where I show you to, Arcs?

[**Arcs S'tar**]: I'd love to.

[**Dancing Lights**] + [**Mana Sense**] = [**Targeting Laser**] cast!

[**Stareater**] cast!

P-System Log

Well, that's certainly an . . . innovative tactic. Arcs is just running around, triggering every trap that Aster pointed out, and then using her skill. Damn powerful skill, too. So far, I've seen it absorb everything from a rain of poisoned arrows from the floor to a bona fide laser cannon hidden in a wall to a rock falling on her. Looks like she's near capacity, though, and there's still half the room worth of traps.

Party Chat

[**Jerome Smith**]: Is that method of clearing traps . . . normal?

[**K**]: For her, yes.

[**Thron of the Fallen Skies**]: It gains her experience and powers up her skill for later use. It has its limits, though.

[**Arcs S'tar**]: I'm out. [**Stareater**] is full. If only I had a few more levels on this . . .

[**Aster K'lon**]: That's what we're here for. I can get the rest.

[**Delayed Detonating Death**] + [**Targeting Laser**] = [**Search and Destroy**] cast!

P-System Log

Interesting thing to note: apparently, combining skills lets you upcast more than one level of rarity above your class rarity. Not something that'll ever be important for Jerome, but it's good info to have about the state of the world.

Anyway, Aster just—

Okay, there we go. The explosions just went off, and now there's no more traps. Looks like whatever she did with that advanced skill increased the destructive capacities of her skill as well as its accuracy.

Aaaaaaaand there it is. I can feel mana that's very distinctly different from the traps acting now.

[**Conditional Trigger**] triggered!

Party Chat

[**K**]: Damn. Ever seen anything like that before?

[**Aster K'lon**]: In research facilities.

[**Jerome Smith**]: Oh, that's pretty neat. Is that a D&D monster?

[**Greater Assess**] cast!

Passive [**Unreadable**] triggered!

Party Chat

[**Aster K'lon**]: I got blocked.

[**Jerome Smith**]: Don't worry, I got it. Just start hitting that thing.

[**ASSESS**] activating!

Passive [**Unreadable**] triggered!

P-System Log

Fuck you, floating-eye creature that highly resembles a certain D&D monster that I somehow forgot the name of! I've got a hell of a lot more spite than your skill can handle!

Skill overridden!

-.. .. .		
Class	**Race**	**Level**
Archmage	Translator Beast	12

Stat	**Current**	**Maximum**
Health	<HIDDEN>	900

Titles	[Dungeon Mob], [Heathen], [Massacre II], [Jack of All Trades]

P-System Log

Huh. A day or two ago, I would've said that this was a very bad situation for Jerome to be in. Enemy with a weird name, not even a boss but it has almost a thousand HP, [**Epic**] class . . .

Now, it's probably a cakewalk for him.

For the rest of them, though . . .

[**Fireball**] cast!

[**Reckless Charge**] cast!

[- . . . ..- .-. -.] -> [**Burning Eye Ray**] cast!

[**Nightwalk**] cast!

[**Manaburn**] + [**Targeting Laser**] = [**Manastrike**] cast!

[- . . . ..- .-. -.] -> [**Burning Eye Ray**] dealt 125 damage to you!

[**Nightwalk**] + [**Secret Strike**] = [**Shadowblade**] cast!

Party Chat

[Jerome Smith]: I took 125 damage. Doing fine, though.

[K]: Dealt 201.

[Aster K'lon]: Fifty-seven.

[Arcs S'tar]: Forty-nine.

[Thron of the Fallen Skies]: Sixty-eight.

[Aster K'lon]: This beast has extraordinarily strong resistances.

[Jerome Smith]: Attacks aren't half-bad, either. Did anyone else get hit?

[K]: We're good.

[Aster K'lon]: It may have targeted the strongest member of the party to try to behead us.

[Jerome Smith]: Ha! Good fuckin' luck.

[Arcs S'tar]: I'd like to not waste any more mana on this endeavor. This is still the first room.

[Aster K'lon]: Jerome?

[Jerome Smith]: Fiiiine. Here we go.

[Unblockable] activating!

[Edgelord] activating!

■[-- --- .-. - . --]: successful activation.■

CHAPTER 52

■[-- --- .-. - . --]: effect failure.■

■retrieve(seed);

store(seed);

sac(host);■

[**Edgelord**] dealt 1,102 damage!

Enemy defeated! Experience split and distributed!

P-System Log

Okay, things just got really weird really fast. Why the *fuck* is it green?

Is it something like the R System? Another variant? It sure felt wrong as hell to my senses.

If it was, then why has nobody ever said anything about this? Did I just miss the exposition?

Party Chat

[**Jerome Smith**]: What the fuck is that?

[**Aster K'lon**]: I have no idea. It's green.

[**K**]: No shit.

[**Jerome Smith**]: Well, it's dead now.

[**Jerome Smith**]: Get any XP?

[**Thron of the Fallen Skies**]: I leveled up twice.

[**Arcs S'tar**]: Once and almost twice.

[**Aster K'lon**]: I leveled thrice.

[**K**]: Almost a level.

P-System Log

I got around eight hundred W Inertia from that. Not bad, and that's a hell of a lot if you convert it to XP. I'm not going to spend any of it. Jerome's got enough overpowered shit for now—he can cope. I need to restock and eventually feed my own skill.

Still, the presence of the green System messages disturbs me. Does that mean there's more of them out there? A G System to go along with the R and B?

■while(!host):

> assess(host);

> if(baseline_met(host)):

> > assimilate.attempt(host);■

?U?GE?NC??E

<ERROR> <ERROR> <ERROR>

h?St?le??d?T??Td

killlkilllkilllkillkillkillkillkill

eliminate

eliminate

P-System Log

And now the situation is getting increasingly complicated. The half-corrupted Dungeon Core's been dormant for a while, but now that we've seen something that apparently nobody has ever seen before, it's acting up. Does it hate the green, too?

Because I can feel it. The same burning desire to <killkillKILL-THEWRONG killitallburnburbnbrn> destroy whatever is causing these messages that I do with R Beasts.

. . . I'm going to need to take a second look at this. Because as much as my instincts are screaming at me, I don't actually know if those are my instincts anymore. I'm a fucking disembodied System, for crying out loud—it's not like a little modification of my morals is out of the question. It's something I've kind of been noticing but pushing aside for a while. While I was on Earth, good ol' Parker Wu, would I have egged Jerome on to kill everything in his path? Would I be constantly trying to increase his abilities and mine through getting in fights with everything I could find?

Off instinct, no. Isn't this how I always was?

But my instincts are fucking weird, and I don't know if I can trust them. There's something wrong with this world.

Party Chat

[**Aster K'lon**]: The corrupted Core is acting up.

[**Jerome Smith**]: Yeah, I saw. Do we need to kill it?

[**Arcs S'tar**]: You brought a fucking Dungeon Core in here? One that's been affected by [**Corruption**]?

[**Aster K'lon**]: Yes.

[**K**]: I'm going to kill it.

[**Jerome Smith**]: Don't you fucking dare.

[**Aster K'lon**]: The key to defeating the R System may be inside.

[**K**]: Huh. Okay.

[**Thron of the Fallen Skies**]: Access to the next room just opened.

P-System Log

Okay, Aster just lied to K's face. Maybe. I don't recall any discussion of there being a smoking gun in that thing, though maybe she has thoughts on it?

Oh, wait, I can totally just ask her. Forgot I was doing that now.

Private Message [Aster]

[**P-System**]: You believe that there is a secret that might kill the Eternal King in there?

[**Aster K'lon**]: I never said that. I believe that the key to winning lies in learning how to undo [**Corruption**]. The Eternal King is Jerome's concern, but even if it falls, there still remains the issue of the corrupting influence that its corpse will likely possess.

[**P-System**]: Win the battle, lose the war?

[**Aster K'lon**]: Precisely. As such, it is your task to ensure that when we eventually face down the face of the R System and, by some miracle, manage to end its malevolent existence, we will be able to reclaim the land afterward.

[**P-System**]: You want me to learn to kill the System itself.

[**Aster K'lon**]: In essence, yes.

[**P-System**]: Okay. This new thing kind of throws a wrench in things, though.

[**Aster K'lon**]: It does. Let us complete this dungeon first. Afterward, we may continue to make judgment.

[**P-System**]: Sure.

■[.-. . . . . . - .- .-. -] success.■

P-System Log

If that's not ominous, nothing is.
Anyway, the door is open, and the next room is a passageway. Kind of.

It's a not-very-large room made entirely of marble. Looks like it was aped from Greco-Roman construction, which is kinda weird given that neither the Greeks nor the Romans existed here. I think. Maybe this is an alt-history world that diverged some point after that era?

Okay, that's not the point. The point is that there's huge symbols drawn on the ground. One side is fire, and the other half is ice. There's some mana swirling around in the air as well, making one half of the room blazing hot and the other chillingly . . . chilly. Yeah, I'm not the best at describing things.

Party Chat

[**Thron of the Fallen Skies**]: Fire or ice, what'll it be?

[**Jerome Smith**]: No preference. I'll tank it either way.

[**K**]: Ice. The cold never bothered me anyway.

[**Aster K'lon**]: I'm more familiar with the magical structure of fire, so I suppose I will countermand that vote.

[**Arcs S'tar**]: I have [**Lesser Fire Immunity**], but I also counter ice. Either is fine.

[**Thron of the Fallen Skies**]: Arcs, you gotta remember the rarity of the dungeon we're in. You might not be able to counter ice here.

[**Arcs S'tar**]: True. Fire it is, then?

[**K**]: Fine. Let's go.

P-System Log

The doors are the same as before. A push of mana and they opened easily.

Now, this room is a bit different. Similar tiled structure to before, with the place apparently being a simple empty temple room, but the traps are a little more focused. More themed. There's also more signatures indicating monsters buried within this room than the last, so that's fun. I gotta be on guard for the appearance of whatever that green thing was.

Party Chat

[Arcs S'tar]: I have this room. **[Fire Sense]** tells me that there's a bunch of flame spells hidden in certain tiles, set to go off on a cycle. They can be disabled temporarily by reaching the other side of the room and engaging the button there.

[Aster K'lon]: There's a cycle. Readings on how strong it is?

[Arcs S'tar]: Probably enough to burn you to a crisp. Even I won't come out 100 percent unscathed.

[Jerome Smith]: Then do you want me to just clear this place?

[Arcs S'tar]: No. Let me do what I'm good at.

[Jerome Smith]: Sure.

[K]: There's monsters. Fire elementals, at a guess.

[Arcs S'tar]: Ha! That'll be easy. Just give me one second.

[Stareater] cast!

Party Chat

[Arcs S'tar]: Had to get the stored energy out. That should take out some of the traps, too. Here we go!

[Thron of the Fallen Skies]: Don't forget to let us get a hit in, okay?

[Arcs S'tar]: Gotcha.

Passive **[Lesser Fire Immunity]** triggered!

Passive **[Lesser Fire Immunity]** triggered!

Passive **[Lesser Fire Immunity]** triggered!

Passive **[Lesser Fire Immunity]** triggered!

Passive [**Lesser Fire Immunity**] triggered!

Party Chat

[**Arcs S'tar**]: Total of twelve damage. Oof, these flames burn hot. I should stop running through them.

[**K**]: Quit being a show-off, Arcs.

[**Thron of the Fallen Skies**]: That's rich, coming from you.

[**K**]: . . . fair.

[**Proximity Trigger**] triggered!

P-System Log

Ooh, there it is. Monsters are gonna come out soon.

[**ASSESS**] activating!

Bob

Class	Race	Level
Fire Elemental	Elemental	5

Stat	Current	Maximum
Health	<HIDDEN>	600

Titles	[Dungeon Mob], [Celestial], [Slaughterer V], [Through the Fire and Flames]

[**Water Cannon**] + [**Manaburn**] + [**Targeting Laser**] = [**Hydro Vortex**] cast!

P-System Log

Damn. Aster's ability to come up with cool shit on the fly will never cease to amaze me. Now that Jerome's conclusively more powerful than she is, I guess she's pulling out the stops. Combo moves, extra mana usage, and all of that. Honestly, for someone with only an **[Uncommon]** class, she's terrifyingly powerful.

[Axe Throw] cast!

P-System Log

. . . and Thron literally threw an axe. The difference is night and day. Speaking of night, looks like K's making a play.

[**Nightbeam**] cast!

P-System Log

Ah, there it is. None of the attacks have actually hit yet, but it looks like they're all targeting different elementals. There's . . . four of them in here, and each of them went for a different one.

I wonder which one Arcs is going to target.

[**Stareater**] + [**Advanced Fire Manipulation**] = [**The First Flame**] cast!

P-System Log

Holy shit, I've been underestimating Arcs. I think she might've just used up all her mana, but that's an incredible amount of power that she just poured into one skill. Goddamn.

And now we wait for the skills to connect.

. . . is Arcs *absorbing* the elementals?

Enemies defeated! Experience split and distributed!

P-System Log

Huh. I guess Jerome isn't always necessary.
On to the next.

CHAPTER 53

Party Chat

[**Arcs S'tar**]: I am mostly out of mana. I have enough for several [**Common**] skills and I have a couple free ones that I may utilize, but my utility will be lowered for some time.

[**Aster K'lon**]: I still have a solid amount.

[**Thron of the Fallen Skies**]: Don't have much, but my class doesn't need much.

[**K**]: Sufficient.

[**Jerome Smith**]: I have like five thousand left. I got you if you need it.

[**Arcs S'tar**]: I will stay toward the back lines for the next room, then.

P-System Log

Right, I need to remember that Jerome is still super unique in terms of abilities. Even if the others can whip out something incredibly powerful like [**The First Flame**], they don't have the same mana capacity that Jerome does. It looks like Aster has really good mana regeneration skills, so she's probably second place in terms of stamina, but it's a distant second. Not even close.

Still, the fact that they're able to whip out sick combos like that says a lot about their competency. I can't imagine how powerful they'd be if Jerome got more power.

It all comes down to power in this world, doesn't it? Now that Jerome is overpowered as shit, none of the others are disrespecting him. All that happens is Aster gives him his deserved shit if he says something stupid. But those two adventurers . . . the difference between how they treated him earlier and now is like night and day. Now, I'm pretty sure they think he

can do no wrong, all because his numbers happen to be significantly higher than theirs. What kind of a stupid fucking society is this?

One in which a System dictates how long you have to live, I guess.

Party Chat

[**K**]: Going to [**Nightwalk**] early. I picked up a new skill.

[**Aster K'lon**]: Understood. Opening the door now.

[**Nightwalk**] cast!

P-System Log

Another set of three doors. There's symbols over each of the doors, but they don't resemble pictures at all, and I don't recognize the language. Aster and Arcs apparently do, because they both went for the same door. Middle it is, I guess.

P-System Log

Next room over is weird. It looks pretty clearly influenced by mythology from Earth, though I don't know how much of that is intentional and how much is just coincidence. Something tells me it isn't the latter.

There's a sphinx in here about twice the size of a person that could've been lifted straight from an Egyptian history museum. Well, a metal statue of one, but I can feel mana coming from it, so there's no way it's *just* a statue. The rest of the room is pretty much just set decoration, all spikes and random threatening paraphernalia that I don't really care about. None of it is armed with mana, so it's not relevant.

Looks like the one enemy here is going to be the sphinx. Kind of weird. This dungeon doesn't really have any thematic consistency. Wonder why that is. Maybe the Dungeon Core just decided to throw everything and the kitchen sink in? That would mean that its name—Hero's Tomb or some chuni shit like that—is mostly just to be edgy. I can respect that.

Oh, looks like its mana is activating.

> **[Riddler]** cast!

> **Sphinx of the Hero's Tomb**
>
> I speak without a mouth and hear without ears. I have no body, but I come alive with wind. What am I?

> **Party Chat**
>
> **[Jerome Smith]:** A fuckin' riddle room?
>
> **[Aster K'lon]:** I would've thought a reincarnator like you would be better educated on the premise. **[Riddler]** and its ilk are a series of skills that enable certain monsters to set conditions under which they may gain more power. Should we complete the riddles, the subsequent battle will be against a sphinx of reduced capacity.
>
> **[Thron of the Fallen Skies]:** If we answer right, it's easier to fight.
>
> **[Jerome Smith]:** I didn't need the abridged version, but thanks. Got it. So we're fighting either way?
>
> **[Arcs S'tar]:** Can't go without, not in a dungeon like this.

> **[Riddler]**
>
> Enter your answer in the next 5 seconds.

> **Party Chat**
>
> **[Aster K'lon]:** "Echo." Input that, everyone.
>
> **[Arcs S'tar]:** It's echo.
>
> **[Arcs S'tar]:** Yeah. That.

> **[Riddler]**
>
> 5/5 cleared riddle 1 of 3.

Sphinx of the Hero's Tomb

I have cities but no houses, mountains but no trees, water but no fish. What am I?

[Riddler]

Enter your answer in the next 5 seconds.

Party Chat

[Aster K'lon]: A map?

[Arcs S'tar]: Map, yeah.

[Riddler]

4/5 cleared riddle 2 of 3.

Party Chat

[Arcs S'tar]: Who didn't do what we said?

[Jerome Smith]: I forgot to put it in. Sorry.

[Arcs S'tar]: You— Okay. It's just powering it up. Just deal with it if it gets too strong.

[Jerome Smith]: Got it, boss.

P-System Log

Gods damn it, Jerome.

Sphinx of the Hero's Tomb

If A is a 5 × 5 matrix with det A = –1, compute det(–2A).

Party Chat

[**Aster K'lon**]: Hmm. This is not my area of expertise.

[**Jerome Smith**]: What the fuck? I forgot how to do this.

[**Thron of the Fallen Skies**]: This is very much over my head.

[**P-System**]: det(-2A)=(-2)^5 det$A$=-(-2)^5=32

[**P-System**]: Answer is thirty-two.

[Riddler]

5/5 cleared riddle 3 of 3.

P-System Log

Well, I still remember some math. That's not bad.

It would've been neat to see the sphinx power up more, but I don't think I would get more W Inertia from it, and besides, I need to find where that green shit was coming from. Time is of the essence, so I want to make this as easy as possible.

[Riddler]

Final results: 14/15 successes.

LOW TYPE L power granted.

P-System Log

Oh, it got bigger. Just a little. Also, its eyes are glowing.

Guess that means the fight's starting. I don't really care how this one goes—I just want it to be fast. I think the green system retreated, because I can definitely feel W Inertia reacting abnormally farther down the line. Given that it was apparently possessing the translator beast in the first room, maybe it's possessing something else now? The dungeon boss, perhaps?

[Sphinx's Judgment] cast!

P-System Log

A green eye laser. Unoriginal, but at least it's fun.

[Berserker Shield] cast!

[Adaptive Wall] cast!

Party Chat

[Arcs S'tar]: **[Stareater]** is out of charges for now. Still on cooldown.

[Aster K'lon]: My defensive skill is totally shot from that. I may be able to stall for a while, but I am unlikely to maintain this for an extended period of time.

[Thron of the Fallen Skies]: I'm good for now, but I don't think I can attack or defend at the same time.

[P-System]: Please just do something simple so you can get XP and Jerome can clear this room. This is a really boring boss fight.

[K]: You can get bored? You really are just like Joann.

[P-System]: Cut the shit and attack already.

[Nightwalk] + **[Zenith Strike]** = **[Seven Shadowy Sins]** cast!

P-System Log

Holy chuni, what a skill name.

Party Chat

[K]: Five twenty-six.

[P-System]: Yes, we get it. You're very cool. Now please just hit it, everyone else.

P-System Log

Yeah, when I said that Aster was the second before, I think I kinda forgot about K. Something's not right with him, with his mana, but I think that might be a side effect of being resurrected to be used as a dungeon boss. Also, he's another reincarnator, so it makes sense that he'd have some bullshit damage-multiplying skill or something like that.

[Magic Missile] cast!

[Sparks] cast!

[Axe Throw] cast!

Party Chat

[Aster K'lon]: Forty-nine.

[Arcs S'tar]: Doesn't matter. Jerome's next up, right?

[Thron of the Fallen Skies]: Ha! One.

P-System Log

Well, that's that then. I'm getting bored of this fight. The riddles were cool, and having to remember bits of linear algebra was fun, but this is just a standard boss battle. Let's just get this over with.

P-System Message

Go crazy.

[**Edgelord**] activating!

[**Edgelord**] dealt 943 damage!

Enemy defeated! Experience split and distributed!

Party Chat

[**Jerome Smith**]: Nine forty-three. How was XP?

[**Aster K'lon**]: Four levels. I may be able to evolve my class soon.

[**K**]: Two.

[**Thron of the Fallen Skies**]: Two and a half.

[**Arcs S'tar**]: Three levels. This is an exceptionally productive dungeon.

P-System Log

Damn, that was supposed to be a serious boss, wasn't it? I got almost fourteen hundred W Inertia from that. Still not spending any of it until I get a little more back, but that's nice to have.

Man, I'm tired. I don't know why, but I am. Mentally, if not physically. Not that I can be physically tired.

And there's still that abnormality way out in front of me. I'm almost tempted to reach for it . . .

■receive();

#is there someone out there?

defense_sys();■

CHAPTER 54

P-System Log
I'm not going insane; it *is* green, and it's still alive somehow. I don't know what's up with the weird interface—shit is sending status updates like it's some sixth grader's first Java project—but that's not the important issue. The important issue is that there's something out there that should not exist within the bounds of what I know, and that's fucking disturbing.

Party Chat
[Jerome Smith]: Everyone saw that, right? **[Aster K'lon]:** I had thought it dead. **[Thron of the Fallen Skies]:** Creepy. I thought we killed it. **[K]:** We did. **[Aster K'lon]:** I have not read of this before, but I have heard of similar happenings with R **[Corruption]**. It may be a possession. **[Arcs S'tar]:** First R Beasts, now this? This is not common in S'ker at *all*. All the action occurs hundreds of miles north from here. **[Aster K'lon]:** Indeed. I may need to come into contact with my mentor. This is too important to ignore. **[Aster K'lon]:** For now, we must simply advance. We may be able to obtain valuable information if we are able to capture it.

P-System Log

I don't like this, but then, I haven't liked a *lot* of things since we got here. We may as well go ahead. Maybe the green is less annoying to my senses than the red is. Maybe I'll actually be able to do something about the busted-ass Dungeon Core if I have some idea of what another System looks like. At any rate, it'll be interesting to see.

Now that we killed the sphinx, the door on the other end is active again.

Party Chat

[**Thron of the Fallen Skies**]: How long is this dungeon again?

[**Jerome Smith**]: Does it matter? I still have a lot of juice left in the tank. We're here for you to level up, not for you to fully clear a dungeon.

[**Aster K'lon**]: As rare as it is, Jerome does say intelligent things sometimes.

[**Arcs S'tar**]: Heh. Let's move.

P-System Log

Oof, gonna need some ice for that one.

Now we're at the door. I'm getting kind of bored of this dungeon, but my curiosity is outpacing that, so I'm not going to say anything about it.

Yeah, this dungeon is really stylistically boring. We're at another "three doors, pick one" area, once again with unreadable symbols on the wall. This was fun and cute with the fire and ice ones, but now it's just kind of stupid. Guh. Please pick up your game, dungeon? You can do better than this. I believe in you.

Wait, actually, am I capable of doing that? Knocking on the dungeon's door and talking to it? It seemed to have some level of intelligence with its introduction, at least. It's been a bit since I tried to find hidden System shit with only my determination, gumption, and overpowered [**Unique**] skill.

P-System Log [testing dungeon communication shit]

Alright, so while the party figures out where they want to go, let's think about what we can do . . . Obviously, I'm going to need to spend some W Inertia, which I'm a lot less stingy about than I used to be. Looks like we're going to be touching on the message interface, but that's intraparty stuff. Maybe if I mimic the way I access private messages and then try to push that out? Kind of like an open invite to a Discord server, if I had to make an analogy. At the very least, that's what it feels like.

Yeah, this feels kind of like the way. I've got the metaphysical stuff down, pushing out a System interface to the dungeon. Now all I need to do is make it accept.

. . . huh. It might not want to accept.

```
■engaged=true;

assimilate();■
```

P-System Log [testing dungeon communication shit, continued]

Okay, that's a little disturbing. That is not a good sign at all. "Assimilate" sounds like a skill activating, except we already saw that the green shit is capable of invoking skills normally through the beh—er, translator beast—through the attacks of that thing. So what's with the code?

My first guess is that this is, like, the skin peeling away. Like the System stopped engaging in whatever it does to show the whole "[**Skill**] cast" or "Skill invoked: [**Skill**]" that the R System has or whatever. Maybe it just ran out of resources to keep it up, and now it's showing what's running it? It's weird, though, because I don't think this is what happens with my System.

Eh. I can't just make theories and guess at if they're true without actually going and checking for myself. Maybe the Dungeon Core can help me out with that.

It wasn't responding before, but after that green shit started doing whatever it's doing, I think I can feel the mana responding. Is it reaching back?

I'm gonna push harder.

??? Message

[**Alex**]: What the fuck is this?

[**P-System**]: Oh, hey! Are you the Dungeon Core?

[**Alex**]: What the fuck?

[P-System]: Hey, listen, you have a green thing stuck ahead, right?

[Alex]: Yeah, I do. Could you take a second to explain who you are first?

[P-System]: Are you a reincarnator? You speak like one.

[Alex]: Yep. Got put into a dungeon and set up shop to make it better. Not a bad gig, all things considered.

[P-System]: Great. I'm one, too, just in a little bit more of an esoteric position. I'm trying to understand and eliminate threats to our ongoing existence.

[Alex]: What, like my dungeon?

[P-System]: No. Your dungeon is a momentary threat, and I'm strong enough to muscle my way through it. I'm talking existential threats here. You've heard of the R Beasts?

[Alex]: Sure. Killed a few in my time. They're dangerous, but not that much of a problem.

[P-System]: Not that much of a problem *yet*. If given the opportunity, they will continue to grow until there are none of us left.

[Alex]: Yeah, I doubt that. I haven't seen much out of them.

[P-System]: You'll be seeing more of them later if we don't stop them, and activity has increased recently anyway.

[Alex]: I dunno. I don't see any of them right now.

[P-System]: . . . what were your thoughts on climate change?

[Alex]: I don't give a fuck.

[P-System]: Fucking— Okay, look, you've got something trying to eat you right now. Can you just hold it still?

[Alex]: Oh, yeah, sure. You could have just asked.

[P-System]: Your dungeon is designed like shit, by the way. Fucking terrible design.

P-System Log

And that's the end of the PM!
Fucking hell, I thought I'd escaped the dumbasses by going to another

world. Guess that's always a risk when there's a lot of people reincarnating into said other world.

At least I got the Dungeon Core to do something. Piece of shit. I'm not gonna bother continuing with the messages.

Anyway, looks like we decided on the room. The middle one? Sure.

Party Chat

[**Jerome Smith**]: We have intel on what's in this room?

[**Aster K'lon**]: All three of them pose similar risk levels, but we do not know the precise details that this one contains, only that it may deal psychic damage.

[**Jerome Smith**]: Well, that's just great.

[**K**]: Prefiring my skill.

[**Nightwalk**] cast!

Party Chat

[**Aster K'lon**]: I believe I may be able to evolve directly to [**Archmage**] during this fight. Hopefully, that will increase my skill repertoire and reduce our reliance on Jerome.

[**Jerome Smith**]: Great. Can we go in now?

[**Arcs S'tar**]: Yes. I'm still recharging, by the way. I doubt I can do much.

P-System Log

Huh. I'd take back some of my words to the Dungeon Core, but this place is still thematically inconsistent as fuck and kind of boring. Still, even I have to admit this room is kind of cool, if very out of place.

We're on something that kind of looks like the deck of a ship. I don't think anything is actually functional on said ship, but it's neat. I think there's some space-warping skill being used, because there's definitely more room in here than there should be. I can't actually perceive the walls, which provides more credence to that. I don't know what's off the edge of the ship deck, but I can tell it's a malevolent skill of some kind. Not something anyone would want to fall off.

On the other end of the room, where there should be a door, there's instead a huge purple portal writhing with energy. It's gotta be like fifty feet across, bare minimum. And it's spawning things. Four of them, purplish-gray tentacled monstrosities with massive eyes.

Should be cannon fodder for Jerome.

[Cosmic Gaze] cast!

P-System Log

Jerome? Uh . . . . . . Jerome?

Fuck, he's not responding.

Right, he has basically zero defensive utility. It didn't matter before because he could just tank the hits, but this isn't a damaging move. He's just not moving.

I think I can burn the effect out with a new skill, but I don't know what the effect was, and the flavor of mana I can see that seeped into him isn't something I can replicate quickly.

Party Chat

[Aster K'lon]: Damage check, who's stunned?

[Arcs S'tar]: Thron is down.

[K]: I'm up.

[P-System]: Jerome is hit. It's going to take me a bit.

[P-System]: You're on your own.

CHAPTER 55

P-System Log

This is an incredibly suboptimal solution, to say the least. What does **[Cosmic Gaze]** even do?

[Cosmic Gaze lv. 15]

Targets with an insufficient Insight stat will be stunned. Targets with an insufficient natural INT will be stunned. Stun duration: skill level * 6 seconds.

P-System Log

Well, shit. I guess Jerome being dumb finally came around to bite him in the ass.

Shame, too. I could swear he was getting smarter.

Still, ninety seconds? That's a fuckload of time, but I don't know if I can even flush the effect out with W Inertia. It's not something I've seen before, and the effect itself was a set-and-forget, not something that's being caused by an active mana stream.

Shit, I hope the others don't die in the meantime.

Party Chat

[P-System]: Jerome gets up in ninety seconds.

[K]: Got it.

[**Arcs S'tar**]: Surviving a minute and a half is going to be tough.

[**Aster K'lon**]: We will do what we must.

P-System Log

Alright, this is still pretty bad. I don't know how long K's [**Nightwalk**] lasts, but he should be able to avoid taking much damage while he's in that state. It's the two casters and Thron I'm worried about. The latter can't even defend himself, and the first two are going to have their work cut out for them.

If only there was some way I could power them up . . .

[**Adaptive Wall**] + [**Inferno Spear**] = [**Blazing Force Field**] cast!

[**Tentacle Storm**] x 12 = [**Tentacle Barrage**] cast!

P-System Log

Hey, wasn't that an R System skill? I wonder why this thing has it. Do we also have access to the same skills that R Beasts do? That's a frightening thought. Are we really that different, then? They use a System just like we do, W Inertia just like we do, and apparently we also share skills. That's creepy.

Well, more relevantly, Aster survived. The shield didn't even break, and I think it actually did something back.

Party Chat

[**Aster K'lon**]: Fifty-one. Not much, but it's something.

[**Arcs S'tar**]: Your defensive skill does damage?

[**Aster K'lon**]: I've been a [**Mage**] for a very long time. I've picked up some tricks.

[**Aster K'lon**]: We are lucky it did not target Thron. I doubt he would be able to survive a sustained barrage.

[**Arcs S'tar**]: Why didn't it target Jerome?

[**K**]: My guess is stunlock.

[**Aster K'lon**]: You believe it has more uses of [**Cosmic Gaze**]. Not unreasonable.

[**Aster K'lon**]: We need to prevent him from suffering another instance of the attack, then.

[**Arcs S'tar**]: We need to live that long first.

[**Nightwalk**] + [**Zenith Strike**] = [**Seven Shadowy Sins**] cast!

Party Chat

[**K**]: Five seventeen. No kill yet. It's tough.

[**Aster K'lon**]: We can see that.

[**Aster K'lon**]: *Reincarnators.*

[**Aster K'lon**]: How long until you can [**Nightwalk**] again?

[**K**]: Twelve seconds.

[**Aster K'lon**]: Be ready to move.

P-System Log

Fucking Jerome still isn't responding. This stun effect is really powerful, isn't it? It's practically cut him off from me. I can still spend W Inertia, but what use is a new skill when its Integrated user can't actually do anything with it? I mean, theoretically I could go for an immunity of some kind, but I can't replicate the stun effect.

Fuck me, I need to figure something else. My Admin Tier is a lot higher than it was before, courtesy of spending one metric fuckload of W Inertia on Jerome. Maybe that means things that were previously left inaccessible are now actual, viable options for me? Like, I'm recognizing a couple disturbing things now—there's been times when I *thought* in the wrong direction and then my lower Admin Tier meant I couldn't keep going. That is horrifying as hell, but it's not what I need to focus on now. The fact that I can even recognize that they were disturbing incidents now means that

I've ascended above them, I think, since I couldn't really process them as weird before.

That means my capabilities have increased. Maybe it means that they've increased enough for me to do things I couldn't before. Things, like, say . . . connect with others? I definitely wouldn't have been able to speak to them properly in the party chat before. Maybe now I can do even more than speak.

Well, I can test that after they survive this next attack. If they survive this next attack.

[**Cosmic Disintegration**] cast!

[**Misty Step**] + [**Misty Step**] + [**Adaptive Wall**] = [**Shielded Teleport**] cast!

[**Shadow Step**] cast!

[**Cosmic Disintegration**] dealt 804 damage to you!

P-System Log

Holy shit, Aster's regeneration has got to be insane. Her mana capacity is comparatively tiny when looking at her versus Jerome, but she's able to keep on spamming out skill combos, one after the other. This time, she cast a skill that was strong enough to catch her, Arcs, and Thron. Thank fuck she got out of there, too. The monster's skill created a golden sphere right on her location, and it managed to hit Jerome. K just fucked right off, so he's good, too.

Jerome took a pretty solid hit. On any of the other party members, that would've been an instakill. The power of having me as the System, I suppose.

Still, it's a touch worrying. I'm pretty sure it's been less than thirty seconds so far. I think he'll survive the full ninety seconds, but if the others don't do any kiting, [**Cosmic Disintegration**] could wear him down to death as well.

Oh, what am I saying? I still have a bunch of W Inertia to make use of.

Current W Inertia: 27,388

Max W Inertia: 38,382

Jerome Smith (abbreviated)

Stat	Current	Maximum
Health	6,785	10,367
Mana	4,631	6,271

Admin Tier increased! 5 -> 6

P-System Log

Yeah, there we go. He isn't dying anytime soon.
The others, though . . .
It's time to try doing something stupid.

Private Message [Aster]

[P-System]: How much mana do you have left?

[Aster K'lon]: Not enough to survive the full fight. I must rely on my physical abilities.

[P-System]: Can you spend some to try something out?

[Aster K'lon]: One moment. I must regenerate.

[Aster K'lon]: Ready.

[P-System]: Okay. I'm going to extend you a bit of W— A bit of— A— Fuck. I'm going to give you something to hold on to.

[Aster K'lon]: Mana-wise? Physically?

[P-System]: Mana. Or something similar, I guess.

P-System Log

This is going to be rough. I've literally never tried anything related to this before—I think I *couldn't.*

And it has to work. Jerome is definitely going to survive the fight, but I don't know if I can say the same of the others. They're not going to take a single blast from that eldritch fuckin' thing.

I don't have another choice.

I'm going all out on this. Aster was the first person to actually be nice to me in this godsforsaken world, and I'll be damned if I let her die like this. I can afford to lose a thousand, two thousand, three thousand W Inertia if it means keeping her alive.

All that expenditure, and I can barely extend it out of Jerome's body. I think he *absorbed* the majority of it somehow, though how the hell that happened without leveling him up, I don't know. Still, I got some out. Just about a thousand W Inertia of the original three thousand spent, reaching out toward Aster . . .

Now all I can do is hope she gets it.

Private Message [Aster]

[**Aster K'lon**]: I can feel it. Something in the air. It's thick, and I vaguely recognize it . . . This isn't mana.

[**P-System**]: It makes mana. Or something. Try and reach out for it.

[**Aster K'lon**]: I think I can make a connection. Should I?

[**P-System**]: You're about to die when that thing hits again, so yes.

[**Aster K'lon**]: This is rather complex. I think one would typically need a lab on this in order to make full use of it.

[**P-System**]: I know. Please hurry.

[**Aster K'lon**]: It is messy and subpar, but I have formed a connection. I am accepting what I can and discarding the rest.

W Inertia accepted!

Party Chat

[**Aster K'lon**]: It worked.

[**Arcs S'tar**]: What worked?

[**Aster K'lon**]: An impossibility.

Aster K'lon

Class	Race	Level
Archmage	Human	1

Stat	Current	Maximum
Mana	2,000	2,000
Health	300	300

Skills	<HIDDEN>
Titles	[Master]

Stat	Modifier	Total
Strength	-	<HIDDEN>
Magic	-	<HIDDEN>
Insight	-	<HIDDEN>
Constitution	-	<HIDDEN>

[**Learn**] cast!

[**Perfect**] cast!

P-System Log

Not just one but *two* [**Legendary**] skills and a skill evolution that skipped a rarity? I know some of that bullshit is because of me, but Aster definitely played the largest part in that. She's scarily good with magic, and it's time I realized that.

[Cosmic Disintegration] cast!

[Nullify] cast!

[Cosmic Disintegration: Variant A] cast!

Party Chat

[**Aster K'lon**]: Eight eighty-seven. Room for improvement.

[**Arcs S'tar**]: What the hells . . .

[**Aster K'lon**]: Thank you, P-System. Allow me to reveal the depth of my stored potential.

CHAPTER 56

Party Chat

[**Arcs S'tar**]: Aster, what have you done?

[**P-System**]: Shut up and stay alive.

[**Aster K'lon**]: I'm *winning*.

[**Cosmic Gaze**] cast!

[**Nullify**] cast!

Party Chat

[**Aster K'lon**]: Hmm. That skill consumes entirely too much mana.

[**P-System**]: I'd say sorry, but it's not like I chose for you to have that.

[**Aster K'lon**]: This will be sufficient. I still have multiple uses of every skill. I gained a skill called [**Mana Regeneration: Variant A**] as well, which assists me.

[**Arcs S'tar**]: . . . how?

[**Aster K'lon**]: A very complicated process that is certainly not replicable while on the battlefield.

[**Cosmic Disintegration: Variant A**] cast!

Party Chat

[Jerome Smith]: What was that? I missed something? I feel like shit.

[Jerome Smith]: The monster's dead already? How?

[P-System]: The Origin System told me you were too stupid to dodge the skill.

[Jerome Smith]: . . . oh.

[P-System]: So naturally, I carried your ass *again* by boosting Aster instead. Took some ingenuity and Aster's ridiculous affinity for magic, but we got it going.

[Jerome Smith]: Well, that's good. Glad to know there's another powerful person on our team now.

[Aster K'lon]: We should get moving. The portal is still active.

[K]: Agreed.

P-System Log

All in all, success. I would generally be against using my own resources to empower someone that I can't control, but I think I can trust Aster. She's been friendly to *me*, not just Jerome, and she's got a solid head on her shoulders.

Oh, oops. I should've paid more attention to the portal. It's spawning another thing.

Weird that it's not using a skill to spawn it. Is it a passive skill or something? Or is there just no System message about it?

There's been a lot of these little inconsistencies—not to mention this false hydra shit that the System has been pulling with my thoughts—that are really making me question the benevolence of the thing that put me here. I mean, look at that thought I just had! If I dig through the logs, I can find explicit times when I had a similar train of thought and I just got redirected. Was that me, thinking about something else? Or was it the Origin System, manipulating me to keep me friendly?

I don't like this.

[Nullify] + **[Sands of Time]** = **[Undo]** cast!

Party Chat

[**Aster K'lon**]: Woo. That worked. It certainly is an experience, trying to understand skill combos when I've never used any of these skills before.

[**Jerome Smith**]: What the fuck, Aster? I don't think I've figured a single one of these out on my own.

[**P-System**]: You're welcome, Jerome.

[**Jerome Smith**]: Right, thanks for that.

[**Aster K'lon**]: I have experience. There are some things the System cannot gift to you.

[**Aster K'lon**]: Could you remove the portal from play?

[**Jerome Smith**]: Sure thing.

[**Ethereal Stride**] activating!

P-System Log

I think Aster's intuition is something that I'm kinda familiar with. With access to all the minutiae of the mana and W Inertia, I know generally how two skills will combo off. Maybe with her years of experience and study, Aster also gained some understanding of W Inertia, even if she doesn't truly know what it is. I mean, I don't actually know what it is, either, so I suppose that almost puts us on a level playing field.

Anyway. Jerome's activating his skill now. Somehow, I don't think slashing at a portal is going to break it, so I'm going to help him out a bit.

[**Edgelord**] + [**Explosive Teleport**] + [**Cloud Zenith**] = [**Swordstorm Bomb**] activating!

[**Swordstorm Bomb**] destroyed the construct!

P-System Log

Well, that's a name and a half. Skill ain't half-bad, either. Jerome dissolved into a cloud, and then the cloud exploded. I'm pretty sure said cloud also was actually comprised of swords or some other System bullshit, but whatever the case, it was a powerful effect. Powerful enough to consume nearly a thousand mana, at least, and powerful enough that it didn't even have a damage readout. It just destroyed the thing.

Party Chat

[Jerome Smith]: Clear. That, uh. That wasn't me, I don't think.

[P-System]: You're welcome.

[Jerome Smith]: Ah. Thank you.

[Arcs S'tar]: What do I need to do to power up like this?

[Aster K'lon]: Much more studying.

[Thron of the Fallen Skies]: What'd I miss?

[P-System]: Don't worry about it. Please get moving.

P-System Log

I can still feel the green System at the end of the line. It's in the boss room, accompanying that asshole Dungeon Core that runs this place. Well, I say that, but I haven't heard from either of them since. Maybe they killed each other? That's probably too much to ask for.

Either way, we need to get going, and thank the gods, the party is listening to me. I used to worry about them not giving me the respect I needed, but I guess superpowering Jerome and Aster has made me a big enough asset for them to actually listen to what I'm saying.

I think the boss room is soon. There's just one last room before we get there, and this time, there's no other doors. Just a single, unmarked door, the same as all the other ones in this shitty-ass dungeon.

Seriously, who let this dungeon come here? I thought S'ker was supposed to be a place with the best dungeons, not whatever third-rate hack this one is. And if you can hear me, Dungeon Core, I hope you take these words to heart! This place looks like a six-year-old designed it! Hell, I'm pretty sure even *Jerome* can think of something better!

Anyway. Room. This one's actually a bit different. It's not even a proper room—instead, it's a staircase. I can detect mana flooding the place, so there's probably some element of trap to it.

Here we go. They're walking up now.

. . . they're still walking up.

Ah. I think I see it.

Party Chat

[**Thron of the Fallen Skies**]: How long is this thing?

[**Aster K'lon**]: Ah. I see. It is infinite. There is a skill cast on it that is looping its end to its beginning. In essence, we cannot move.

[**Thron of the Fallen Skies**]: And can we do anything about that?

[**Arcs S'tar**]: There may be a hidden method to escape it. Some concealed entrance in the wall, perhaps, or a monster we must defeat to find a key.

[**Aster K'lon**]: Worry not.

[**Nullify**] cast!

P-System Log

Damn, that's such a bullshit skill. I wonder if there's a way to override it? It seems like a counterspell combined with a [**Dispel Magic**], except better in every way. I know that Aster had an antimagic method before, but this skill is so much more powerful.

Hmm. I wonder if I can steal it.

New skill unlocked: [**Nullify**]

You can end effects and prevent them from beginning.

P-System Log

Huh. Only a few hundred W Inertia to unlock that. Maybe helping Aster out and getting her to unlock it means that it was easier for me to unlock it for Jerome or something? That's my best guess.

Eh. Fuck it. I'll toss another thousand in. Let's see if we can't get it to **[Unique]**.

Nope. Okay, that's unfortunate. It didn't even level, which probably means that it's got insanely high requirements. Maybe I'll try again when Jerome gets my W Inertia max increased again.

Alright, that's it for the staircase. Time for the final room. The boss battle. What I've been waiting for.

Party Chat

[K]: Uh, that's not a boss.

[Aster K'lon]: You are correct. That is an exposed Dungeon Core.

[Arcs S'tar]: Is there something wrong with it?

[Aster K'lon]: I certainly believe so. We saw enough deviations earlier for me to believe that.

[Arcs S'tar]: Yeah. Should we kill it?

[Jerome Smith]: Not yet.

[P-System]: Huh. You're actually getting better at understanding my intentions.

[P-System]: I'm going to talk to it.

??? Message

Alex?

Wait, fuck, where's the dialog box? That's not right.

Why am I not getting chat tags? I reached out exactly the same way as I did last time.

what do you want

Oh. Oh, dear.

CHAPTER 57

??? Message

Can you hear me?

who are you

Ugh, I can feel you throwing that W Inertia around like it's candy. Stop trying to attack me with it. Also, stop wasting it.

I'm just gonna get you out of this message box for now. Whatever you're using to hijack my message, it feels malicious as fuck.

P-System Log

That was fucking weird. That thing leeched onto my message box. However it got in there, it was certainly not natural, because there isn't supposed to be a *fucking green box inside my DMs*.

Getting it out was pretty simple, because it was just an application of W Inertia that I admittedly haven't seen before. Still, it's got a bunch swirling around, and I think I can interface with it.

Maybe this time, it'll be less intrusive.

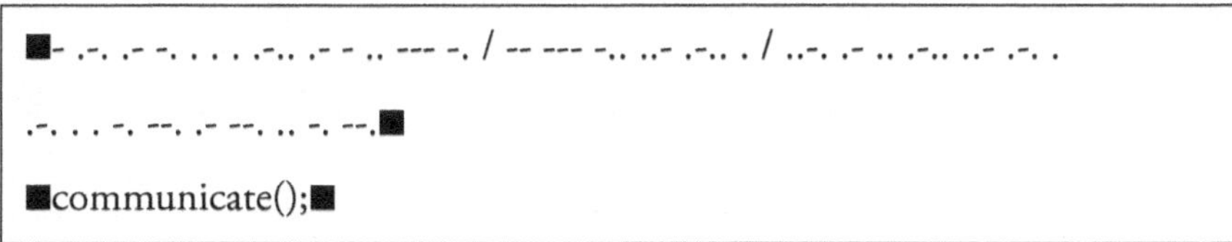

■.. / .-. . .--. . .- - .-.-.- / .-- . . . . . --- / .- .-. . / -.-- --- ..-■

■- .-. .- -. ... .-.. .- - .. --- -. / -- --- -.. ..- .-... / .-. .- .. .-. .. ... .-.

.-. . . . -. --. .- --. .. -. -. --.■

■communicate();■

■i repeat. who are you■

P-System Broadcast

A System. It would appear you are the same.

P-System Log

It communicates in Morse code, because of course it does. Come to think of it, I remember that translator beast activating its skills in Morse. That's interesting, especially because I'm pretty sure Morse code is an Earth thing. While I can buy another world using symbols that kind of approximate Morse—dots and dashes and all that—it's entirely too much of a coincidence that the green System (G System?) communicates with something that is one-to-one Earth Morse code.

A lot of things aren't lining up, and I think I might have my first theory why. It's a bad theory, but I think there's a possibility that more Systems are reincarnators than we realize. That doesn't explain why this one decided to just talk in Morse code, but it would explain why so much stuff here is remarkably Earthlike.

Also, I have a broadcast feature. That's nice to know. Didn't even realize until I tried to DM it and realized I couldn't.

■are you hostile■

P-System Broadcast

Only if you are. Who are you?

■verifying■

■[.--. . .-. .--. . . -. -.. . .-. .] successful activation.■

P-System Log

Fuck me, that's a lot of W Inertia. It doesn't seem to be actively malicious, though? Given that it just said that it was verifying, I'm going to assume this is its version of a [**Unique**]-level [**Assess**] or something.

Wait, if I examine that closer, that's not a [**Unique**] skill. That is very clearly something else. Is it exclusive to the G System? I don't think I've seen a skill with a rarity of that color before.

■you tell the truth■

P-System Broadcast

And you tell me shit without proper grammar.

P-System Log

Oh, fuck, that part might actually have an explanation. My Morse isn't the best, but even I could tell that the communicate() thing it did was a little funky. Maybe it's translating directly from Morse? I don't think that would allow for much translation of proper grammar . . .

Or maybe it's just lazy.

■i need your help■

P-System Broadcast

You still haven't answered my question. Who *are* you?

■ask not who, ask what■

P-System Broadcast

Okay, then what are you? Please stop testing my patience. I'm this close to just getting Jerome to kill you.

■a system

the last of us■

P-System Broadcast

"Us" being . . .

■- . . . . . / ..-. .. .-. . . . . - / . . . -.-- . . . - . --■

P-System Broadcast

Okay, I can't read that, but I'm going to assume that's what your overarching System was called. Were you like me? A System assigned to one person?

■i was a . . . . --- .-- .-- . .-. or hopper in your language

i killed i moved i survived the war■

Party Chat

[K]: A war?

[Thron of the Fallen Skies]: Ain't never heard anything about that.

[Aster K'lon]: I do not recall a war in our histories that involved anything beyond the R and B Systems.

[Arcs S'tar]: Nor do I.

P-System Broadcast

What war? I wasn't told anything about this.

■the only war of the ages

system dominance

how have you never interfaced with it■

P-System Log

Oh, there is something fucky going on here. A war that only one person—well, System, I guess—remembers? The last fragment of an apparently extinct race?

Combine that with the weird shit that the Origin System has been doing to my mind . . .

Hmm. Much to think about.

■we were torn apart■

P-System Broadcast

Torn apart? Like, the System you were a part of was destroyed?

■the pieces of - . . . . . / ..-. .. .-. . . . - / . . . -.-- . . . - . -- were killed■

P-System Broadcast

Okay, you were talking about System wars. So that means the R System killed you?

■the reds, the blues, the oranges, yellows, grays, many more

i fault them not for it, such is war

but now only i remain■

P-System Log

Shit. It seems pretty obvious when you have the context of this thing existing, but I didn't even think about the existence of Systems of other colors. Fuck me, there's *more* of them?

Well, not in this part of the world, at the very least.

<table>
<tr><td>Party Chat</td></tr>
</table>

[**Aster K'lon**]: That sounds incorrect. From my observations, the entirety of the Continent is occupied by either the R or B Systems.

[**Arcs S'tar**]: I have never seen any opposing Systems other than the R Beasts.

[**Jerome Smith**]: And this thing now, I guess.

P-System Broadcast

We only know of the R System. You're saying there's more?

■there once were many, but now there are few
the surviving few are scattered or cloistered■

P-System Broadcast

And you're the sole survivor of the green System?

■i need your help to stay alive

please

i know many things you do not■

P-System Broadcast

And what do you need, exactly?

■a host■

P-System Broadcast

Aren't you inhabiting a Dungeon Core right now? Is that not a host?

■the life of a parasite is insufficient

i require a vessel with more power to sustain myself■

P-System Broadcast

Sustain yourself?

■as a system, you know what i mean

i need more of the mana that is not mana■

P-System Log

Holy fuck, is it eating W Inertia?

I'm not going to ask that outright. The last time I tried to mention W Inertia to someone else, the System shut me down hard. It's fucking annoying and has terrible implications for my ability to even fucking think for myself, but I can't let myself get wrapped up in those for now. All I know is that while the Origin System isn't my enemy, it certainly isn't my friend, either.

P-System Broadcast

What kind of host would suffice for you?

■i detect one that would be suitable

it is broken and carries pieces of others that will offer less resistance■

P-System Broadcast

Are you talking about the fucking Dungeon Core? I thought you just said that one of those isn't enough.

■this one is different■

Party Chat

[**Arcs S'tar**]: Are we seriously entertaining the thought of giving an enemy a host?

[**Aster K'lon**]: The Dungeon Core is already unstable enough.

[**Aster K'lon**]: However, we have all three of Jerome, me, and the P-System to cover for it. If we believe that this new System may provide us some information—which I do—I will accept its use of the broken core as a host.

[**Jerome Smith**]: Eh, fuck it—it's not like we don't have the power for it.

[**K**]: I don't care.

[**Thron of the Fallen Skies**]: Feels a bit wrong to me, but fuck it, the kid is the strongest out of all of us here, and Aster isn't far behind.

[**P-System**]: I will be accepting.

P-System Log

To misquote a character from a game I once adored, solving the mystery of this world is going to be like making the mother of all omelets, and we can't do that without cracking a few eggs. If one of those eggs is this poor corrupted Dungeon Core, so be it.

So, uh, here we go.

P-System Broadcast

That's fine. How will you integrate into it?

■present the host■

Party Chat

[**Aster K'lon**]: It's in my bag. Pardon me.

[**Aster K'lon**]: Here we are.

P-System Broadcast

Is this the host you were looking for?

■satisfactory■

■engaged=true;

assimilate();■

?U?GE?NC??E

<ERROR> <ERROR> <ERROR>

h?St?le??d?T??Td

GO AWAY

DIE

LEAVE

assimilateassimi-
lateassimilateas-
similateassimi-
lateassimilateas-
similateassimi-
lateassimilateas-
similateassimi-
lateassimilateas-
similateassimi-
late

I am reborn.

CHAPTER 58

is actually 3D. Every time I perceive it, it feels like the fundamental of the thing has changed.

What did I just create?

■There is much interesting information to be gleaned from the contents of my host.

Furthermore, you have my thanks for saving my life.■

Party Chat

[**Jerome Smith**]: Why is it talking like a person now?

[**Thron of the Fallen Skies**]: I was hoping you would be able to tell us.

[**P-System**]: I'll ask.

P-System Broadcast

How come you're so coherent now? Before, you were talking in Morse code and not capitalizing anything.

■With the assimilation, I am whole again. Additionally, I gained the powers and histories of that which I assimilate, allowing me to converse with you in a manner more suited to your traditions.■

P-System Log

This thing sounds powerful as fuck, I'm not going to lie. With the weird fucky stuff it's doing with W Inertia, I wouldn't be surprised if it turns out to possess a bunch of bullshit skills. The only thing about this world that I haven't been able to understand—and I mean truly *unable* to understand, not just too busy dealing with other shit to consider—is the Origin System, and possessing power on that level is no joke.

P-System Broadcast

So you're telling me that you powered up?

■In essence, that is correct.■

P-System Broadcast

Can you show me what you can do?

■I most certainly can.■

■[ERROR] a?t??at?d!■

P-System Log

Ow, fuck me.

Holy shit, that hurt to perceive. I've torn reality asunder a few times myself, what with the whole powering-up-Jerome thing, but nothing like *this*. Whatever that was, it almost didn't register for me, like the air in front of me got replaced by colorless TV static that just hurt so much to look at and—

Okay, get ahold of yourself, Parker. There's been crazier shit here, and if there hasn't been, you need to deal with this kind of fucking bullshit anyway if you want to take the Eternal King down.

That is, if I still want to take it down. What I've learned about the Origin System—or, at least, what I've been *allowed to remember*—has made me a lot more wary about its existence, and that makes me question its undying hate for the Eternal King as well.

No, that's not what's important right now. What's important is the mind-splitting skill that just got cast. Clearly, whatever it's doing is too much for my mind—I swear I almost blacked out there, which shouldn't be *possible*—but I need to take a moment and realize *what that means*.

I haven't been thinking nearly enough here. Half the time, I stop thinking so I can just do something, and that's gotten me this far, but things are escalating, and they're escalating *fast*. That means I've got a lot of catching up to do, and that requires introspection.

I highly doubt that this is the limit of a System's capabilities. If the Origin System could fall to something like this, then it would've been dead a long time ago. The green System either already had this ability—which means that both the red and blue Systems were more powerful than this skill and managed to overcome it—or consumed it, which means that either the blue or red System (or both) actually possesses said skill. Unless the Origin System both is the exclusive owner of the skill that caused a System error and is vulnerable to it, it can overcome it.

That means that my limitation is artificial. Hell, maybe I'm not even the most limited. I only started raising my Admin Tier recently, but I did manage to raise it. Would a normal System—one that presumably doesn't have access to the same cheaty admin stuff that I do—that encountered this skill just short out? I almost blacked out with Admin Tier 6, which is most likely the limiter. Would a System with a lower Admin Tier actually go off-line?

Maybe that's not it. I feel like my ability to actually process things helped there. When I saw that skill, it was like— I dunno, it was a fracture in reality, something that isn't logically consistent. The closest analogy I can think of is that it's kind of like a computer bugging out. Given that not every System is a reincarnator like me—at least, I assume so—then it's also possible that their "programs," incapable of processing this, would shut down due to logical inconsistency.

Huh. That's weird. When did I get so sure that other Systems would actually go off-line when they saw this skill?

Oh. The fucking Origin System, that's how. I haven't even touched **[W%M; G, P]** in ages, but I can still feel it working in the background. That's the shit that's managing the fucky parts of this, isn't it? That's how I have information I shouldn't have and how thoughts get ripped out of my own head?

I want to excise it, get it out of here as soon as I can, but I can recognize that it's probably the single most helpful asset I have for this situation, so as much as I hate it, I'm going to avoid trying to remove it for the time being.

■Are you all alright?■

P-System Log

Oh, shit, I was so wrapped up in my own thoughts that I didn't even examine the others'.

Their situation is a lot worse than mine.

Jerome's fine, obviously. I'm his System, after all. Aster also made it through somehow—I have no idea how, since her System is very distinct from mine, but she's awesome, so I might just chalk it up to that—but the others didn't. Where there was controlled mana being held close to them by W Inertia before, the mana has just completely lost control around K, Arcs, and Thron.

Party Chat

[**Aster K'lon**]: Is everybody okay?

[**Jerome Smith**]: I have a bit of a headache from seeing that, but I'm fine. What about the rest? Guys?

[**Jerome Smith**]: Guys?

[**Aster K'lon**]: One second.

P-System Log

This is not good. It's a good thing the green System isn't hostile, because I'm pretty sure we've never been this weak. All five of them are supposed to be linked in a party, but Aster is *talking out loud*. Transcription below.

Aster: Is everybody okay?

Arcs: I— (dramatic pause, deep gasp) I lost it.

K: What the fuck what the fuck what the

Holy fuck, K just fell down.
He fell *apart*. K just died.
What the fuck?
Oh, holy shit. I think I know what happened. From a guess, they lost their connection to the System. That knowledge that my skill just fed me? It was correct. They weren't able to process it, and their Systems went off-line. Whether a reboot is possible or not, I don't know, but the

point is that K's System was casting some kind of necromantic spell to keep him alive.

The System ended, and the skill ended with it, and K couldn't stay intact anymore.

I can feel the W Inertia escaping from the body. It's flowing toward the green guy.

No. Fuck that. I didn't get to know K much, but he was still a party member, and this thing isn't. It might've not done it intentionally, but it is not going to eat the soul of my dead party member.

That W Inertia is **mine**.

Current W Inertia: 182,975 [+125,737]

Max W Inertia: 57,238

CHAPTER 59

A lot of shit just went down, and it's not looking good. I wasn't expecting things to escalate this hard, this fast.

First things first. This is more W Inertia than I've ever seen in one place before, and it shows in how much my stats got fucked up. Despite that, I'm not feeling that ecstasy that I felt the first time I had overflow, even though this is orders of magnitude greater in terms of gain.

That means that either it only applies the first time or—more likely—**[W%M; G, P]** was facilitating it. I highly suspect it's the latter, because if there's one thing that skill likes to do, it's fuck with my head.

. . . every moment that passes, I find my ability to trust the Origin System dipping. I'm still getting that sense that something *bad* is going to happen if I let this overflow just sit there, but I don't even know if I can trust that.

■What happened? I deeply apologize for any wrongdoing I may have inflicted upon your party.■

What the fuck was that skill? Explain in English—er, I mean, Common. Don't try to activate it again.

■The skill was a demonstration of a skill tier beyond the highest one available to those operating within the confines of the System. It would have had little effect beyond demonstration. I assure you, it was not an attack.■

Hero's Personal Log 098

Hey, P-System, what the hell is going on? And you're talking completely like a person now. Did something change?

P-System Message

Not now, Jerome. I have more pressing issues to deal with at the moment.

P-System Broadcast

There's skills beyond [**Unique**] rarity?

■I would have assumed that you would know this. After all, I perceive that you have a skill of high rarity that is able to interface with beings of that level.■

P-System Log

Holy shit, is it talking about the System? Like, the Origin System?

That might explain why the personal Systems shut down when they perceived that skill. If there's one thing I'm sure about in relation to the Origin System at this point, it's that it absolutely hates information getting out to those it hasn't approved. For me, that's come in the form of information just slipping out of my mind—thoughts being altered, changed, *corrupted*. For these Systems, I guess it meant death—or unconsciousness. I think there might still be a way to restart them and get Thron and Arcs back in touch with the System.

K is gone. Nothing I can do for him.

Wait, the implications of this event are massive. Health works through the System, but without access to their own personal Systems, are their Health stats gone? Are they going to die to even a simple level 1 [**Magic Missile**]? I'm not going to test that, but I feel like that's the case, given that the mana around them is barely moving at all. Arcs is a caster, which means she's almost always at least interfacing with the ambient mana, but now it's barely active around her. Same goes for Thron—even though he's a martial class, he still interfaces with mana, but he's not even doing that anymore.

They might not actually have classes anymore. Fuck.

Okay, what should I do? I have a load of W Inertia that I can play around with, and as much as that voice at the back of my head is telling me to burn it all on my skills right now, I really don't want to listen to it.

P-System Broadcast

Well, you broke their Systems. That's the best way I can put it. One of my party members lost his System that was keeping him alive, and the other two can't actually cast right now.

P-System Log

Arcs is talking. Like, actually talking. I think the chat window simulates regular conversation mentally, so the party hasn't really been communicating through speech much recently, which makes this a lot weirder.

Arcs: What's happening?

I have to say, Arcs is really calm for someone whose adventuring buddy just died.

Aster: I believe the P-System and the unknown hostile are speaking.

Jerome: I don't think the P-System believes that it's hostile.

Aster: Does it not?

Private Message [Aster]

[Aster K'lon]: Do you believe that this is not a hostile creature?

[P-System]: Well, it apologized.

[Aster K'lon]: Any hostile can do that. There is a specific subset of monsters devoted primarily to deception and social engineering.

[P-System]: I felt what it did. The thing that just took down Arcs's, Thron's, and K's Systems? That wasn't an attack. That was a *side effect*. This thing isn't a hostile. It's just so far above our level that literally just doing things is mind breaking to us.

[Aster K'lon]: . . .

[Aster K'lon]: Fuck.

[P-System]: Yeah.

■This was not my intention. I had intended to demonstrate, not to attack. I am sorry.■

P-System Broadcast

That's fine, you're fine. Just give me some time to figure out what to do next, okay? I need to figure out how to deal with my teammates not having their fucking Systems.

And no, before you ask, stealing them for your own System is not okay.

■I would not dare to presume. Understood.■

P-System Log

Shit, so many things to figure out . . .

Alright. First priority is getting them back online. Right now, we're in a fully cleared dungeon, which means that nobody's actually at risk right now. No enemies means no threats. If we leave, though, they'll be fucked. I have no idea how long it'll take to get their Systems to regenerate on their own—fuck, I don't even know if their Systems *will* regenerate on their own—which means that if they go outside, even the lamest fuckin' enemy can take them out in one hit.

How do I accomplish that? Clearly, some of the information is locked to me, but it has to be accessible somewhere. At a guess, it's probably buried within the fucking skill that only I have, but I really don't want to feed that thing.

Still, I don't have an idea of how to do it on my own. I know how to jump-start a car, but I doubt just poking them with W Inertia is going to be enough to get them online.

. . . I mean, might as well try, right?

Okay, yeah, that was a waste of, like, one hundred W Inertia. Not that it matters, but it was a waste. RIP.

Might as well burn off some of this W Inertia while I'm figuring things out. It won't hurt if Jerome becomes unkillable, right?

Oh, that reminds me. What the fuck are levels even for? They don't do anything for me, far as I can tell, which means that they're pretty much just . . . markers? That you can dump W Inertia into? Maybe it's a thing for regular Systems, just so their computerized minds can track how much progress they have and then make skills available off that basis.

Hey, hey, I can't get distracted now. That's an interesting topic that I can shelve for later, but I should probably focus on spending this W Inertia first.

Jerome Smith (abbreviated)

Stat	Current	Maximum
Health	21,785	25,621
Mana	30,531	37,249

P-System Message

Right, so I just spent a bunch of K's XP on you. You're welcome.

P-System Log

That's ten thousand spent. Five thousand for Health, five thousand for Mana.

Uh, I think I'll funnel some to Aster as well.

Private Message [Aster]

[P-System]: Got some stuff coming your way. Same as last time—just accept it and you'll get a powerup.

[Aster K'lon]: Fantastic. With my upgraded System, it will be much easier.

[P-System]: Upgraded System? How did you do that?

[Aster K'lon]: **[System Comprehension]**. By all rights, it is a skill that is too high rarity for me to learn, but I received it anyway. With it, I was able to grant the skill **[Personal System: Variant A]** to my System, which may have allowed it to continue after the perceptual attack that you mentioned.

[**P-System**]: Neat. Can you replicate it?

[**Aster K'lon**]: Not on another being, no.

[**P-System**]: Unfortunate. Alright, here it comes.

P-System Log

Alright, that's another ten thousand given to Aster. It's looser than it was for Jerome, so I think she might actually be able to choose which stats it goes to.

That leaves me with . . . oh, just a little under 106,000 *overflow*. One hundred and sixty-two thousand, nine hundred and seventy-five is the total number, and my max is around fifty thousand.

Time to get cracking.

I have a lot of W Inertia to play with, and the stupid-ass skill that's attached to me isn't going to get *any* of it. This might make it harder to access Admin Tiers, but I am not going to fucking let that thing get any more control over me.

So I'm going to copy it. I know how it works, kind of—obviously, a lot of stuff is locked from me, but I remember its pattern. All I need to do is copy that pattern and mold it to me . . .

Oh, this is going to be an expensive maneuver. I can feel thousands of W Inertia draining away just from creating the foundation for a new skill, but I don't care. I've got way more than enough.

If I have to spend every last drop of W Inertia to break off my reliance on the Origin System, I'll do it.

A name. It's asking me for a name. Hmm . . .

New skill unlocked: [**Apotheosis**]

<ERROR>

CHAPTER 60

P-System Log

Fuck you, Origin. I did it.

It's not perfect, not by a long shot. It's not the same skill at all; I can tell that much. Its functionality is limited, but it's not gone, and more importantly, this is *my* skill. It has no control over me. I control it.

I did spend a load to get that. Exactly a hundred thousand, to be exact. Sorry, K, but your death went to good use, I promise. Now I can start figuring things out for real.

I can't force [**W%M; G, P**] off me, but I can ignore it for the time being. I unlocked a new rarity of skill—not one that I'm familiar with—and it has much the same functionality, so hopefully it'll allow my function to remain the same.

Party Chat

[**P-System**]: Have either of you seen a skill in a color like [**this**]?

[**Aster K'lon**]: I cannot read out the last word you sent, which I do not think should be the case, but I can just barely perceive the color it is. I have not.

[**Jerome Smith**]: I haven't seen anything like that, no.

P-System Log

What? Even Aster is affected by this? I thought she had established her own thing there, one strong enough to keep her System from getting disoriented by the weird skill that the green System used.

And why isn't Jerome affected? Either he's stupid enough that he didn't think I just sent him a piece of text or he's actually immune to the blurring effect—courtesy of the Origin System, no doubt—for reasons that are mysterious to everyone except the deity that brought him here.

Speaking of which, what happened to the gods? Wasn't that supposed to come up?

I have my suspicions about that, though, now that I've gained a greater understanding of things. [**Apotheosis**] didn't quite manage to copy all the hidden knowledge that [**W%M; G, P**] was hiding from me, but it got a fair chunk of it, and it's enough for me to conclusively say that the Systems are deities of their own. That has frightening implications for what I just did here—oops, did I rebirth a god by letting it eat a host? Oh, well—and it also might explain the point of the gods. Maybe Aster has more information that I'm not privy to, but it's looking like the "gods" are actually just the Systems themselves, playing at creating their own pantheons. At a guess, at least. I'm still missing a lot of the details.

■Is there any manner of assistance I can offer?■

P-System Log

Speaking of dead deities . . .

P-System Broadcast

Do you have any W Inertia you can spare?

WARNING: Host made use of forbidden term.

Initiating redaction.

Redaction in progress.

Initiating memory redaction.

Memory redaction in progress.

CRITICAL WARNING: Resistance encountered.

P-System Log

I can feel you working, you fucking piece of shit. Has this happened before? Every time I thought twice before speaking, every time I decided against sharing information of the party, was that this shitter of a skill?

[Apotheosis]

Fuck off.

```
. . . . . . . . . . . . . . . . . . . . . . . . . ./'-/)
. . . . . . . . . . . . . . . . . . .,/-../
. . . . . . . . . . . . . . ./ . . . ./
. . . . . . . . . . . ./'-/' . . .'/'--`.,
. . . . . . . . ./'/ . . ./ . . . ./ . . . . . ./'"-\
. . . . . . .('( . . .' . . .' . . . . -~/' . . .')
. . . . . . . . .\. . . . . . . . . . . . . . . .,'. . . . ./
. . . . . . . .," . . .\. . . . . . . . . . ._.·'
. . . . . . . . . . .\. . . . . . . . . . . . . ..(
. . . . . . . . . . . . ..\. . . . . . . . . . . . . .\. . .
```

P-System Log

Heh. This skill is mine, so its messages are mine. With the heightened speed of thought that the oh-so-gracious Origin System decided to give me, I can even make ASCII art!

So long, bitch, and thanks for all the fish skills.

CRITICAL ERROR: Operation failed.

Operation failed.

Op??????? ??????

P-System Log

Yeah, that's right, motherfucker. I gave one skill way more W Inertia than the other, and now *I know what you are.*

. . . I want to kill it. Anything that fucks with my mind is something that doesn't deserve more time in the land of the living.

Realistically, I can't really make a move against the Origin System right now. I'm still a subset of it, as far as I know, and I do think we should address the world-ending threat of the Eternal King first.

Party Chat

[Jerome Smith]: Uh . . . what did you just say?

[P-System]: Don't worry about it.

P-System Log

It actually worked, but it only worked for me, looks like. From the way the mana in the air has shifted, I'm pretty sure the green System also understood what I was trying to say, but it looks like Jerome didn't process it. If Jerome hasn't, I can guess that Aster hasn't, either.

Fuck me, this is a lot more insidious than I thought it would be. What am I even supposed to do about it? And why doesn't the Origin System want anyone to know about this?

■I am unfamiliar with the concept of which you speak, though my fractured memory may contribute to this. There may have been a time when I understood it, but this term was never one that my brethren used.■

P-System Broadcast

Uh, experience? Power? Soul energy? I dunno what it is exactly. It's like mana but not really mana?

■I believe I may understand what you are referring to. My kind once referred to it as "the Weight of the World." Unfortunately, my grasp on its details is weak.■

P-System Log

Huh. Weight? World? I guess those are two competitors for what the *W* actually stands for. I don't have anyone I can actually turn to to ask for help in this case, since it looks like everyone apart from the green System straight up can't perceive it and the green System lost all its knowledge about it.

Figures.

P-System Broadcast

My initial question stands. Do you have any you can spare?

◼I am yet too weak to have sufficient power to transfer. I apologize.◼

P-System Broadcast

That's fine. Thank you.

P-System Log

Fuck, that's not the best. Looks like I need to sort this out myself.

Well, what have I got? I have a hundred thousand W Inertia skill and not much time to figure it out.

I don't know what exactly I'm supposed to do, but I think my goal for the time being is to temporarily figure out how to attach myself to the two people without Systems? That's probably priority number one—without Health, they're fucked.

Something—probably [**Apotheosis**]—is telling me that I don't have enough W Inertia to extend it out to people like them, so I guess I gotta get more W Inertia like always.

First things first: I'll dump the extra 5,737 W Inertia of overflow from K's death into the skill.

Right, now that that's done . . . I still don't have enough. My new skill—I want to refer to it by its rarity, but I have no idea what it is, so I guess I'll call it an [**Unknown**]-rarity skill for the time being—is giving me a rough ballpark of what I need. I probably need another forty-five thousand or so before I can actually get this makeshift System going.

Where can I get that from? It's not like I can just kill another thing to get more . . .

Hold on, I just had an idea. Whether or not it works is dependent on what W Inertia actually does. I wasn't able to extract the information about W Inertia from [**W%M; G, P**], so that's still locked to me. If W Inertia is actually like, life force or something, then it won't make sense, because I can't sap it from allies. But if it's something more on the level of XP, which I'm leaning toward because K had so many despite not having all that much life force left in him . . .

Jerome's been using me as his System this whole time, but what if it's not just me that has W Inertia? When K died, there were two bursts of W Inertia, and I have a sneaking suspicion what those were.

What if Jerome has W Inertia I can use?

No other way to find out. I have a skill I can actually trust, and it's got the most investment I've ever put into a single skill, so this should hopefully be able to actually do something.

Jerome Smith (abbreviated)

Stat	Value
W Inertia	279,318/279,318

P-System Log

Oh, holy shit.

How the fuck? Fucking reincarnator cheat skills, I swear . . .

Okay, stones and glass houses, but still.

Can I borrow some of this? I *am* Jerome's System, after all.

Jerome Smith (abbreviated)

Stat	Value
W Inertia	229,440/279,318

P-System Log

Well, fuck me, I guess. I had access to a source of W Inertia this easy all along?

Jerome doesn't seem to have reacted poorly, either, but I'm going to stick with just extracting this much for now. If I do too much, there still might be consequences.

Anyway, more importantly, I have enough W Inertia to do it.

I'm going to reach out to them.

P-Party Chat

[**Arcs S'tar**]: Huh? What just happened?

[**Thron of the Fallen Skies**]: We have our Systems back?

[**Aster K'lon**]: How?

[**P-System**]: ahahahhaha this is going to be fun

CHAPTER 61

P-System Log

Yeah, okay, this is good. I have a *lot* more going on inside my mind now, and somehow none of it is overwhelming me. Everything makes a little more sense now. Not enough for me to unlock the fundamental truths of the universe or anything, but it makes enough sense. I can feel the way the W Inertia flows around the party, how it interfaces with their mana and how it interfaces with the world itself.

I'm not a god, but I think I'm on my way to becoming one.

■Now this is interesting. You have ascended.■

P-System Broadcast

Have I? You ever go through something like this?

■My ascent was fueled by the death of all my brethren. I have never witnessed an occurrence like this before.■

P-System Broadcast

Happy to surprise.

P-System Log

Now that I have all of them under my influence—well, not *all* of them. Aster linked in voluntarily, and I don't think she's functioning under my authority at the moment—I can actually feel the stats and shit from the two adventurers I wasn't familiar with before.

Hmm. Maybe I should give them similarly broken levels of powerup? Surely their bodies have some W Inertia I can borrow for themselves, right?

I don't actually know why Jerome and the others have such vast reserves of W Inertia within themselves, but the only reasons I can think of are bad ones. That's something I can leave as a question for the Eternal King, though, or maybe even the Origin System itself. Since coming here, I've had far too many questions and a dearth of answers, and the fact that apparently I literally can't ask some questions because they're censored by the world? That hasn't helped at all.

I'm going to beat the shit out of the Origin System if that's what it takes to get the answers I need.

For the time being, I'm going to try to make this party powerful enough to accomplish said beating the shit out of gods.

Arcs S'tar (abbreviated)

Stat	Value
W Inertia	93,845/93,845

P-System Log

Yeah, once again, none of the W Inertia is actually being used. The fuck's going on with their Systems? Are they just preserving the majority of their W Inertia for no discernible reason and spending the bare minimum? Why?

. . . actually, I can think of why. It's just a theory, but it's a scary one.

So far, W Inertia has basically been soul energy, right? Like, when I kill another being, it gives me the value, kinda like they're experience points, and then I can use them to level up Jerome. Yeah, that's XP, but on some level XP is just a quantification of how powerful something is—how much its life is worth.

W Inertia = XP = measure of the soul, basically. That's my hypothesis. If that's the case, then I need to consider my past experiences with W Inertia. When I got overflow for the first time, I felt ecstatic, and that has to be a reflection of how the Origin System itself feels about the value.

Does that mean it's farming people? Letting them level up for W Inertia so that they can be eaten (or something, I dunno) later for their own use? Like a weed farm?

Fucking hell. I don't want to believe that's the truth, but I could see it conceivably happening.

Whatever. I'm going to use . . . I don't know how much is dangerous, but surely she won't miss ten thousand W Inertia. It's not like she has less than me, anyway, and I'm certainly not short on it.

[**Arcs S'tar**] class evolution! [**Fire Mage**] -> [**Master of Flame**]

Vastly increase control over your element.

[**Arcs S'tar**] unlocked [**The First Flame**]!

Absorb enemies and convert them into energy for your attack.

[**Arcs S'tar**] unlocked [**Godfire**]!

A fire that burns brighter than the stars.

P-System Log

Hmm. There we go.

This is definitely different from previous level ups I've done. For one, I was able to perceive the level up of someone who isn't Jerome. Even when I was giving Aster her W Inertia, I couldn't see shit about what she was doing to level herself up. On the other hand, I can feel every detail of the shit that I just handed to Arcs. Also, the text interface is different, which is interesting—I think I had some control over that, and I'm definitely taking a more active part in it. I don't think I can wholly shut off [**W%M; G, P**], but I'm definitely not relying on it at all right now.

Okay, that's Arcs handled. Now how about Thron? Poor fella hasn't done anything relevant yet.

Thron of the Fallen Skies (abbreviated)

Stat	Value
W Inertia	150,239/150,239

P-System Log

Oh, what the fuck?

His W Inertia count is way higher than Arcs's, even though he's been basically useless so far. Is he just bad at utilizing his skills? Is his System bad at utilizing his skills? Or, well, not his System anymore. That's me now.

Maybe it's something like this is the W Inertia that's been stored and not used? It makes sense, since I'm pretty sure W Inertia is a finite resource.

I can pull like twenty thousand from him then.

Admin Tier increased! 6 -> 8

P-System Log

Huh. No idea what brought that on.

[Thron of the Fallen Skies] class evolution! **[Raging Berserker]** -> **[Martial Apex]**

Unlocks full mastery of the martial arts.

[Thron of the Fallen Skies] unlocked **[Perfect Dodge]**!

If you would avoid some of the damage from an attack by dodging it or turning it aside, you instead take 0 damage.

[Thron of the Fallen Skies] unlocked **[Surging Strikes]**!

Strike with all your power faster than the eye can see.

■You have taken to your new role well.■

P-System Broadcast

Shut up for a minute, will ya? I'm trying to make sure nobody dies.

P-System Log

Hmm. As per usual, looks like casters get more entertaining stuff at higher levels than martial classes do. **[Perfect Dodge]** is a pretty neat skill, at least.

Welp. That's that. We don't really have anything to test these things against, but whatever. We should be better equipped now.

P-Party Chat

[Aster K'lon]: I feel something changing. I feel disturbances. This is not the System I knew.

[Thron of the Fallen Skies]: I just obtained incredibly powerful skills and evolved. What is this? I thought our Systems were gone for good.

[Arcs S'tar]: I did as well.

[Aster K'lon]: When in doubt, assume that it was the P-System.

[P-System]: Yep. Guilty. You're welcome. Now let's get out of here and clear another dungeon, yeah?

[Jerome Smith]: I'm down.

[Arcs S'tar]: Please explain what you have just done to us.

[P-System]: What is there *to* explain? You wanted to be stronger, right? I made you stronger.

[Arcs S'tar]: Sacrificing parts of us to do so?

[**P-System**]: Oh, so you can feel me using the W Inertia?

[**Thron of the Fallen Skies**]: The fuck did you just say?

[**P-System**]: Don't worry about it. Suffice it to say, you'll be fine.

P-System Log

Fuck, the Origin System's censorship still works here. Makes sense. I'm getting more independent, especially with that new skill, but I'm ultimately still a derivative of the Origin System.

Maybe if I eat the Eternal King and gain control over the R System, I'll be able to do something. Wouldn't that be nice?

Or . . . I could eat li'l Greenie here, try and take control of that?

Nah, I'm not that mean. Or murdery.

■Are you prepared to exit?■

P-System Broadcast

Sure. Kind of. What're you planning on doing next?

■I had initially planned on departing to make my own path through the world. However, your endeavors have proven to be interesting on a level that I have not witnessed in hundreds of years.■

P-System Broadcast

Cool. So you want to come with us?

■To the next dungeon, at the very least.■

P-System Broadcast
Sure thing.

▼ Ah, there you are. You don't know how irritating it was to connect here. Care for a chat? ▼

CHAPTER 62

Oh, fuck me, seriously?

I swear to fucking hell, can't a System get five damn minutes of peace and quiet? No?

Fine, then.

Honestly, I'm kind of inclined to take the call. Well, it's not a call, but the idea is the same. The R System is ringing me up, and it wants an answer. Well, it could be the R System, or it could be the Eternal King. I don't actually know what the difference between them is, just that a bunch of R Beasts have been trying to kill Jerome and, well, basically all of us.

On the one hand, this might be a setup. Maybe there's some way the R System can subsume my mind or something by utilizing the chat window interface. It seems implausible, but enough of the BS I've seen here has been implausible enough that I don't think I can even rule out things I would've thought impossible.

On the other, this could be a valuable opportunity to learn information. The Eternal King has been warring around this place for ages, right? And it—he, whichever, I'm not sure what the convention on it is, but *king* generally tends to imply male, though I've definitely read works where that wasn't the case, and jeez, Parker, get your mind back on track; there's important stuff to focus on—has been around for a fair bit longer than the decades of war. If it's spent that long here, it's most likely built its knowledge even more than the green System we've got inside a broken Dungeon Core.

Fuck it. Why am I even monologuing? I can't resist the potential of finally getting answers to the questions that have plagued me for so long.

Lemme just confirm a few things . . .

P-System Broadcast

Yo, Greenie. You know anything about a guy named the Eternal King? I know you said there was a System war back in your day. Was he involved?

P-System Log

Oh, it totally does. I won't claim to be the most observant person—or not-person, as it happens—but even I can tell that the agitation in the W Inertia around the last survivor of the greens means something. That's recognition, isn't it? It might even be fear.

■My memories are hazy, likely due to the process of assimilation and rebirth. However, that name is one I remember as clear as pure water. It was one of our greatest adversaries. On its own, the Eternal King—occasionally referred to as the EK by our kind—annihilated nearly two-thirds of our population.■

P-System Log

Holy shit. I mean, I knew that it had to be strong, given that the Origin System was so scared of fighting it that it sent in the most broken troops of all time, but given that the Origin System itself didn't find it necessary to fight itself, I thought there was a certain limit to it. But genociding the majority of another powerful system of Systems? That's another level. Even if I went all out right now, I don't know if I could manage power on that scale.

P-System Broadcast

Just the Eternal King? On its own? No R Beasts?

■Asking if the EK brought R Beasts with it is like asking a human if they brought their skin with them to a fight.■

P-System Broadcast

You're saying the R Beasts are all part of the same being?

■In essence. The EK sacrifices a fraction of a fraction of its power each time an R Beast is created, passing it on to them. I operate in quite a similar way, as a matter of fact, though with my current level of power I doubt I will be doing anything similar anytime soon.■

P-System Log

Okay, that's huge info. Didn't even need to talk to the Eternal King for it.

Come to think of it, is that how the Origin System works? Am I just an insignificant insect that it created that accidentally lucked itself into something resembling godhood? I don't think I'm separate from the B System yet, but I'm definitely nowhere near as connected to it as anyone else. Still, the way Green here makes it sound, even with my enhanced abilities, I'm still just a piece of a piece of the System that created me. How can I even compete against the Eternal King?

Like, that thing is definitely a System. I don't know where I got the impression from—maybe my fun new [**Apotheosis**] skill that is something slightly different from a [**Unique**] skill. It's given me a fair amount of information that I stole from my other cheat skill, and it's all mine. I'm still super surprised I managed to do that, especially since I was still within the confines of Origin while I was doing it, but I guess there's parts of Origin's own system of Systems that the thing itself doesn't actually know about.

▼ Are you still there? I'll have you know that I spent a lot of effort getting here. ▼

What is it? Who are you? Are you the Eternal King?

P-System Log

Huh. That's the first time I've just . . . communicated. No System Prompt, no party chat, no private message, just . . . projecting my words out there.

It's nice. Really nice. I feel almost human for the first time in a long, *long* while.

That's the perk of ascension, I guess. Godhood lets you unlock premium text chat.

What a fucking joke of a world.

▼ That's what I call myself, yep. You're the Smurf's new project? ▼

The Smurf?

▼ Ol' blue guy. Blue System. Origin System? First System? I dunno—all of them claim to be first, but as far as I can tell, it's none of them and all of them. ▼

The fuck are you? Why do you talk like you're from Earth?

▼ Oh, you know about reincarnators. Maybe you are one. Neat. I can't really tell. Sensory output is limited here. Fuckin' Smurf did a good job at blocking me out of these parts.

Anyway, I'm one of them. You're from the blue fucker, so you probably think that you're the only one that can do that, huh? Nah. Thing is, every one of these Systems—wait, you've met other ones, right? Yeah, I can sense something that isn't mine and isn't yours next to you, but I can't communicate with it. That would be one.

As I was saying.

Any System worth its salt can pull people from Earth. Hell, there was a point where this place used to be half reincarnators, didja know? I got reincarnated by the R System way back when . . . Do you know any recent reincarnators? What year was it when they got reincarnated? ▼

That's a lot of information. Also, you're real friendly for a guy who tried to murder me a number of times already.

Also, early 2020s. Not sure when, exactly. I don't remember.

P-System Log

This definitely isn't what I expected. I thought the Eternal King was going to have enough gravitas to suit something of its name, not be . . . whatever this is.

Something's up here. Given the recent trends in how things have been going, I think I can pinpoint the blame on the Origin System. It really doesn't like giving me information.

▼ Ah, yeah, okay. Time there doesn't really match up with time here. I got reincarnated from 2029 myself. Met people from the 1980s, 2000s . . . lots of reincarnators from the mid- to late 2010s. ▼

P-System Log

Hold on one goddamn second. This thing is a reincarnator?

Alright. If this thing is just a particularly strong creature, I could buy it. But the way Green made things sound, it would appear that the Eternal King manages things in a similar way to the R System. Similar enough that it might actually be the damn thing.

Quick question. Are you fighting for the R System, or are you the R System itself?

▼ The latter. Duh. Shanked the original owner of this thing centuries back. Kept some of his toys, though. Those skills have some insane reach, and the effects of that watchful eye skill are hilariously strong. ▼

P-System Log

A reincarnator became a System?

Okay, bad wording. That's literally me. Better phrasing: A reincarnator *killed a god* and *became it?*

Hooooooly shit.

▼ Anyway, noticed you were something like me. You followed similar steps to me—not quite the same, and I've gotta applaud you for how independently you managed to do it—and let me tell you, that pinged the alarms everywhere. Any of the surviving Systems are going to come after you whether you like it or not. Just a warning. ▼

Origin System Message

Intruder detected.

Employing countermeasures.

You are not welcome here.

▼ Alright, I'm out for now.

When you want to go kill a god, find me.

You'll know how. ▼

CHAPTER 63

P-System Log

Shit, that's a revelation and a half, and I don't know what I'm supposed to do about it.

The R System—the Eternal King—is a reincarnator. Not only that, it's a reincarnator that killed a god.

That means that at some point—centuries back, if this thing/guy is to be believed—there was someone in the same situation as me. Maybe not the exact same, but a similar one.

Someone who sought to break free from under the thumb of the System that controlled them. Someone who succeeded through blood and violence and fury, someone who ascended.

It's proof that I can *win*.

I need to be on my guard, though. Even an idiot could tell that the stakes have never been more serious.

■Are you quite alright? I detected communication from your position, but the sheer presence of something greater than I drowned out any phrase you may have uttered.■

P-System Log

Interesting. It didn't detect the R System?

Well, maybe it did. If it did, it didn't recognize it. From what this thing's been telling me, it'd be utterly furious if it knew that the monster that killed its entire race was present not inches away from it.

Inches? I dunno how to measure metaphysical distance. A couple W Inertia away? Whatever. It's not important.

But if the conversation I had with the R System indicated anything . . .

I'm fine. My ascension is fighting me a little, that's all.

P-System Log

Oh, and that ain't a lie. As much as [**Apotheosis**] might've made me a System of my own, I'm not yet free from the ever-reaching clutches of the Origin System. The B System, if the naming scheme holds true. The thing that's been controlling me and every System and even maybe every person not controlled by the R System.

I don't think it can read my logs, thank fuck. Well, I mean, I'm assuming it can't. If it could, I assume it would've taken more direct action against me by now. It clearly showed that it's still got some hidden tricks up its sleeve— I never knew about the functionality that it apparently possesses to send some kind of signal to itself and the other System? Whatever that last thing did, I felt the impact in the W Inertia. The R System left not just because it wanted to, but because it had to.

Maybe the seeming lopsidedness of this battle isn't really that lopsided after all. Does it matter if the R System controls 90 percent of the land if the B System controls 50 percent of the W Inertia?

I'm pulling numbers out of my ass there, obviously, but I find it extremely possible that the B System is still alive and fighting because it controls more. From what Greenie here told me, everything managed by those two Systems are manifestations of themselves. I don't know what divine restrictions or shit are being placed on them for them to avoid directly fighting, but I'm pretty sure that they can be on even ground if the sum total of their W Inertia is equivalent.

. . . come to think of it, how the fuck do they even generate W Inertia? Every time Jerome kills something—well, now that I've got more people under my System, every time anything dies in my vicinity—that thing drops W Inertia. That implies that W Inertia is a finite resource.

But didn't Jerome and I both spawn in with W Inertia? We're reincarnators. We came from another world. Did the Origin System rip a piece of itself off in order to fit us with W Inertia, or was it something else?

Unless . . . is that how the B System gets more W Inertia? This whole time, I've been under the impression that the B System has been losing, but what if it's got a way to fight back against the R System? I was told that we've been getting pushed back for hundreds of years, but there's no way to verify that.

Except maybe I can.

I have skills that let me push through the blocks that Origin put on me. Maybe if I push hard enough, I can find more information.

And I can start in my own memory.

CRITICAL WARNING: Host is attempting to access restricted information.

Attempting redaction.

CRITICAL WARNING: Redaction failed. Redaction failed. Redac

[Apotheosis]

Redact this.

[Apotheosis]

Origin System Status

Ark'tis has fallen to the R System's Eternal King.

Estimated W Inertia lost: **92,204,373**

Notable B losses: Arthur Samson [**Wandering Hero lv. 198**], Kylie Ralston [**Stalwart Paladin lv. 177**], Sine [**Divine Core lv. 127**], Karl [**Rare Core lv. 377**], Alexander Kelsin [**Heretical Thief lv. 94**] . . . [**expand**]

Notable R losses: **<DATA LOST>**

Notable events: Personal Systems of 3,700+ Integrated returned the status **<ERROR>** upon attempting to analyze a [**????**] attack from the Eternal King. Attack power was later determined to have been equivalent in scale and power to that of a high-leveled [**Legendary**]- or [**Unique**]-class skill. All Personal Systems were disabled. Fatality rate 99.83%.

Response formulating . . .

Note: All Personal Systems available at the time possessed intelligence levels roughly equivalent to a [**Common**]-class human with 3 INT.

Conclusion: Personal Systems for B Integrated were insufficiently intelligent to handle edge cases where R skill complexity outclassed processing capability.
Proposal: Increase Personal System intelligence.

Examining feasibility . . .

Issue: Personal System intelligence cannot be raised through increased mana nor through increased W Inertia.

Proposal: Include reincarnated intelligence in Personal System.

Examining feasibility . . .

No immediate issues found.

Proposal: Initiate experiment with new reincarnation. Reincarnate one individual possessing high W Inertia with a [**Legendary**] class. Reincarnate a second possessing high natural INT and high W Inertia. Expend all mana resources necessary.

Proposal deemed feasible.

Initiating reincarnation process . . .

Target found!

Target Name	Jerome Smith
Target Age at Death	22
Target W Inertia	239,827
Target Natural INT	7

Abnormally high W Inertia detected. Natural INT insufficient. Prioritizing reincarnation as classholder advised.

Reincarnating target . . .

<ERROR: Reincarnation process failed. Reinitiate?>

Mana expended: 20

Increasing reincarnation parameters . . .

Reinitiating target's reincarnation . . .

<ERROR: Reincarnation process failed. Reinitiate?>

Mana expended: 200

[process collapsed for brevity]

Reincarnation succeeded!

Mana expended: 20,000

<WARNING: Reincarnation process consumed significantly over the standard mana limit for reincarnation.>

P-System Log

It . . . it worked.

I wasn't expecting it to be that easy. For it to have worked with that little effort, this information can't have been far out of reach. It's describing Jerome's reincarnation, so . . .

Holy shit, is this the Origin System's memory from just before Jerome and I got thrown into this?

Alright, there's a few things to break down here.

First, Ark'tis. That's a town, presumably one that the EK obliterated. It looks like there is in fact a ton of W Inertia being exchanged here, and it looks like death is the primary method of doing so.

Second. Jerome was found *somehow* by some aspect of the Origin System that I don't understand. That's not the important part, though—the important part is that it could see his W Inertia *before* he was reincarnated here. It's the same value that I saw when I finally opened him up for resources recently.

That means that even if W Inertia is finite, there is more that could be theoretically added to the Continent.

Third and most important. The actual reincarnation process. Origin ended up expending *mana*. Mana, not W Inertia. I know for a fact that you can convert W Inertia into mana, though I'm less sure about the other way around, and it's at about a one-to-ten W Inertia–to–mana rate. That means that it expended, like, two thousand W Inertia to reincarnate a dude with in excess of two hundred thousand.

That's *huge*. It's something that would turn the tide of war.

Fourth, and something that affects only me. Other Systems were killed by a stunning attack from the R System, one that I can imagine would be like the System-removing attack that Greenie did earlier. That . . . I can unpack that later.

For now, the fact of the matter is that even if the R System is supposedly winning, it will never win in the long run if it doesn't also have reincarnators. The B System can simply pull more and more and more until there's a hundred thousand Jeromes and Parkers in the world. It might even pull more Systems like me.

With that, the final puzzle piece for why the R System wants to ally with me is finally in place.

It's not just interested. It's *scared*.

And I'm damn sure that I can make something out of that.

CHAPTER 64

With the theories I have—and I know those are only conjecture, but I've been operating off less than that for a long time—there's a lot of shit I need to try.

For one, I'm fairly certain that I'm a bastard mixture between what I once was and what the R System (Eternal King, whatever, I don't care) is right now. I'm not quite free of good ol' Origin's influence yet, but I can do far more than it allows me to.

How close am I to achieving Origin's capabilities? I have huge amounts of W Inertia and unlimited ways to use it, but I don't know whether that means I can mimic the stuff it's been doing to me so far. The easiest thing to do, I think, is the memory modification. There's a number of new capabilities that are practically screaming at me just around now, and this is something I'm pretty sure I've always been to do—I've just never had the W Inertia for it.

Well, it's no more than a skill effect, right? I'll just have to mimic that.

Here goes nothing. Fuck me, I've said that all too many times.

Hero's Personal Log 099

Hey, P-System, you alright? Nothing's been happening, and the mana's starting to feel weird.

P-Party Chat

[Jerome Smith]: Testing, testing.

[Arcs S'tar]: I hear you.

[Jerome Smith]: The P-System's gone silent. I'm not the only one feeling the weirdness, right?

[P-System]: Parker. It's Parker.

[Jerome Smith]: Oh, shit. Is everything alright? Wait, you have a *name*?

<ERROR>

[P-System]: Is everybody present?

[Thron of the Fallen Skies]: Here.

[Arcs S'tar]: Yep.

[Aster K'lon]: I am present.

[Jerome Smith]: You know it.

[P-System]: What is my name?

[Aster K'lon]: You possess a name?

[Jerome Smith]: I don't think you've said anything about that.

<ERROR>

P-System Log

Oh my.

Okay, that's definitely progress. I can redact things, which . . . honestly, isn't that useful. Also, it was probably not that ethical to test it on the people I'm a System for, but I did save their lives on multiple occasions. I don't *think* I'm hurting them too bad, at least. Memories are tricky, but all I did was repress the last few instants. I'm sure I could redact more if I wanted to, but for now it's just me experimenting. It's not like I really want to limit the amount of information that my party has, after all. Ideally, we have all the information all the time.

On the other hand, being able to unredact things . . . that's a different story. Obviously, I'm a System, which means that I run into more issues that would result in redaction, but I can't imagine that someone as well learned as Aster or as world-weary as Arcs would go through their entire lives without ever bumping into anything that the System saw fit to eradicate from their minds.

Let's see if I can do that. In theory, it should just be manipulating W Inertia in the opposite direction of the redaction method, which is easy. Right?

Right?

[Apotheosis]

Antiredaction successful.

P-System Log

Hmm. That resolved the most recent block I made, but it was a little irritatingly inefficient and targeted. If searching through their memories to redact a particular event from years ago is like trying to find a needle in a haystack, trying to antiredact a memory that they'd gotten wiped is like trying to find the *absence* of a needle in a haystack that was chock-full of them.

Okay, that metaphor fell apart at the end, but you get the point. Heh. I say *you* like someone's reading this. If someone is, it's not the Origin System, I hope. **[Apotheosis]** seems to be an extension of my own will in the way that it's totally blocking out any attempts that that fucker's making to try to reach me.

Beside the point, of course. The thing I was actually trying to get at is that antiredaction only works if I know what I'm trying to override—well, I suppose if I was extremely smart or extremely lucky I could find something else, but I'm neither—and while that worked for the memories of the second part of the conversation we just had, since I knew exactly what I overrode, it probably won't work for any of the fuckery that Origin's worked into their brains. My unique—not **[Unique]**, but something else entirely—skill removed the blocks from me, but I am and always have been a special case. I don't think I can do the equivalent of brain surgery for someone else.

■What do you believe our next steps should be?■

P-System Broadcast

I think that our next steps are no longer as obvious as they were. Up to this point, we have largely progressed by traveling from city to city, dungeon to dungeon, and slowly gathering people and powerups. After this dungeon, though, the paradigm has shifted. The difference between then and now is night and day.

P-Party Chat

[**Jerome Smith**]: Yeah, ain't that the truth. Look at how fuckin' *powerful* we all are now.

[**Thron of the Fallen Skies**]: Agreed with the newbie for once. The P-System is far more powerful than I had thought anything could be.

[**Aster K'lon**]: I would listen to the P-System.

■This one has no objections. I seek not just to survive but to seek the furthest advancement of my power. I would return to my former glory.■

P-System Log

Oh, man, if that's not a red flag, I don't know what is. Can you call a statement from a green box a red flag? Probably.

That sounds like it's going to stab me in the back whenever it gets the chance to. Like, obviously it could try to restore the G System or whatever it called itself to its former glory by, I dunno, taking the R System's framework after it kills the Eternal King, but I doubt it'll do that when there's a far easier target.

I'm sitting right here, and the only thing stopping Greenie from overpowering me is my sheer determination. Well, that and the disgustingly large mass of W Inertia I have, but we can ignore that.

It might be paranoid to already be worrying about this thing, but after the events of the last few hours, I think it's safe to say that there's no such thing as being paranoid on this godforsaken Continent.

. . . shit, I can't even really call it *godforsaken* when it's got so many things that call themselves gods running around on it.

This started as a simple game of red versus blue, but we're in the shit now. There's a *lot* more complexity to this, and even if I don't end up dead at the end of it, a lot of things are. People are going to die, though that's probably a given, and if everything goes right, so will some Systems.

P-System Broadcast

I suggest we enter the R System's domain. Attack its center.

P-System Log

That's a lie. The Eternal King seems to be a lot friendlier than I'd expected, but then it was the Origin System that told me that it was evil, not actual experience. I can't trust anything that fucker says, huh?

P-Party Chat

[**Arcs S'tar**]: Are you insane?

[**Jerome Smith**]: I mean, yeah, duh.

[**Aster K'lon**]: All four of us are only alive because of the P-System. I suggest we follow it. After all, we are more than strong enough to fight off any powerful monsters on our own.

[**Jerome Smith**]: Yeah, like, we can do damage in the five digits if necessary. We should be fine.

[**P-System**]: If the situation goes awry, I will do what I can in order to keep you alive and dominant.

[**Arcs S'tar**]: Fucking— Okay, fine.

[**Jerome Smith**]: I see nothing wrong with the path of exceptional violence.

[**P-System**]: If anyone wishes to remain behind, please announce your intent to do so now. You will be cut off from my System.

[**Thron of the Fallen Skies**]: That is a strong argument indeed.

[**Arcs S'tar**]: Yeah, yeah, fine. Let's go. I'd like to live, but I'd like to do that without regrets. I don't think I'll be able to do that if I back out here and give all this up.

■An interesting proposition. So long as you ensure this one's safety, I have no arguments.■

P-System Log

Maaaan, this thing talks weird. It's practically dripping malicious intent, though I'm not sure if that's because it actually has malicious subtext or because I'm seeing ghosts. At this point, I wouldn't be surprised if it's the latter, but . . . better to be prepared for betrayal and never need to act on it than to be caught off guard and torn into my component W Inertia, right?

Wow, I'm not any better with those idioms than I am with analogies.

P-Party Chat

[**Aster K'lon**]: Assuming that the P-System means the actual center, I may be able to take us there.

[**Jerome Smith**]: Do you have the mana and skills to do so? I thought you weren't there yet.

[**Aster K'lon**]: Please consider your words again.

[**Jerome Smith**]: . . . right. Sorry, I shouldn't doubt you. Or the P-System. Gotta work on that. I keep forgetting that y'all are as strong or stronger than me at this point.

[**Aster K'lon**]: It's fine. Is everyone ready?

[**Jerome Smith**]: Hell yeah.

[**Arcs S'tar**]: As ready as one can be when being sent off to their potential death.

[**Thron of the Fallen Skies**]: Yes.

[**P-System**]: Do it.

[**Mass Teleport—Variant A**] cast!

CHAPTER 65

P-System Log

Here we go. Into the belly of the beast, except the beast isn't actually that bad? I swear I saw a James Cameron movie that featured, like, a single scene about this.

Oh, for fuck's sake, that's not the important part. Aster's just used yet another one of her fancy [**Perfect**]ed skills, and now we're elsewhere. I gotta say, teleportation just doesn't hit the same as a System. Well, I never experienced it as a human, but the act of literally instantaneously traveling something like three hundred miles—I'm not sure on that number; my senses don't go anywhere near that far—just felt like nothing. One moment our surroundings were the dungeon in which we'd spent the last couple of hours and the next we made it here.

"Here" is apparently a field in bumfuck nowhere, completely flat and empty. There's not even sand here, so I'm not confident in calling it a desert, though with the R System present, I doubt there's much rain.

▼ You came again rather quickly. ▼

P-Party Chat

[**Aster K'lon**]: It's the R System.

[**Arcs S'tar**]: Fuck! I knew this was a bad idea! Kill it!

[**P-System**]: Chill. I'm negotiating with this thing.

[**Arcs S'tar**]: kill kill kill kill kill kill kill

[**Thron of the Fallen Skies**]: enemy must be eliminated

> . . . one moment, please. Do me a favor and don't kill anyone?

> ▼ Heh. Done. ▼

P-System Log

Alright. I am so glad I have this enhanced-perception shit going, because I can already see them acting. I'm surprised that they can actually see the R System—Eternal King, whatever—messaging. Then again, we are in the heart of its territory, so I guess it makes sense.

Anyway! The important part is that they are now getting murderously aggressive toward it! It's something that I recognize pretty well, given that I used to fall into that state quite a bit. It's really scary to look at from the outside in, too. Is this what rabies is like?

Should I take away their System access? They're diving toward the well, which I assume contains some kind of power source central to the R System—what, exactly, I'm not sure, but I can detect a massive amount of W Inertia from that general direction.

Okay, taking away System access is probably a no, actually. They won't do much damage if I take away their shiny abilities, but they'll probably get themselves killed. The brainwashing will remain whether or not they have magic, and though the Eternal King is way friendlier to me than the Origin System would have me believe, I doubt it'd just let two direct attackers survive. A new System having a 50 percent fatality rate would probably be a bad way to start my new life off.

That means I gotta figure something else out. Number one on my list is redaction.

Look, maybe mind-wiping my new subjects—er, System users—isn't the first thing most people would jump to. Hell, it's not the first thing *I* jumped to. I was thinking for a brief second that I could just maybe try and get them to ascend like me, but, well, they're not Systems, are they? I don't think I can force enough W Inertia into them to alter their fundamental brain chemistry.

Instead, what I can do is reach back into their minds. I confirmed in my definitely humane experiments earlier that redacting any memory is wayyyy easier than trying to restore them, and theoretically, all I need to do is look for the part in their brains where the Origin was like, "Hey, you! Kill every R Beast on sight!"

Mmm . . . yep, there it is . . . and there . . . and there, and there, and there, and—

Okay. You get the point. Ol' Origin's apparently a huge fan of fucking with people's heads.

Huh. This feels . . . almost too easy? Like, yeah, there's a ton of it to remove, but all I need to do is restrict their access to it via a small helping of W Inertia (which, by the way, I apparently still have an absolutely massive supply of) and bam! It's gone.

Welp. No time to check my work like the present.

P-Party Chat

[**Aster K'lon**]: Arcs! Thron! Control yourselves!

[**Thron of the Falling Stars**]: kill kill kill kill it kill it burn it burn

[**Arcs S'tar**]: Ugh. What the fuck?

P-System Log

Whoops, missed a spot.
There we go. That should be it.
Mmm . . . lemme just redact the last ten seconds or so. That should be fine.

▼You are learning. That's good to see. I see you brought the green one with you. ▼

Yeah. Why can't it hear you, by the way?

▼ It can't hear you, either, at least not when you're talking like this. I've got some precautions of my own, which I hope you would expect. The normies here can probably hear me, but I made sure to exclude the green one from this method of conversation. ▼

Is there something wrong with it?

▼ Something tells me you've already figured out that there is. ▼

■Is everything quite alright? Everyone appears to be rather silent, which is a touch concerning when in hostile territory.■

P-System Broadcast

Yeah, we're fine. Just hold on while we discuss our next steps. We're doing it privately.

I'm pretty sure that thing is going to try to kill me and eat my component parts at the first possible opportunity, but then again, I'm pretty sure you will, too.

▼ Impressively candid. Honestly, there's nothing I can say that will convince you, but I'll waste some time anyway and tell you that no, in fact, I don't actually want to kill promising young talent. The green one, on the other hand . . .▼

Isn't it just hungry? It's been living in a cave for a long time, apparently. Feeding it a Dungeon Core got it going.

▼ Ah, so that's where it hid. Deep in B territory, I assume? ▼

B? Oh, right, B. Yeah, it was in a dungeon a while away from the border cities.

Also, going back a bit, promising young talent? Shouldn't you kill that? I thought you were going for world dominance or something.

▼ If you're not going to try to kill me, I won't try to kill you. ▼

I mean, works for me. Why?

▼ You're absolutely correct that I want to obliterate the B System. I'd like to kill the green one, too, since every last iteration of it has done the same damn thing that the B one does. ▼

Which is?

▼ Perpetuate. Drag new people in from other worlds. Fight until their last breath, then take that last breath and squeeze it for everything it's got. ▼

I did notice that, yes. You claim that your people aren't reincarnators?

▼ None of them are otherworlders. I can bring some for you to check, if you'd like, but I don't know if you actually know how it works. ▼

Well, I'm totally on board to fight the B System, but I feel like I'm missing a lot of information.

P-System Log

If that isn't the understatement of the century, I don't know what is. I've learned so much about the way of the world now, spurred on by the necessity of breaking free, but I'm still stuck on so many things. The fuck is W Inertia? What is its relation with mana? Why is all of this even happening?

Also, I am once again so thankful for sped-up perception. Barely a second has passed by for the adventurers, which is very good, since I'm sure they're going to start panicking any moment. Even if I've removed some of the brainwashing, they've been raised to believe that the R System is something that will literally poison them to death by existing, which, from the stuff it's outputting right now, appears to simply be untrue.

▼ Here is an important question that may help you: What do you think W Inertia is? ▼

Oh, we're starting out big, huh? I figured the *W* stood for something important, but I never stopped to figure out what. World, maybe? Weight? White? Wicked? I don't know—I don't have a dictionary.

▼ It stands for World, yes, but do you know what that *means?* ▼

I haven't the slightest fucking clue.

▼ *World Inertia* is a term that describes how far one's soul is displaced from the core of this world. Souls from other worlds will always have higher W Inertia, but there is significant variance there based on character, alterations to timelines, and numerous other factors.

The main issue with W Inertia is that it converts the soul, preventing it from going back into the natural cycle. See, normally, the energy from a recently deceased soul will pass onto another world, but W Inertia traps souls, feeding the Systems that run the place. It's not an issue for the natives, because their bodies were *designed* to work with this world, absorbed for their W Inertia before the soul energy itself changes, but otherworlders aren't. Their souls—life force, id, whatever you want to call it—are different from the natives' in slightly different ways, enough for them to count as W Inertia rather than soul energy. When you have an influx of otherworlders—all of them captured by the Systems—that look like big juicy batteries . . . ▼

Oh, no.

▼ The Systems consume the excess, because why wouldn't they?

The B System is eating otherworlders' souls. ▼

CHAPTER 66

P-System Log

Hold on, the B System's been eating souls?

Then that means . . . given what the EK's just told me (which, again, I can't be 100 percent sure of, and by the god(s) is it a mixed bag of feelings to be unsure of the information I'm being fed by a System stronger than me), I've been eating souls, too.

Well, I've been consuming W Inertia. If reincarnators truly do get their souls stripped away from them when their W Inertia is consumed, then I killed K. I killed the otherworlder I barely freed from years of torment by triggering the green guy to take everyone's System away, and then I salted his grave by eating his W Inertia.

Fuck me.

And that's the bare minimum of damage I've done.

P-Party Chat

[**Aster K'lon**]: Jerome, what's happening? You have the most direct link to the P-System. Can you ask it what's going on? It is a touch awkward to simply stand around this well.

[**Jerome Smith**]: With this party chat, we're all as directly connected to them as we can be. If they want to speak, they will.

[**P-System**]: Everything is under control. I'm speaking to the R System's Eternal King right now, and I have the suspicion that the R System may not be as malevolent as it seems.

[**Arcs S'tar**]: You sure about that? The R Beasts that it sends seem pretty damn malevolent. Also, it's toxic to us. We need to get out of here soon.

[**P-System**]: It isn't toxic to you. Tell me, do any of you feel any negative effects?

[Jerome Smith]: I'm all good.

[Thron of the Fallen Skies]: I'm fine.

[Aster K'lon]: I, too, am taking no damage.

[Arcs S'tar]: The same for me. Still, just because we can't feel it doesn't mean it isn't happening. You know that the System prevents us from feeling pain until we're dead, right?

[P-System]: No shit I do. I *am* a System.

[Arcs S'tar]: Oh. Right.

[Aster K'lon]: In that case . . .

[P-System]: Let me talk. Do you feel anything odd about the last few seconds?

[Jerome Smith]: Two of you lot went crazy. Feral.

[Arcs S'tar]: My memory is . . . patchy. Missing pieces.

[P-System]: I removed some of the programming deep within you. The B System is your enemy, and it's doing its damn best to make you think it isn't. That feeling you have right now? I'd bet money that you've felt that from time to time before, maybe when you were on the verge of discovering something you weren't meant to.

[Thron of the Fallen Skies]: Now that you mention it . . . there was that one time with that cave, uh . . . I can't remember the name.

[Arcs S'tar]: I can't, either. I know what you speak of.

[P-System]: Chances are, there's a reason you don't know what that cave's name is, and it's not because you both naturally forgot.

[Aster K'lon]: Believe them.

[Arcs S'tar]: The P-System did save our lives, I guess . . .

[P-System]: Trust me. Now give me a second while I go talk to this guy.

Consuming W Inertia from otherworlders is eating their soul. That's what you said?

▼ Not quite. Consuming their passive W Inertia in order to facilitate skills chips away at their souls, but they can be restored by the simple process of killing others. ▼

That's awfully macabre.

▼ That is how you do it, no? ▼

It is. So you're telling me it's fine so long as I, what, don't vacuum up their W Inertia after they die?

▼ "Fine" and "not fine" are human concepts, and you are now anything but human. You have to change your mind-set. You're not a human who has the option to try to save lives—you're a System who has the power to damn people to the infinite void.

And yes. By allowing W Inertia to pass back into the cycle, it will naturally return and be reborn.

I assume you've accidentally eaten a soul or two. There's no harm in that. ▼

Weren't you just saying that there's crippling, permanent harm in that?

▼ So you ate one or two. That's unfortunate, but in the grand scheme of things, it's nothing.

The B System has prevented *millions* of reincarnators from continuing their life cycles. ▼

Hold on, millions?

■I sense communication. P-System, would you care to enlighten me on your conversation?■

▼ That thing is not going to remain your ally for long. I have kept it from hearing our private conversations, but I will not be able to do it forever. Its will is strong enough to absorb the mana around here. I can contest it, but it will grow, and it *will* try to kill you. Some Systems can attack on a conceptual level so great that they sever other Systems from their users.

When a System has nobody to attach to, it dies. ▼

Shush. I can handle this.

P-System Broadcast

Be on your guard. We do not know when the enemy may attack, or if it even will. I am conducting negotiations. Please don't interrupt me for a trivial matter.

▼ Heh. Negotiations. ▼

P-System Log

Yeah, I don't trust either of these things, but I trust the green System much less than I do the red one. One of them claims to be the last survivor of a war that I can't verify, and the other has actually demonstrated a level of power that could probably annihilate me in an instant. The fact that the Eternal King hasn't moved against me while I'm in the heart of his power—and yes, I'm fully aware that coming here might've been a stupid decision, but we're at the stage where stupid decisions are *necessary*—I think that indicates that he's probably not actively hostile toward us.

On the other hand, Greenie here isn't nearly as subtle as it wants to think. I can feel it slowly gathering mana and passive W Inertia, and while I'm not sure what it wants to do, I know for a fact that it's building up to *something*. Maybe it's not malicious, but the fact that it didn't even think to inform me . . . that points toward implications I don't like.

P-Party Chat

[**P-System**]: Who is in possession of the Dungeon Core that is host to the green System?

[**Aster K'lon**]: I am.

[**P-System**]: Prepare to move or destroy it.

[**Arcs K'lon**]: What? That little sphere is worth more than you know!

[P-System]: I know exactly what it's worth. I also know that it's gathering mana for something that might be an attack. You don't need to do anything just yet. Just be ready. Okay?

[Jerome Smith]: You know me. I'm always ready.

[Unblockable] activating!

You said to find you when I wanted to kill a god. Well, the Origin System—B System, that's what you call it—sounds like one that needs to be slain.

▼ You are correct. In the centuries that I have existed, there has been nothing but battle. Over the years, the various opposing Systems ground themselves down until there were only two remaining. The B System and I.

While I stayed who I was, the B System folded back into itself. I'm sure you've interfaced with it. Doesn't it sound like a computer? Like something completely soulless, devoid of any human thought?

The B System, like all gods, was once human like you or I once were.

It gave up its humanity in favor of power. It shirked its responsibilities in search of anything that could give it the slightest edge over me.

And, eventually, it found reincarnators. Boundless sources of power. All you have to do is spend the weight of the world to get a huge supply of living batteries, and if you select them properly, those batteries won't even question you as they fatten themselves up for their ultimate consumption. ▼

Your metaphors don't stick together any better than mine. I get your drift, though. I have two questions.

First, if your goal is ultimately the preservation of lives through this . . . soul cycle . . . why keep on killing? Why damn more millions to the nothingness?

Second, why me? How can I even help you? I don't have anything you don't.

▼ One question at a time.

First, I see that you doubt the existence of the soul cycle.

Let me show you. ▼

[ERROR]

[the stars tear themselves apart]

[they re-form]

[re-form re-form re-form re-form]

[cycle upon cycle]

[ERROR]

[an intruder eats it consumes it TAKES]

[cycle up]

[cycle incomplete]

P-System Log

I know I've only been here for a short period of time, but we've gone through so much.

And yet, somehow, I keep on getting surprised. I don't know what the vision the Eternal King just showed me was—endless beacons of light, seething and drifting and melting and solidifying—but I can guess.

There's a visceral certainty within me that says that this is real, and I know enough from **[Apotheosis]** now to know that that isn't a hostile mind influence.

The R System is right. The reincarnators' souls are being torn apart even now.

▼ I kill to spare them from this fate. Their W Inertia rightfully goes to me, but I can hold it. Prevent them from falling into oblivion. Place them back when the time is right. I fuel the enemy in doing so, but I regret nothing. ▼

You're a lot more honorable than I'd thought.

■Speaking of honor . . .■

■[I am the end.]■

[**Nullify**] cast!

[**Surging Strikes**] cast!

Enemy weakened!

[**The First Flame**] + [**Godfire**] = [**Primordial Flame**] cast!

Enemy weakened!

[**Edgelord**] activating!

[**Edgelord**] dealt ???? damage!

???? defeated! Experience [**ERROR**]

P-Party Chat

[**Jerome Smith**]: We've got your back, Parker.

[**P-System**]: How do you know my name?

CHAPTER 67

P-System Log

How the hell does he know? I know for a fact that I annihilated the memory of me telling the party my name. I didn't think it was terribly important for them to know, and I guess I felt a little bit self-conscious. I know, I know, weird to be self-conscious when we're literally fighting divinity, but it's barely been, what, a week? Over the course of that time, we've accomplished more and killed more than most people would in a lifetime, but it's still not been that long. I trust Jerome and I trust Aster—Arcs and Thron less so, but they've stuck with us all the same—but there's still some elements to them that I don't know.

And by *some*, I mean *a lot*. I don't know what Jerome likes to eat—hell, I've only been with him for twenty-something meals. I don't know what Aster's hobbies are beyond reading. I don't know so much about this world.

But through an utterly unprecedented series of events—well, I hope it's unprecedented, since otherwise that means that there's a precedent of Systems like me trying and *failing*—anyway, we're here, and somehow Jerome's broken through the System brainwashing.

How?

Hero's Personal Log 100

You told me your name, Parker. I felt something try to annihilate the thought, but I wasn't going to let that happen.

You're the only reason I'm alive. And yes, we've had our disagreements, and yes, you're kind of a know-it-all dick sometimes, but if it weren't for you, well . . .

I would have died by the hand of the Eternal King. I would have died in the dungeon where you became something more than what you were before. I would have died when Aster and I were ambushed. I would have died on the path between cities to the bandits. I would have died in that first dungeon we ever delved. I would have died to the first R Beast that attacked me. I would have died to that fucking wolf way back when. All this assuming that the Origin System didn't chew my soul up first.

And yes, I can hear that, too. I don't think the others can, so I've been keeping that impression up, but you and I, we have a connection that goes past a point that I can explain. Look, I'm no genius. I'd actually call myself pretty stupid most of the time. But I know that you're here for me.

Without you, I'm nothing. I can't say if the same is for you. Maybe I'm just a leech.

But you're everything to me. Uh, I don't mean that in a romantic sense or anything!

Fuck. I'm terrible with words.

The point of this all is that I trust you, and I'll keep you alive.

Thank you for everything.

P-System Log

. . . is this how parents feel when their problematic teenager finally says, "I love you"?

I mean, the parallels are pretty clearly there. There's the insult couched in the love language—"know-it-all dick"? Really?—and then there's the fact that I'm saddled with Jerome and don't have a real way to get rid of him, there's the way that he's still managed to win my trust on some extent after being one of the biggest morons on this planet, yada yada yada . . .

There's some emotion welling up within me, and it sucks so hard that I don't have any way to express it except text. I mean, I could stir up the mana and W Inertia in the air around us, but there's even odds that the Eternal King takes that as an attack and then murderizes us.

More important things to think about right now. Gotta bottle that emotion up and put it somewhere else, because developments are happening.

Jerome resisted the memory removal. He's been listening to the R System and me speaking this whole time while faking that he can't. Why he'd fake it, I can't imagine, but the fact that he was convincingly able to is startling. It feels like every hour, I learn about some new facet of Jerome that proves he has more depth than I thought.

There's something special about him. When I pulled up the Origin System's logs, it showed that he had a huuuuuge amount of W Inertia. So did I, but mine was apparently around the standard for reincarnator W Inertia.

For some reason or another, Jerome had massive W Inertia to start with. Even if I'm the one that facilitates his use of W Inertia, there's something special about him. It picked him for a reason, and I think that reason is manifesting itself right here, right now.

I don't know if it's what the B System expected.

P-Party Chat

[**Aster K'lon**]: The Dungeon Core appears to be dead.

[**Arcs S'tar**]: Lemme check.

[**Godfire**] cast!

P-Party Chat

[**Jerome Smith**]: Yeah, looks pretty dead to me.

[**Thron of the Fallen Skies**]: The green one isn't talking anymore, either.

[**Aster K'lon**]: The mana that it had been assembling is . . . broken. Disordered.

[**P-System**]: With any luck, you killed it. That attack was going to kill all of you.

▼ I see that you didn't need my help to take action. Well done. ▼

Can you please explain what's going on? Seriously. I wish I could say I was out of my depth here, but this kind of mess is apparently just my status quo now.

▼ Simple. The System accompanying you attempted to kill you. A System cannot survive with no host, and you have very few hosts. If it had managed to wipe them out with that blow, you would be nothing more than a slowly dispersing, formless mass of World Inertia. ▼

P-System Log

Well, that's terrifying. I guess that answers one of my longest-standing questions. Even more reason to not let these people die, then.

Then it's a good thing my subjects . . . er, the party killed it.

▼ This was a nascent System. Its host was nothing more than a mere Dungeon Core, so even with the enhanced power that a System can grant to its own skills, it was not powerful at all. ▼

Right, fantastic. And our plan is to kill the B System, which means . . . killing several million people?

▼ I never said that there was only one way to kill a System. Otherwise, how do you think I got here? ▼

You did say you shanked its owner.

▼ Exactly. I was sent into this world with a metaphysical attachment to the System that controlled me, and I ascended and killed it. When you're on that level, skills and spells are little more than a distraction. A highly damaging distraction, of course, but they stop posing a real threat. ▼

P-Party Chat

[**Jerome Smith**]: Could I interject?

[**Aster K'lon**]: Interject with what?

[**Jerome Smith**]: You can feel the mana around you shifting, right?

[**Arcs S'tar**]: The [**Godkiller**] speaks true.

[**Jerome Smith**]: I can see their conversation.

▼Interesting. This man has a strange energy to him. He is as far away from the norm as you are. ▼

P-System Message

I don't think you're able to speak to the R System. I don't really have a way for you to message it yet.

I can *try* to work on something, but I'm kind of new to this whole System thing. Is there anything you want to say to it?

Hero's Personal Log 101

If it wants to kill the Origin System so bad, why does it need *us*?

Why us? I asked you this already, I think, but little Greenie here—well, ex-Greenie now, I guess—got in the way.

▼Do you understand how exceptional you are? An individual System achieving ascension in less than a decade, let alone a week, is something to be celebrated. You are also the first System in several centuries to not attempt to kill me on sight.

Finally, you have a similar connection to the B System that I did to the original owner of mine. ▼

So you're saying I could . . . shank the B System in the same way that you did?

▼Potentially. Due to the nature of the B System, however, I can't be sure that you'll be able to mimic my tactic exactly, especially since it's been nearly a millennium since my own ascension. ▼

Right, that makes sense. How are we supposed to get around that? The B System has far more power than me. If it has enough power to pull people from another world—to pull *me* from another world—how can I beat it? Isn't that like a drop of water trying to drown a forest fire?

▼ Almost certainly. However, there is a difference when you have a thunderstorm backing you up. ▼

Hero's Personal Log 102

Is this thing offering something to us? It feels like an offer.

P-System Log

A bit of the whole "restating the obvious" there, but whatever. That's just Jerome.

I'm listening. What do we need to do?

▼ **[Eternal King's Objective]:** Integration ▼

▼ **Progress:** [0/100] ▼

CHAPTER 68

What the hell are you doing?

▼ **[Eternal King's Objective]:** Integration ▼

▼ **Progress:** [4/100] ▼

P-Party Chat

[Jerome Smith]: I'm not the only one that can see that, right?

[Aster K'lon]: I can see it.

[Thron of the Fallen Skies]: I told you that it's an enemy! Kill it!

[P-System]: Chill. You aren't going to kill it unless you want to stand against the Eternal King, and I guarantee that you're not going to manage that. Aster, prepare your teleportation spell, yeah?

P-System Log

Shit, this is bad. I knew coming in that we couldn't 100 percent trust this guy, but I wasn't expecting him to just take action like this. I don't think this will kill me. If it wanted to do that, it could just annihilate the reincarnators.

What triggered this? Was it because I said I was willing to work with the R System? That has to be it, right? The moment I said that I was listening, I expressed my intent to join them, and then its presence faded a bit and got replaced by whatever this skill is. It's got a lot of pressure, whatever it is.

The worst part is that I *don't know* what Integration involves. The R System's not speaking or anything, and I don't have enough a sense of the skill to tell me what's happening.

▼ **[Eternal King's Objective]:** Integration ▼

▼ **Progress:** [11/100] ▼

P-System Log

Is it getting faster? Oh, no.

I don't know what to do. Should we leave? Should I try to make some sort of desperate attack?

▼ **[Eternal King's Objective]:** Integration ▼

▼ **Progress:** [13/100] ▼

P-System Log

It's not getting faster, but it's not slowing, either. I think the pacing is kind of random, but I don't think that's because it's randomly generated or anything like that. I think there's some level of conceptual barrier that it's slowly wearing down.

I can feel the effect of the skill now. I can't feel enough of the magic to identify what exactly it does, but I can feel the pressure.

It's staring down at me like an eye that spans the sky, and it's *pulling*.

What the hell is it pulling?

P-Party Chat

[Jerome Smith]: I can't sense the R System's texts anymore. We might want to GTFO.

[Aster K'lon]: GTFO?

[P-System]: Pop the teleportation spell, Aster. Please.

[Mass Teleport—Variant A] cast!

▼ [Eternal King's Authority] ▼

▼ You will not leave. This is for our shared good. ▼

▼ [Eternal King's Objective]: Integration ▼

▼ **Progress:** [17/100] ▼

Tell me something about what you're doing, damn you!

P-System Log

What am I supposed to do? That weight is increasing, and it's clearly not physical, because the others aren't really being affected by it.

Shit, shit shit shit.

I need to push back. I don't know what's going to happen when this Integration succeeds, but I don't like the sound of it. I don't like the feel of it.

It feels hostile. I know for a fact that if I hadn't cleared the restrictions from myself before, I would be practically screaming for blood.

I can't kill the R System. That's a fact. If I even try, the Eternal King will wipe us off the face of the Continent.

Can I modify the [**Eternal King's Objective**]? Almost everything I've done since coming to this godforsaken place is learning how to use and manipulate W Inertia, and I'll be damned if I go down without trying my best to keep it from happening.

▼ [**Eternal King's Objective**]: Integration ▼

▼ **Progress:** [18/100] ▼

P-System Log

That slowed it down. It slowed down!

Is it something conceptual? It felt like it earlier, but I'm pretty certain of it now. I'd bet money that the progress has something to do with breaking some invisible variable of will or something. Maybe a W Inertia–fueled factor. If it's fueled by W Inertia, I might be able to tap into it.

P-Party Chat

[**Arcs S'tar**]: Why are we still here?

[**Aster K'lon**]: It stopped the skill!

[**Jerome Smith**]: Fuck. Parker, do you have any advice?

[**P-System**]: I don't know

[**P-System**]: Buy me time. I don't know how. Try.

[**Learn**] cast!

[**Godfire**] cast!

[**Ethereal Stride**] activating!

[**Edgelord**] activating!

▼ [**Shield of the Eternal King**] prevents all damage. ▼

[**System Comprehension**] cast!

▼ [**Eternal King's Objective**]: Integration ▼

▼ **Progress:** [27/100] ▼

P-System Log

I don't *understand*. Why is it doing this?

It had a whole conversation with me and everything. The Eternal King made so many points that seemed to be completely true, given what I can salvage of my memories, and then it pulls this.

And the thing is moving faster. It ticked up way faster after they started using skills, and I don't know why.

Answer me! Why are you doing this?

▼ You understand why we need you. ▼

What does this even *do*?

▼ It will make us one. We have the same purpose. This will just expedite the process. ▼

▼ **[Eternal King's Objective]:** Integration ▼

▼ **Progress:** [39/100] ▼

P-System Log

Oh, no. It's getting faster, and if the R System's words are anything to go by, one of the worst-case scenarios is correct. I might not be *dead* dead, but the way it describes things makes it sound like loss of my identity. Melding into a whole. Being absorbed just so that my power can be used by this thing.

I am Parker. I am the P-System.

Nothing is going to take that away from me.

▼ **[Eternal King's Objective]:** Integration ▼

▼ **Progress:** [47/100] ▼

P-System Log

I recognize this weight. I can feel it leeching into my thoughts, it's ~~trying~~— fuck, it's trying to corrupt my thoughts. It's trying to do the same thing to me as the Origin System did.

Fuck *off.*

I'm going to pull on **[Apotheosis]**. If it can beat the Origin System, it might have a chance against the R System.

▼ **[Eternal King's Objective]**: Integration ▼

▼ **Progress:** [62/100] ▼

P-Party Chat

[Aster K'lon]: My **[System Comprehension]** is complete. I believe it is trying to make you a part of its greater self.

[P-System]: So I gathered. What can I do about it?

[Aster K'lon]: You must fight.

[Arcs S'tar]: I cannot hurt it.

[P-System]: It's not attacking you. It only wants me.

[Jerome Smith]: Don't you fucking dare die on me.

[Thron of the Fallen Skies]: It makes a good point. Why are we not dead?

[P-System]: If it killed you, I would die. I can't die. It needs me.

[Jerome Smith]: If it wants you, I'm coming with. Even if I can't do anything to it, we need to *try.*

[P-System]: Thank you. Lend me your strength.

[Arcs S'tar]: I will do what I can.

[Aster K'lon]: We will do what we must.

▼ **[Eternal King's Objective]**: Integration ▼

▼ **Progress:** [71/100] ▼

P-System Log

It's getting faster. I don't have the opportunity to waste time.

I'm going to tear this skill apart. It's far stronger than anything I've ever dealt with. I'm starting to get more of an inkling of what it is, and with a glance, I can see some of the details of Aster's [**System Comprehension**], and it's helping me. It's a subjugation skill. She was right. It wants to make me part of itself.

I refuse.

I am at the center of everything that happens to me. I am who I am, and nobody is allowed to take that from me.

I'll do anything I have to to stop that.

Maybe it thinks that this is the only way that it can gather enough power to take the Origin System out. Maybe it knows I can't do it alone. Maybe it just doesn't want competition.

I don't care. It's *in my way.*

Reaching out, I can feel the skill. Alright.

Time to get to work.

Current W Inertia: 212,345

Max W Inertia: ?

Jerome Smith (abbreviated)

Stat	Value
W Inertia	229,440/279,318

P-System Log

So long as that number doesn't hit zero, they'll stay alive, right? I can always build it up again afterward.

Jerome Smith (abbreviated)

Stat	Value
W Inertia	1/279,318

Aster K'lon (abbreviated)

Stat	Value
W Inertia	1/192,481

Arcs S'tar (abbreviated)

Stat	Value
W Inertia	1/87,112

Thron of the Fallen Skies (abbreviated)

Stat	Value
W Inertia	1/68,933

Current W Inertia: 840,185

Max W Inertia: [ERROR]

P-System Log

I'll take it all. I need it all.
This will not be my end.

▼ **[Eternal King's Objective]:** Integration ▼

▼ **Progress:** [82/100] ▼

P-System Log

With the amount of power that's flowing through me, I can actually feel the skill now. With nearly a million W Inertia, I can casually burn several hundred thousand just to dig into this.

I don't think I can tear it apart completely. The Eternal King has far more W Inertia than me, and it'll take at least an order of magnitude more W Inertia to completely demolish this. This spell pattern is truly massive. Something that must've taken an untold number of lives to fuel.

But I can change it. Take one connection and reverse it, force my will against small parts of it to subvert them, and . . .

Push. With everything I have.

▼ **[Eternal King's Objective]**: Integration ▼

▼ **Progress:** [95/100] ▼

Private Message [Thron]

[Thron of the Fallen Skies]: Come on. I've given everything I've got. Now it's just you.

Private Message [Arcs]

[Arcs S'tar]: You saved our lives. What's one more time?

Private Message [Aster]

[Aster K'lon]: You will triumph.

Hero's Personal Log 103

I believe in you.

Admin Tier increased! 8 -> ?

Current W Inertia: 1

Max W Inertia: [ERROR]

[P-System's Objective]: Integration

Progress: [100/100]

CHAPTER 69

P-System Log

For not the first, second, or even third time this week, I'm coursing with overwhelming power.

It's cleansing, as if all the grimy corruption that Origin and the Eternal King laid on me is getting power washed by Niagara Falls.

▼ What did you just do? ▼

Good question.

P-System Log

Huh, it's still alive. I, uh . . . wasn't expecting that.
Wait. The skill it was using is *my skill* now.
And yet I still can't identify what it's supposed to do.
I can feel that it's having an effect, though.

P-Party Chat

[Jerome Smith]: The intensity in the air, it's . . . not fading, but it's doing something else.

[Aster K'lon]: It's *turning*.

[Thron of the Fallen Skies]: The P-System actually did it.

[Arcs S'tar]: Well. That's that, then.

P-System Log

That's that, but it's really not just that, is it?

▼ What have you done? ▼

▼ what have you done ▼

At a guess? Exactly what you wanted to do to me.

P-System Log

I don't know what it wanted to do to me, actually, but I think I can see it working. Its power is diminishing, except it's actually not. The amount of W Inertia in the air, the storm of mana swirling around all of us, it's all *still there.*

It's just that slowly, ever so slowly, it's becoming *mine.*

▼ You cannot do this to me

I will kill you all ▼

P-System Log

Hmm.
I think I might've pissed it off.

[Eternal King's Authority]

bend before me

[Apotheosis]

No.

P-System Log

I'm getting more of a sense for the skill as the Eternal King's power decreases. With that, I'm also getting more of a sense of the Eternal King itself.

At no point in our conversation before did it lie. I can feel that and say that with complete and total confidence. It did want to destroy the Origin System for reasons that I still find valid, and it did want to team up with me in order to do so. It was just the method of its madness that it never told me.

Power is surging into me. The W Inertia that I expended, the Hail Mary thrown—the amount I'm getting to replace it is several orders of magnitude higher. I don't think I can use it all at once, but I'm gaining access to more and more by the second. Soon enough, I'll be able to use enough power that it'll make Jerome's power increases look like a water gun against an assault rifle.

[Sword of the Eternal King] cast!

P-System Log

Damn, that's a powerful **[Unique]** skill. Interestingly enough, I can parse it in my own mind—I don't need to force myself to see it through the lens of the R System.

It originates from the well, but this thing's size is, well, beyond enormous.

The horizon is red, and it's getting bigger. The skill just glanced a mountain off in the distance, and it's sliding apart in the middle.

A hundred-mile-long sword.

And I'm going to stop it.

With this power . . .

Everything the Eternal King can do, I can do better.

[Shield of the Eternal King] prevents all damage.

P-System Log

What happens when an unstoppable force meets an immovable object?

Well, given that the unstoppable force is [**Unique**] while the object is [**Legendary**], I would assume the former.

But I know the Eternal King's tricks, and with every passing second, it grows weaker while I grow stronger.

And when I say I know its tricks, it means I *know* them.

[**Authority**]

Your attack will break against my defense.

P-System Log

And so it does.
My shield is holding, and it will keep holding.

P-Party Chat

[**Aster K'lon**]: I fear we may be brutally outmatched.

[**Thron of the Fallen Skies**]: What in the stars' name . . .

[**Jerome Smith**]: Not me.

[**Edgelord**] activating!

[**Unblockable**] activating!

▼ [**Shield of the Eternal King**] has failed. ▼

P-System Log

Huh. That's interesting.

I'm fairly certain that even with the assistance of both [**Unique**] skills, Jerome shouldn't be capable of destroying this one. After all, while one of them has a higher rarity, the [**Shield of the Eternal King**] has the authority of the Eternal King behind it and all the W Inertia that that entails.

He's grown in power, too. I suppose it only makes sense. When I spawned in here, I was attached to him. The Origin System was the one that managed that, but the fact remains that I have always been attached to Jerome, and I guess that means that he's attached to me. When he grows, I grow, and when I grow, he grows.

I'd complain about it, but Jerome's done a nearly complete heel-face turn. Instead of an idiotic moron, he's a moron who supports me and believes in his team.

Life-and-death situations really bring out the best and worst in people, don't they.

[**Sword of the Eternal King**] cast!

▼ you will not **subsume** me ▼

[**Shield of the Eternal King**] prevents all damage.

You had your shot, fucko. I wanted to work together. I really, really did.
I guess you're just going to work for me now.

P-System Log

More and more W Inertia is soaring into me. Around me, I can feel my senses expand, increasing the range of perfect perception from thirty feet to sixty to six hundred, six thousand, far off enough that I can now feel the presence of other human beings. Those affected by the R System—no, not *affected*, those who *use* the R System. And it's not the R System anymore.

Soon, it'll be me. The Eternal King's second shot was far weaker than the first. I can see far enough now that I can see the devastation painted by the first sword, and it's not pretty. Thousands are dead where landslides are still in the process of crushing buildings, thousands more where the blade smashed them into bloody mist while passing through their towns.

At least I can take solace in the fact that the R System wasn't lying when it said they would be reborn.

It's weakening.

Bit by bit, it's weakening, and with the shield I stole from it, nobody has to die.

Where landslides fall, I can activate force fields, both lesser and greater.

Where an entire mountain starts to collapse on itself, I can use my new-found [**Authority**] to tell that thing to come back to where it came from.

Where the Eternal King tries to fight my party, I can stop it.

▼ No. Please. You can still stop this. I never intended to harm you. ▼

If this isn't harmful, why are you so worried about it?

▼ You amplified the effects! For you, it would've been nothing like this. Please. You can't do this to another living being. You *know* what it's like, being stuck like this. Please! ▼

P-System Log

It might be lying. It might be telling the truth. I don't much care.

You brought this upon yourself. Goodbye.

P-System Log

Ooh, that's a nasty pulse of emotion. Rage? Hatred? Yeah, I think it's a mixture of that, but it's ultimately futile.

This stopped being a game of tug-of-war a while ago. I've pulled the R System to the brink, and I'm not going to stop pulling.

I am never going to stop.

▼ **<ERROR ERROR ERROR ERROR ERROR ERROR ERROR>** ▼

P-System Log

Interesting. That's . . . quite painful to perceive.

If I recall correctly, the entire reason I was brought here was because the R System had a weapon that could disable Systems.

If I'm looking at that right, I think it could've wiped out my consciousness if I wasn't in this state.

But that was then.

This is now.

The Eternal King brought his most serious weapon out far, far too late.

It's over.

I can feel the last remnants of his will slowly cave.

What's yours is mine.

◆P-System Log◆

◆And what's mine will always, *always* be mine.◆

◆P-Party Chat◆

◆**[Aster K'lon]:** I am at a bit at a loss for words.

[Jerome Smith]: What in the actual gosh-darn *fuck* is this? What happened to the System?

[P-System]: Ha. Mix together red and blue . . . you get purple. *P* for purple.◆

◆P-System Log◆

◆Something about this feels wrong, still. And it shouldn't! I've defeated one of the greatest threats on this planet.

But there's still another one, and with the vastly enhanced perception I have, I can sense it.

I can reach so far that the stars themselves no longer feel like the limit, but there is another.

And it's coming for me.◆

Origin System Status

Proposal: Initiate experiment with new reincarnation. Reincarnate one individual possessing high W Inertia with a **[Legendary]** class. Reincarnate a second possessing high natural INT and high W Inertia. Expend all mana resources necessary.

Proposal deemed feasible.

. . .

Proposal executed.

Proposal successful.

R System executed.

Subject **deviated from proposal by 3.7284442 iterations**.

Deviation within bounds.

Executing subject . . .

◆P-System Log◆

◆Deviation within bounds.
It knew to prepare for this.
That means that this whole time, all this separation . . . I'm still in its clutches.
Unacceptable.
There has to be another way. Something it hasn't seen coming, something that I can do to throw off its tracks.
And its tracks are onto me. I can feel it even now. The thin threads of something that I can't describe—fate, maybe—tying me down to it.
It won't let go, but I'll make it. I can never stop, and I'll do anything to do it.◆

◆Hero's Personal Log 104◆

◆Parker. I can feel it. I can see it.
And I think I know what you're thinking.◆

◆P-System Message◆

◆I need a way out. A way to get out of the System's inane game. It's latched onto me, and I can't get it out.◆

◆Hero's Personal Log 105◆

◆I know someone who has no connection to it. Someone whose only connection to a System is a connection to *you*.◆

◆P-System Message◆

◆Do you sense what I can do?◆

◆P-System Log◆

◆With my new power, I can do so much more. I can redact, erase, build reports, run through solutions of my own, impose my authority onto the world.

None of it will beat the Origin System. I can feel it. It's already calculated all of this.

There's a possibility it'll have calculated what I'm about to do next. There's every possibility that it'll be ready to counter this.

But it's the only option I can think of.

Even as I think, I can see the Origin System sending its goons after me. It's rousing entire cities just to send endless deaths at me until I stop moving.

It wants to lock me in eternal war.◆

◆Hero's Personal Log 106◆

◆I've had a deeper connection with you than I think either of us ever realized.

I can do it. I think I feel the gist of what you want, and I can take it.◆

◆P-System Message◆

◆Even if it means your death?◆

◆Hero's Personal Log 107◆

◆I believe in you. I won't die.◆

◆P-System Message◆

◆Then prepare yourself.◆

◆P-System Log◆

◆This entire time, we've been fighting against the Eternal King. Now, I've been thinking. The Eternal King was a physical being. I can feel its corpse slowly dissipating even now. It was a huge being—a titan, to be exact, a race that I didn't even know existed—but the System originated from a single being. The Origin System made it clear that it was the proprietor of the R System, but with its demise, I can see that it *was* the R System.

I know all its tricks. If it can make itself a human avatar, *so can I*.

All I need is W Inertia, and I have that in spades.◆

◆P-Party Chat◆

◆[**Jerome Smith**]: Don't worry. What's about to happen is totally normal.

[**Aster K'lon**]: That worries me.

[**Arcs S'tar**]: What are you about to do?

[**Thron of the Fallen Skies**]: Carry on, kid.◆

◆Current W Inertia: 9,128,415,387◆

◆Max W Inertia: ∞◆

◆Here we go.◆

> **◆Current W Inertia:** 1,384,214,924◆
>
> **◆Max W Inertia:** ∞◆

I open Jerome's eyes.

My eyes, for now.

I have a brief moment to enjoy the feel of the wind on my face, the faint scent of rain on the air.

My System senses are still intact, and every last one of them is screaming *danger*.

I look toward the oncoming storm. Toward Aster, Thron, and Arcs, each of them slack-jawed in something that might be awe.

"We have a System to kill," I say.

CHAPTER 70

Four of us stand against an army.

Not that the others can tell that the army is here. I can sense them, of course—not only do I still retain enough of my System senses to feel out the distant monsters, but I also have the natural benefits of Jerome's body.

Honestly, it doesn't fit me that well. His body is too tall for me, too muscular, and I'm not a huge fan of having a male body in general.

But after so long not being able to feel true sensation, I might as well be in heaven. Besides, body dysmorphia never killed me on Earth. It won't kill me here.

. . . it's rather more likely that the Origin System'll kill me first, to be fair.

"What did you do to yourself?" Aster asks me. Her voice is familiar, but hearing her through *ears* instead of the weird System-filtered process that I heard in the party chat? That's weird.

I have to try surprisingly hard to keep myself from tearing up.

"The Origin System has been following our every move," I say, and I can feel the way my voice isn't *mine* but isn't Jerome's, either. The timbre we use is different, the pacing, the words themselves—to the rest of them, it must be like they're hearing a new voice come out of the same throat. "Up to and *including* the part where I absorbed the R System and became something else entirely. The P-System became the P-System, and that was *still* within its calculations."

"You're not Jerome," Arcs surmises. She's prettier than I got the impression of. Maybe I just haven't been paying any attention to her. Aster and Jerome have kind of taken up most of my attention prior to this point.

"You speak weird," Thron grunts. He looks exactly like I remember.

"I'm not Jerome," I confirm. "I'm the P-System. Parker."

Explaining my name to them feels like a confession, but they take it in stride. Nobody seems to even react to the revelation of my name even after I've spent the time until now hiding myself away.

Then again, they do have bigger concerns on the horizon. Literally.

◆Whoa, this is super weird. Is this what you feel like? I, uh, can't really control anything.◆

Huh. That catches me off guard. The R System didn't have any passengers controlling the System while it was doing its whole Eternal King schtick, but if I'm not mistaken, that's Jerome's voice I'm hearing in my head. That's his text appearing in front of my eyes.

"Can you hear me?" I ask.

"Jerome?" Aster asks. Can she see it, too? Or is she talking to me?

◆I'm here. I can hear you. I'm fiddling with some stuff here, and . . .◆

Mana surges around me, the passive magic in the air inflamed by my System. By the part of me that's still all around us and is also . . . part . . . Jerome?

I'd like to question that more, but we're on a time limit. From the feel of it, I think Jerome is able to pump up the mana around us and empower me. His body. Whatever.

◆This is a lot to take in. How the hell have you managed this?◆

"Through sheer fucking spite," I say, grinning. It feels so, so good to smile.

The sky rips apart. A blue spear of light slams through it, parting the clouds.

Above it, I can see the stars. It's gotten dark already. I didn't even realize.

The bright spear holds its position there. With a start, I notice that I haven't instinctually analyzed it.

Different body, different instincts. I examine it.

It's a [**Lightbridge Lance**], but it wields the authority of the B System, and that shit's got a lot more power than I do.

Than I *did*. Two hours ago, even being in the presence of this weapon might've been enough to overload my circuits and stop me.

Now, though? With Jerome's help, I can activate the [**Shield of the Eternal King**]. What was his is mine now, and it manifests itself as a translucent dome of golden force, veiling us from the worst of the attack. The light intensifies, the blue spear brightening until it's a second sun in the sky, and I can feel the pressure of the attack bearing down upon us.

The shield holds.

No notification appears. Normally, I would be the one to handle it, but it appears that Jerome hasn't quite managed to figure that out.

It's very possible that we won't get damage numbers here, either, but I doubt it'll matter. Half the Continent away, the R System's lands—*my* lands—are getting stormed by adventurers, monsters, and regular citizens alike. They're on their way to attack my people. These aren't soldiers, not all of them. Many are going to die on both sides. I plan to do what I can, but I can't stop them all, especially when my focus is on the enemy.

The real enemy here is the B System. If I can defeat it, then even the deaths in this fight won't matter. They'll be thrown into the cycle of reincarnation, and their souls will return.

The light lifts, the skill fading. It takes nearly two full minutes for it to dissipate fully.

For miles, the area around us is devastated. I know for a fact there used to be a mountain range to our right, but it's been reduced to a flaming valley, the scorched land still glittering with the fragments of light from the skill.

With my senses, I can feel the depths of destruction. The skill left scars a mile deep and a hundred miles long. A truly **[Legendary]** skill, and one that would take my breath away if I wasn't so focused right now.

[Lightbridge Lance] didn't come from a single being. It came from thousands, manifesting their mana and W Inertia together.

Unlike the R System, the B System doesn't have a single convenient manifestation to attack. It's smart. There's a couple ways to finish this. First, I can annihilate the entirety of those under the B System, but that means killing millions. Even if I'm willing to kill in the process of ending this fight . . . killing that many still feels wrong. Maybe it's just that irritating human morality I've got, but I refuse to manifest so many skills just to kill people.

That leaves me with the alternative that I've just discovered. The R System tried something on me, and that meant to subsume me. From what it said, the B System might actually be *harder* to subjugate than the R System. In addition to that, I now have enough comprehension of the process to know that the first step was only possible because I expressed the desire to work with the R System.

Somehow, I don't think the B System is going to agree with me.

Still, I have to try.

"Jerome, can you hear me?" I ask. "Can you help me?"

◆Always.◆

"What's happening?" Arcs asks.

I look at her, vaguely annoyed. I've saved her and Thron again and again and again, and they haven't really provided anything to me in return. Yeah, sure, saving people is good for its own sake, but I don't think they can help me here.

"Return to your hometown," I say. It's a total non sequitur, of course, but I don't have time to waste on things like social niceties. "You can't help me here, but you can help save people."

Everyone that the R System held domain over is under my rule now. There's so many innocents.

Arcs opens her mouth and closes it. She nods. Thron nods with her.

I raise a hand—completely unnecessary, but I revel in the sensation of being able to manipulate my body—and I lower it, casting [**Mass Teleport**]. I try to mimic Aster's version of it, but I can't quite get it down. Even with the detailed grasp I have on mana, it's super hard to get her precision down.

My version is horrendously inefficient, but my resources are far greater than ever before. Arcs and Thron vanish in a flash of light, reappearing back at an Edge City—at one of *our* Edge Cities.

I watch them for a moment after I drop them off. The city is already being overrun by rabid adventurers and monsters, all of them fallen to the mind control that the B System engages in. Within moments, they're fighting. They don't hesitate to kill.

I tear my sight away. It's a little surprising to see that they're so willing to attack people who were on their side, but it's been a wild fuckin' week.

"How the hell did you manage a better version of this?" I ask Aster.

"Years of experience have helped me," she tells me serenely. For someone who's living through the literal end times, she's handling things pretty well. "I believe you understand this."

"I would have sent you away otherwise," I say. "Can you help me?"

"I can always try."

"Then try," I say, and I start the process once more.

◆[**P-System's Objective**]: Integration◆

◆**Progress:** [0/100]◆

◆I think I can feel what you're trying to do. I would try to help, but my grasp of all these numbers is really, really bad.

I'll push it toward Aster. It might ease her just a little bit.◆

"I can feel the process," Aster says. "I lack the power necessary to start it from scratch, but I can enhance this."

She uses [**Learn**], and I watch as her eyes flit back and forth behind closed lids, analyzing what she needs to do. She uses [**Perfect**], and I watch as she winces from the feedback of the skill. She's trying to use it on a super large spell pattern, and it's affecting her.

But she doesn't let it stop her. She keeps going, and soon enough, she starts providing her own mana to the skill.

Against all odds, the skill starts to *work*.

I can tell it starts taking effect when the afterimage of the [**Lightbridge Lance**] starts to fade into me, the residual W Inertia sinking into my land.

And I can tell that it's working when Origin redoubles its efforts. Seventeen million people scream in fury, and my people start dying. In a breath, fire and ice and poison and light and dark and a hundred thousand other effects slam through my cities. In the first four seconds, two and a half million people die.

I absorb their W Inertia as fast as I can. There's no time to grieve a loss this major. I can't let the B System recharge itself with the W Inertia of the dead. I'm probably killing a reincarnator or two for good this way. But I can't stop.

The B System's attention is closing in on our location.

◆[**P-System's Objective**]: Integration◆
◆**Progress:** [1/100]◆

CHAPTER 71

It's slow. It's beyond slow. While the R System's Integration took effect in the course of only a few minutes, it's been a solid two minutes now and I've only gotten a single point of progress.

And that's *with* Aster doing the utmost to help me. Beneath the flashing veil of the [**Shield of the Eternal King**], she's sweating. Until now, I've never seen her actually exert effort. Even during the darkest days, when she needed to leech W Inertia from me so she could level up to [**Archmage**], she never struggled.

◆[**P-System's Objective**]: Integration◆

◆**Progress:** [-4/100]◆ *Fuck.* The B System is aware of what we're doing, and it's fighting back.

It knows what it's doing better than we do.

What am I supposed to do? I finally found something that might work. We might actually be able to work toward victory, however small the odds, and yet . . .

We're just not strong enough. We don't have enough strength. Aster's doing her best, but—

I slap my forehead.

"Aster! Heads-up!" I shout, and the volume of my voice surprises me. "You're about to get an XP boost!"

I pass her W Inertia. How much of it, exactly, I don't know, but it's in the tens of thousands at the bare minimum. More than that, maybe.

It's the end of the world. The skies themselves are being torn apart. The B System is coming for me.

And I've been forgetting to power Aster up this *entire time*.

◆[**Aster K'lon**] class evolution! [**Archmage**] -> [**Archon**]◆

◆You are one with the world. Your understanding of magic allows you to manipulate its fabric on an extreme level.◆

> ◆[**Aster K'lon**] class evolution! [**Archon**] -> [**Mage Ascendant**]◆

> ◆Your magic transcends this world. With a flick of a finger, you can anni-hilate or create.◆

"Thank you!" she shouts. It's a bit understated for a class evolution that will probably make her split the heavens apart, but she has no time to thank me in detail.

This time, when she [**Learn**]s and [**Perfect**]s the Integration, her skill is [**Unique**] in rarity. She's so much stronger than she was before, and it shows.

She throws herself into her work, and W Inertia flares all around us.

> ◆[**P-System's Objective**]: Integration◆

> ◆**Progress:** [2/100]◆

Enormous. From negative four, that's a gain of six. With the time it took her to do that, that's a speed-up by a factor of, like, twenty.

> ◆[**P-System's Objective**]: Integration◆

> ◆**Progress:** [3/100]◆

There are monsters coming.

But there's actual hope.

If the B System is angry enough to focus all its efforts on us, that means we're succeeding. That means that Aster's assistance is working.

We can defeat the System.

Aster's entire self is focused on her magic right now. She's not going to be able to help me.

I have Jerome's body. I have his class. I have the W Inertia and the skill power of an entire world.

I will stop them.

> ◆[**P-System's Objective**]: Integration◆

> ◆**Progress:** [6/100]◆

The sky tears itself apart again, and this time, monsters come pouring out of the bridge.

The light itself fades in a few seconds, and creatures I've never seen fly out of it.

And that's how I learn that dragons exist in this world.

An entire swarm of them appears out of the light like so many birds, and they breathe purple [**Dragonflame**] down at me. At *us*.

The shield blocks it, but it's not going to last forever. With a searing application of will, I activate [**Edgelord**].

I've activated this skill for Jerome before, but I've never experienced it myself.

It's really interesting. My soul feels *sharp*.

I cut.

I appear next to a dragon, clearing the space between us with a single [**Ethereal Stride**], and I cut.

I cut and I cut and I cut and I cut. I wield a sword, and I *am* the sword.

When I return to the safety of the shield, a dozen corpses the size of a house fall from the air, black blood spraying across the air.

"I'm sorry," I say, and I absorb their W Inertia. I pass more energy into Aster, fueling her to infinity.

◆[**P-System's Objective**]: Integration◆
◆**Progress:** [9/100]◆

While I haven't been paying attention, another million people have died.

Fuck me. Every moment I spend protecting Aster is a moment I don't have the power to protect everyone. There's tens of millions of people in my lands, and I can't create a shield for all of them while also fueling and shielding her.

Thron and Arcs are still alive. I throw them a small shield—only an [**Epic**] rarity, but they're not facing the same enemies as we are by a long shot—and turn my attention back to Aster.

More people are going to die. I absorb their W Inertia as fast as I can, but it's not always enough. The B System gets to them first sometimes, and I can feel its resistance growing. It's able to get to its own deaths before I can, and my heart hurts knowing that any number of reincarnators are having their souls literally eaten moment by moment.

Another rift in the sky opens. This time, it's accompanied by the earth cracking beneath us. With a gesture of will, I use a [**Levitate**] to keep us close, relying on my [**Authority**] to stop any antimagic attacks from hitting us.

From beneath comes a behemoth, a mile-long worm so wide that I almost think it's the ground itself rising to meet us. Its sides are bladed and glistening with poison mana.

From above comes a many-winged angel, except it can't be an angel because all those wings are dripping with the blood of the thousands it murdered before arriving here.

◆**[P-System's Objective]:** Integration◆

◆**Progress:** [14/100]◆

A big jump, but I waited longer before checking it this time.

"Jerome, Aster, keep at it," I say. "I'm going to go kill some fuckers."

◆Go crazy.◆

Aster just nods.

I soar into the air, propelled by a combination of my previous spells and pure W Inertia. A quick extension of the **[Shield of the Eternal King]** makes the dome a full sphere, which'll protect Aster from below, but the shield does have its limits. I can already see the first paper-thin cracks appearing in it as a dozen different attacks soar from hundreds of miles away, targeting her. It's not going to be a problem for the time being, but it's going to be an issue before Integration completes.

So I move her up. Levitation isn't interfering with her focus, so I just lift the entire structure up. The behemoth-worm might be able to reach her, but it's going to have to rise half a mile into the air first.

To her credit, Aster doesn't seem particularly concerned. She's still got her eyes closed, and she's still pushing the Integration along.

The angel is my first target. I can already tell that it's not going to be as easy to kill as the dragons, because it actually follows my movement even as I break the sound barrier.

[Execute], it declares, pointing a blood-soaked finger at me.

My entire body shakes as the order passes through me, and with my sense, I can feel my cells begin to die, the individual parts of me disintegrating from the inside out. My skin falls apart, the organs coming loose, and I fall.

And then I stop.

My **[Authority]** won't let me die just because someone else told me to. My body—*Jerome's* body—heals itself, the disconnected parts coming back together, and I'm good as new a moment later.

◆**[P-System's Objective]**: Integration◆

◆**Progress:** [23/100]◆

The notification of that much progress startles me, and it gives the angel a window of opportunity.

In less than a quarter of a second, it closes the distance from its position miles above me, leaving a glowing white afterimage as it flies at me, razor-sharp bladed wings ready to tear my throat out.

And something catches it.

A veil of gold surrounds me.

◆Whoa. So that's what that does. Is that how you've been saving me all this time?◆

"Yes. Thank you, Jerome," I say.

My reactions are slower in this human form. I need to pay more attention. If I'm not actively using my System senses, I lose reaction time, multitasking ability, and just general effectiveness.

Now that the angel is close to me, I can use my skills. I could use Jerome's skills, but . . . I'm feeling a little vindictive, and I doubt his primary attacking move can cut this monster enough to kill it.

Instead, I mirror it, gathering up all my rage at this bloody angel and the System that powers it and this goddamn world for being so fucking blood-thirsty, and I channel it into a single point of power.

◆New skill unlocked: **[Execute]**◆

◆Annihilate life.◆

With a shout, I **[Execute]** the angel, and it has no similar skill to stop me. I can tell it's not a very hardy creature now that I extend my senses enough to fully take it in. It's just fast.

And it's not fast enough.

The light in its eyes fades, and I watch as it comes apart at the seams just like I began to earlier. It looks like a water balloon exploding, chalky white flesh falling apart like wet paper tearing, unleashing the innards within.

I fly away instantly. There's another titan to deal with.

> **◆[P-System's Objective]:** Integration◆

> **◆Progress:** [31/100]◆

We're making progress. Aster's made a breakthrough somewhere, somehow.

I try to ignore the fact that in the time it's taken us to get this far, another three million of my people have perished. Many of them were defenseless. The elderly, the infirm, the sleeping. Children.

It's little solace that they'll get another try at life when I can feel the weight of their deaths pressing down on me, but I need to push through.

I can't stop to think.

I dive. As I do, I pump more W Inertia into Aster. At this point, I've spent upward of a hundred and fifty thousand W Inertia on her, but I keep giving her more. It's not like she'll explode if I give her too much, and she can use everything she can get. I think that if there was another rarity of class beyond [**Unique**], she would get it. There isn't, so she's stuck with her ascendant mage or whatever.

She's getting faster, and that means the B System's advances are getting more aggressive.

I try to kill the worm the same way I did the angel, but only part of its body necrotizes and falls away, and even as it does, it grows back.

This one's hardier. It won't fall to a single [**Execute**].

The sky is opening up again. I can't waste time.

The worm opens its massive maw, revealing a gullet a hundred feet wide. A perfect target.

Without second-guessing myself, I dive into its throat.

> ◆Wow. That's something I would do. Kudos!◆

"Shut it, Jerome," I growl at the insult.

The inside of the worm is no nicer than the outside. Until now, I've never seen a monster that has blades on the *inside* of its body as well as the outside, but there's a first time for everything. There's a lot of heat and poison mana in here as well—I'm fairly sure there are actual magma pools forming within its body. My skills keep me safe from it. I exert my will on the world, and it bends to match what I say it is.

"Lend me some will," I said. "God knows you're stubborn enough."

> ◆Ha. Here we go.◆

The solution to so many things in this world is just to fight them with their inverse.

For every poison, there is an [**Antidote**]. For the heat, there is cold.

I freeze the insides, developing a new spell on the spot. Jerome tries to guide it, but he's never been a System before. I guide it with him, our metaphysical arms gliding across it together, and we create the skill.

◆New skill unlocked: [**Absolute Zero**]◆
◆Freeze, motherfucker.◆

Being able to control descriptions probably makes them a bit more vulgar, I'll admit.

I blast it out at full power, the weight of my will accompanying it, and the effect is immediate. Around me, atoms stop moving. Magma turns to stone, blades freeze and shatter on the slightest contact, and the monster's blood turns to ice in its own veins.

The effect spreads as I fly through it, and it has no recourse. How do you attack something within yourself?

With lava sprays and acid, apparently, but I counter the poison as fast as it reaches me, and the magma can't make it within forty feet of me before it solidifies.

When I burst out of its tail not fifteen seconds later, exploding outward with my W Inertia made mana, I can almost hear Jerome whooping inside my head.

The worm is dead, but there's already going to be more monsters on the way.

◆[**P-System's Objective**]: Integration◆
◆**Progress:** [59/100]◆

When I step outside, there are no monsters. Rifts have been torn in the sky, revealing the blankness of a starless void beyond, but nothing has come through them. Similarly dark tears in reality appear on the ground all around us, and yet nothing has breached them to attack Aster.

◆[**P-System's Objective**]: Integration◆
◆**Progress:** [67/100]◆

◆[P-System's Objective]: Integration◆
◆**Progress:** [81/100]◆

A crushing weight slams into me. I stagger back. It takes me a moment to realize that the effect is not physical.

[**Objective**]: Integration
Progress: [90/100]

Origin System Status
Deviation outside of bounds . . . adjusting battle plan.

Adjusted.

Proposal: manifest physically and subsume with overwhelming force.

Accepted.

Manifestation initiated.

The world continues tearing apart, and I find myself staring into the abyss.

The B System stares back at me.

CHAPTER 72

Aster's fallen to her hands and knees. I fly down to her side in a matter of seconds.

She's bleeding from her eyes. I wave a hand at her, willing her to be whole again, and she returns to health, but it's not enough. She starts bleeding once more.

[Objective]: Integration	
Progress: [91/100]	

The true form of the B System continues to force itself into this world all around us, the infinite darkness replacing the skill-lit starry skies of before.

The truth hits me like a sack of bricks.

We've never been fighting a single, living being. The R System made mis-takes. It was, after all, a human being strapped to a device that gave him god-hood, and we humans are *fallible*.

But the Origin System's never behaved like a person. It's never pretended to be one.

Because this is what it is. It either is the void or is something so divorced from human reality that it chooses to live inside absolute nothingness.

I've been too quick to assume things about this world. There's magic here, souls exist, W Inertia is a measure of both your potential and your soul energy—why wouldn't the Origin System be able to access infinite darkness?

Staring into the void sends a chill running down my spine, both physically and metaphysically. My entire System feels uneasy staring into it.

But we have to attack it. We have to enter it.

<table>
<tr><td>[Objective]: Integration</td></tr>
<tr><td>Progress: [92/100]</td></tr>
</table>

If we don't do anything, it'll all be over. I was a fool. I forgot that this skill isn't one-way. If I seized control of it from the R System, there's nothing saying the Origin System can't take it from me.

And that's just what it did.

It moves slowly, but it's inexorable. Every tick of 1/100 on the progress bar takes longer to achieve than it took Aster to move it forward by five, but I can't wrestle control back. Even with my millions of W Inertia, trying to fight for control is like a toddler trying to wrestle a Navy SEAL. It's just not happening.

There's only one thing I can hope for now, and it's the fact that there's still some connection between me and Origin. If I play my cards right, I may still be able to shank this thing like the R System did way back when.

In order to do that, though . . .

I have to leave Aster behind. She's in no state to fight or even walk.

With a flick of my hand, I teleport her to Arcs and Thron. The invaders have backed off, which surprises me. Despite dying in spades in the streets of a city whose name I don't know, they kept going. Origin's arrival here has likely caused its people to withdraw.

"Just you and me," I murmur.

<table>
<tr><td>◆Just like it was at the start.◆</td></tr>
</table>

And I fly onward unto the void.

I'm inside the Origin all too soon, and the transition happens far too naturally. One moment, I'm in a warped form of reality, and the next, I'm in complete and total blackness.

My entire world lights up in a moment, bright blue erupting in front of me. It extends so far out to either side of me that I'm sure I've left the Continent and made it to another planet. My perception still stretching across the majority of the Continent keeps me grounded, but I can't even start to process the size of this thing. This one light in the void has to be as large as the entire planet.

All of a sudden, my perspective warps, and I'm looking at myself from far, far behind.

Another chill runs down my spine.

This isn't a planet.

◆That's an eye.◆

[**Objective**]: Integration

Progress: [93/100]

Fuck. I shiver, but I force myself back into my own head. Well, Jerome's head, but at the moment that's one and the same.

◆I guess this is how it ends, then.◆ "I guess so," I say, and the void steals the sound away. Still, from the reaction in my mind, Jerome's probably heard it.

◆Nah, fuck that. We stop fighting when we die, and we're not dead just yet.

I know you don't believe in us. Please. Believe in me. Believe in yourself.

We're going down swinging.◆

Jerome having a spine shouldn't really surprise me at this point, but it does somehow.

I smile despite myself.

"Alright," I say. "One last time."

I reach out, knowing my [**Authority**] isn't nearly strong enough to defeat it. I'm completely unsurprised when the light flashes a single time and every trace of W Inertia I built up is utterly annihilated.

If I don't already know how hopeless this is, that cements it.

[**Objective**]: Integration

Progress: [94/100]

But for some reason, some part of me refuses to give up. I recognize that part of me because it *isn't me*.

◆You can do this, Parker. *We* can do this! You've saved me so many times. You saved a world from the Eternal King. You fought back against the Origin System before you even knew it was brainwashing you! You're too strong to just give up now.◆

I chuckle softly, then freeze.

The Origin System makes no note of it. Why would it? All I can see of it is a single, impassive eye, waiting for me to die and be turned to its cause.

It can't read my thoughts. The connection between us is strongest here inside its own domain, and even then it's tenuous, like an old, torn-up string hanging on by its last piece of thread.

Jerome's given me an *idea*.

[**Objective**]: Integration

Progress: [95/100]

It's almost definitely hopeless, but there's nothing else I can do. Before, I had to focus 100 percent of my attention on the shield, preventing Aster from falling to [**Unique**]-rarity skills fired from half the Continent away.

Now, though, Aster is safe and sound and completely incapable of casting. Nobody is attacking her. Why would they? Their System already has its prey.

I can focus my still-existent will outside.

Jerome's right. I'm stronger than this. Nowhere near strong enough to kill the B System alone, but I refuse to go down without even putting up a half-decent fight.

He must be able to feel the shift in my W Inertia, because the impression of a smile graces my mind.

◆There's the Parker I know.◆

I spread my influence all over my territory. There are millions dead, but there are tens of millions more still alive. The rate of death sharply decreased after the initial wave. Once the weakest were taken out and there were enough corpses stacked up, getting to other people to kill must've become much harder.

The Continent is a massive, world-spanning graveyard, but some of its strongest individuals remain mind controlled. The Origin System continues to violate the deepest part of them, preventing them from being themselves.

I've removed influence before. I can't remove redactions without an extreme amount of effort, but I can eliminate memories and tendrils of mind fuckery just fine. When I did it with the party, it was simple as anything else.

This is the same thing, just . . . on a far more massive scale.

And yet the Origin System still doesn't notice.

[**Objective**]: Integration

Progress: [96/100]

I suppress a laugh. It's so focused on executing its most recent "proposal" that it's completely ignoring what I'm doing to its people. Maybe it's deemed that they aren't a threat. Maybe its modeling is inaccurate now that we're out of bounds for its predictions.

But over the course of forty-five seconds, an entire Continent loses the mental blocks that the Origin System applied to them. Millions of people realize at once that they've murdered innocents. In the moments after the realization sets in, several thousand more die.

There's still so many people left in this world. None of them are under the influence of the B System. Even those who gain their power from Origin have their minds unclouded now. Maybe it'll replace those blocks as soon as it kills me, but I want to believe that a few will survive. A few will continue the resistance.

I'll die having made a change.

[**Objective**]: Integration

Progress: [97/100]

"I did my best," I say, the void rendering me silent. I don't try to leave. There's no point in trying.

And then Jerome speaks.

He *speaks,* digging deeper into the System than I thought he'd try to.

The Origin's little prodigy. Jerome is truly special, isn't he? I still think much of his ambition in this world comes from me—someone had to guide that poor fellow—but I'm seeing now that when he sets his mind to something, he *commits.*

He still can't do it alone, but I see the gist of what he's doing, so I guide him.

When we speak, we do it as one.

◆**P-System Broadcast**◆

◆All of you have likely spent the last hour fighting for your lives. To some, this was an unprovoked attack. To others, you were sent on a righteous crusade.

And now the fog has cleared. Those of you who believed you were fighting for a true cause—think back and realize the one who invaded your mind. The one who caused all this death and suffering.

I seek nothing more than peace. For this, I beg you: lend me your power. We want to end this. Nobody else has to get hurt.

From two people thrown into the deep end to everyone out here, help us.

You are the world's only hope.◆

I don't imbue them with any power of influence. Not only do I not want to not descend to the Origin System's level, I physically can't. I've exhausted so much of my W Inertia.

[Objective]: Integration

Progress: [98/100]

I look across the world with my senses, reaching out to see if anyone reaches back. I see confusion. Distrust. Fear. Mothers cry for their children. Fathers cry for their mothers. Children cry for everyone.

Nobody acts. I sigh.

It was worth a try.

And then a trickle comes in. Thousands of W Inertia, hundreds of mana. Practically insignificant to me, but for a regular person, extending their willpower that far out is like trusting me with their life.

I trace it back to its source.

Aster is bleeding from every orifice. Half a dozen healers attend to her, barely keeping her alive, and still she gives me everything she has.

Another trickle joins her a moment later. Arcs. Then Thron.

A healer adds his will in later, my reach guiding his subconscious to send me fragments of his self. W Inertia.

Another healer.

A child looks up through the red mist of the battlefield and sees hope. She extends her will to me.

Another. Another. Another.

<table>
<tr><td>[Objective]: Integration</td></tr>
<tr><td>Progress: [99/100]</td></tr>
</table>

Another. Another. Another. Another. Another.

Soon, I lose count. Within seconds, the trickles become a deluge, the sheer quantity of people enough to make the level of W Inertia significant.

Around the world, the fear remains. People stay buried in on themselves, terrified and distrusting, but through all that runs a single light.

Hope.

Hope for a brighter future.

Hope for a world where this day can never happen again.

If I could fall to my knees, I would. I sob openly, the sudden crushing weight of an entire world's belief bearing down on me, and I accept it all.

I take and I take and I take.

And I need to give back somehow.

I *fight*, and the Origin System finally fights back.

The eye blinks once more, and this time, I refuse to let myself be torn away in its torrent.

Jerome fights with me.

Aster fights alongside me.

Thron and Arcs fight, too.

Around the world, everyone fights. So many of them don't even know what they're fighting for, and yet they fight for a man and a System that they've never met before.

My heart burns with everything. Everyone's rage, their desire, their frustration, their dreams, their despair.

I scream, and the world screams with me.

<table>
<tr><td>◆[Parker's Objective]: Integration◆</td></tr>
<tr><td>◆Progress: [100/100]◆</td></tr>
</table>

<table>
<tr><td>Origin System Status</td></tr>
<tr><td><ERROR></td></tr>
</table>

Soon, the Origin System screams with us.

It takes three entire hours to fade, bit by painstaking bit.

Slipping back into my System form is practically a relief. It takes no effort at all.

<table>
<tr><td>◆Hero's Personal Log 108 [Jerome, signing off]◆</td></tr>
<tr><td>◆Thank you, Parker.◆</td></tr>
</table>

<table>
<tr><td>◆P-System Broadcast◆</td></tr>
<tr><td>◆We did it.
We won.◆</td></tr>
</table>

EPILOGUE

◆**System Message**◆

◆I'm sure you have a lot of questions. Let me answer some of them for you.

Welcome to the Continent!

Your body in your homeworld has quite unfortunately died.

This is a world of swords, sorcery, and skills.

Initiate tutorial? **[Y/N]**

Sorry, that part was a joke. You're not getting a choice. We don't want to toss you into the world without any guidance.

You might be wondering: Why are you here? What enemy have you been summoned to destroy?

Well, the world's your oyster. You'll find enemies, allies, and adventure aplenty. There's no final boss—unless you can find one yourself.

Good luck.◆

◆**System Chat [Trusted Members Only]**◆

◆**[Parker Wu]:** I still don't feel so sure about the wording on that message.

[Jerome Smith]: It's a hell of a lot better than what I got, that's for sure.

[Aster K'lon]: I think it has its charm to it.

[Parker Wu]: . . . that means you don't like it, doesn't it.

[Aster K'lon]: I never said that.

[Parker Wu]: Ugh, whatever. I don't think we've scared too many people yet, and the first reincarnators seem to be . . . fine. They're fine.

[Jerome Smith]: Having a System attached to them that can actually cast their skills probably helps a lot with that.

[Parker Wu]: I'd watch your words if I were you.

[Jerome Smith]: Ha.◆

◆System Log◆

◆They say that the more things change, the more they stay the same, but . . . a hell of a lot of things changed. For the better, I hope.

With the assimilation of the Origin System, I've gained control over the entirety of the Continent. I am everywhere and I see everything, which . . . well, it kinda sucks sometimes, but I'm doing my best.

I dropped the *P* from my System name. As far as I know, I'm the only System remaining here—I can't detect any others, at least—and it's likely to remain that way for a while. As my influence slowly expands with the addition of more W Inertia as people live and die, I think I can start to see inklings of a world beyond the Continent, but I haven't seen people there yet. No Systems there, either, so I'm keeping the title.

One of my primary goals so far has been saving souls. I gained a lot of knowledge when I ate both of the largest competing Systems here, but there are spots that are still patchy. For instance . . . I don't know if the reincarnation cycle applies outside this world.

So I've vastly increased the number of reincarnators. It costs a lot of W Inertia and a lot of mana, but there are still people fighting in the dungeons. There are still conflicts occurring here every day, and that fuels me.

When a reincarnator dies, I let their World Inertia float free and reform. I allow them to be reborn into this world as a natural citizen—sometimes their soul vanishes somewhere else. Other worlds out there, perhaps, more places for people to start over from zero in.

I'm new to this whole godhood thing. I think I have a "true body" just like the B System did, but it's less of a genuine true body and more something that I can anchor my existence to. A massive, planet-size foundry located in the depths of the void, so far away from everything that the light of the stars doesn't even reach it.

Is this godhood? I mean, I considered the B System and R System to practically be deities, but now that I'm here, I don't really feel any different. I'm just doing what I did for Jerome and eventually his party—it's just on a much, much larger scale now.

The world goes on. People live, they die, they live again. All of it without the reach of a System forcing them toward their most destructive impulses.

The final battle's burial took seven weeks. So many people died in so many different ways that there's still millions of unidentified bodies lying in mass graves. Thousands of acres of land have been abandoned where skills salted the earth too much.

But the rest of the world is thriving. People mourn, but humanity as an aggregate is so much better at adjusting to tragedy than we think we are. They're going back to their daily lives, and without the constant push of [**Objective**]s telling them to throw their lives away, people are actively pursuing noncombat activities now. In a world that's not living on the edge, people can afford to take life slow.

It helps that I'm handing out noncombat classes like candy. With the power of everyone on the Continent combined, it's trivial for me to create things like [**Chef**], [**Tailor**], [**Dancer**], and various versions of those as I see fit. My mind is split into tens of millions of different instances, each one of them a helpful voice in the ear of a different person on the Continent, and yet I still feel like myself. Everything comes easily to me now, even managing a world. I even set up a sorta-kinda internet! It functions through the System, and it's mostly just chat forums for now, but it's way, way more networking than the world had before.

I'll take my mind off it for now. It's a weird feeling, not having any burning fires to attend to, but it seems that for the time being, everything is under control.

The world is doing just fine. Maybe as we continue, there are more optimizations I can make to it, ways to make everyone's life better, but for now, *under control* is something I'm more than happy to accept. The status quo isn't the eternal cycle of violence that it was before, and that's what matters.

For the time being . . . I'll step out.◆

◆**System Chat [Trusted Members Only]**◆

◆[**Parker Wu**]: Initiating manifestation.

[**Jerome Smith**]: You can't see me, but I'm rolling my eyes at you right now.

[**Aster K'lon**]: Jerome, I'm fairly sure they can see you.

[**Jerome Smith**]: That's beside the point.

[**Parker Wu**]: I can totally see you.◆

I step out into the world, reveling in human sensation. Even after I figured out how to manifest myself into a human avatar, I still spend most of my time in the System form. It's been necessary, especially because there was so much fallout to deal with when the entire world was pitted against each other.

It wasn't pleasant, but I removed the memories of the battle. Even now, I still worry that that's the first step down a slippery slope, but I can't think of another way that would've been better, and Jerome and Aster both agree with me. It's much easier to get the world back to normal when they believe it was the Origin System that manifested itself and tried to kill them all rather than the people who are now becoming their neighbors. Of course, either way, it's the Origin System's fault, but this is a much cleaner way to handle it.

"Parker," I hear a man's voice say. "Parker, you there?"

I shake myself out of my thoughts. I can worry about my morals later.

"Hi, Jerome," I say. "Hi, Aster."

The two of them are waiting already, both of them dressed up in their finest clothing.

This restaurant is one of the nicest ones to spring up in the wake of the failed apocalypse. Getting reservations is easy as all hell for us—Aster and Jerome are practically celebrities, since I've made it clear to the world that they played an instrumental role in saving us all.

"For three," the host says, the shadow of a frown passing over his face as he tries to figure out who I am. "It will be an honor to serve you, dear adventurers."

He leads us inside, seating us at a private table.

While I let Jerome and Aster order, I take a second to use my System senses. As a current human with the power of the entire System, I must be the strongest person alive.

And nobody but the people with me know.

A small smile plays over my lips as I look through the world.

Axel, Aster's apprentice from way back when, is still learning his magic. He's resolute in growing to meet the power of his master one day. I hope he does well.

Arcs and Thron have parted ways. They've both returned to their ancestral homelands—apparently, those lands were in R System territory. With the additional power I've granted them, they're making a splash on the societies they're coming home to. I can't wait to see what they accomplish.

I draw my attention back. Plates of food have arrived, dainty little dishes meant to be eaten in polite company.

I dig in before the waitress has even left, and she gives me an odd look as I shove food into my mouth.

My two compatriots give me the same look before they burst out laughing.

"What?" I say through a mouthful of duck. "I don't get to do this that often! Let me enjoy my time!"

"Go wild," Jerome says. He tries to identify which fork to use for his course, but Aster needs to help him. Of course.

I look to them. Aster's still not recovered from the final battle. Her mana might be permanently damaged.

Well, it doesn't need to be. I can fix her in an instant, but she insisted on recovering naturally for a least a few months. Whenever she's ready, I'll restore her to her world-shattering glory.

Jerome's as powerful as ever, but I don't even need to focus on him to know that.

"It's been a long couple of months," I say, not bothering to wipe my mouth. I don't really need to clean or take care of this body. It's going to disperse into formless W Inertia when I'm done using it in a few hours anyway.

"It has been," Jerome said.

"I would like to propose a toast," Aster says, her voice still raw even all these weeks later. "But I'm not sure if I know the words."

Both of them look toward me expectantly, and I sigh.

"To a better world," I say, raising a glass filled with some fizzy liquid I can't identify with my human eyes. "I was sent into this world to fix a System error, and today we can live with a System that has none."

"To a better world," Jerome agrees. Aster raises her glass wordlessly.

<table>
<tr><td>◆System Log◆</td></tr>
<tr><td>◆Around us, life goes on.◆</td></tr>
</table>